Gingerbread and Guilt

Peta Tayler

HEADLINE

First published in 1995
by HEADLINE BOOK PUBLISHING

First published in paperback in 1995
by HEADLINE BOOK PUBLISHING

10 9 8 7 6 5 4 3 2 1

ISBN 0 7472 5011 1

Typeset by Keyboard Services, Luton, Beds

Printed and bound in Great Britain by
Cox & Wyman Ltd, Reading, Berks

HEADLINE BOOK PUBLISHING
A division of Hodder Headline PLC
338 Euston Road
London NW1 3BH

For my mother

Prologue

'What? I don't believe it!'

Her voice was hard and sharp. Emotion – possibly, he thought, the most powerful emotion she had ever experienced – stripped away the layer of urbane charm that usually surrounded her, an unctuous and creamy smothering of meringue insulating the solid core of permafrost in the middle.

'It can't be true. There must be some kind of mistake. You've got the wrong will out, or something.'

'I'm afraid not. This is your grandfather's will.' Long years of practice made his voice slower and deeper than usual, deliberately calming. It had no effect.

'Let me see, then. Let me look at it.'

'Of course.' He ignored the implied insult and handed her the document, its stiff folds crackling as she nipped it out of his grasp. Her long, varnished nails were as aggressive and predatory as a crab's claws. He leaned back in his chair, and watched her, and rejoiced.

It was not, of course, apparent. Had she looked up, she would have seen nothing but courteous attention on his parchment coloured face. Fastidiously shaved, his skin was remarkably unlined for his age, a fact which his wife in mock exasperation and envy put down to the immobility of his expression.

'Hugh never frowns, he never laughs, he hardly even

smiles,' she would protest, her eyes gleaming within their nest of laughter-induced wrinkles. 'Just a twitch of an eyebrow, or a curl of a lip, that's all. A statue, my dears, positively a statue. That's why I have to keep pulling faces, to redress the balance.' And her mobile mouth would stretch into the wide, generous smile that had been the first thing he had learned to love in her.

Yet for all her clowning it was only Mary, and through her their children, who had seen beneath his impassive façade the humour, the idealism, and the romance that made his legal work both a despair and a delight to him. Mary, had she been there, would have known that within that immaculately tailored suiting, beneath the beautifully laundered shirt and the carefully chosen tie, the real Hugh Prendergast laughed, laughed with abandon and even joy. Laughed, and said in the language of the playground, 'Serves you right, you rotten cow. Nothing for you, nothing at all, so sucks to you, Angela bloody Johnson-Smith, sucks to you with brass knobs on.'

It was not a long will, but she read it through carefully as though by some happy chance he might have missed that all-important 'and to my Granddaughter, Angela . . .' She was, he saw, angry or worried enough to hold the document at arm's length and to screw up her eyes, both of which actions were aids to focusing her vision she had trained herself to avoid. Beneath the porcelain finish of her exquisitely applied make-up it seemed to him that he could detect hairline cracks, a subtle loss of elasticity and tone that no amount of tinted foundation and delicately applied blusher could hide. Even her hair, tactfully coloured and streaked to a softer, more mature version of the vivid red-gold it had been, suddenly looked brittle and brassy. Her lips were parted. There was a rime of spittle in their corners, almost obscene against the brilliant red lipstick, precisely outlined with deeper maroon, that matched the equally vibrant red of her wool suit.

Angela snapped the pages flat, took stock of their position and brought them back to her lap, at the same time closing her eyes and then opening them wide. She began, with rather more difficulty, to read the will again. Her skirt, fashionably short, revealed the hard bones of her knees, the calves that were as slim as a schoolgirl's but somehow so unappealing in their sheer-stockinged elegance.

Hugh thought of his wife. At fifty-three Mary was only one year older than Angela, but even ten years earlier she would never have worn this sharp little suit with its armoured gold buttons. Neither thin nor fat, Mary would look admiringly at such clothes but buy, for herself, things in which she felt comfortable: skirts and dresses of jersey that moved and gave, big soft pullovers, plain cotton shirts and T-shirts and recently, with a laugh, leggings. 'So comfortable, darling, with a long top. I don't know how I'll ever bring myself to put on anything else! Can you bear it?' And he had replied, of course, that yes, he could bear it very well, and maybe she should get a pair for him.

The will was slapped down on his desk.

'It's perfectly ridiculous, of course. It will have to be contested, set aside.'

'On what grounds?' His tone was mild, hiding his jubilation.

'I'd have thought that was rather blindingly obvious. He was senile, that goes without saying. It happens all the time, some harpy of a nurse gets her claws into a dotty old man, makes a fuss of him, perhaps even gives him a bit of . . . you know what I mean.' Her mouth screwed downward in disgust, she unscrewed it carefully and widened her eyes again. 'I don't recognise the name, but still . . .'

No, he thought. No, but then you wouldn't remember the names of any of his nurses. If you ever met them – and how often did you visit, these last few years? Twice a year, if that? – you wouldn't have seen them as people, just as expensive servants you would have preferred him not to have. No, you wanted him tidied away into a convenient 'home'. Well, he fooled you there, and he's fooled you better now. Ha, as he used to say. Or, rather, Ha!

'If you would just look at the will again, Mrs Johnson-Smith,' he suggested. She stared at him, refusing to pick it up again. 'You will see,' he continued as if she had done, 'that it is dated nineteen sixty-seven. Twenty-five years ago. I hardly think that a claim that he was senile would carry much weight.'

'Plenty of people are senile at seventy-six.'

'But not Alastair Johnson. He was,' Hugh pointed out with a careful lack of triumph, 'still running the farm. Very successfully. You probably remember that it was only the previous year that he sold Long Meadow and Castle Meadow to the developers.' For an amount of money which, at the time, had seemed almost unimaginable to a younger Hugh Prendergast, newly qualified and hoping very much for the offer of a partnership.

'Of course I remember,' she snapped. 'It was the year that I—' Her mouth clamped shut so firmly that he was almost certain he heard her expensively crowned teeth chop together. She would not, could not, connect her own wedding to the sale, or to the writing of the will.

'That you married,' he said gently, to punish her. 'I handled the settlements.' She had forgotten that. To her, almost visibly glowing with the triumph of having landed an Honourable, he had been of no more account than the assistant at Harrods where she had had her wedding list. Rather less, in fact.

'The Hon. John Smith,' Alastair Johnson had said,

rather grimly. Hugh, who had only just met him, ventured that it seemed a very suitable match. The prospective groom was, at thirty-four, neither too old nor too young for his twenty-seven-year-old bride, and though he could not have been called wealthy he had some inherited capital, a pleasant London flat and a cottage in the country, supported by a safe and moderately lucrative partnership in a firm of accountants.

'Suitable? Ha! Suitable for what? A doorstop? A fire extinguisher? A hot-water bottle? No, not that. If Angela has her way they'll have genteel twin beds with pink satin covers.' Hugh had remained, with some difficulty, impassive in the face of this tirade, rightly suspecting that his client was trying to embarrass him. 'The man's a bore,' Alastair had said gloomily, 'and she'll make a doormat of him, make no mistake. Well, she'd better have a good lump sum now, to keep her quiet. Better than waiting for me to die, which I don't intend to do at her convenience. And then . . . we'll see. Ha!' So now, thought Hugh, we're seeing. Ha! indeed.

'The settlements,' said Angela, who shortly after her wedding had attached her grandfather's name to her husband's uninspired 'Smith'. 'I suppose that's what it means by "well provided for". My God, a few thousand pounds . . .'

'One hundred and fifty thousand pounds. The equivalent, in today's terms, of about ten times that amount. One and a half million,' he concluded kindly, as if he thought her incapable of adding a nought and moving a comma.

'Peanuts, compared to what the estate is worth now. And you know it. I suppose, if you handled the settlements, you wrote this – this criminal document? There's such a thing as undue influence, you know.'

'There is indeed. But not, I am happy to say, in this case.

That is why your grandfather chose to use me, rather than one of the senior partners. He scarcely knew me, and I didn't know him or his family. I was asked to handle your settlements, so that he could at least see that I was competent.' He ignored her snort. 'Then, having discussed his wishes with both the senior partners of the time, he instructed me to write the will. He was very clear about what he wanted. The notes are still in the file, both in his own handwriting and in that of the senior partner.'

She bit her lip, unmindful for once of her lipstick.

'He knew I would contest it.' It was not a question, but he answered as if it had been.

'He knew that there is always a danger, when leaving what might be called controversial instructions for the disposal of his estate, that future claimants – your children, perhaps, had there been any – might wish to contest the will. He did not want there to be any distress, or unpleasantness.'

'Unpleasantness!' Her voice had risen to what almost amounted to a screech. Hugh saw the effort she made to moderate it. 'I am, naturally, greatly distressed,' she said, more calmly. 'Not so much by the loss of the money—' She closed her eyes for a moment. Like hell, he thought inelegantly. You've been counting on that money for more years than I can remember. Never thought, did you, that he'd last so long? I remember your face at his hundredth birthday party, last year. 'Not so much by the loss of the money,' she repeated, 'but by the unkindness, the cruelty, even. His only grandchild, his only natural heir . . . I cannot believe that this will can stand.'

She stood up, reaching for bag, gloves, umbrella. It was proving to be a very wet spring, so far. He rose to his feet, looked down at her, waited.

'I will fight it,' she said, her voice bitter. 'You may be sure of that.'

'Oh, I am. Perfectly sure.' Before he had finished speaking she was gone. She had tried, he knew, to slam the door behind her, but she would have been frustrated by the door stay that now hissed gently as the heavy old wood quietly closed the last few inches. He sat down again, picking up the will from the floor where the wind of her departing had flung it, and smoothing it between his fingers.

'She'll fight it,' Alastair Johnson had said, wheezily, from his bed the last time Hugh had visited. It was an oak four-poster, foursquare and solid, and every time he saw it Hugh wondered how it had ever been moved down from the bedroom where it had been made more than two hundred years earlier. It had, nowadays, an air of raffish surprise to find itself in the downstairs annexe, originally the dairy, laundry and outhouses but then charmingly converted, first into farm offices and now into a self-contained suite of rooms. From it the old man could look out over the well-tended fields and hedgerows of his farm, across an attractive cobbled courtyard, framed by the empty stables, that was bright almost all the year round with tubs of carefully planted shrubs and flowers. 'She'll be sure to fight it. The harpy. Dear little Angela. She'll fight you every inch of the way. She'll say I'm senile, or I was.'

'Well, you weren't then, and you aren't now.' Hugh had stretched out his legs from the comfortable armchair beside the bed and reached a lazy hand for the glass of malt whisky that waited, as ever, on the small table at his elbow. Alastair, forbidden by his doctor to drink anything but weak brandy and soda, enjoyed his malt vicariously.

'I don't remember things as well as I used to.'

'Nor do I. Nor does anyone. You remember what you want to.'

'Yes. Yes! Ha!'

'What are you remembering now?'

'Not remembering. Just imagining her face. Angela! The only angelic attribute she possesses is her complete lack of sex appeal.'

'Vindictive old devil,' murmured Hugh, without heat.

'Vindictive – of course I'm vindictive. And why not? She was a whining baby, a nasty child, and has grown into a spoiled, greedy woman. I warned her mother, I told her how it would be . . .'

'Yes, I'm sure you did.' Hugh remembered Joan, who had descended from disappointed middle age into querulous illness so quickly that Angela, busy with an absorbing social life in London, had scarcely had time to notice the onset of disease before her mother had died, as meekly and tidily as she had lived. Angela, typically, had been outraged.

'Why didn't you *do* something? Send her to America, or Switzerland, or something?' she had stormed at Alastair. 'She was your daughter, your only child!'

'Why didn't you? She was your mother, and you were her only child, too.'

'Me? What could I have done? You're the one with all that money.' She had dissolved into tears then, and with irritated pity he had not pointed out that what she could have done was to have given her mother what she had craved, her presence and her support that might have made the pain and the indignity of dying more bearable. Nor did he tell her that money could not buy health, that he had expended a small fortune in telephone bills to speak to specialists all around the world who had all said, in varying tones of pity and regret, that they could do nothing more than was already being done.

'She's well provided for.' The old man's voice, with its undertone of uncertainty, had recalled Hugh from his reverie.

'Very well provided for. Even after buying the Manor, Mrs Johnson-Smith must have had a sizeable sum to invest, which will be bringing her in a handsome income by now.'

'Smith. Mrs Smith. Johnson-Smith, pretentious rubbish. Only because she can't bring the precious "Honourable" into everyday conversation. Bloody snob. Ha!'

'As you wish. If you are not happy, however, there is nothing to prevent you from leaving her more.'

'I'm not changing that will.' Observing signs of distress in his client's breathing, Hugh was quick to soothe.

'You don't need to, that's not what I meant. But a simple codicil, another lump sum . . . nothing could be easier.'

Alastair Johnson subsided into his pillows, and concentrated on breathing for a moment. A lifetime in the open air had tanned his skin beyond the ability of a few years in bed to fade it, but recently it had begun to look yellowed, much the same colour as the rim of sandy hair, still thick and vigorous round the tonsured baldness of the crown, that was all that remained of the wiry shock of red curls that had been so much a part of his character.

'No,' he had said at last. 'No. No need. No children to bring up, put through school. The Hon. John's doing all right, isn't he?'

'Very well, I should say. With his training in accountancy he built up that business he took over very well, and it's due to go public in a month or two. Then he'll probably be richer than you.'

'Good. Poor fellow. Some compensation for being married to that harpy for twenty-five years, eh? Always felt sorry for the Hon. John.'

'You needn't,' said Hugh laconically.

Alastair's eyes, as sharp as they had ever been, flicked towards him.

'Like that, is it? A mistress? Don't blame him. I told you she had no sex appeal. Ha!'

He chuckled, coughed, fell silent. Outside, the stable clock struck seven. Hugh drained his glass – he was later touched to learn that Alastair had left instructions that he was to be given the remaining bottles of Auchentoshan – and stood up.

'Time I was going. Mary will have supper ready. She sends her love, by the way.'

'Send mine. Bring her with you, next time.' There was always, Hugh thought, going to be a next time in Alastair's book. There was an expectant pause.

'I suppose,' said Hugh, knowing what was expected of him, 'you wouldn't like to tell me who she is? This woman who is to inherit everything?'

'A life interest, don't forget, in trust for . . .'

'For her child, or children . . .'

'If born in nineteen thirty-seven, don't forget that bit.'

'As if I could. So, are you going to tell me? It will make my job a great deal easier, when it comes to finding her. Or the child.'

'Tell you? Why should I tell you, if I've not done so all these years? I'll say no more now than I've said before. She's a part of my life, of my past. Someone I owe a debt to: a debt that none of this money can repay or put right. A bit of unfinished business, if you like. Mine, and Robert's. You'll find out, soon enough. And why should I make your job any easier? God knows you've had enough money off me in fees all these years, you legal bloodsuckers. Earn your keep, for once. Ha!'

Deeply satisfied, the old man had raised a hand in farewell. Once he would have given a handshake, firm and brisk. Now he knew that his hand was cold and the bones brittle and light to the touch, so he preferred not to. Hugh half saluted in return, his lips turning up into a smile that Mary would have been astonished to see.

It was a game they played, the two of them. Hugh knew

that nothing would make Alastair Johnson divulge who this Frances Mortimer was, or why she would in the near future inherit the lovely old farmhouse and the portfolio of investments that brought in an adequate, even handsome, income for its upkeep. The hint today, the mention of Alastair's long-dead son, had been the most he had ever given. An unfortunate affair, presumably, and yet if he thought enough of her to leave her his fortune, why had the couple not married in the first place? Robert Johnson, dying in early manhood, had never had a wife or, he suspected, the inclination to acquire one.

It was a mystery, a pleasant one except that the solution would only be found after the death of his old friend. Finding her would not, he assumed, be particularly difficult even if, as was likely, she had subsequently married. If the worst came to the worst, he could insert one of those cryptic little advertisements in the newspaper. His main worry was not that he might not find her, but that once found, she might prove to be unworthy.

Alastair had died in his sleep two weeks later, and Hugh had been both profoundly saddened and almost religiously thankful for so easy a passing. Now he sat at his desk and thought, yet again, how glad he was that his old friend had died in his own bed, in the house if not the room where he and his father and grandfather had been born, in the lovely rambling timbered farmhouse that had belonged to Johnsons since the beginning of the seventeenth century.

There was a brisk tattoo of footsteps. He just had time to register that such a high-heeled sound would never be made by his secretary, who was like his wife in favouring comfort over fashion, when the door was pushed open again.

'I came back,' Angela Johnson-Smith informed him unnecessarily. 'After all that, you never told me who the hell she is. Who is this bloody woman, this Frances

Whatever, this damned bitch who is stealing my inheritance from me?'

'It is Frances Mortimer's eldest child, if born in nineteen thirty-seven, who is actually to inherit . . .' Oh, the pleasure of being the precise, pernickety lawyer.

'Some little bastard, no doubt. His, I suppose.'

'Or your uncle's.'

'My uncle? I haven't got an . . . you mean Robert? But he died in the war! And besides, he was . . . Good God, is that it? Poor old Pansy Robert managed to get some girl "in trouble"?'

Hugh lowered his eyelids for a moment, his strongest expression of distaste.

'I regret that I am unable to tell you.'

'Unable, or unwilling?'

'Unable,' he said, with a mixture of relief and disappointment. 'But of course,' he added blandly, 'if I had not been unable, I should certainly have been unwilling.'

She stood looking at him, her red suit glowing like an ember in the dark doorway.

'I'll fight it. Up to the High Court, if necessary.'

'That is for you to decide. I should warn you, however, that you have no chance of winning. You will not, naturally, believe me when I tell you so, but there are no grounds on which you could successfully fight it. I suggest you consult with your own solicitor, and you will find he will tell you just the same. If you choose to contest the will, only two people will benefit. Your lawyer and, of course, myself. You will be left considerably poorer, since you will almost certainly have to pay all the legal costs, which would be extremely high. Good day, Mrs Johnson-Smith.'

Chapter 1

Afterwards, looking back, it always seemed to Frances utterly extraordinary that the morning had begun just like every other morning. Retrospectively it seemed to her that every moment, every act should have been rimmed with light, heavy with portent and significance. As a punctuation in her life it was more than a semicolon or even a full stop; it was closer to a heavy exclamation mark, or perhaps two, one upside down like the beginning and ending of a Spanish phrase.

How could I not have known? she wondered. I should have been like a bride on her wedding morning, like a person setting out on a long and arduous journey. I should have thought, next time I clean my teeth, next time I get dressed, I will be . . . I will be what? Different? Translated? But am I? Isn't it just that I was so busy, before, that I never noticed myself? Left myself to sit quietly in the corner, like a good child disregarded by the adults? Or did that me, that part of me that I found, simply not exist before, like the soul of a child that has yet to be conceived?

She woke early, as she always did now. Even with her eyes closed she could see that there was daylight coming through the thin curtains, unlined through indifference and parsimony. So, she had cheated the World Service of one listener, at least. Through glowing wisps of self-satisfaction she sought among the crevices of her mind, exploring for flavours like a tongue savouring a complex mouthful of unfamiliar food. As usual she caught the feeling of the book she had been reading before she recalled what it was. Warm, familiar and safe, an old friend. Trollope, then. Good.

Encouraged, she moved her body, shifting beneath the down duvet that still, after twenty years, seemed so luxurious. Deliberately she summoned up the bed of her childhood with its mattress – one half of an old double that sagged towards what had been the middle so that her small body always rolled to the outside edge. And oh, those sheets, carefully sides-to-middled but still catching on toenails – and, horribly, on scabs on her knees – neatly folded over stiff harsh blankets. Cream, and army grey, heavy to lift and to lie under, and yet somehow never quite warm enough in winter. Not, at least, in the large-roomed, draughty Rectory where discomfort, even unnecessary discomfort, was regarded as a force for good in an ungodly and decadent world.

Properly awake now, she stretched carefully, then reached out for the bedside clock. Half past six. Quite a respectable time, an ideal time, really, she thought happily. Early enough that she need not feel compelled to get up, but quite definitely morning. She felt irrationally triumphant at having managed to sleep through the night. It was a detached kind of triumph, as though she were a nursemaid whose infant charge had finally gone through without a two o'clock feed. Well done, dear. Good girl.

She gave a snort of laughter. Really, to be feeling so self-satisfied over a few hours' sleep was quite ridiculous. It was not as if any painstaking effort on her part had gone into it. At least I can still laugh at myself, she thought. That must count for something. But then, I have always been able to do that. I suppose it comes of being on my own: there's nobody else to laugh at.

Her mind ranged over friends, neighbours, acquaintances. It could not be denied that they, too, frequently afforded her much secret amusement, but that was only on the surface of things. Her own head was, naturally enough, the only one she could get inside, and that was where the funniest bits were, popping up like carp in a pond, or like the rude-sounding bubbles of a mud geyser. I suppose the truth is, she thought ruefully, that I am self-absorbed. Impossibly Self-Absorbed, she put it pompously, writing a report on herself. Oh, well.

'Come along, Frances. Time to get up, dear.'

Her mother's voice, gentle and a little harried. The same words, every morning, and it occurred to Frances that her mother had never known, all those years, that her daughter had been awake for at least an hour already, waiting for the right time to get up. Before that call would not have been the right time, for Father would have been in the bathroom, and it would never do for Frances to catch a glimpse of that male body, chastely clad though it might be in striped pyjamas of a curiously stiff cotton. After the call, of course, would be equally wrong, for that would be lazy.

Now the call came only in her memory, for the voice had been stilled for more than forty years. Even so, it was an effort to disobey its summons, and yet she felt compelled to do so. Could it be that she was experiencing, more than fifty years too late, a surge of adolescent rebellion? What fun! And how much easier, now, when she had only memories to rebel against. Her eyes closed, she sought sleep again, but knew that she was really too wide awake, and in fact was longing for her cup of tea. Soon she would make it, but not yet. So there.

Of course, she said wisely to herself, the elderly need less sleep, and I am, after all, elderly. Old, I suppose, but that sounds so much worse, so terribly final. No, I shall remain elderly. Maybe I've always been elderly, for I've never needed much sleep. All those mornings, waiting to get up. All those evenings, waiting to go to sleep. Which was worse, winter or summer? Summer was so tantalisingly light, with the birdsong and the sounds of life outside floating in through the window, and the temptation of the shelf of books. Nobody ever checked, I could have been reading, and yet I never did. Then in winter, it was so dark and I was sometimes frightened, because to have a light on, or even a nightlight in a saucer of water, would have been unnecessary luxury. Did I imagine it, or did Mother move around more than she needed to, those dark nights? Did she know the comfort of that golden gleam when the living room door opened, the friendly sound of voices, or the wireless, or even just the clack of heels on the hall floor?

Tea. And book. She smiled to herself, feeling the book invade her mind, little ghostly figures flitting and drifting along its corridors: Archdeacon Grantly, Mrs Proudie, the Warden with his cello, Mr Slope, even the insipid Eleanor – phantasms that appeared and reappeared like painted horses on a roundabout. They were her world, her undemanding friends, giving her their words and feelings but needing no part of her in return. Knowing that she would soon be with them again she deferred the moment, like a child leaving a final titbit on the side of her plate. I am a greedy woman, she thought. A glutton, really. And why not? If what I experience when I am reading generally seems more real, even more important to me, than my everyday life, who does it harm? Not me, certainly.

Frances turned on to her side and sat up carefully, the way the nurse had shown her, lowering her feet to the floor and sitting still for a moment. Her feet, protruding from beneath the flowered cotton of her nightie, gave her a renewed feeling of pleasure. Lumpy, of course, and by no means beautiful, they were mercifully free of corns or bunions, and she could still reach to cut her own toenails. Odd, that something one had taken for granted for so many years should bring, now, such heartfelt thankfulness. Only the other week she had heard, on the radio, the voice of a woman who had been unable to leave the house for months because she could not get a chiropodist, and her toenails were so long they were cutting into her. All those years of doing exercises with the children, she thought, and now I am rewarded.

Putting on her slippers she stood up, and put her arms through the sleeves of her dressing gown. At five foot eight she was tall for a woman of her generation, and although she would have preferred a robe that reached her ankles the practical cotton towelling hung only to her calves, a singularly unbecoming length for someone of her age. All her life she had been slim, and though age had not thickened her body she was perhaps now more bony than slender, while early discipline ensured that she held herself straight and tall. After tying her belt securely she stretched her arms up and out.

'Come on, now, children!' she said to the rows and rows of faces, more than she could count. 'And bend, and stretch, and bend, and stretch. Harder, now! Reach out with your arms! Bend your knees! And one day, in about sixty or seventy years' time, you'll still be able to cut your own toenails! Won't that be nice?' Giggling, she went to the window and pulled back the curtains.

The sky, as she had guessed, was heavy with clouds, but the air was mild and she pushed open the wooden casement, trying to ignore the fact that it was severely in need of a coat of paint and wobbled, rather ominously, when she forced it over the place where it stuck in the frame. The house was an old one, of traditional Sussex style. Originally a timber-framed building filled in with wattle and daub, the outside walls had been reinforced with brickwork up to the first floor, and tile hanging above. The old wisteria that clambered rather too freely along the back of the house was bursting into its first flowers, the buds hanging down like miniature bunches of grapes against the leafless stems.

The cat, lying in wait for her on the other, more accessible, windowsill as he did every morning, looked at her accusingly and mewed, his mouth opening wide and pink. The deep golden orange of his fur glowed even on this dismal morning, clashing wonderfully with the mauve flowers. He stood up on his back legs, front paws scrabbling for purchase against the small-paned window, trying as always to reach the open toplight. Very rarely, when she was feeling particularly sentimental, she let him in and allowed him to sit on her bed, and he always hoped that this treat would be repeated.

'Go downstairs,' she said firmly, ignoring the fetching stripe of soft white fur down his proffered belly. 'It's damp out there. Your feet will be muddy.' He mewed again.

The garden was looking at its best, with the wisteria and the early-flowering azaleas, and though there were plenty of weeds in the borders and the lawn needed cutting, it was still lovely enough to remind her, yet again, that May had always been her favourite month. She drew in a deep breath of the scented air, then went downstairs to put the kettle on.

While waiting for it to boil she opened the back door. The cat, who had begun his descent of the wisteria as soon as she turned away from the window, shot inside and took up his usual inconvenient position in front of the Aga, just where she had to lean across him to make the tea. And as always, she gave in and fed him to get him out of her way.

The tray was already laid, her favourite cup and saucer, (not a mug), the teapot warming on the Aga, the knitted tea cosy, relic of some long-forgotten church bazaar or fête, the milk jug. Was she ready to rebel far enough to put the milk bottle on the tray instead? Not really, she decided rather sadly. And besides, it would make the tray so heavy, and if it should fall, which it easily might, it would be a whole pint wasted, and to clear up. Otherwise, of course, she might well have done it.

She carried the tray back to her bedroom, to the bedside table that awaited it. The air that came in through the open window was chill, damp and wintery, and she climbed back into bed, which welcomed her with residual warmth. The first of May, May Day, no less, and this year the Saturday of a Bank Holiday weekend as well. All those cars, nose to tail, heading for the beaches, poor things. And the Russians, of course, with their parades. Funny how I can only think of Russia in black and white. I really ought to be able to put some red in, somewhere. And do they still hold those parades, in the new era of *glasnost* and *perestroika*?

Now the first, the best cup of tea of the day. Oh, the luxury of it, and the joy of savouring it while reading in bed. As always, Frances found herself thinking of her mother as she poured it. Not that she had ever known this pleasure, except when she was ill. Tea in bed was something unheard of, effete, almost sinful, in Father's eyes. And to be reading, when she could have been doing something useful! Every day, as she sipped, Frances sent an apologetic, sympathetic thought to her mother's memory. You would have liked it, you really would. Except, of course, that you wouldn't have allowed yourself to. Oh, dear. Poor Mother.

The second cup, never quite as good but still enjoyable, was poured. Today I really must start sorting those books.

Yes, I certainly shall. I can't keep putting it off. It's ridiculous to have the shelves in that state, everything doubled up, and then I can't find anything when I want it. And I had better wear something sensible, that tweed skirt, and perhaps that old dark green cardigan over my blouse. I'm sure to get dusty.

Later, washed and dressed, she stood before the mahogany-framed dressing table mirror that she kept, for convenience, on the tallboy that held her clothes in neatly ordered heaps, and brushed out her hair. Released from its night-time plait it was still thick and long, almost to her waist, though the colour had faded from its uninspired mid-brown to an indeterminate grey. A hairdresser, she supposed, would have urged her to tint it brown again, or lighten it to silver or that curious mauve that elderly ladies seem to favour, but one of the huge benefits of keeping it long was that she would never, as long as she lived, need to go back to the hairdresser.

She remembered childhood visits. The cold, scary feel of scissors against her neck, the fear of their points snipping into her ear (only once, but never forgotten). The prickly torture of little bits of hair stuck in the neck of her wool vest and liberty bodice. Her mother, she believed, would have allowed her to grow her hair long. 'Such pretty hair,' she would murmur, brushing the cropped little head, 'such pretty hair.' But Father, ever on the watch for vanity, decreed otherwise, and it was many years before the comparative freedom of wartime allowed Frances, at last, to let her hair grow.

Her fingers twisted and pinned automatically, the spotted grey surface of the mirror unnecessary as she fastened the heavy knot neatly at the back of her head, quite high up so that it would not catch on her collar. She scarcely bothered to look at her face, knowing that it too had hardly changed in the last ten years. The pale skin was perhaps a bit more lined, the grey eyes more faded, but none of her pupils, of any previous vintage, would have had any difficulty in recognising her. The hairstyle had been already out of date when she had adopted it, and this, together with the strong, classic bone structure of her face, gave her appearance a timeless quality. Looking in the mirror, she could still see hidden within the present day reflection the same Frances who had looked into this same mirror over her mother's shoulder and yearned silently for long pigtails that she, like the other girls at school, could fling over her shoulders with a satisfying thump.

It was after nine o'clock by the time she finally set to work on the books. Telling herself that she must have a proper breakfast before tackling such a task, she had scrambled an egg – I shall have an egg for my breakfast, she thought with a smile – to supplement her usual bowl of porridge. Somehow the eating of an egg necessitated an extra slice of toast with marmalade, and then there was more washing up, which she did with more than usual care. But once the bedroom and kitchen were tidy there was no further excuse for procrastination, and she stood helplessly in the dining room surveying the shelves that rose, floor to ceiling, on two of the walls.

Come on, now, she told herself. The first step, that's all it is. She closed her mind to all the other steps that must inevitably follow, and the goal to which they would lead, and set to work, starting on a middle shelf because it was the easiest to reach. Now then, three piles, or four? Books I cannot bear to part with, that's easy. Books to give away. Books to sell – how awful! Like putting one's friends up for auction. But some of them are worth quite a bit, and I will need all the extra, if . . . Books for the church fête – thank goodness it's only next month, so they'll be gone. I don't mind that so much, I wonder why? I suppose because it's always the same people who go to church functions, the same old faithful few, no matter how many posters are put up to advertise them. And everyone says, what a pity the rest of the village didn't come, but the truth is we are all glad because it's just us. So I would know anyone who bought them, and of course the money will go to a good cause, which makes it better, somehow.

By ten thirty, in spite of several times finding herself standing lost in a book, having just opened it for a moment to see inside and been ensnared by the seduction of the printed word, two shelves were empty, and there were four heaps around the room, one of them significantly larger than the other three.

Well, it stands to reason that a lot of my favourite books would be on those shelves, being the easiest to reach, she told herself comfortably. When I do the higher ones, and the ones near the ground, there are sure to be plenty I can get rid of. But I'd better get these in boxes, before I do any more. What a good thing I saved so many in the shed.

Moving briskly, with the conscious virtue of one who has started an awkward or an unwelcome task, she opened the back door, then started back. A young woman, a girl, really, stood on the step, her hand raised so that when the door opened she looked, for a moment, as though her fist was lifted to strike Frances in the face. Arrested in the act of knocking, the girl fell back, equally startled. With her hand still raised she quickly tried to compose her face into a suitable expression. With the vulnerable mobility of her youth a complicated selection of expressions flitted across her face, to be replaced by a kind of helpless blankness. For what expression could possibly be suitable to such a situation?

'I'm so sorry, I hope I didn't frighten you. I knocked at the front door, but nobody heard . . .' Her voice was breathless, high-pitched with nerves, and with the sharp consonants and clear, rounded vowels of an expensive upbringing. Received Pronunciation, thought Frances, remembering an article in a Sunday paper, or even Augmented Received Pronunciation, like Prince Charles. Her auburn hair, cut in a neat bob to hang to her shoulders, was brushed straight back from her face, caught and held at the sides by tortoiseshell combs. Her face, with its smooth, faintly tanned skin, was innocent of make-up, except perhaps a little mascara. The dark lashes served to heighten, rather than disguise, the pinkness of the eyelid rims and the faint puffiness that spoke, as did the purple shadows beneath, of a sleepless and tearful night. Within them, however, her eyes were clear; an unusual shade of light brown, almost gold, that nearly matched her hair, beneath startlingly dark straight brows. She was faintly, hauntingly, familiar. One of her old pupils? It seemed unlikely, but Frances smiled a tentative welcome, just in case.

'I'm Amy,' she said, and Frances searched her mind, which as always on such occasions let her down, coming up with no one she had ever met called Amy.

'Amy . . . ?' The girl's look deepened to discomfort, she withdrew a little, looking away, checking for a house number that was not to be found, at the back door, then returning to Frances's face with entreaty.

'I'm . . . you're . . . that is, are you M-Miss Frances Mortimer?' Her tongue stumbled over the honorific that was suddenly so hideously, so embarrassingly, inappropriate.

'Miss Mortimer?' Surely none of her ex-pupils would address her in any other way? 'Yes, I am.'

'Oh good.' The girl stopped again, looking at her with anxious hopefulness. 'I'm Amy,' she said again. 'Amy Knight. Well, Hamilton-Knight really.'

Once again Frances scrabbled through the names in her mind. So many children, over the years, so many registers called and reports written. But Hamilton-Knight? Surely not. No name like that had ever passed through her little village primary school.

'I'm so sorry, I'm afraid I don't remember . . . Did I teach you? After all these years . . . my memory, you know . . .'

'No.' Unexpectedly the girl's eyes had filled with tears. 'No, you didn't teach me. We've never met before.'

'Then I'm afraid I don't really see . . .'

'You're . . . that is, I think you must be . . . I mean, I'm your granddaughter.'

'My granddaughter? But that's ridiculous! I've never . . . oh. Oh yes, I see. Oh dear.'

Extraordinary that she could actually have forgotten. And more extraordinary that the most powerful emotion Frances should feel was embarrassment. Not for herself, but for the girl, Amy. She shivered with the kind of cold sweat that is the aftermath of a dreadful social gaffe. Frances looked at the girl and saw her own desperation mirrored there before she – Amy – dropped her head so that her hair swung forward to hide her burning cheeks. Her confusion was momentary, however. With courage she raised her face and smiled with an assumption of ease that attempted to put her companion's peace of mind, politely, before her own.

'I'm sorry. It's a mistake, just a mistake. I'm so sorry, I'll go away, I'm sorry . . .' Amy's voice was breathless still, but firm and already distancing her, though she had not as yet moved away.

'No, no!' Frances, putting out a hand to detain her, could not bring herself actually to touch. 'It's me, I'm sorry, it's my fault. It's just that I hadn't expected . . . it's all rather a shock.' With a certain theatricality that a part of her mind was aware of, and mocked, she put her hand up to her breast, her heart. Amy, as if she had been given the correct cue, achieved a real rather than an assumed composure.

'Are you all right? I'm dreadfully sorry, I should have thought . . . of course it's a shock; do you need to sit down? Shall I call a doctor, or get you a glass of water or something?'

'No, I'm all right. I'm not ill. But you'd better come in.'

'Are you sure? I quite understand if you'd rather I went away.'

'No, of course not. Come in.' Trying to make up for her earlier behaviour, Frances flung the door unnecessarily wide, stepping back with an expansive gesture. Amy stepped over the threshold, wiping her feet like a conscientious child, though as far as Frances could see the soft navy leather of her shoes was spotless.

'I should have phoned, I'm sorry.' Her voice sounded concerned, and her eyes were carefully but unobtrusively trained on Frances, who felt sure that if she should suddenly collapse in the throes of a heart attack this self-controlled girl would not panic, but would take control of the situation without blinking.

'No, no – and I don't suppose you knew the number, anyway. It doesn't matter. I'll make some coffee – I was just about to have some, and it's such a cold day, isn't it? A pity, really, being a Bank Holiday, but it often happens like that. Do you like milk? And sugar? And what about a biscuit?' Frances heard herself chattering feverishly, not knowing how to atone for her lapse, scarcely allowing herself to think of the reality of the situation. Amy stood immobile in the middle of the kitchen, careful not to make any kind of invasive movement.

'Yes, milk, but no sugar, thank you.'

'Shall we stay in here? It's much warmer, with the Aga, and the other room is rather a mess.'

'Oh, yes, of course. That's fine.' Amy cast a covert glance at the door, as if wondering what was in there. Maybe, she thought, there's someone there, a friend, or a neighbour, or the Vicar even. And she wouldn't know how to introduce me, how to explain me. Oh dear, I shouldn't have come. I wish I hadn't. But the coffee was steaming in mugs on the table, and she, whom Amy hardly knew how to name even in her own mind, was waiting for her to sit down.

'You didn't know? About me, I mean?' Amy gripped the straps of her bag tightly. Her hands looked younger than the rest of her. They were small, the skin soft and smooth, the nails well tended but innocent of polish, cut tidily short in a business-like, practical manner. She wore no rings, but the watch beneath the cuff of her sleeve looked expensive – a twenty-first birthday present, perhaps?

'Know what about you? Oh yes, I see. No, I'm afraid I didn't. I'm sorry.' That's all we seem to be able to find to say, she thought. I'm sorry. I'm sorry that I'm sorry. Pull yourself together, woman. She gave herself a little shake. 'You knew about me, though? That your mother was—'

'Adopted?' The word fell like a judiciously tossed pebble, sending out its little ripples and frissons of emotion. 'No. At least, I only learned about it last night. But it doesn't matter, that's not the problem. At least, I wish I had known about it, but only because I could have said, at school . . .' She glanced sideways swiftly, sensitive to the danger of a tactless word. Frances grinned.

'My mother is really related to the Romanovs? A woman with a mysterious past?' Amy nodded, her smile half shamefaced. Of course, she was a teacher, she thought. She understands about the things children do. 'And you're how old, now? Younger than I would have expected.'

'I'm twenty-three.' Amy at last sat down, hooked the bag over the back of the chair. Like her shoes it was of soft, fine leather, surely the real thing, as real as the pearl studs in her ears that matched the discreet gleam round her neck, just visible beneath the white silky shirt and baggy V-neck navy pullover that had the understated sheen of cashmere. Her dark green wool skirt hung in beautifully cut loose pleats that swung round her slender legs in their sheer navy tights.

'So you've finished with school, gone to university or college, perhaps?'

'Yes.'

The answer was bald, and Frances found herself unable to go on. Ridiculous to be making light conversation at such a time. And how is your mother, my illegitimate daughter? Well? I'm so glad. And your father – you have a father, presumably? – is well, too, and making plenty of money by the look of you? Splendid.

There was an anguished silence, and in desperation they both sipped their coffee. It was strong and bitter: in the stress of the moment Frances had used too much coffee. She put down her mug decisively.

'This is horrible. Let's throw it away and start again. I don't like strong coffee, and I'm afraid I'm one of the generation whose answer to any kind of crisis is to make a nice cup of tea.'

Amy looked up, and smiled uncertainly.

'Well . . . I don't really like coffee either.' Their eyes met, and suddenly they were laughing, a little hysterically, perhaps, but surely that was allowable, under the circumstances? Frances moved the kettle back on to the hotplate and began the familiar, comforting ritual of warming the pot, measuring out the tea. Amy, moving with more ease now she had something to do, took the mugs of coffee to the sink and washed them out. She picked up the tea towel from its rail on the Aga.

'How cosy it is. We've never had an Aga. Granny always said they're messy.'

'Well, they can be, but this one is oil, not solid fuel. Rather extravagant, but lovely and warm, and of course it heats the water too. And it purrs.'

Amy listened with her head on one side, the tea towel dangling forgotten from her hand.

'So it does! How lovely!' Her hair swung smooth and glossy against her cheek, and Frances saw with approval that she moved with the natural grace of a well-exercised body. 'It's almost as good as a cat.'

'Well, I have one of those too. He's probably hiding.'

'I don't blame him. I expect you would have done the same, if you'd known.' Amy sounded quite cheerful about it.

'Yes, I might have done, but where? The cupboards are too full of clutter for me to fit into. In the shed with the boxes? Or under the bed, perhaps? Not very dignified at my age.'

'No, but awfully *sporty*. Or like one of those farces where people pop in and out of bedrooms.'

They grinned at one another, and this time the silence was easier.

What do I say? thought Amy. How do I ask what I want to know? And what do I want to know?

What do I say? thought Frances. Well, Amy, I suppose you would like to hear why I gave your mother away at birth. How I 'got into trouble'? Oh dear.

Amy was stirring her tea unnecessarily, and for all her control and her obvious maturity Frances suddenly saw her as a child. And children, she thought, are what I know about, younger than this, certainly, but still children. Direct the child's energies into constructive channels, she thought. It was true then, and I suppose it still is.

'Perhaps you'd like to help me?' she said in tones of calm authority. 'I am sorting out my books.'

Chapter 2

'What a lot of books!'

Frances stifled a sigh and waited for the next drearily inevitable question, Have you read them all? Don't say it, she begged in her mind. Don't damn yourself, not yet! Not when we haven't learned anything about one another. I don't know you, but I know me. Intolerant old woman. Intolerant young woman, come to that. Intolerant child, only I always knew how to hide it. She wanted to say something, to fling some kind of conversational gear-change into the waiting air, but a stubborn habit of mind refused to allow it. Better, after all, to know the truth at once. She waited.

'We never had books at home.' The wistful comment filled Frances with guilt and dismay. Dismay, that she should have expected to be irritated by this child, this flesh and blood of hers. Guilt, irrationally, that she should have grown up in a bookless household.

'Not even for you, when you were little?' Some of her horror must have been apparent in her voice, for Amy's was overloaded with reassurance.

'No, no, of course I had shelves full of them, we all did. And Mummy read to me every night, for years. But there were no grown-up books,' she continued, sublimely unaware of the childish phrase. 'Cookery books, of course, lots of those. And stacks of magazines. But no' – she picked up the nearest book at random – 'no novels. Or poetry, or anything like that. How funny, I never noticed, never even thought about it before.'

'Children don't, I find. By and large they accept their family and their home as normal, however bizarre the arrangements might be. Oh, I'm sorry! I didn't mean . . .'

Amy made a small, dismissive gesture, and Frances saw in that movement the practised social ease that came from what her mother would have called 'a good upbringing'.

'It's all right. It is bizarre, of course, now I come to think of it. And even more so to you, when you obviously love reading. I don't read much, myself, though I did when I was at school and at university, of course, and Mummy—' she stopped with a little gasp, like a hiccup, then continued valiantly, 'Mummy reads all the time. Daddy used to say that she always had her head in a book. It used to irritate him.'

Used to? Was that the problem, then? Well, let it pass for now.

'What did she read? Cookery books?'

'No, all sorts of things. Historical, and thrillers, and proper books too, like Dickens.'

'Goodness. Where did she keep them, then? In the attic?'

'No, in her bedside cabinet. Tidied away. Oh, I see what you mean – no, they were library books. Always library books, four at a time. What do you want me to do?'

'Do?' Frances dragged her mind back from the startled appraisal of someone who loved to read but who possessed no books. She herself, although she used the library, was unable to resist buying copies of her favourites, and had been known to buy at a jumble sale something she already had at home, because she couldn't bear to see an old friend lying neglected and unwanted. To her, books were rather more necessary than furniture, even than food. To enjoy only borrowed books seemed unnatural, almost immoral, like having an affair with someone else's husband. 'Oh, with the books. Well, I'm sorting them, you see. This pile is for the church fête, these are to be given to friends, and to the hospital, and this pile is for selling.'

'Oh.' Amy's tone was carefully noncommittal.

'Yes. I am getting too old for this house, and more particularly for the garden,' said Frances with the kind of brisk cheerfulness that she particularly disliked in other people. 'The old chap who used to cut the grass and do the heavy work has retired, and it seems impossible to find anyone else. I mean to sell it, before it gets too much for me and starts to look run-down, and move into somewhere smaller. Possibly,' she made herself say, 'into one of those sheltered flats. With a warden. I believe they can be quite charming. Only, of course, there won't be room for all my books.'

'No, I suppose not.' Amy looked around her, fighting down an incipient feeling of sadness. This, after all, was not a familiar safe refuge but the strange house of an unknown woman. 'That sounds very . . . very sensible.'

'Yes. That's what people have always called me. Sensible. Sensible Miss Mortimer.' She drew a deep breath. 'And you would not believe how tired I am of being sensible.'

Amy gazed at her, the golden eyes wide and startled. Had her arrival, she wondered, precipitated some kind of crisis? Was this epitome of a retired teacher, with her baggy cardigan and tweed skirt, her thick stockings and her no-nonsense hairstyle, about to break out with a long-suppressed brainstorm?

'Um . . .'

'But I am afraid that the habit is too strong in me. So if we go and fetch the boxes from the shed, which is what I was about to do when you arrived, perhaps you could dust the books, and pack them up?'

'Yes,' said Amy with relief, 'oh, yes.'

For a while they worked in silence. At first this was natural, even comfortable, as each busied herself with her task. Then, inevitably, the minutes began to stretch themselves unbearably, getting longer and longer until Amy, surreptitiously checking her watch, was dismayed to see that only twenty of them had passed. She longed for something to break the silence – a sneeze, say, or a clap of thunder, anything to fracture the solidity of their not speaking. She felt as though the air had gelled around her like aspic, so that soon she would be unable to move at all, set in a firm, quivery mould. She looked down at her feet, almost expecting to see a neat garland of parsley. I must say something, she thought. Ask for the lavatory. Remark on the weather. Oh help, I wish I hadn't come.

I must say something, thought Frances. She, after all, is the one who took that first momentous action, turning up here. So there must be something she wants, needs. Questions she wants to ask, and doesn't know how to begin. Come on, Miss Mortimer. It's up to you.

'I suppose—'

'May I—' said Amy at the same instant. 'Sorry.' She laughed nervously, and knew she was blushing. All her normal composure and social ease seemed to have left her, quite suddenly, in a way she had thought she had left behind with adolescence. Frances put down the book she was holding.

'Look, this is difficult for both of us. I know there must be hundreds of things you'd like to ask, and I suppose I would too, only I don't know where to start. But it's too – too raw, too sensitive. I feel as if someone had taken off all my skin.'

Amy was grateful.

'Oh, yes, so do I. Do you want me to go away?'

'Only if you can't bear it. But why don't we just forget our – our relationship – and pretend? Pretend we've just recently met, which is true enough, and that you've kindly offered to come and help me sort through my books because you've got a few hours to spare. No more than that. We'll leave your mother out of it, for now. It can be just you and me, getting acquainted a bit, speaking as chance-met strangers. What do you think?'

'"Human kind",' Amy quoted shyly, '"cannot bear very much reality."'

'Eliot, yet! I thought you said you didn't read?'

'Did it for A level,' said Amy. 'English, French, History. An A and two Bs. The A was for English.'

'Well done. Of course in my day,' said Frances, picking up her book again and rifling absently through its pages, 'it was Matriculation. Much the same, I suppose. And then – university, you said?'

'Yes. I read English. It was fun, but pretty useless, really. For getting a job, I mean.'

'So is almost anything, I gather. I mean, the papers are full of people graduating from Oxford and Cambridge with first-class degrees, and ending up as house painters, or without any kind of work at all. Fortunately, I happen to believe that education is never wasted. The mind is like any other part of the body – it needs regular exercise. So you didn't get a job?'

'Well, yes, I did, as a matter of fact. With the BBC. I'm a studio manager, on the radio side. Fairly lowly, really, but great fun.'

'It sounds it. What do you actually have to do?'

'Oh, follow the producer's every whim, really. Sort out microphones, recording levels, that kind of thing. And sound effects.'

'Ah!' Frances was fascinated. 'Rattling tin trays? Clopping coconut shells together?'

Amy smiled.

'It used to be, but it's all digital now. More reliable, I suppose, but less romantic. I spoke to someone recently who said her happiest memory was trying to produce, between three of them, the sounds of a full-blown Roman orgy. Modern technology has a great deal to answer for. It's a very junior post, but still . . . Only it had nothing to do with my degree. My brother helped.'

'You have a brother?' Surely that question was no more than natural, but how avid, how intrusive it sounded in Frances' ears.

'Yes. Robin. He's thirty-one, eight years older than me. He's a producer, with Radio Four. Drama.'

'How interesting,' said Frances, despising herself for the triteness of the response. She longed to know more, but could not bring herself to ask.

'Yes. Then I have a sister, she's called Sarah. She's eleven years older than me, and married. With two children,' Amy continued doggedly. 'I don't see very much of her. Or of Robin, really.'

'I never had any brothers and sisters.' Frances felt it was her turn to give. 'I always wanted them, of course, but then you always want what you don't have. I should probably have hated them. Or them me.'

'Why?' Amy, who liked her brother but found herself unable to communicate with him, and who found her sister both boring and hard to like, was interested.

'Because I was always so bossy. If I had been older I should probably have bullied them, and if I'd been younger I'd have been trying to keep up with them. Or, preferably, overtake them.'

Amy laughed, the first spontaneous and natural sound Frances had heard from her since they had laughed together in the kitchen.

'Are you still bossy?'

'I do my best to control it. Of course, for a teacher it's an occupational hazard, if not a positive asset.'

'Who did you teach? What age, I mean?'

'Primary. In a little village school, which meant that I had them in my class until they were about seven. There were only three classes. And for the last fifteen years, until I retired twelve years ago, I was also the headmistress.'

'In this village?'

'No! That would have been disastrous. In a village about ten miles away. Near enough to reach easily, far enough away that I could keep clear of village politics. As far as that's ever possible.'

'I always wanted to go to the village school. It was in one of those old Victorian buildings, and I used to look at the children there and envy them like anything. It looked so cosy. And they all played together, after school. All my friends were miles away. I could only see them if it was a proper invitation, and someone drove us.'

'If it was a Victorian building it was probably anything but cosy,' said Frances with feeling. 'Were you lonely, then?'

'Oh, no!' Amy was quick to defend. 'I had friends round all the time, or went to them. My mother never minded. I mean, she used to make jokes about being a taxi service, but all the mothers did that. It's just that I would have loved to be able to creep through a gap in the hedge and have a friend there. Only there wasn't a gap, and if there had been all I'd have found was sheep.'

'If there was a gap in the hedge, they'd have found it first.'

'Mm. My mother always said that sheep are incredibly stupid, but they have a sort of low cunning. I used to find that very funny.'

'I went to the village school, but I didn't have many friends there.'

'Why? Too bossy?'

Frances laughed.

'Not that. Oh, I was, but only inside my head, if you know what I mean. No, my father was the rector of the village. Not the vicar, you understand. The rector.'

'Is there any difference?'

'Not really, but he insisted on the correct title. He was disappointed, I think, that he never moved up, not even to rural dean, let alone archdeacon, or bishop. He was a very proud, ambitious man who believed to the depths of his soul that pride and ambition were sins against the Holy Ghost.'

'Goodness. How uncomfortable.'

'Very. I don't believe he ever reconciled himself. Nowadays we would probably consider that he was mildly schizophrenic, in the non-clinical sense. It made him rather difficult to live with.'

'It must have done. He sounds awful. Oh Lord, I'm sorry!'

'You needn't be, he was. Awful, in the sense that he inspired awe. No one ever fell asleep during his sermons, and the parish was known for its well-behaved choir! And he had a lot of good points, too. He was both kind and generous – no one in genuine need was ever turned away from his door, and he'd often sit up all night with a sick parishioner. He was never unfair, or spiteful, and he never asked from others what he was not prepared to perform himself. But he had no sense of humour, no appreciation of pleasure or joy, and he didn't know how to love, or at least how to express love, and although the village held him in profound respect, they never felt any affection for him.'

'Did you?' Amy was encouraged by such openness.

'No. Only, perhaps, my mother . . . but even for her the respect came first, and I'm afraid it stifled the affection, in the end.'

'How sad.'

'Yes, very sad. Though I did not, of course, realise it at the time.'

'And you were sent to the village school? Wasn't that rather – unusual?'

'Oh, very. In those days, girls of our class—'

Amy winced.

'You cannot, by ignoring it, pretend that something does not exist,' Frances pointed out gently. 'I know very well that you have been to a private nursery, pre-prep, and preparatory school, and then a public school. Not only your accent, but your appearance and your – for want of a better word – your *savoir-faire*, publish the fact. When I say girls of my class I am speaking as we spoke then, which I believe to have been more honest than this make-believe of classless political correctness.'

'Sorry.'

'Don't apologise. We are all products of our time. Anyway, as I was saying, in those days girls like me were not, as you have recognised, generally sent to the local village school. My father, typically, insisted that I should be a part of the community and not be sent away. Equally typically he was careful to see that I didn't learn to speak like my classmates, and he would not allow me to visit the homes of the other children or invite them to play with me at the Rectory.'

'But that's . . . that's *crazy*!'

'Of course it is. And most unkind, as well, though he was quite unable to see it.'

Amy looked at her in horror.

'You must have been so unhappy.'

'Not really. In fact, not at all. Children accept things, as I said. Sometimes I was teased, and sometimes I was ignored, but mostly we all just accepted. I played with the others in the playground, and said goodbye to them at the end of the day. I envied them, but no doubt they envied me my good clothes and food, and my grand home. And of course there were a few young people that my father considered suitable friends, so there were some parties and festivities I went to. I had a pony. And I had my books. No, on the whole, I think I had quite a happy childhood.'

Amy looked unconvinced, but disinclined to argue.

At twelve o'clock, Frances went briskly to the small freezer in her big walk-in larder, and took out two labelled margarine pots which she put to defrost in the microwave before tipping the contents into a casserole and putting it in the Aga oven. Two scrubbed potatoes followed on.

'Beef casserole, that great standby of those who cater for themselves,' she said. 'Rather wintery food, but it's not very summery outside. Spring greens all right? I hate frozen vegetables, except peas.'

'Oh yes, thank you,' said Amy, who was still young enough to take it for granted that an older person would provide a meal of some kind for her. 'You're very well organised.'

'I quite enjoy cooking, but after years of school dinners I'm afraid my taste buds have atrophied slightly. I'm always thinking I should try something more exotic, like one of those takeaways everyone seems to eat, but I never quite have the courage. Besides, that sort of food is better when there are more of you, I understand. More different dishes.'

Amy, who for almost twenty-four hours had felt so sick that she had been unable to swallow, was amazed to find that she was starving. Frances watched with approval as she ate the casserole, soaking up the rich gravy with the fluffy baked potato and having a second helping of undercooked greens. She produced a gooseberry crumble, made the previous day, and a pot of thick cream to go with it.

'Goodness, do you always eat like this?' enquired Amy artlessly.

'Not every day, but it is a Bank Holiday weekend, and then I don't often have a guest to lunch. I don't suppose I shall want anything much tonight, though. Soup, an omelette, or something like that.'

Amy said nothing, but the hand that held her spoon shook a little so that it clattered against her plate. She had not, as yet, allowed herself to think of the day coming to an end. The hastily packed case, that still lay where she had flung it, that morning, on the back seat of her little car, suddenly assumed monstrous proportions as if it had swollen into something the size of a school trunk. She swallowed the rest of the crumble without chewing it, and felt it slide slowly down her throat like a boulder through mud.

'Shall I wash up?' she said briskly, pushing back her chair so that it screeched protestingly over the quarry tiles of the kitchen floor. 'Do you generally have a rest after lunch? I know a lot of people do.'

'Thank you. I don't always, but I think I might put my feet up for an hour today.' It seemed to be accepted between them, Frances thought, that Amy would be there for the afternoon at least. It was, in any case, quite obvious that she had not achieved whatever it was she had hoped to find, learn or say. 'Why don't you go out for a walk? It's brighter than it was, and some fresh air would blow away some of this morning's dust.'

Amy was relieved to have the next hour, at least, planned and accounted for.

'Yes, I'd like that.'

'Good. If you turn right out of the gate, there's a footpath signed up about fifty yards down that runs across the fields and through a small wood. It's full of bluebells at the moment, so it's worth seeing, and if you want to carry on the path comes out in the centre of the village. You can either come back the same way, or take Coppice Lane which will bring you back to the crossroads further down from the footpath. I don't know about you, but I hate to come back the way I went, however pretty it is.'

'Can I fetch you anything from the village? Is there a shop?'

'Yes, please. I could do with a loaf of their brown bread, and half a dozen eggs. Let me give you—' She fumbled for her purse.

'No, no.' Amy blushed frantically, more embarrassed by the mention of money than by anything that either of them had said. 'Don't worry, it's the least I can do, really . . .'

It seemed kinder to let her pay, and certainly, thought Frances looking at her, she looked well able to afford such small items.

'Thank you. There's a very good village shop that specialises in home-baked French bread, and wonderful cheeses. Little village post office stores have to have something extra, nowadays, to attract customers from further afield. It's the only way they can keep going.'

'I know. Ours – in Oxfordshire, where I lived – turned itself into a little tea shop. They do fabulous home-made cakes, but it only really pays during the summer. They're always threatening to close, and then the village gets in a panic and buys everything there, for a bit, instead of going into the big supermarket.'

It was going to take a long time, Frances reflected as she went up to her bedroom, for them to learn anything about one another at this rate. Still, it was another little nugget – the family had lived in Oxfordshire. She stumbled on the stair, her grip tightening on the handrail and on the book in her other hand. She clutched it to her as if it had been a baby. Her refuge, her respite. For the next hour, she told herself, she would escape into Barsetshire where everything, even unhappiness and disaster, was serene and ordered.

Half an hour later she laid the book down, as gently as if it were fragile porcelain, on the bedside table. This extreme gentleness was a reaction against the urge, as powerful as it was appalling, to fling the well-loved novel, with its rubbed leather binding and tissue-fine pages that smelt of dust and leather and that indefinable smell of old book, across the room with all her strength. It had failed her. Something that was to her as natural as breathing or walking had suddenly become artificial, unreal. The characters, who usually made way for her to slip in among them as an invisible, yet participating, member of their circle, had turned their two-dimensional selves sideways so that they were not even cardboard cutouts, but thin, almost invisible lines.

It's the shock, she told herself. You've had a dreadful shock. Enough to make you ill, at your age. Send your blood pressure up, or give you a heart attack. You can't expect to carry on as normal. Resolutely she closed her eyes. Her body felt heavy, aching, and yet restless. Little tremors ran along muscles she had forgotten she possessed. Her eyes itched, she rubbed them and then pushed the lids down harder so that her ears buzzed and abstract red and orange patterns flashed on her retinas.

Behind them, in her head, she saw pictures. Herself, as she had been then but still clad in the sensible tweed skirt and green cardigan, nursing a tiny, white swaddled bundle in her arms, gazing down at it. Then the ridiculous figure running, running down a lane with her hair falling from its restrained bun. Then a church porch and herself, again, stooping with a hurried and furtive action, laying the baby down on the stone and then backing away, step by step, her arms still reaching for the silent bundle.

But this is ridiculous! she thought. Victorian melodrama of the worst kind. I scarcely saw the baby, after that first instant when they held her up and slapped her, and she cried. I never even saw her properly dressed, just wrapped up when I held her for that instant, before they made me . . . I won't think of that. It's gone, it's a long time ago. But that's not how it was!

Then, without warning, she fell asleep. Not the light, refreshing doze of an afternoon nap but deep, drowning. She woke to the sound of her bedroom door being pushed open, and the knowledge of someone standing looking at her. She felt too hot, her mouth dry and her head thick and heavy. Opening her eyes she saw Amy, her hair lit by a nimbus of sunlight from the landing window behind her.

'Have I woken you? I'm sorry, very sorry. Only I got back nearly three-quarters of an hour ago, and the house was so still and quiet that I thought . . . Oh, I don't know . . .'

Frances pushed back the covers, and sat up.

'I know,' she said. 'You thought I'd died of shock, or something.'

'No. Yes. Yes, I suppose I did. I suppose it's only a year since Granny died, and . . . and I was frightened, really. She – oh, it was dreadful – she—'

'Not now,' said Frances firmly. 'Not yet. Go and put the kettle on, and we'll have a cup of tea, and you can tell me.'

'Oh.' The girl braced her body, as for an ordeal, and Frances cursed herself.

'I'm still half asleep,' she said more gently. 'I was more tired than I realised, and I slept very heavily. It's not that I don't want to hear.'

Amy nodded, and gave a valiant attempt at a smile.

'Of course. I'll go and make the tea. And there's a cake,'

she added with determined cheerfulness, 'from the shop. A chocolate cake.'

'Lovely,' said Frances, who disliked most cake, and particularly chocolate. 'That will be a treat.'

Chapter 3

'My grandmother killed herself, you see. She committed suicide.' As if, thought Frances, the first phrase was inadequate to the occasion, as perhaps it was. She took a sip of tea to wash down the mouthful of cake. As always with chocolate cake, it seemed to be glued to the roof of her mouth in a cloying lump, like sickly mud.

'How very sad,' she said inadequately. 'Was she ill?'

'No. At least, they said the balance of her mind was disturbed,' said Amy with the glimmer of a smile. Frances smiled back.

'Ridiculous, isn't it? I mean, of course it must have been disturbed. Phrases like that are meant to comfort the relatives, reassure them that it wasn't their fault.'

'Mm. Well, it wasn't, of course. Their fault, I mean. But it wasn't particularly reassuring, either.' She spoke, Frances noticed, as though she herself was not a relative, as though she looked from the perspective of an observer.

'Were you close to her?' Even in this conversation the word 'grandmother' seemed impossible to say. Amy reached out and cut herself another large slice of cake. It was almost black with chocolate, with a rich buttercream filling, and she had already eaten two slices with every sign of enjoyment.

'No, not really. I was so much younger, you see.'

Frances, who didn't, crumbled the cake on her plate.

'That made a difference?'

'Well, I was a kind of afterthought, I suppose. I mean, she was thrilled to bits with Sarah and Robin, came and stayed for weeks on end and changed nappies and things, but of course she was older when I was born, and wasn't really up to that sort of stuff. And by that time Robin and Sarah were old enough for her to take them out, and away on holidays. Especially Sarah. Robin didn't really like it, he preferred being with his friends, but Sarah loved all that high life. So Granny was too busy with them, and I don't suppose she wanted to go back to the baby bit again.' She took a bite of cake. 'This is delicious. Nearly as good as – as at home. Would you like another piece?'

'No, thank you. Did you mind?'

'Mind what? Oh, that Granny didn't make such a fuss of me? No, not a bit. Actually, to be honest, it was rather a relief. I mean, she was very generous and everything, and of course she was always very kind to me, but she did rather swamp people, if you know what I mean. Sarah never minded, I think she rather enjoyed it, and Robin – well, Robin's different. He just slides out of the way of things, quite quietly. You couldn't swamp Robin.'

'But you would have been swamped?'

'Yes. I wouldn't have known how not to be, and I would have hated it, and been awful, I expect. Mummy used to protect me, I think. Organise things for me to do, make sure I was busy, so I wasn't free to do things. And once I was old enough, Sarah was leaving school and doing all sorts of glamorous things that Granny found far more interesting. So of course when she died I was terribly sad, naturally, and shocked and everything else, but it didn't really affect me like it did Sarah, and Mummy. Well, Mummy mostly. Sarah just cried a lot, and went on and on about it, but Mummy went all silent and peculiar. I thought it was just grief, for a long time. After all, they were very close. At least, they were always doing things together, and talking on the phone, and things.'

'That sounds like close to me.'

'Yes, but looking back, I can't remember Mummy ever actually *telling* Granny anything. Not anything important to her, how she thought or felt.'

'I expect she told your father, instead.'

Amy laughed.

'Oh, no! Daddy wasn't at all like that! Anything to do with emotion made him go all stiff and silent. I don't think I ever remember him saying or doing anything that was genuinely, spontaneously affectionate towards any of us, even Mummy. He never forgot our birthdays, or anything – he was meticulous like that, kept a birthday book and always had a box of suitable all-purpose cards to send – but the things he gave us were never anything that we wanted or even liked. I think he went to Harrods and asked for something suitable for an eight-year-old girl, or whatever.'

'Did you mind?' Frances knew only too well the symbolic importance of such things for children.

'Not really. It was irritating, sometimes. But he used to buy them on account, so Mummy used to wait for a week, and then quietly take them back and exchange them for something we did want. She never said anything, or criticised him, and we all told ourselves that we did it not to hurt his feelings. A kind of unspoken pact of secrecy, not to admit even to ourselves that our father didn't know, or much care, what sort of people we were. He classified everybody, by age, and class, and income, and gender and so on. Quite detailed, in its way, but only the outward details. Sad, really. And that's why Mummy didn't discuss much with him. He wouldn't have understood, it would be like speaking to him in Swahili, or Mandarin. No, she told things to us, occasionally. Not so much to Sarah, but to

Robin, and to me when I was old enough. But she didn't tell us much,' she finished bitterly. 'Not important things, anyway. Not about you, for one thing.'

Frances steered her away from this to the part she was half longing, half dreading, to know.

'It was your mother's mother, then, not your father's, who died. Killed herself.'

Her, thought Frances. It was her. Down a long tunnel she saw a tiny figure. She had never properly met her, never had a conversation with her but there had been those glimpses, from time to time. Impressions, really. A fur coat, mink, of course. An afternoon dress of fine silk, with a fur stole. A cleverly cut suit. And all of them, all of them shrouding a body that was thickening as hers did, that rounded imperceptibly week by week until the slender legs seemed scarcely enough to support the proud swell of pregnancy.

How greedily she had watched her, seeking chances to hide and peer from behind curtains, through shop windows and even, once, through the railings into the garden. She had not, of course, been supposed to know, but she did. She was aware, always, that she herself was spied on, examined. She would catch a flicker of movement, a flutter of a hem, a drift of expensive perfume in unexpected moments. An avid face on a bridge, turning away as she looked up from the canal side. A reflection in a lake. A shadow, a *doppelgänger*, that she was forbidden to know or to notice. Except for those two, dreadful meetings. And never, now, to be known except as a memory.

Amy was finding it easier to talk.

'Oh yes. Daddy's parents died ages ago, before he was married. No, you see, I thought when Mummy was so peculiar it was just that she was so upset about Granny. Grief can do that, you know,' she said earnestly. 'I mean, she used to say some really odd things, sometimes, but I never thought . . . I just felt I should make allowances. And then, of course, Daddy went off.'

'Your father left home?' The statement had come out so offhand that Frances wondered if she had misheard.

'Yes. Though as a matter of fact he hadn't really lived at home properly for ages. Several years, five at least.'

How, Frances wondered, did a husband not live properly at home? Improperly, of course, her flippant mind replied. She made an indeterminate, questioning sound.

'He lived in London during the week, and came home sometimes at weekends. He had a mistress, of course. I didn't realise at the time, but I assume Mummy knew.'

'Didn't she mind?'

'I don't know. I suppose she couldn't have done, or she'd have said something. It all seemed very normal. You'll think I was very naïve, but I just took it for granted that he was working hard, all week, and that it was easier not to do the journey every day. I never thought about things like who looked after him, and washed his shirts, and cooked for him. I expect I just assumed, if I ever thought about it, that he ate in restaurants, and sent everything to the laundry. But then, after Granny died, there was a frightful row and he moved out.' She firmed her lips for a moment, and the pink, faintly swollen lids came down to hood her golden eyes. 'It wasn't that things were so very different, only Mummy just didn't seem to *care* that he'd gone! Or that she had to sell the house and move into a horrid little cottage, or anything! It was . . . I can't explain it, but it was so *awful*. And the worst of it was that because she didn't seem to care, one couldn't do anything to help her. It was a kind of rejection, one felt totally excluded from what she was feeling.'

Silently, Frances reached across the table for Amy's cup, and filled it again. They were coming, she sensed, to the heart of the problem. Amy lifted the cup and drank thirstily. She was fighting hard to keep her equilibrium, and Frances respected the effort she was making.

'Thank you. That was all more than a year ago, and I thought I was over it, but now it's all come back, all that strangeness. I got my job with the Beeb, and moved into the flat at Primrose Hill – Granny bought it for Sarah, ages ago, and it sort of got passed on to Robin and now to me. And a few weeks ago, I met this man.'

Ah, thought Frances. This man. Here we go. She pushed the remains of her cake firmly away from her, and refilled her own cup.

'He's called Michael. He's a writer, he's not very famous yet, but he will be soon, when he's finished his novel. And he wrote a really *brilliant* play for the radio. That's how we met. And he's – he's—'

'The one?'

'Yes. Oh, yes. You do understand, don't you? I mean, he's not the first person I've ever fallen for, in fact at university there were several, and every time I thought it was the real thing, but this is different, it really is! And I think he thinks so too, although he hasn't said so yet. He's older than me. Nine years – that's not so much, is it? Not enough to be a problem. I like it – all my other boyfriends have been about my age, and they always seemed so young, somehow. I suppose,' she said wisely, 'I'm looking for a father figure. But why not?'

She paused to draw in a breath, her hand unconsciously flat against her diaphragm. When she spoke again her voice was higher, cracking occasionally, and the words poured out. Frances felt that she was expelling them as quickly as they could be articulated, in case the flood should suddenly be blocked by the very urgency of the need to communicate.

'I went home, yesterday, for the Bank Holiday weekend, because he had a deadline for an article for a magazine and

I thought I'd tell Mummy, and she'd be so happy, and then perhaps on Monday he'd be able to come and meet her, he said he might, but she wasn't happy at all, she was, oh, bloody, and she shouted at me, and I was so sure she'd have been pleased because he really is great, and *suitable*, he was at school with Robin, for God's sake, and they were friends then though they lost touch later and he remembered Mummy and everything and said how nice she was, only all she did was scream at me that I couldn't marry him, she'd never allow it, and she wouldn't say *why* or anything, and I thought she'd gone mad and I was so frightened, so I just . . . I just left . . .' Her voice was rising, quickening. She drew in a breath. 'I'm gabbling, I'm sorry. It's difficult to talk about it.'

'You ran away from it?' Frances kept her tone neutral, but Amy looked up defensively.

'I suppose so. At least, I didn't say I was going. But I'm not a child! I don't even live at home any more – not that that beastly little cottage was ever my home, because it wasn't and I couldn't ever think of it like that – but I'm an adult now! I've got a job and a flat and I look after myself, I don't have to say where I'm going all the time.' She paused, breathed. 'I couldn't stay,' she said more calmly. 'I couldn't risk losing my own temper, saying something unforgivable. And I needed to be doing something. To be my own *Deus ex machina*, perhaps. Not just sit there waiting to have some dreadful secret explained to me that was going to change the course of my life, like some kind of puppet.'

Frances nodded, understanding completely, but returning always to the severely practical.

'Does anyone know where you are? Michael, for instance? Or your brother?'

'No. I didn't really know . . .' Amy pushed the cake crumbs on her plate into a neat line with infinite care. 'I wasn't sure, on the way, whether I'd see you or not. I just drove down, and I suppose I thought I'd look at the village, and perhaps the house, and then . . .'

She had wanted, Frances could see, to find out what kind of person her unknown grandmother might be, before she committed herself to a visit. If she had found her living in a run-down council house she would probably have shuddered, and put me out of her mind, she thought without rancour. And I don't really blame her. How could she find a common meeting ground with someone whose experience of life would seem, to her, bounded by bingo and bus trips? That such a woman might be far better fitted to understand, to comfort and advise was something that Frances was ruefully aware of, but it was unlikely that Amy would have been.

'She will be worried about you.'

'I know. I'm afraid that, at first, that was what I wanted. A kind of punishment. I'm over that now, of course, but . . . I can't ring her just yet. I know that sounds childish, but I really can't, at the moment.'

'I cannot tell you to do anything,' said Frances crisply. 'I would hesitate even to suggest. I'm not sure that I can tell you anything at all.'

'But I wanted . . .' Amy's eyes brimmed, her voice died away.

'You wanted what? To find out why your mother disapproves so strongly of your boyfriend? How could I possibly know? I know nothing of either of them.'

'But you *must*! You must know something. She was so peculiar, so – I've never known her to be like that, never! And you're the only thing, the only other peculiar thing! It *must* be connected!'

Frances removed both the plates and put them out of reach.

'Right. Now, take a deep breath, hold it while you count to five, then breathe right out. Close your eyes. Now do it again.' Obediently Amy breathed. Her eyelids, though swollen, looked so fine they could have been transparent, the skin beneath her eyes was faintly purplish, bruised. 'Now, tell me again exactly what your mother said.'

'She didn't *say* anything.' It was the voice of a sad child. Frances hardened her heart.

'You know what I mean.'

'Well—' Amy's hands, with nothing to fiddle with, gripped each other. 'I told her I had met someone special, and she was pleased, you know, all happy and smiley and how lovely, darling. Not tell me all about him – she never says things like that – but waiting for me to say. So I told her about his writing, and how we'd met at the Beeb and had been spending more and more time together, and what he looked like, and things. That was all right. In fact, it was great. But I'd saved up the best bit for the end – you know?'

'I know. And that was the bit . . . ?'

'Yes. I said, guess what, he knows you, and she laughed and looked blank, and said she couldn't remember meeting any paragons recently, and I said not recently, but when he was little and he was at prep school with Robin. Oh!'

She sounded as though someone had stuck a pin into her.

'What?'

'I've just thought! I wonder if that was it . . . but surely they'd have been so young . . . she *couldn't* think that, could she? I mean, not *then*. And then his parents split up, and he went back to Australia with his mother, so . . .'

'I don't,' said Frances patiently, 'have the faintest idea what you're talking about.'

Amy looked at her, startled.

'No, of course you don't. I'm sorry, I suppose I was just thinking aloud. Only, I just thought, I wonder if it's because Michael was a friend of Robin's . . . but it was so long ago.'

'Why should that make any difference?'

Amy looked at her dubiously.

'Well, the thing is, Robin's, well, he's gay, actually.'

She kept her eyes fixed on Frances in a mixture of defiance and appeal, wondering what reaction this might bring from this elderly, old-fashioned spinster who appeared to have stepped, entire, from between the pages of a book by Miss Read. Her own world took most aspects of sexuality very much for granted, but she was still young enough to think that the old are, like little children are supposed to be, innocent to the point of imbecility. 'But not at all effeminate,' she amplified. 'I mean, he doesn't flap his hands and talk all precious. Really, you'd never know – in fact, none of us did, for ages.'

Frances blinked. Gay. As always, she spared a thought of regret for the loss of a word that had once been so innocent, so charming in its connotations. She saw that Amy was looking anxious.

'I hope you're not shocked? He really is very nice, I'm sure you'd like him.'

'I'm sure I would. All the gay men I've ever met have been extremely pleasant, good companions, interesting, cultured . . .' Was she overdoing it? She had only, in fact, known one practising homosexual in her whole life, as far as she was aware, and while it was true he had been all of these things she could hardly consider him a representative sample. There was Robert, of course . . . poor Robert . . . could there be any connection? Was such a thing, by any chance, hereditary? She remembered newspaper articles, a supposed revelation by researchers that there was a genetic link, and its violent rebuttal by others. Her mind recoiled from the idea, because it carried with it a suggestion of her own involvement, or even responsibility. This was not the time, however, to be worrying about such things, and she pushed the thought away to be mulled over later. Amy's face, however, was filled with gratitude.

'Oh, I'm so glad you said that! Some people can be so horrible about it, especially now with Aids and everything. And, of course, I know that older people find it harder to accept these things . . . Was that rude of me? I didn't mean to be. But I know Granny would have been horribly shocked, and all her friends if they'd known about it.'

'She didn't know?'

'No. Well, none of us did, unless Mummy . . . but I don't think she really knew, though she might have wondered . . . but she'd never have told Granny. I'm glad you're not all stuffy and narrow-minded.'

'I think that older people – most older people – are harder to shock than you realise. Your grandmother led a very sheltered, protected life, but most people of my age who went through the war have seen and experienced enough not to be very surprised by things. They don't necessarily like them, naturally, and old people frequently feel at liberty to say what they think, because they are old. Homosexuality – well, sex in general, as you might say – was very little spoken of among my generation. But that's not to say it wasn't going on!'

'No, of course.' Amy looked dubious, however. The idea of one's grandparents having sex is even more embarrassing than the idea of one's parents doing it, she thought, and goodness knows that's bad enough. Her thoughts returned to her mother, and she shivered. 'But Mummy—' she began. 'My mother,' she corrected herself, striving for some objectivity, 'never seemed to be shocked by anything. I mean, she went to all sorts of films like those terribly clever French ones that are really obscene, only it's artistic of course, and never batted an eyelid. My friends at school used to be really jealous, because I could tell her all sorts of things and she never minded. But this . . . she really freaked out!'

It was the loss of control, she thought, that had really frightened her. In all her life, though she had seen her mother argue, and cry, and shout sometimes, she had never seen her like that. The wide, screaming mouth, the body that could not remain still but strode around the room, fists clenched and then stretching, reaching as if for something to tear, to smash, to destroy. She felt giddy, unreal, that something she had never thought about but which had been a solid foundation in her life should disintegrate like this. Her throat tightened and ached, the eyes which already felt sandy and hot filled again with sticky tears, thick as the mucus that streamed from her nose. Appalled, she fumbled for her bag, for a handkerchief.

'Here.' A large, no-nonsense man's handkerchief was put into her hand. Gratefully she blew her nose, mopped her eyes, and tried to control her hiccuping breathing. The linen smelled of garden-dried, freshly ironed laundry, and was tremendously comforting. She was thankful that there had been no attempt at physical comfort, no hugging and patting, which would have filled her with embarrassment.

'Sorry.'

'You don't have to apologise. It's rather early in the day, and very soon after tea, but I think we could both do with a brandy. At least, I could.'

'Yes, please. Could I have something in it? I don't like it neat.'

'Will soda do? That's what I generally have. I don't like the taste of whisky or gin, but this seems to agree with me. They say, as a matter of fact, that it's the alcoholic's drink, though I can't see why.'

'I thought the whole point about alcoholics was that they drank anything they could get their hands on.'

'Well, we'll risk it just this once.'

Frances handed her the glass, and Amy took a large swallow. The bubbles burst in her mouth, and she could feel the warmth of the spirit going down into her stomach. She drew a deep breath.

'Better?'

'Much, thank you. Sorry about all that.'

'There's no need to apologise. I don't cry much myself, but then I don't have a great deal to cry about. If you've got a good reason, which it seems you have, then it's probably a case of better out than in.'

'Like being sick.' Amy gave the ghost of a laugh.

'Mm.' Frances, moving smoothly and quietly, cleared away the remains of the tea from the table. Amy, she saw, was more than halfway through her drink already. 'Finish that, and I'll pour you another.'

'Oh dear, I suppose I shouldn't—'

'Amy.' Frances faced her squarely, leaning forward with her hands on the table. It was the first time she had called the girl by her name. 'Where were you intending to stay tonight?'

The amber eyes dropped.

'Well, I hadn't really . . . I suppose I wondered . . . but I could go back to the flat . . .'

'You may stay here if you want to, you know.'

Amy, who had been holding her breath, breathed out and looked up again.

'Thank you. I'm afraid I did hope I could, and I've got my case in the car, I expect you've guessed. Heaven only knows what's in it, though. I was in such a state when I packed, this morning, that it'll be a wonder if I have anything I need.'

'In a state because of what your mother had said?'

'Yes, and because – because I'd just found out about you. I mean, about her.'

'This morning? You found that out this morning?'

Amy took another gulp from her drink, and stared down into the glass.

'Well, in the night, really. But it was this morning, of course. I couldn't sleep.'

'So you talked? You, and your mother? And she told you?'

Amy was silent. Frances pulled out her chair, and sat down again, slowly.

'Amy?' Thirty-five years of teaching had formed that voice. Amy, reluctantly, looked up. She fixed her eyes on Frances' hands.

'I couldn't sleep,' she repeated. 'I kept thinking about what she'd said, and how she'd said it. Screamed it. I'd gone to my room and locked the door. She knocked, later on, and called me, but I couldn't . . . I couldn't . . .' She swallowed. 'So I didn't answer, and she went away. And I went to bed, but . . . so much later, I came out and went to her desk. There's a drawer. She keeps things in it, important things like passports and birth certificates, we all knew about it, bits of our hair when we were babies, and our first letters, and things, it's not locked, and I thought . . . I thought . . . so I pulled it out. There were lots of things, all our letters from school in bundles, a few photographs, her passport . . . and an envelope. An old one. It was Granny's. I could smell her scent on it, it was creepy, as though she was there. And inside it, some papers. Official ones, things in French, and another one, in handwriting. Signed.'

'The agreement.' Frances felt a wave of nausea, her skin damp and clammy, a buzzing dark before her eyes. Suddenly she, too, remembered the scent. It had been on the paper, clinging to it where hand and wrist had rested. She had written it herself, that other she, and Frances . . . Frances had signed it. Even now, the words burned, 'never to attempt to see, to find, to contact the child . . . never to speak of it . . . as if it had never been' . . . all those nevers. And she had signed it. 'With my name on it.'

'Yes. How could you do it?'

'I had to.' It was a whisper. She tried again. 'I had to. It was . . . the only way.'

'Yes,' said Amy, who couldn't begin to understand.

'But was that all? You couldn't have found me from that. No address, and so long ago . . .'

'No. But there was another paper, new, in Mummy's writing. Just the address, that's all. I thought she must have been to see you, and not told any of us. Told me. But she didn't, did she?'

'No. No, she never came to see me.'

'I didn't really think it through very clearly. I just copied it out, and packed my things, and went.'

'Then? In the night? Without saying anything?'

'What could I say?' It was a cry of despair. 'I couldn't tell her I was coming here, could I? I'm not even supposed to know about you.'

Frances was silent. The things she could have said – that Amy had no right to search her mother's private papers, that she should not have run off in the night without leaving some kind of message, were, she knew, unnecessary. She might not have known the girl for more than a few hours, but she knew very well that, brought up as she had been, she was already wrung out with guilt. She waited.

'I suppose I'd better phone her, hadn't I?' The resignation was tinged with anxiety.

'Yes, I think you must. If only to say that you are safe. Would she know that you had found out about me?'

Amy blushed.

'No. I – I put everything back exactly as it had been, very carefully. And I wiped the drawer, and the desk.'

'For fingerprints?' Frances, in spite of everything, was both touched and amused. She was also relieved, for it seemed to her that with that gesture Amy had revealed that she was, in some degree, playing a part, acting out some kind of drama in which she was both protagonist and audience.

'I'd rather not tell her where I am, though. I need – we both need – a little time to get myself back together.'

Frances agreed.

'No, probably better not. In fact, certainly, for the moment at least. Later . . . well, we shall have to see, shan't we?'

Amy went to the telephone on the dresser, glancing for permission and receiving a nod. With her hand on the receiver, she looked up.

'What should I call you?' she asked, rather shyly.

What indeed? thought Frances. Granny and its like were clearly ineligible; Miss Mortimer too stiff, too much like school; Frances, to one of her generation, too informal.

'Call me Mée,' she said, on an impulse.

'May? Like the month?'

'No, it's what the Belgians say for Granny, Mée or Mémé. I expect the French do too.'

'Oh.' Speculation stirred in Amy's eyes, like carp in a pond. 'Yes, that's nice. But I shall think of it as the month too, because that's when we've met. And it's an anagram of my name, too.'

'So it is.' Frances smiled. 'Now, make your call.'

Amy picked up the receiver, and dialled.

Chapter 4

Persephone put down the telephone. Her hand was shaking so much that the receiver clattered on the holder, and it took her several tries to position it properly. Almost immediately, it rang again, and she snatched it up.

'Hello?' Her voice was scarcely more than a croak. 'Hello?'

'Mother?' Sarah's voice was sharp. 'Is that you?'

Who the hell else would it be? thought Persephone wearily.

'Yes, darling.' Persephone sucked in her cheeks, trying to force some moisture into a mouth that was as dry and acid as cheap fino.

'It's me. Sarah.' As usual, Persephone refrained from pointing out that there was, in fact, only one person in the world who was likely to call her Mother. Sarah had decided, at sixteen, that Mummy was too babyish. Their grandmother's early training ensured that the word 'Mum' was as unlikely to cross their lips as 'toilet' or 'lounge', so Robin called her Ma, and only Amy still kept to Mummy. Persephone's thoughts shied away from Amy, wincing as from the exposed nerve in a tooth.

'Yes, darling,' she said again. 'How are you?'

The question, so automatic, was instantly regretted. Sarah, like the grandmother for whom she was named, always gave this automatic courtesy a full and detailed answer.

'Well, as a matter of fact, I'm not too good. I've had this awful tight headache, you know how I get them, just across my forehead, and I didn't sleep a wink last night. Honestly, not a wink. It's tension, of course. I really don't know how long I can stand this. I mean, it's just more than I can bear.'

Or I, thought Persephone.

'Poor you,' she said vaguely, into an expectant pause.

'And then, of course, there's my back,' announced Sarah in tones of mingled pride and doom, like someone introducing a terminally ill relative. 'I haven't been able to play tennis all week, it's been such agony. I told Edward I'd have to have Mrs B. for another half-day, I simply can't cope with the ironing, you know how my back man said that the kind of half-bend one does over ironing or hoovering is the *worst* possible thing for people with my problem.'

'He didn't object, did he?' Persephone, who thought she could have become quite friendly with her son-in-law if she had ever managed to get to know him, tried to remember the last time Edward had objected to anything.

'Well, no, but he looked pretty glum. It's all very well for you, I said, going off early in the morning and not getting back until half past eight or nine, but I'm stuck in this house all day, and if I don't get out I shall go mad! I mean, I *know* there's a recession, and all that, but I don't see how anyone could regard Mrs B. as anything other than a *necessity*, with this great big house and the boys, and as for the garden – well, I can't even begin to think about that!'

Persephone found that she was standing bent over the phone, which was on a small table in the hall, in precisely the position that Sarah's back man had forbidden. She straightened up and reached behind her with one foot for the chair, carved oak with a cane seat that had looked so attractive in the spacious hall of the Lodge, but which had taken on a surprised and affronted air when placed in the small, rather dark hallway of the cottage. Sitting, she tucked her feet up on to the rail out of the draught that nothing seemed able to stop seeping in round the front door, and tried not to hear the ominous tearing sound as the small rent in the edge of the cane seating became a few strands bigger.

Sarah was now well under way on the well worn path of He Doesn't Appreciate Me and There Must Be More To Life Than This. Really, thought Persephone, it's so corny one could almost laugh, except that I don't know whether I'll ever be able to laugh again. This is my child, she told herself severely. My first born. That dear little chubby, dimpled baby that I sat and watched so adoringly for hours, she was so perfect, so wonderful. And if she has grown into a spoilt, peevish, demanding woman, whose fault is that? Mine, all mine.

'. . . and he says we can't take the boys to Greece this year, because the skiing was so expensive, and that we'll be lucky if we have two weeks in Devon, or Wales or some ghastly hellhole, and I said, but I *need* the sun, there's no point in having a holiday unless it's somewhere warm, and he just *looked* at me, honestly, Mother, I could have *screamed*!'

You probably did, thought Persephone wearily. But then who am I to blame you for screaming?

'Why don't you get a job?' she asked mildly.

'A job?' Sarah's voice was as blank as if her mother had suggested she get an armadillo. 'What on earth do you mean?'

'I mean, darling, that with Charlie at prep school, and William at pre-prep until four, you could look for a part-time job and earn some money. If you could contribute to the cost of the holiday . . .'

'Contribute! My God, Mother, when I think of all the holidays we've had that he hasn't had to pay a bean for, I hardly think he can expect me to *contribute* now! Besides, what could I do? My shorthand and typing are all to pot, and anyway, it's all computers and stuff now, and I know I could never understand them. And how could I find the time? I must keep up my tennis, if I *ever* get my back right, that is, and there's my bridge classes I've signed up for, and then Charles's matches to go to. And I couldn't have poor little Wills turning into a latchkey kid.'

Persephone, who knew that William went to play with friends after school at least three days of the week, decided yet again that she was unequal to the struggle of persuading her daughter to confront the real world. Sarah, encouraged by her grandmother to feel that two or three holidays a year were not only necessary but normal, was finding that living on the straitened income of a London solicitor, without the buffer provided by her grandmother's money, very hard to come to terms with.

'Talk to Edward about it. See what he has to say.'

'Talk to him! You must be joking! By the time he gets home all he wants to do is to eat, and slump in front of the television. And then half the time he goes to sleep in the chair! How can I possibly talk to him?'

There were times when Persephone found her deliberate policy of non-interference in her children's lives very hard to stick to. Edward, she knew, had wanted some time before to move nearer to his work, but Sarah had refused to leave Gloucestershire, on the grounds that the children were so well settled at school, that all their friends were there, and that she couldn't think of moving to a smaller house even if it did mean getting rid of the mortgage. Edward, as ever, had accepted her decision and continued to spend nearly two hours, morning and evening, driving to the station and fighting his way into London. He no longer,

Persephone knew, bought the first-class season ticket that his former income had allowed him. Solicitors, particularly those whose firms relied mainly on conveyancing for a living, were feeling the pinch of recession as well.

A wailing, slightly muffled by the telephone but rapidly growing louder, interrupted Sarah's complaints.

'Oh Wills, for heaven's sake! No, it's not broken, at least only a tiny bit. No, I won't buy you another one. It's Gammy on the phone, do you want to say hello to her? Here.'

Her voice was succeeded by the sound of heavy breathing. William was mildly asthmatic, and this tendency was always aggravated by having his brother home from school. Charlie's prep school, and William's pre-prep department of the same establishment, arranged their half-term dates quite arbitrarily to fit round the dates of Common Entrance, so that this year it was ridiculously early.

'Hello, darling. Are you having a nice half-term?'

'No.' William's husky voice was uncompromising. 'I'm not. I hate having Charlie home, he's horrible. He won't play with me, or anything, he just keeps talking about boys at school and saying I'm too babyish to understand anything. I think he's a prat. Can I come and stay with you?'

'Don't be silly, darling. Gammy hasn't got room for you in her little house.' Sarah's voice penetrated clearly, she was obviously quite near the phone. She might just as well have said 'her little hovel', thought Persephone. Sarah had not yet forgiven her mother for leaving the Lodge, the rather grand house where she had been brought up, and moving into what she described as a fifties monstrosity. Persephone looked at the front door, with its round stained glass window depicting a sailing ship in clear, nursery book colours, and sighed.

'Of course you can, William. I've got plenty of room, and

even if I hadn't, you could always sleep in a sleeping bag somewhere, couldn't you?'

'Cool! Can I do that anyway? On the floor?'

'I expect so, if Mummy says you can come. She's probably planned lots of lovely outings.'

'And you won't invite Charlie, will you?'

'Of course I shall. But not at the same time. I like to enjoy you both properly. Is Charlie there?'

'Great. See you, Gammy.' William had not answered her question, but his brother was obviously hovering nearby, as, after a short interlude of grunts and mutters indicative of a struggle, he spoke.

'Hello, Gammy.' His voice sounded subdued, but he obviously had his mouth right up against the mouthpiece and it echoed hollowly in her ear.

'Hello, darling. Are you having a good term, so far?'

'It's all right. Thank you for your card,'

'Did you like it? I thought it would make you laugh, though it was rather a rude one for a grandmother to send. Have you some exciting plans for half-term?' Persephone made it a rule never to put a direct invitation to the boys, to make them feel pressured into coming to see her. As a result they regarded it as an honour, and were always begging to come. Now, however, there was a pause.

'I dunno.' Another pause. 'If I . . . Could I come and see you, Gammy?' His voice was perhaps a little strained. She injected as much warmth as she could summon into her own.

'Of course, darling, you know you are always welcome, I love having you here. When it's convenient for Mummy, of course.'

'Mm.' Again he hesitated, as if on the verge of speech, but all that came out was 'Bye, Gammy,' before the receiver was laid down with a crash and taken up by Sarah.

Gammy, she thought. Somehow it had been impossible,

when Charlie had been born, for her to be called Granny. That name belonged exclusively to Lady Singleton. For a while they had experimented with Grandma, but when Charlie's baby vocabulary had come up with 'Gammy' they had seized on it with some relief. People used to talk about having a 'gammy leg', when I was young, she reflected. I think I must have a gammy brain. How could I have said he could come, when I've got all this business of Amy hanging over me? When I don't even know where she is?

'Oh, Mother,' Sarah was saying with irritable patience, 'I do wish you wouldn't say Wills can do things like sleep on the floor in a sleeping bag. It's so bad for his asthma. That little house is so dusty.'

'So was the old one, but I suppose that was upper-middle-class dust.'

'I beg your pardon?'

'I do clean my house quite regularly, you know.' Persephone bit her lip, aware of a stunned silence at the other end of the line. Such acid remarks were not at all her usual style. 'Sorry, darling. I'm afraid I had a very bad night, and I'm a bit crabby.'

'Oh, Mummy!' It was rare for the childish name to cross Sarah's lips. 'Are you all right? Do you want me to come down?'

Her concern brought a rush of tears to Persephone's eyes. Sarah, she thought, though she had many faults, still had her heart in the right place.

'No, no, darling. I'm fine. Just a bit tired, that's all. But not too tired to have the boys, if they'd like to come.'

'Well, we'll see. I'd better go, they're clamouring for food again. Heaven knows what they feed them at school, Charles never stops eating the entire time he's at home. You're sure you're all right?'

'Quite sure. Go and give some worms to the chicks. Is it worms tonight?'

'Spaghetti hoops, so near as makes no difference. And fish fingers, and chips, and cake, and ice cream, and Coke – all the things I swore I'd never let them have, when they were little. Still, at least I don't have to regurgitate it for them.'

'Ugh, disgusting! Oh, by the way, have you spoken to Amy recently?'

Persephone hoped that her offhand tone did not sound as artificial to Sarah as it did in her own ears.

'Amy? No, not for ages. Why? I thought you said she was spending the weekend with you?'

The trouble with Sarah, thought Persephone, was that while she rarely listened to anything others said to her, you could never absolutely rely on her not to have taken in what you had said you would be doing.

'Yes, but something came up and she had to dash off. I thought she seemed a bit . . . well, never mind. I expect I imagined it.'

'I should ask Robin. He sees more of her than I do. If you're worried, that is.'

'Worried? No, of course not. You know I never worry about anything much.'

'I know. I wish I could do it. I worry about *everything*.'

Persephone hastily said goodbye, to forestall any tendency Sarah might have to unload any more of her numerous worries. And of course I worry, she thought. I worry all the time. I just don't tell them, because I know what a burden it is, to have other people worrying about you. And now I'm worried about Amy, worried sick, and even though I know she's safe I don't know where she is, or who with, but at least she isn't with Mikey. Oh dear, Mikey. Michael. Such a dear little boy. And, it seems, such a nice man. Oh. Oh.

She found that she was hunched down in her chair, her head on her knees and her arms clasping her updrawn legs.

Foetal, she thought. Back to the womb. And not even a womb with a view. Not even a womb's-eye view. Pull yourself together, you stupid woman. You're fifty-five, five and a half decades, not five and a half years. She straightened her back and thumped her feet down on the new, hard, corded carpet (*very* hard-wearing, madam) that still, after six months, had the dusty beige smell of the factory about it. Resolutely she stood up, and walked the three paces to the sitting room door.

The room was pleasant, and if her children found it distressing to see the familiar, gracious pieces of furniture from the Lodge in so humble a setting, she was glad of their comforting presence. The cottage had two downstairs living rooms, one on either side of the central passage that was the hall, with stairs leading up at the far end to the two bedrooms. The kitchen, and over it the bathroom, were at the back, overlooking the small square of garden. Persephone, resolutely making the best of things and fighting the insidious idea that she didn't really care much where she lived, had used the last of her savings to put a neat little conservatory on the back adjoining the long narrow kitchen. This, already softened by pots of scented pelargoniums and trails of ivy and jasmine, formed a little dining annexe to the kitchen and allowed her to turn the remaining downstairs room into a kind of study or library.

'But Ma, what are you going to put on all these shelves?' Robin had protested, helping her to erect the stark but functional shelving that was all she had been able to afford.

'Books, of course,' she replied patiently.

'But you've got shelves in the kitchen for your cookery books.'

'I know I have. When I say books, I mean *books*. Novels. Thrillers. Romances. That kind of thing.'

'But surely you get all of those from the library?'

'Not any more. I'm going to buy them. At jumble sales.' She cast him a defiant look, and he laughed.

'No need to look so guilty! You can shoplift them from the barrows in Charing Cross Road, if you want to. Are you coming out of the closet, Ma dear? Join the club.'

'In a way.' She had not told him her true intention, which was that she meant to try to write something. That was too private to discuss, even with Robin.

'But why wait until now? Dad wouldn't have minded you buying books, would he?'

'No, I don't think so. Oh, I don't know.'

'I do. I detect the fell hand of Granny. What did she do, combine reading lessons with potty training, or something?'

'Well, she always thought reading was rather a waste of time, unless it was schoolwork. Reading was for when you were too ill to do anything else, or on a train, or something.'

'Poor old Ma, an anally retentive bookworm. Never mind. I shall bring you all manner of unsuitable books to fill these monstrosities, only you must promise me not to read them. Mothers aren't supposed to read pornography. You must just use it to impress the coven.'

'I doubt I'll ever do that.' Too used to her son's habitual method of referring to the village branch of the WI even to notice it, she had nevertheless left some of the dubious volumes that, true to his word, he had bestowed on her at each subsequent visit lying in prominent places around the cottage. The only effect, as far as she knew, had been that some of her old friends had taken to treating her even more gently, as though she were a fragile invalid, and she concluded that they thought her recent troubles had driven her a bit funny in the head.

Perhaps they had. Pushing the sitting room door shut behind her to exclude the draught from the hall, she drifted round the room. It was chilly, and she looked at the remains of the previous evening's fire sitting sullenly in the grate. Apart from the conservatory, her only other piece of major alteration to the cottage had been to pull out the hideous fireplace, tiled with what looked like decaying liver round a meanly sized arched opening surrounded by dog-biscuit bricks, and put in a wider grate in a simple pine surround. There was kindling in the basket, and logs, but she looked at them and shook her head.

At least, she thought, straightening the candlesticks on the mantelpiece and lining up the row of pewter mugs so that they were exactly equidistant from one another, at least Amy phoned. I may not know where she is, or who with, but at least I know she is safe. Her strained face looked suddenly much older as she caught sight of herself in the mirror in its carved frame that hung on the chimney breast. Even her hair, which with its new grey streaks was usually the most vibrant part of her appearance, looked subdued: less red, less curly. The hazel eyes behind her glasses were bloodshot.

She sat down in the armchair, and summoned up the short conversation. Her own attempts at apology, uttered in a flatly toneless voice because she was terrified of bursting into tears, had been cut short by Amy's brisk 'Sorry I went off in a rush.' It had seemed even more impossible than usual to ask where she was, but she had ventured an 'Are you all right?' which seemed, under the circumstances, permissible.

'Yes, I'm all right,' Amy had replied. 'I'm staying the night with a friend – no one you know, really, at least . . . well, no one you know properly. I'm not quite sure how long for. There are things I want to . . . well, you know.'

'Darling, I'm sorry, I'm so sorry . . .'

'Not now, Mummy. I can't talk about it now. I'll ring you tomorrow. Or the next day.'

That had been all. And more, probably, than she had any

right to expect after last night. Looking round the room, Persephone was almost astonished to see it unchanged. The soft primrose walls as fresh as before, the slate-blue and primrose curtains with their woven stripe and prettily curved and braided pelmets hanging in pristine folds, the carefully arranged pictures and cushions still in their allotted places. It seemed as though her own violent emotions should have stained and sullied the subtle colour-wash of the paintwork, tattered the fabrics, starred the glass with cracks and splinters. The room looked back at her, an unbearably smug witness to her fantastic loss of control.

'Oh, shut up,' said Persephone to the room. 'Mind your own business.' In the corner the grandfather clock, too big for the room but too beautiful to leave behind, ticked and tutted its disapproval. From its place on her desk the framed photograph of Lady Singleton, her mother, smiled inscrutably. 'I don't know what you've got to smile about,' Persephone told her sourly. 'After all, you didn't do any better, did you? You didn't even tell me I was adopted, did you? At least Amy's my own daughter, even if . . . I mean, why not tell me? Or, if you didn't want me to know, why not destroy those awful old bits of paper, instead of leaving them for me to find after you were dead. After,' she pointed out bitterly, 'you'd killed yourself. And left me here, wondering who the hell I am, like some kind of ancient teenager examining my navel. I may have despised myself before, but at least I knew what I was despising. Now, I can't even do that. We haven't even been introduced, me and I. You can't despise someone you haven't been introduced to. I want to hate you, and I can't even do that properly any more. You're not mine to hate. And you're not even here. I can't even ask you, tell you, scream at you like I screamed at poor little Amy.'

Suddenly that familiar smile was more than she could

endure. Pulling herself to her feet she went to the desk and put the photograph face down in the drawer. Then, of course, the drawer was too full to shut, so she took out the brown envelope and carried it through to the kitchen.

The late afternoon sun had dipped low enough in the sky to find the chinks in the lumpy cloud cover, and now came into the south-west-facing room, gilding the filigree leaves of the rose-scented pelargonium, and casting fine-cut shadows on the soft grey walls and cupboards. Persephone became aware that she was growlingly empty. After her hysterical outburst the evening before she had taken herself off to the bathroom and vomited, explosively, until her retching brought up no more than glutinous, bile-flavoured saliva. The muscles of her stomach and jaw still ached from that sickness, and the shock of finding Amy gone in the morning had driven all thought of eating from her head. Now she opened the refrigerator, shrinking from the sight of the steak and the leg of lamb she had bought, small fatted calves for her youngest and, secretly, best-loved child.

In the end she put an egg to boil, made a pot of tea and cut some brown bread for toast, sublimely unaware that in Sussex, Frances and Amy would dine on much the same nursery fare. When it was ready she carried it through to the conservatory and ate slowly, chewing each mouthful conscientiously before swallowing, like a well-brought up child with a strict nanny. After a second slice of toast she felt better, and pushed the plates away so that she could, once again, take out the contents of the envelope.

It was not something she found herself able to think about in a direct fashion. It was necessary to approach it carefully, as if she were playing Grandmother's footsteps, or finding her way through a maze. One approached the central point by going away from it, as often as not.

The most extraordinary thing, really, was that Sarah, her

mother as she still must think of her, had been able to keep it a secret. From the papers it appeared that she had been born in Belgium, in Bruges, a city which she had never visited but which was known, she recalled vaguely, as the Venice of Belgium. Sarah, Persephone knew, had spent some of the early years of her marriage in Brussels with her husband, who had been in the Diplomatic Service. Persephone had always understood that she herself had been born in Brussels at that time, two years before the war. Then, of course, they had been obliged to return to England, and in all the confusion the papers relating to Persephone's birth had, Lady Singleton said, been lost or destroyed.

Lady Singleton's husband, some years older than she, had taken his considerable expertise to the Ministry. Sending his wife and child to the relative safety of his native Oxfordshire, Sir John had remained in London, and Persephone remembered him as an occasional weekend visitor, always welcome because he brought some excitement and even glamour to their quiet village life, but also rather alarmingly masculine and stern. Her mother, whom she was accustomed to regard as all-powerful and all-knowing, seemed to shrink in his presence, to deflate slightly so that Persephone, at five years old, had had the alarming fancy that if she were to prod her mother with a finger, the dent in her flesh would remain, as if in dough or plasticine.

At the time it had been rather frightening, and had led her to regard her father with fearful respect, though all her memories of his behaviour with her were of someone quiet and kindly. Now, from this new viewpoint, she wondered why he, alone of all the people she had ever known, had exercised this unwitting control over his wife. It was partly, she thought, that although Lady Singleton had great inherited wealth in her own right, it was *his* position in the world, coming from his birth rather than from his own family money, that had raised her to that all-important 'ladyship'. That, certainly, was a big factor in her life, for although it was seldom mentioned Persephone knew that Sarah's family had made their money recently and rather dubiously, in trade. That Sarah should find this obscurely shameful was one of the many things that Persephone had always found impossible to understand about her.

A stronger factor, however, was almost certainly that he alone must have known that Persephone was not their natural child. The fact that Lady Singleton had been able to keep this a secret for so many years must mean that she had confided in no one. Persephone could not imagine how such a thing could be possible, but certainly the birth abroad and the subsequent turmoil of the war had helped, and the early death of the man who must have known at least some of the truth had enabled the deception to survive.

When the building in which he had a small flat took a direct hit, one night in 1943, she had been more shocked by the revelation of his disobedience in not having taken shelter in the Underground than by the fact of his loss, which at that time meant little or nothing to her, in terms of everyday living.

It was his death, she now saw, that had enabled her mother to carry off her deception. That her own adoption had been arranged privately, had possibly not even been properly recorded, was fairly clear from the contents of the envelope. The strange little agreement, written in a hand so young as to be almost childish, yet still unmistakably Sarah's, showed that this was no Adoption Society arrangement. That a young widow, deprived of the protection and help of her husband, should have lost her child's birth certificate and other records in the removal from Brussels, or in the destruction of her London home, would have occasioned no surprise, and with an extensive acquaintance in government and diplomatic circles it would have been relatively easy to obtain a replacement, though erroneous, birth certificate.

Frances Mortimer. Persephone looked again at the signature at the base of the agreement. It had been surprisingly easy, too, to find her. Unwilling to go to the dramatic length of hiring a private detective, she had started in the most obvious place. Lady Sarah had said, on the few occasions when she could be induced to speak of her own childhood, that she had been born in Sussex, and brought up there by two elderly aunts who had both died before she, Persephone, had been born. As a starting point, Persephone had consulted telephone directories for Sussex in the local library, and to her astonishment had found F. Mortimer, and an address in a village near Lewes.

The rest had been easy. She had driven down to Lewes and found a hotel there. The house was not difficult to find and was, she was obscurely relieved to see, a pretty place in the traditional Sussex style, tile-hung down to the level of the ground-floor ceilings, the brick below painted white, and pleasantly shrouded with honeysuckle and wisteria. She had loitered in her car in the entrance to a field not far up the road, pretending to drink morning coffee from a Thermos, and had seen the elderly occupant, tallish and active looking, coming from the rear of the house and out into the road. In sensible shoes, a tweed skirt and a warm, if dull, coat, she had carried the kind of stick that is more likely to be used for thrashing down nettles than for support, and was obviously out for a walk.

As she came level with the car Persephone had glanced towards her, and received a faint smile and a 'Good morning' to which, in a shaky voice, she had responded. Then, in terror at her own daring, she had started up the car and driven back to Lewes. She had returned home the next day, feeling both guilty and relieved, and resolved to put the whole matter out of her mind. That her natural mother, still using her maiden name, had never married seemed obvious. That she would not welcome the intrusion of an unknown and unwanted daughter into what was obviously a respectable and quiet life seemed equally obvious.

For a while, Persephone had succeeded in forgetting the whole thing. The consequences of Sarah's death, and the subsequent removal from her life of her husband with all the upheaval that this entailed, had driven other considerations from her head, and it was only later when she was settled in the cottage that she had had time to think of it again. Now, in the aftermath of Amy's appalling revelation, and her own equally appalling reaction, she fastened on this distraction as a means of hanging on to her sanity. The problem Amy posed was beyond her strength, at the moment, to deal with. Perhaps, she thought, if I can come to terms with this, I will become a new person. Stronger, wiser, even. At least I shall know who I am.

The comforting feel of food inside her, and the warmth of the cups of tea, filled her suddenly with lassitude. Her eyes began to close of their own accord, her body felt limp and boneless. She should, she knew, go upstairs and get back into bed, but even so small an effort seemed as far beyond her as climbing a mountain would have been. The wooden chairs round the circular wooden table that she had herself stained and distressed until they were the patchy soft green of old bronze had cushioned seats, tied on at the back. With her head feeling like a lump of lead she pulled clumsily at the ties of the chair beside her, pushed the papers to one side so that she could put the cushion in their place, and with a sigh let her head and folded arms fall forward on to softness, and oblivion.

Chapter 5

There was a hand on her shoulder.

'Ma? Wake up, Ma.'

Persephone tried to lift her head, but found her neck so stiff it was locked solid. Her lips seemed gummed together; she parted them stickily.

'Robin?'

She was not really querying his identity, and as she had known he would do he answered what she had meant, not what she said.

'You must have fallen asleep at the table, Ma. Don't sit up, just put your head straight and I'll rub your neck.' His fingers, warm and strong, probed the muscles of her neck and shoulders, the pain an exquisite pleasure. He had once had a brief affair with a man who taught therapeutic massage, and though they had soon found themselves incompatible he had at least acquired a useful skill, as he had informed her with a wry grin. 'Sarah phoned me, after she rang you. She seemed in a bit of a state, said you weren't yourself. I hadn't any serious plans – at least, the ones I had made fell through – so I thought I'd come and check up on you.'

It wasn't true. He had been coming anyway, despising himself for doing so and yet heading back to her with the childish instinct to run home at moments of crisis that he had thought he must long have grown out of. Until now. Until that call, the familiar voice, once so loved, that could still stir his feelings and bring an ache to the back of his throat, and behind his eyes. Harry. Oh, Harry. Impatiently he banished the memory, pushed it away, locked the door.

'I have to be in Oxford some time tomorrow, anyway.' He gave her neck a final stroke. 'There, is that better?' He stooped and planted a kiss on the back of her neck. Of all her children he was the most demonstrative, the one who found it most natural to express his affection physically. Persephone pushed herself upright, rolling her shoulders and lifting her face to kiss him.

'Aah, better, lovely. Oh, Robin, it's very sweet of you. I'm perfectly all right, you shouldn't have worried.' He looked strained, she thought. What on earth had Sarah said to him? As her eyes searched his face, he smiled.

'Well, I wasn't very worried, actually. But you must admit it is unusual for Sarah to fuss about anyone but herself, or the brats.'

'Oh, Robin.' There had never been very much love lost between Sarah and Robin. Sarah, who would have been delighted to have an older brother bringing home eligible friends, had had very little time for one three years younger. As adults, when they might have grown closer together, she had been both shocked and disgusted by the revelation of his sexual orientation, and had for a time refused to allow him to be alone with Charlie and William.

Persephone had felt compelled to remonstrate with her, a thing which she had not done for years, and the result had been a full-blown row after which Sarah had divided her attention between her father and her grandmother. This, since the whole family had conspired to keep Lady Singleton in ignorance of Robin's homosexuality, had in the end proved too much of a strain, and things had been patched up. Robin, however, still felt uncomfortable with his nephews, and was inclined to be bitter against his sister.

Though he liked children, his taste, as he had pointed out to her, had never run to small boys, and he had loved her sons not only as his relatives but as substitutes for the offspring that he would never, in all probability, be able or willing to father.

'What time is it?' Outside the conservatory it was pitch dark, and only a few lights showed where Robin had switched them on to find her. Now he went to the kitchen door, and turned on the concealed lighting under the cupboards and in among the plants, so that the rooms sprang to life.

'About ten o'clock. You must have been asleep for hours, the whole house was blacked out when I got here, except for one lamp in the sitting room. Are you sure you're all right? You look very pale.'

'Well, you know I always do.' It was true that Persephone's creamy skin seldom had much colour and never tanned to more than a faint dusting of gold. She had always been thankful, however, that she was not cursed with the greeny-white skin of so many redheads. She put up a hand and pushed vaguely at her unruly curls. As a younger woman she had spent endless time and money straightening them to a more fashionable style, but now she was amused to find that the tight curls with their tendency to go frizzy in damp weather were considered trendy. The young assistants at the hairdressers were openly envious of what they had to resort to endless perms to achieve.

She leaned back in her chair, picking up the cushion and hugging it to her for the residual warmth it contained. She still felt dazed with sleep, and rather shivery. He glanced at her, and filled the kettle. His movements were deft and economical. Even as a small child he had never been clumsy, had seldom broken or dropped things. With blurry eyes she watched him empty the teapot and take out the caddy, knowing that she never drank coffee this late in the evening. He was, as ever, beautifully dressed. Even in casual clothes he always looked immaculate, to Persephone one of the few little giveaway signs. His dark brown hair, so like his father's, was well cut and only slightly long. Secretly, Persephone thought that the currently fashionable ponytail would have suited him very well, but she knew better than to say so.

'No Amy?' She was not deceived by the careless tone. 'I thought she was coming for the weekend, isn't that what you told me?'

'Yes, she was, but . . . Have you seen her recently, Robin? Spoken to her?'

''Fraid not. Glimpses in corridors, that kind of thing. Big place, the Beeb. And I'd got the idea she had a new man in the offing, so I kept out of the way.'

Yes, thought Persephone, he would do. While making no secret of being gay, Robin was still extraordinarily sensitive in his dealings with his family. Deep down, she knew, he feared that he might cause them embarrassment. No matter how often she had begged him to, he consistently refused to bring any of his lovers to Oxfordshire when he came for weekends, though he was happy for her to meet them when she visited London. He would not risk any awkwardness for Amy, in the early stages of a new romance, and would certainly keep out of her way even though he was, at present, living a celibate life since the stormy departure some months earlier of his previous companion, an American, back to the States. That had been the longest relationship yet, and though he had made light of it she knew that he had suffered in the break-up.

'Something the matter with her? Problems with the new boyfriend?'

'In a way.' Persephone put a hand up to her head. 'I'm sorry, Robin, it's something I just can't talk about. All I can say is that the problem is me, not her.'

'Fair enough.' He accepted it easily, as she knew he would. Fanatically careful of his own mental privacy, he was equally careful of other people's rights to secrecy. He poured a large cup of tea, strong and milky as she liked it, and put it down in front of her. 'Wrap your laughing gear round that,' he said lightly, fetching his own mug of instant coffee and sitting down opposite her. 'What's all this?'

In the act of gulping thirstily at her first mouthful, she swallowed too quickly and felt the liquid burn its way down her gullet. She put the cup down, splashing the tea as she did so. He had already reached out to the papers, scattered over the table where she had pushed them from her earlier, and picked them up. Seeing her face he put them down, squaring them up with eyes averted and then covering them with the old foolscap envelope.

'Sorry,' he said.

Persephone felt that she was rejecting him, and it was suddenly more than she could bear.

'It's all right, it's not really private. It's something I found when I cleared out Granny's things, after she died. I didn't tell anyone about it at the time, because . . . well, I don't really know why, except that it was so extraordinary that I could hardly believe it, so I sort of put it out of my mind.'

His hand smoothed over the envelope, but he did not attempt to look at the papers.

'You don't have to tell me, you know,' he said. 'Don't feel you've got to, just because I saw them for a moment. I saw that one of them was in French, but that's all. It doesn't matter.'

'I think it does. I'm sick of having secrets. We didn't tell Granny about you, all that time, and think how awkward that was, when she used to go on and on about when is Robin going to get married and settle down. And Daddy, pretending about Susan and that our marriage was still all right, and me going along with it. All of that. And now I find she was keeping the biggest secret of all, all these years.'

'Worse than me being a pansy?' he asked wryly.

'Much worse, to me. At least, I think so. At least you *know* what you are.'

'Does anyone, really? No, don't answer that. What are you saying? You don't know who you are? Don't tell me the sainted Sir John wasn't your father! Did Granny have a naughty no no, and foist you on to him?'

'No – at least, yes. He wasn't my father. But she wasn't my mother either. I suppose, if you're a pansy, I'm probably a bastard.'

'Strewth.' He looked at her as if he'd never seen her before. 'But you looked like her.'

'Not really. Not facially, not in the bone structure or anything. Only the hair, and that was dyed. Hers, I mean.'

'Well, it would have been at her age, of course, but – when she was younger? When you were little?'

'She used to go for her "treatments", every month. I never thought. But I looked at the photographs of her as a child, and a young woman. Black and white, of course, but even so . . . I believe she was blonde. I believe she dyed it, later on, to look like me. After all, red hair is one of those instant things, isn't it? The first thing you notice about someone, an obvious likeness.'

'That puts a whole new slant on matching accessories, doesn't it?' He sounded flippant, but she could tell he was shaken. 'But surely, when you applied for a passport – don't you have to show a birth certificate then? Wouldn't it have said?'

Persephone explained her theory about the birth in Belgium before the war, the bombed flat, the supposedly lost papers.

'She knew a lot of useful people,' she pointed out. 'I

should think it was easy for her to pull a few strings, and get a new one. Why should anyone doubt her? And with my father dead, of course . . . He must have known, surely?'

'Presumably. But she could have asked him not to tell anyone, or something, and then of course he was killed. As you say, she knew everyone, and it wouldn't have done any harm that she was so stinking rich, either.'

'Mm.' Lady Singleton, who had inherited one fortune from the elderly maiden aunts who had raised her, gained a second after Sir John's death. He, to everyone's amazement, had left his considerable inheritance outright to his young wife with no trusts, and no strings attached. Very much later that was seen to be a pity, but at the time Lady Singleton had impressed everyone by the businesslike way she had handled her investments, so that the original sums had grown considerably over the years.

'Can I look at these?' She nodded her assent and sat sipping her tea while he read through the documents, pausing longest over the handwritten agreement.

'This one's extraordinary. She must have done it herself, without consulting anyone. The language is a kind of semi-legal mishmash, isn't it? Rather touching, really, if it weren't so close to home. And she signed it, didn't she, your, er, bio-mother?'

Persephone smiled.

'Good word. Yes. Frances Mortimer.'

'I wonder how she felt. Do you think they met? Handed you over? It's almost beyond imagining, isn't it? I wonder . . .' He glanced at her.

'What she's like? Well, she's certainly never been a redhead, at least. Quite tall, thin, long mousy hair in a bun, very old-fashioned and a bit prim. Country clothes. Speaks properly.'

His mouth fell open.

'You've met her? Good God, Ma! How could you keep

all this quiet? It's riveting! I feel as though I'm living in a soap opera!'

'I know. I think that's why I didn't tell anyone, I started to feel like a character in *Neighbours*, or something. But I didn't meet her, I saw her, that's all.'

'How did you find her? Don't tell me, Philip Marlowe, Private Investigator.'

She laughed.

'No. Persephone Hamilton-Knight, amateur sleuth, my dear Watson! It was ridiculously easy, because she's never married. At least, she still uses the same name. I started in Sussex, where Granny lived with the aunts, and found her in the telephone book. Not in the same part of Sussex – they were down near Arundel and this was just outside Lewes. I drove down, and just loitered in the car in the lane near the house. She came out for a walk, and said good morning to me.'

'Is that all? I'd have pretended to have broken down, or something, and asked if I could telephone.'

'I was terrified. I ran away. Sorry to have been so feeble.'

'Don't blame you. I should think Granny's ghost was gibbering at you from every corner. But how do you know she was the right one?'

'I suppose I don't, really. But still, right name, right sort of age, right part of the country . . . I just assumed. But I didn't feel any kind of familiarity. I couldn't see any likeness to any of us, or anything like that.'

'No red hair, anyway. And you didn't tell anyone? Not even Dad?'

'He wasn't exactly there to tell, by then.'

'No. He didn't hang about long after the funeral, did he? So that wasn't why he left?'

It was Persephone's turn to stare her amazement.

'No, of course not! Why would that make any difference?'

He looked down into his mug, swirling the dregs of the tea leaves.

'Just wondered. I was always afraid that . . . oh, never mind.'

'That what? That he left for some other reason? Other than Susan, I mean?'

'Yes. After all, Susan had been around for years, and he still didn't make the break, did he? And I thought perhaps it was because of me. Pretty egocentric of me, I suppose.'

His brown eyes, that like his hair were so like his father's, were shadowed. Persephone reached out both her hands to him.

'Oh darling, of *course* not! I mean, we didn't tell him about you earlier, partly because he was hardly at home and when he was we never talked of anything that mattered, and mostly because you didn't want Granny to know and we couldn't trust him not to blurt it out. You *know* that. And when we did tell him, after she died, he took it very well, you know he did. Better than we expected, really.' Persephone suppressed her firm conviction that George had accepted the news so well because, at heart, he cared little for his children as long as they were successful and he could boast about them to his cronies. 'Did you feel guilty about it, all this time? I'm so sorry, love.'

He gripped her hands.

'Only at first. But after a while it seemed to me that you were far better off without him, in any case. I mean, you didn't seem to be particularly upset, or to miss him, and frankly, Ma, he wasn't a very good husband, was he?'

Or father, she thought. Poor old George.

'Not very,' she agreed gently. 'No, as a matter of fact I was rather relieved when he went. It was a lot of upheaval having the divorce, of course, and I did rather hate leaving the Lodge, but on the whole it was the best thing.'

'So, since we're opening our hearts, why did he leave? Don't tell me. Money. Or rather, that's why he didn't leave sooner, isn't it?'

'Yes, of course. I never said anything, because it didn't seem right to run him down to any of you. The stupid thing is, I didn't really realise, until afterwards, that he only kept up the fiction of our marriage because he didn't want to lose out on Granny's money. Looking back, I must have been incredibly naïve.'

'But when you were first married – didn't he love you then? And you him? You don't have to answer that, if you don't want to,' he added quickly.

'I don't think I knew what love was, not properly. I used to read romantic novels, like Georgette Heyer, but always knew that real life couldn't be like that. I was hideously *sensible*, you know. Daddy seemed – well, suitable, Granny thought he was wonderful, and I liked him. He was fun to be with, in those days.'

'And did you . . . ? No, sorry, forget I asked that.'

Persephone was amused.

'As a matter of fact, we did. But I didn't enjoy it much, I was too scared of being caught or getting pregnant, so I couldn't relax at all. I thought it was uncomfortable and rather boring, but of course I pretended it was wonderful, mainly because I didn't want to hurt his feelings. I'd read, you see, that men are very sensitive on the subject of their performance in bed.'

'Oh, Ma! That's dreadful! Of course, you were far too young to be getting married. I suppose that was Granny, again. Why didn't you stand up to her?'

'I didn't really want to, not then. She had told me all my life that she knew what was best for me, and I believed her. Of course, it was only nineteen fifty-five, so all the liberation of the Sixties was way after my time.'

'Why was Granny so keen to get you hitched? Most

mothers would have been discouraging a nineteen-year-old from marrying, not wheeling them down the aisle.'

'I think she thought it was all I was good for,' said Persephone without self-pity. 'I was a bit of a disappointment to her, really, never managed to be the kind of person she wanted me to be. So she decided to find me a suitable husband who wouldn't interfere too much, and get to work on grandchildren instead. I may be wrong, but I've thought about all this a lot recently, and I think that's how it was. Of course, she didn't know Daddy wouldn't inherit the title, then. That must have been a bit of a blow to her. No, she thought he was the best I was likely to find, and she encouraged him for all she was worth.'

'Practically an arranged marriage. Unbelievable.'

'Probably no worse than many other marriages. We got along all right for quite a long time, after all. And I had you three, and that makes everything worthwhile.'

If I had my time over again, she thought, would I do the same thing? Quite probably. I suppose George and I did love one another, in a tepid kind of way. The worst thing was that we never laughed at the same things, and we were never really friends. George, of course, was of the generation that had been brought up to believe that it wasn't manly to have feelings, still less to speak of them. If we could have talked about things, would it have worked?

If I could have told him how little I enjoyed our sex life, perhaps? The trouble is, I thought then that it was my fault, that I was frigid or something. And I had nothing, then, to compare him with, no helpful magazine articles or books to teach me about erogenous zones. Poor old George, I hope Susan has managed to teach him a thing or two. I suppose it must have been pretty dull for him, too, with me pretending less and less as time went by, never initiating or suggesting anything.

Of course, Robin's right. I should never have let Mummy

organise me into marrying George in the first place. Looking back, she was wanting to found a dynasty, I think. With only me at her disposal – why didn't she adopt a son, I wonder? – she wanted to get me settled before I tried out my wings, and perhaps learned a bit of independence. And George, a rising young man at Lloyd's, not too well off so that he could easily be controlled, must have seemed just right. Poor old George again. He sold his soul for her fortune, really, and then in the end it all came to nothing. Funny really.

'What's the joke?'

Persephone had not realised that she was smiling.

'Oh, nothing, really. I was just thinking of poor old Daddy, waiting all those years for Granny to leave me her fortune, and then to have it all swallowed up in Lloyd's losses. And he couldn't even complain, because he was responsible for getting her on to those syndicates in the first place.'

'Another of life's rich ironies. Did you mind, about the money, I mean?'

'Not as much as I would have done earlier. But I was beginning to feel a bit like Marley's ghost, dragging a chain of cash boxes around after me. It was nice, of course, being rich, or at least fairly rich and with a rich, generous mother. And she was incredibly generous, after all.'

'Oh, yes, embarrassingly so. It was the most awful burden, all that gratitude.'

'Yes, wasn't it? She never understood that. She never actually *said* After All I've Done For You, or anything like that, but it was always there like a hologram floating in the air, making you do what she wanted. Oh dear, I shouldn't be talking like this. Especially now she's dead. I mean, it was the ultimate sacrifice, wasn't it? Only it didn't work.'

She remembered the telephone call from the housekeeper, hysterical with shock, the policemen, polite but suspicious. How quickly their suspicions had evaporated when they realised. And George, tearing up that suicide note that she had left, so clearly written for the coroner, so that it had had to be pieced together like a jigsaw. 'The stupid bitch!' he had raved. 'The stupid, bloody bitch! Why couldn't she at least have made it *look* like an accident! Suicides don't bloody well count!'

It had been as simple as that. With losses on her syndicates so unimaginably huge that it seemed clear that they would eat up every penny of capital she possessed, Lady Singleton had made her dramatic gesture believing that the estate protection plan would cover the losses. No one, naturally, had ever thought to warn her that suicide invalidated that particular form of insurance.

Furious with Lady Singleton and, by association, with her daughter, George had flung out of the house and back to his mistress in London. In his bitterness he had demanded a half-share of the value of the Lodge, which had originally been bought with money supplied by his mother-in-law but which he had, he said, been keeping up for all those years. Persephone, bewildered and shocked into a state of complete numbness, had found that she couldn't find the energy to fight him. The divorce had gone through quickly, the Lodge had sold surprisingly soon, and she had on other people's advice stayed in the same familiar village and bought her present cottage.

'Come back, Ma.' Robin's voice recalled her to the present.

'Sorry, darling. I'm not sure I'm properly awake even now. I think I'd better go to bed. Are you staying? The spare bed is made up, of course. Amy scarcely slept in it.'

'Doesn't matter if she did, I don't mind Amy's sheets. Yes, I'll stay until some time tomorrow. Of course, if you want me, I can easily put off Oxford.'

'No, don't do that, darling. I may go away, myself. For a night or two.'

They looked at one another. He did not ask, and she did not say, but his careful hands gathered up the papers once again, tapped them square against the table top, and pushed them back into the envelope. He handed them to her across the table.

Why not? she thought. Robin would come with me, if I asked him. But it wouldn't be right. Bad enough turning up as a long-lost daughter, without bringing a long-lost grandson as well. Of course, I should be tackling the problem of Amy, but I can't face that just yet. Maybe, if I can find out more, it will be easier to deal with. Maybe. Please.

What should I do? thought Robin. I don't want this, I don't want to be worrying about Ma, taking care of her. I want her to do that for me. To make everything better. Oh, God. As if she could. And now I can't even tell her, ask her . . . not now. Not yet. Why did this have to happen to me, to us, to her, to Harry? Above all, to Harry.

Chapter 6

Rather to her own surprise, Persephone slept deeply and dreamlessly, waking the following morning completely refreshed, with only a slight roughness in her throat and redness round her eyes to remind her of the excesses of the previous thirty-six hours. It was early, before seven, and she lay in bed for a while savouring the Sunday quiet, thankful for the physical wellbeing that made it so much easier to deal with the emotional turmoil. Even the thought of Amy, this morning, was bearable. She had, after all, plenty of friends. Besides, she was twenty-four, with her own life and job, not an inexperienced adolescent running away from home.

Of tremendous comfort, also, was the knowledge that Sarah had taken the trouble to worry about her, and that Robin – dear Robin – had come to see her. There was no sound from his room, but knowing that he was there made the whole house seem full of warmth. She had not seen much of him, in the last few months. Since Harry had gone storming back to the States he had kept away, and she had suppressed her longing to try and comfort him with the certainty that he would not welcome her intrusion into his private grief.

Now that he was here, it seemed a pity to go away. The food in the fridge would feed him just as well as it would have done Amy – better, in fact, because Amy was still young enough to care little what she ate, so long as there was enough of it, whereas Robin enjoyed cooking and was an appreciative and knowledgeable person to cook for. The idea of chasing down to Sussex after the phantasm of self-knowledge appeared, in the saner light of day, both self-indulgent and foolish. Let sleeping dogs lie, she thought, turning over and burying her face in the pillow. Let sleeping mothers sleep.

Twenty minutes later she sat up, pushed back the duvet, and got out of bed. The decision to go back to sleep had banished all lingering traces of drowsiness. She knew, too, that she was simply making excuses; that she must sooner or later confront her past and that now, if ever, was the time. After all, she thought wryly as she made her way to the bathroom, since I'm going to be in a stew anyway until I've sorted out this business with Amy, I might as well get all the anguish over with at the same time.

She bathed and dressed quickly, packing a few clothes and an overnight bag at the same time, and went downstairs. A cup of coffee and a slice of toast later she went back upstairs to clean her teeth and make her bed. Cases in hand she hesitated outside Robin's room, longing to speak to him, to ask him to go with her. She remembered his appointment in Oxford and went resolutely downstairs to write him a note.

The roads were almost empty. Nine o'clock on a Sunday morning of a Bank Holiday weekend, too early for the families going out for the day. Even the route was familiar enough from last time, and the accustomed manipulations of driving provided just enough activity to allow her mind to range.

She thought about her mother. About, she corrected herself, her adopted mother, Lady Singleton. Sarah.

For the first time in her life, she found herself able to look at her objectively. As a woman, a human being separate from her role and her relationship with Persephone herself. Also for the first time, she felt pity, sadness, and a complete lack of the guilt that had been the driving force of her life until now.

All her life, her mother had given her things. As a small child this had seemed normal, and of course in her early childhood the restrictions of rationing had seen to it that she had very little more than the other children at her nursery school. They lived relatively simply in a small cottage – Mother had not wanted to risk being landed with evacuees. After the war, however, she and her mother had moved back to Sir John's large country house that had been taken over during the war and used by some mysterious and secret branch of Intelligence.

At the age of eight she was already well aware of the unspoken bargain that was to dominate her life. Up to this point it had not been overtly stated, but it was inherent in Lady Singleton's whole attitude to her that, where much had been given, much was expected in return. There was, always, a burden of gratitude that Persephone never queried until later, when after Lady Singleton's death she discovered just what, in fact, the gift had been.

The discovery that, even by the standards of the exclusive little girls' preparatory school she attended, she was perceived as overindulged horrified her. It took only two or three days to realise that her hand-smocked and embroidered dresses, her little fur coat, her nursery full of toys, and the tailored jodhpurs and jackets she wore to ride her pony were regarded with awe and envy by her peers. Thankful that for school she wore the same navy pinafore and blazer as all the others, she begged her mother for some plainer clothes to wear when she was invited out to tea. For the first time in her well-behaved little life, she saw real anger in her mother's face.

'Well, really, darling, when Mummy thinks of all the

trouble she has gone to, with all the restrictions there still are, to see that her little girl has everything of the best, it makes Mummy quite unhappy to think that it's not appreciated.'

Persephone felt something shrivel inside her with a kind of internal quaking.

'Oh, I do appreciate it, Mummy, really I do. It's just that the other girls . . .'

'The other girls are all nice children from nice homes, otherwise Mummy wouldn't have sent you to that school, but they have not all had the advantages that Mummy wants for her little princess. Hand-me-downs are all very well in large families, but Mummy has only one girlie, and she wants her to have everything of the best. If the other girls are envious and spiteful, then perhaps Mummy should think about a governess, instead.'

'Oh, no, Mummy! Please, no! The other girls aren't unkind, honestly, it's just that I'm . . . well . . . different.'

'And so you should be!' A velvety satisfied look banished the anger, and Persephone felt a warm gush of relief that made her eyes fill with tears. 'Mummy's little girl is very, very special. She doesn't want to be just an ordinary child, like all the others, does she?' And Persephone, who longed with all her heart to be just that, shook her head. Impossible to explain that it was bad enough to be afflicted with her wild mop of red curls and her peculiar name, without having the additional handicap of being considered grossly spoiled.

She reacted by withdrawing, more and more, into a private dream-world. This habit was exacerbated by her poor eyesight. Lady Singleton had been affronted, even annoyed, to learn that her precious daughter was short-sighted. For some time she made Persephone do eye exercises, and told her that if she would only concentrate harder she would be able to see properly. In the end, of course, the pressure from teachers who complained that even in the front row Persephone could not see the blackboard, made her give in and order some glasses. An expression of dissatisfaction came over her face every time she saw them, however, and Persephone formed the habit of wearing them only during lessons or when she was reading in her own room. As a result she saw the world around her as a misty blur which had less reality than the imaginary one.

She was surprised to find that because of her red hair people expected her to have a quick temper, made all the more violent by being, as she heard one mother whisper to another, 'spoiled to death'. As a result she became very quiet, rarely raising her voice above a murmur and never expressing an opinion on anything. The other girls found her insipid, but harmless, and she gained credit in their mothers' eyes, if not in theirs, by getting a reputation for beautiful manners.

Lady Singleton was gratified to find that her daughter was well liked, and pleased by the other mothers' praises, but her expectations for her daughter were very high. When, in later years, Persephone read *Dombey and Son*, she found herself torn between laughter and tears at the exhortations to Mrs Dombey to 'make an effort'. Just so had Lady Singleton encouraged her, convinced that by making an effort Persephone could be top of her class instead of somewhere in the middle, could win prizes at gymkhanas or tennis matches, could play the piano, take the lead part in the school play, sing solo in the choir, or win the French essay prize. Persephone would get a part in the play or a place in the choir, might win a blue rosette at a gymkhana or get a pass grade in a piano exam, but she was always miserably aware that these achievements fell short of her mother's hopes. And where tennis was concerned she did not even do that well, for her poor eyesight and nervous fear of missing the ball made her so startlingly inept that Lady Singleton forbade her to play any more.

'If you can't do any better than that, Persephone, then Mummy thinks you had better not play at all. Of course, if you would only make more of an effort . . . I was very fond of tennis, at your age.'

'I'm sorry, Mummy. I do try, but I just can't seem to hit the ball, somehow.'

'Well, it can't be helped. But it does seem a pity . . . tennis is such a good game socially. Tennis parties in the summer . . .'

Persephone hung her head.

'Perhaps if I practised against the board, I'd get better.'

'No.' Lady Singleton was decisive. 'It would be a waste of time, I'm afraid.' From then on she would say, dismissively: 'Tennis? Oh no, Persephone *isn't* a great one for games. Of course, she's very sensitive, very artistic, you know. She simply loves coming to galleries with me, and of course she just adores going to concerts.' And Persephone, who had rather enjoyed netball because the ball was big enough to see, found herself cast in the role of infant aesthete.

She left school at seventeen, astonished to find that both staff and girls were genuinely fond of her and that, though she gained no academic prizes and had not even reached the less than dizzy heights of deputy prefect, she won the Headmistress's Cup. This amorphous prize purported to be for a girl who had made a significant contribution to the life of the school, and was actually presented to someone who was acknowledged to be a pleasant girl who had gone through the system without doing anything more dreadful than forgetting to change into white socks for the afternoon.

Lady Singleton decreed a year at a finishing school in Paris. Afterwards, Persephone thought wistfully that she could have had a lot of fun there and even learned to speak French had not her mother decided that she, too, would spend the year in Paris. She took an apartment near the Bois de Boulogne, furnished throughout with ornate carved and gilded furniture that made Persephone feel she was living in a museum, and dressed them both in clothes from the fashion houses that were the envy of Persephone's female contemporaries, and which attracted a host of polished, exquisite, cosmopolitan young men of whom Persephone, whose knowledge of the male sex was confined to the fathers and, occasionally, the brothers of her school friends, was terrified.

At the end of the year they returned to London. Lady Singleton, who had thoroughly enjoyed Paris, made plans for a Season to culminate in a splendid ball for her daughter's coming out. Persephone, who dreaded the whole thing and would secretly have loved to do a secretarial course and get a job, smiled and agreed. She was, she knew, a disappointment. Every time she failed to have the kind of success her mother craved for her, she was miserably aware that she was failing to repay her mother adequately for everything that had been lavished upon her, that she was not giving value for money. She thought, not infrequently, that if she had been a shop-bought item she would long since have been returned to the shop and a refund demanded. At the time the thought was no more than a rueful fancy, but later she was to wonder whether Lady Singleton had not, at times, been tempted to do just that.

The season progressed, and she struggled through the endless round of luncheons, tea parties, cocktail parties, dinners and dances. In her Paris clothes, with her brilliant curls carefully cut and styled, she attracted quite a lot of attention, and Lady Singleton took on a glow of satisfaction that almost made the discomfort of nerves and boredom worthwhile. And when, after a few weeks, George's attentions became so marked that it was quite obvious that he was seriously interested in her, Persephone felt that for the first time in her life she was being a success. For George, though he was not particularly well off, was good-looking, polite, and above all, well connected. Though he never mentioned it himself, it was well known that George Hamilton-Knight would inherit an earldom on the death of a distant cousin who, though only fifty-five, was said to be in such poor health that his demise was only a matter of time.

In the pleasure of having, at last, come up to Lady Singleton's expectations, Persephone scarcely thought to wonder whether she really wanted to marry George. He was kind and, if not particularly amusing, at least cheerful company; she did not find him intimidating, and above all she was so grateful, so very grateful to him for liking her and pleasing her mother. He said that he loved her, and so of course what she felt for him must be love, mustn't it? There was none of the heart-stopping excitement she had read of in books, her pulses did not race at his touch, and she did not find herself lying awake at night thinking of him, as she had done of the film stars she had worshipped as a schoolgirl. But at nineteen, Persephone told herself wisely, she was old enough to know that that kind of thing was only for books, and silly young girls. Real love was getting married, and making a home, and having babies. When she thought of having babies, her heart seemed to expand into something warm and soft and nest-like, and she was even more grateful to George.

They had a country wedding, though Lady Singleton was heard to speak of St George's, Hanover Square. Further reflection, however, convinced her that it was better to be a big fish in a small pond, and certainly the opulence of the flowers, the clothes and the catering were discussed, in a ten-mile radius of the village, for several years. Lady Singleton presented the happy couple with a beautiful house not far away.

'Jolly good of the old girl,' said George, expansively. 'Of course, later on, there'll be the family house to move into, but until then . . .' He paused, delicately, to make it clear that he wasn't wishing to hurry his cousin into his grave. Lady Singleton was less discreet.

'Of course, darling, when you move into your own house you will hardly need this one any more. And what fun it will be, doing it up together! Mummy will have to do some studying, to make sure we get all the colours just right – it's sure to need decorating, after all!' When moved, Lady Singleton was still inclined to refer to herself in the third person.

Persephone, afterwards, was to look back on this halcyon period as the high point in her relationship with her mother. Later she was to despise herself for it, but at the time she basked in the gilded light of Lady Singleton's approval, and gained at last enough confidence to stand up to her on rare occasions. After all, she thought, once I am married I will be away from her – the word 'free' lurked like a brightly coloured goldfish in the muddy pool of her ideas – and I will lead my own life, make my own decisions. Choose my own clothes, even.

The family house, however, never materialised. George's cousin, to Lady Singleton's chagrin and George's secret fury, made an unexpected marriage with his nurse, and proceeded to have twin sons. Persephone, six months married and already pregnant with Sarah, had already learned that her cage, though it had expanded slightly, was still firmly locked. Lady Singleton invariably accompanied her on every shopping trip. George, whose rise at Lloyd's was less meteoric than he had hoped, was only too happy to have a well-dressed wife at no expense to himself.

'After all, Perse,' he said, leaning back in the armchair his mother-in-law had bought and lifting a glass of whisky (bought by the case and put down on her account at Berry Bros.) to his lips, 'the old dear can well afford it. No use looking a gift horse in the mouth, is there?' His expression was astonished and pleased, as if he had just invented the cliché and it had sprung, fully armed and glossy with newness, from his head. 'I mean, it's not as if she doesn't enjoy it. Never happier than when she's spending money on us, bless her heart. It would be a shame to spoil her fun. Like,' he affected an American accent, 'taking candy from a baby. Eh?'

'Yes, I know. But George . . .'

'Mm?' His eyes were wandering back to the television screen.

'Oh, nothing.' He was right, she told herself. Her mother's delight in her pregnancy, which was great enough to transcend her disappointment over the fact that her daughter was unlikely, now, ever to be a countess, had been intense. Lady Singleton, for once bereft of words, had wept, and Persephone had been both astonished and moved. And how impossible, after that, to resent the fact that her mother bought (and chose) every item for the coming baby, from the pram to a teddy bear. A nursery, complete with hand-painted furniture, a specially commissioned mural of a woodland with animals that was featured in *Country Life*, and a life-sized rocking horse, was created. Persephone, who went through a dreamy, vegetative stage in mid-pregnancy, painstakingly sewed some little Viyella nightgowns which she then hid away. Lady Singleton engaged a monthly nurse and Persephone felt quite sure that she would compare them despisingly with the exquisite creations bought from the White House.

In the ten years after Sarah's birth, Persephone learned

that just as marriage had not freed her from her mother, her own motherhood could not either. At thirty-one she felt no more adult than she had at nineteen, and the advent of Sarah and, three years later, Robin, had if anything tightened Lady Singleton's embrace.

Sitting in the car, her mind ranging back over the past, Persephone wondered why she had accepted it all so unquestioningly. At the time it had seemed so normal, so logical, above all so inescapable. Somehow she had never really doubted her mother's right to control her life. She had always, without realising it, felt purchased, but it was only now that she properly understood why.

With that understanding came, surprisingly, sympathy. The very strength of her mother's will to mould and create her spoke of a kind of desperation, a need that had never been completely satisfied unless, perhaps, by the child Sarah. Now that it was over she saw something pathetic in it. Though she might never have known the misery of infertility she was imaginative enough to guess at it, and to realise the blow to self-esteem for a woman like her mother, who could buy almost anything in the world that she wanted except a child of her own.

That, after all, was the problem. Persephone had not been, could not be, her own child. If she had been, would things have been any easier? Would Lady Singleton have been more able to accept her imperfections, to allow her to be herself? Probably not. But she might not have been quite so single-minded in the trying.

The M25 rolled interminably by, mercifully free of lorries and, for once, without any traffic jams. Almost before she was ready for it Persephone came to the turn-off, and realised with horrible suddenness that she was in Sussex. On the motorway she had felt safe, isolated in her little metal box and allowing the outside world to pass by her in a blur of verges that could have been anywhere in the country. Now, on the winding road, she was facing the end of her journey.

I must be practical, she thought to herself. Go to Lewes first. Find a hotel. Unpack. Change into something a bit more respectable? Maybe not. These jeans are perfectly all right, and the jumper too, and it's not as if she looked particularly smart – not like . . . No, it's not fair to make comparisons. It's easy to be smart when you've got plenty of money.

The money, though, that was a lot of the problem. If her mother hadn't been so wealthy, surely things would have been different. Simpler. But it was there, she'd always had it, couldn't manage without it. Well, she couldn't, could she? That hurt. It still hurts. That in the end I, even the children, weren't enough for her when the money went.

Or did she think that we wouldn't love her, when she had nothing to give? Surely not. Surely you can't know someone all their childhood and adult life, and not know that about them? That I'm not that sort of person. That my children aren't either. I don't suppose I'll ever stop wondering about that. Or feeling guilty, that I didn't guess what she would do. But how could I? Did she do it for herself, or for us? She certainly thought she would save her money, by dying like that. If it was for us, what a burden. How can I bear it? How can I not?

The miles seemed to pass too quickly; she slowed her speed, drove like the elderly Sunday drivers she always disliked at home. Still the numbers on the signposts diminished: Lewes 9; Lewes 6. She began to feel sick again.

Why am I going to see this woman? All that stuff I said about finding myself, getting to know myself, is a load of eyewash. I know who I am. I have already defined myself. I don't need – have never needed – a voyage of self-discovery. Whatever genetic inheritance I may have, I am formed by my past and my present, and my expectations of the future. No, it's not me I need to know, it's her. The woman I have called Mummy all my life. I need to understand what drove her, so that I can be at peace with her memory. I need to forgive her. And, perhaps, to feel forgiven. Only there's no one to ask, no one to tell me. I can only guess, and imagine, and try to empathise.

Lewes 3.

And let's be honest, I'm curious. I want to know – who wouldn't – who my . . . what was Robin's phrase? Bio-mother . . . who my bio-mother and bio-father were. If I can find that out, and learn how I feel about it, perhaps it will be easier to talk to Amy. Please, God, if you exist, if you're listening.

A road sign, with a frog. No, not a frog, a toad. I remember it from last time. Beware the giant toad. I'm there.

Lewes.

Chapter 7

Amy wriggled down in her armchair. Its chintz cover was faded and worn, its shape bulgy like an old soft toy, but it was extraordinarily comfortable. The cat, at first disgusted to find a stranger in the house, had relented after she had fed it some crumbs of chocolate cake. Now he prowled into the room, surveyed it with a comprehensive glance, walked to the middle of the floor as if considering where to settle. Frances called him, so, ignoring her, he padded over to Amy and jumped on to her knee. She stroked him and he arched his back, lifting his tail to her touch, then settled in a warm heavy heap across her legs.

After their early supper Frances had lit the fire in her sitting room.

'It may be May,' she said, 'but it certainly isn't summer yet. Besides, I like the look of it, don't you?'

The rest of the room, like the chair, was shabby but comfortable. All the furniture had come from the Rectory, solidly made, unpretentious oak for the most part, and real feathers in the upholstery of sofa and armchairs. The walls were painted an uninspired ivory against which the faded pinks and greens of the chintz glowed warmly in the firelight, and tendrils of wisteria were silhouetted in the French windows against the dull sunset. It was neither fashionable nor particularly smart, but it was very homely with piles of books on the small tables, and odd little vases of flowers here and there, some from the garden and some obviously picked at random on walks, judging by the preponderance of wild flowers and leafy twigs. Like a nature table at nursery school, Amy realised with a touch of amusement. Once a teacher, always a teacher, seemingly.

The sofa and armchairs were grouped in a friendly huddle round the fireplace. Amy dragged sleepy eyes from the hypnotic dance of bright flames among the kindling, and became aware of something absent.

'I've only just realised, May – you don't have a television!'

Frances stifled a smile. Amy had spoken in the awed, somewhat awkward tones of someone commenting on another's physical disability, as if she had only now noticed that Frances had only one arm.

'No,' she said apologetically. 'I'm afraid I've never been very interested in watching the television. I love the radio, and listen to Radio Four a lot, and I adore going to the cinema, but television just never gripped me.'

'Goodness.' Amy stared at her. 'Do you think it's because of your strict upbringing?' she asked sympathetically. It was obvious that she considered this an aberration, but Frances was quite used to such a reaction. One helpful village acquaintance, noticing the same lack, had been moved to recommend a psychiatrist she knew – 'Really most sympathetic and helpful, my dear, and of course nowadays there is absolutely no reason to feel embarrassed.'

'No,' Frances had answered with a straight face. 'Nobody is called mad these days, are they? We all just have hang-ups.'

Now, she felt obliged to reassure Amy, child of her time to whom life without a television, let alone a video, was deprivation if not derangement.

'I don't think so. I do all sorts of things I was brought up not to do – like having a drink, and reading at the table, and – well, other things.' Other things, like having an illegitimate daughter. Like Jean-Pierre, she thought. 'I don't object to television, I just don't seem to want to watch it much. Actually I do have a little portable one, in the cupboard in the spare room. Sometimes I watch the adaptations of things I like – did you watch *Bleak House*? I enjoyed that so much. So if you can't face life without a daily dose of *Neighbours*, feel free to go and watch it. Though of course you've missed it for today.'

'Oh, no. I don't watch it myself, very much. I loved it when I was little, of course, but now I hardly ever bother. Besides,' she added innocently, '*Neighbours* isn't on at weekends.'

Frances managed not to smile.

'I expect you're out most evenings, with – Michael, wasn't it?'

A dreamy smile lit Amy's face.

'Yes. Nothing very special – I mean, we're a bit old for discos and we don't like going to clubs, though we did go to listen to some jazz once.' Oh, the delicious flavour of that word 'we' in her mouth, the careless assumption that they were a couple. 'We go out for a meal, or a drink, or sometimes just for a walk. I've never much liked walking in London before, but with Michael it's special. He's lived in Australia since he was nine, you see. London is still foreign to him; foreign, and special. You know how you make an effort to look at places when you're abroad, and never look at the castle or the cathedral on your own doorstep? He looks at things, and notices things, and somehow I see it all quite differently, when I'm with him. After university he travelled in the Far East – he lived in Japan for two years, imagine! – and in parts of Europe, but somehow he never got back to England. He was doing travel writing for a magazine, you see, and he more or less went where they sent him. Such amazing places!'

'How wonderful,' said Frances with real envy. 'And does he mean to continue travelling? Does he still work for the magazine?'

'Only freelance. He – he says he wants to settle down,' said Amy, blushing rather charmingly. 'He says he never realised, until he came back, how much his roots were in England. He'll still do some travelling, of course, but his base will be here.'

'You've discussed it all, then?' Really, thought Frances, it's hard to see what there is to object to in him – he sounds perfectly normal and open.

'We discuss everything. We seem to have so much to talk about, all the time, it's amazing.'

'I know. As easy as if you'd known one another always, and wanting to tell each other everything you've ever thought or done, to make it true.'

'You do understand, don't you?' Amy smiled across without turning her head, which was pillowed on a fat cushion as she sat curled up sideways in the wide lap of the armchair. 'Not everyone does.'

'You don't forget. However long ago, and even if things didn't work out, in the end you remember the happy times, those first few weeks or months. Hold on to them, my dear. Not everyone is as lucky as you. Some people never experience it at all.'

'But you did, didn't you?'

'Oh yes.' Frances laid her own head back against her armchair, her particular one that had a high back that suited her own, rather tall, body. Her eyes were half closed as she looked into the fire. 'Yes, I was one of the lucky ones.'

'But . . . it didn't work out for you? I mean, you didn't marry him, did you?' The question was spoken with the unselfconscious inquisitiveness of a child, and for once Frances found that she did not mind.

'No. He died.'

'Oh dear! I'm so sorry!'

'Don't be. We were very happy, for those months we were together. But I don't know that it would have lasted. He had been badly hurt, you see – lost a leg, in fact – and, besides, he was married.'

'Oh. But he could have got a divorce, couldn't he?'

'Not easily. He was a Catholic. A Belgian. Not very devout, but his wife was. I don't suppose she would ever have agreed to divorce him. We never even discussed it, never talked about the future. The present seemed enough for us, then.'

'It sounds very romantic.' Amy, tired from a sleepless night and emotionally overwrought, had tears in her eyes. 'Like an old film.'

'I suppose it was. Certainly it seemed that way at the time. Unreal, almost as if you could step back from it and watch it happening. But things were like that during the war. If he hadn't died . . . I sometimes think I would be looking back on it, now, and thinking of it as rather a sordid little interlude. That, after all, is certainly how it would have seemed to his wife, wouldn't it? Such a classic situation, too, the injured man and the nurse. Corny, really.'

'Oh, no! Not corny! But so dreadfully sad!' The tears were flooding over her lower lids now, weeping easily for Frances as she had not allowed herself to do for herself. Frances spoke bracingly.

'Well, it was sad at the time. But I'm afraid that old phrase about Time the great healer is true. To be honest, I hadn't thought of him for years, or only fleetingly. Don't look so shocked. You can't mourn for ever, and it was all so very long ago. Talking to you has reminded me, that's all.'

* * *

So long ago. And yet, how easy to summon it up. The old hospital with its dark, inconvenient corridors smelling of disinfectant, and bedpans, and the lingering effluvium of yesterday's boiled cabbage. Herself, a very immature twenty-three, proud of her probationer's uniform and terrified of the work that it represented.

What a struggle it had been to persuade her father that she should nurse! At the beginning of the war she had been only nineteen. Matriculating a year older than her contemporaries, she had not long left school and was still bewildered by the lure of freedom that this milestone carried with it. Her companions at school had moved on, one or two to university, a few into nursing or teaching, the rest to learn shorthand and typing, or merely to stay at home and wait for Mr Right. Frances had not felt herself to be clever enough for university, even if her father could have been brought to consent to her going, and since by this time her mother was showing the early signs of the illness that was, a few years later, to kill her, it seemed that her future lay in home and parish work.

There was, at first, a certain novelty to this. After two years at the little boarding school to which her father had, reluctantly, sent her, there was a pleasure in the prospect of being at home. To help mother run the house, to plan meals and pick flowers, to help with the Sunday School and the Brownies, these were enough, for a few months, to occupy her energy and, more or less, her mind.

The events of the outside world scarcely impinged. The Rector, an old-fashioned man, did not care to have a wireless in the house, and though *The Times* was delivered daily it was taken at once to his study. Occasionally in the evening, if he were not occupied and his mood was expansive, he would read extracts from it to his wife and daughter as they knitted or sewed, but it seemed to Frances that she learned of the impending war from the headlines she noticed when polishing her shoes, or wrapping up some item of rubbish, both of which activities involved the use of old newspapers. She was to find, in later years, that the most interesting articles and items of news were always and only to be found on the pages that were being scrumpled up to light the fire.

In the beginning, the war had seemed rather exciting. The arrival of evacuees, and the subsequent installation of four tearful children in the empty rooms of the Rectory, promised a new outlet for an instinct that had been roused by working with the Sunday School. As the months went by, however, many of the children drifted back to London, and those who stayed adapted themselves to their new surroundings, and scarcely needed her any more.

Her mother, though frequently unwell and sometimes in more pain, Frances thought, than she would admit, was in her element organising jumble and sales of work, obediently eking out frugal meals with produce from the garden, and establishing in the new intimacy of shared hardships a closer relationship with her neighbours than she would ever have believed possible. As the months turned into years Frances felt herself to be increasingly useless, unnecessary even, and all the time the call for women to do their bit in factories, in the services and on the land was becoming stronger.

Of the three of them, it was her father who was the worst affected by the war. With his own memories of what he could only refer to as the Great War still haunting him, he regarded all acts of aggression with horror. Believing, because he had wanted so much to be convinced, in Chamberlain's assurances of peace, the start of hostilities had come as a shock to him.

While committed, passionately, to loving his neighbour in the abstract, he found the invasion of his home by children who were not always perfectly clean, and whose language and table manners were an affront to his standards, almost unbearable. The heartfelt and secret gratitude he felt that he was, himself, too old to go and fight filled him with shame and, though he would never have admitted it, he found the restrictions of wartime rationing just as distressing. Ascetic by inclination and as an act of self-denial, he had still been used to good plain meals built around joints of meat, and while he would never dream of putting both butter and jam on his bread at the same time, it had never occurred to him that the butter might scarcely be there at all, or that there would not be a slice of home-made fruit cake to follow it.

He felt mortified that his own body should betray him by such unpatriotic weakness, and as a result punished it even further by insisting on giving away his small allowances of sweets and other luxuries, which soured his temper and made him irritable.

Frances, no longer a schoolgirl but a young woman of twenty-two, longed to escape from the stifling atmosphere of the Rectory. While she did not expect that her father would allow her to enter any of the services, she begged him to allow her to work as a land girl. His strongest objection, and one which she had not foreseen, was that she would be wearing trousers.

'I am, I know, old-fashioned, but it would greatly distress me to see a daughter of mine displaying herself in such unfeminine garments. If you want to work on the land, there is plenty that might be done with our own garden,' he pointed out. 'You have no need to leave home to do it. Besides, it is not suitable work for a woman.'

Frances, who longed merely to leave the stultifying environment of the Rectory, saw that he was not to be moved. While legally an adult, she still found it hard not to be ruled by him. If only, she thought, he would *say* that after all that had happened in the past, she owed him her obedience, that she had proved herself not to be trusted, that he had cared for her, forgiven her. The weight of his forgiveness lay intolerably on her spirit, there could be no relief from it because it could never, as long as they should live, be spoken of again.

Wiser, after her first attempt, she enlisted her mother's help.

'I must be useful!' she said, scrubbing ferociously at the stained sink in the kitchen while her mother sat at the table, scraping a mound of carrots from the garden. 'I'm not really needed here any more. Unless it's as company for you. I don't want to leave you, Mother, but I must do something.'

Her mother, hearing the desperate note in her voice, nodded.

'I know, dear. It's not enough for you, this life.'

'Is it enough for you?'

'Of course!' She was surprised to be asked. 'But I have your father to care for, and the house, and the parish. I don't need anything else.'

Frances was silent. It was only much later, after her mother's death, that she had understood how much her father had needed her mother's quiet, undemanding presence, and that she was in fact the stronger of the two, the invisible prop that supported his shallow-rooted self-confidence. At the time she felt only pity, the pity of the young whose life is ahead of them, iridescent and glowing in the fantastic colours of the imagination. Her mother scraped, the blade of the knife moving steadily over the carrot skin, removing as little as was consistent with hygiene. The noise set Frances' teeth on edge, and she was beginning to hate the sight of carrots.

'What about nursing?' her mother suggested after a pause.

'Nursing? Ugh!'

'I know, it's not really your cup of tea. But for Father – I think it might be the only thing he would consider suitable. You would be living in a nurses' home, after all, and looked after, and then it is a *womanly* thing to do. Not like working on the land, or in a factory.'

'I suppose so. I'm not very good with blood, though. You know it makes me feel funny just digging out a splinter. I wouldn't be much use if I kept fainting all over the place.'

'Well, you've never actually fainted, have you? And I should think you would become accustomed. After all, at the beginning you probably wouldn't have much to do with wounds and operations and things. I expect you'd be kept busy emptying bedpans, and making beds. Not all that pleasant, but probably no worse than mucking out a barn. Think about it.'

Frances had thought, and it had not taken her long to realise that her mother was right. The Rector, when approached, though not enthusiastic had not given an instant veto. And in the end, as her mother had predicted, the suitability of the work both from the point of view of femininity and of his Christian values had won the day, and Frances found herself a probationer at what had once been a sleepy cottage hospital, now enlarged with rows of Nissen huts to provide space for wounded servicemen.

The reality of those first few weeks proved very much as her mother had predicted. Frances spent them in a daze of exhaustion. Her legs ached, her feet hurt, her hands were chapped and red from disinfectants and scrubbing, and her stomach was constantly in turmoil from the sight of the wounds when she helped to change dressings. Worst of all, she lived in constant fear of doing something wrong.

From the moment she got up, and began to wrestle with her cap which must be gathered at the back by hand and then secured with elastic and safety pins, to the time when, hungry but unable to eat, she eased her throbbing feet out of her lace-up shoes, she seemed unable to do anything right. The needle which she had to force through the stiffly starched calico of the cap invariably ended up ramming itself up her nail or into her fingers, which meant blood on the clean cap and, too often, a septic hand. In the wards the beds she made came out crooked, the bedpans she scrubbed were pronounced unhygienic, she called the patients by the wrong names and was often in the wrong ward altogether.

Three months later she was still exhausted, but much of the anxiety had worn off. She could find her way blindfold round the hospital, mysterious names were no longer mystic incantations, but instruments or parts of the body. The patients, too, seemed easier. She had learned to deal with depression, anger, rudeness, flirtation and (occasionally) physical molestation with equanimity and cheerful friendliness. No longer did she blush at their jokes or turn away her eyes when she gave a bed-bath. The adult male body, once so strange and even uncouth with its blatant possibilities for sexuality, became a familiar object, to be cleaned and cared for with no more and no less consideration than one might accord a small child, or an injured animal.

'Nurse! Nurse!' The cry was always in her ears, even in her sleep when she would start awake, sometimes, thinking that she was being called. 'Nurse!'

'Oh hush, Jimmy. You'll wake the rest of the ward. What is it, can't you sleep?'

Jimmy, the ward comedian, was always in the forefront of anything that was going on, his long pointed nose quivering with pleasure as he bustled round on his crutches.

'Sleep? 'Course I can't sleep! I'm not a baby, am I? Too early for sleep. Now, if you could just help me up, we could be off down the pub for something that'd help us both sleep. Eh? Eh?'

'Pass out, more like. Shame on you, Jimmy, trying to lead me astray. What would Sister say?'

'Sister wouldn't like it. But then, Sister wouldn't get it? Eh?' He wheezed into laughter. 'I couldn't half do with a fag, too.'

'Not now, Jimmy. I'll make you a hot drink later, if you're still awake.'

'Right you are, Nurse. What's a nice girl like you doing in a place like this, that's what I want to know.'

'That's what I want to know too, most of the time.'

It was a stock response, to please him. In fact she found she enjoyed night duty. On quiet nights she could knit, or study, and there was a special kind of intimacy that came in those long dark hours. It was not uncommon for a man, silent and even morose during the day, to find his tongue loosened, his thoughts binding together into words and flooding out.

'That chap in the side ward's awake, too, I reckon.'

'Is he?' Jimmy seemed to possess an almost uncanny instinct for those who needed help, and though his jokes could be rough, even crude at times, they were never malicious and he was quick in the defence of those who were suffering. 'I'll go and look at him, if you'll settle down.'

'And a cuppa later?'

'And a cuppa later. If you're good.'

'You know me, Nurse, I'm always good. Now you be a good girl too, and if you can't be good, be clever.'

'Not much hope of that. I'll have to stick to being good, won't I?' She left him chuckling to himself in the dark.

The side ward held only one bed, and was kept for those more seriously injured. She scarcely knew the occupant, who had returned from theatre two days earlier and had spent most of his time in a drugged sleep. The door was ajar, and she crept in.

His eyes were closed, but he was not asleep. In the dim glow from the shielded lights she studied his face. Not particularly handsome but strong and clean-cut. Lying on his back, his arms and hands neatly arranged outside the pristine folds of the sheets, his breathing was slow and regular, the well-shaped hands relaxed. Only the slightly compressed lips and the frown between his dark, rather heavy eyebrows gave away his wakefulness. She glanced at the name on his notes.

'Mr Vandenbrugge?' Even now, after six years, her tongue did not hesitate over the pronunciation of his name. His eyes opened and the tight lips relaxed into a small smile.

'Very good! You must be the first person since I got here who has known how to say my name.' His voice held no trace of a foreign accent, it was clear and well modulated with the clean vowels of an expensive education. 'Are you perhaps familiar with my country? You know Belgium?'

His eyes were black in the dim light, dark as velvet against the pale skin.

'I spent some months in Belgium, when I was a girl.'

'When? You're only a girl now.'

She shook her head.

'Not at all. I'm twenty-three.'

'Well, I'm thirty-five, so to me you are a girl.'

'A nurse,' she corrected.

'Does that make a difference? Yes,' he conceded, answering himself, 'I suppose it does. The uniform, at least, lends dignity. Like a nun.'

'Nurses aren't like nuns!' she objected. The Rector, firmly Low Church, regarded Rome and its ways with horror.

'Not altogether, but not so dissimilar, either. The

insistence on obedience, for instance. Don't think I haven't heard you. "Yes, Sister. No, Sister. Sorry, Sister. Right away, Sister." He mimicked the breathless, frightened tones of a junior nurse, then drew in his breath in an involuntary gasp of pain. She took his wrist, fingertips on his pulse in an automatic gesture that she often used to cover the straightforward human instinct to hold a hand. His eyes closed again, but he turned and moved his arm so that his fingers gripped hers. His grasp was hard enough to hurt and she found this obscurely flattering, as though she were being initiated into an exclusive society by some kind of rite of passage. She kept her own grasp firm, continuing it when his own eased while with her other hand wiping the sweat from his face with a small towel.

'Do you want something for the pain?' She kept her eyes on his face, did not look down to the mound where a cage held the bedclothes away from his legs. From, rather, the stump where his left leg had been amputated above the irreparably shattered knee. He twitched his head in a silent negative.

'No more drugs,' he whispered. 'They make me . . . dream.'

She would have removed her hand, but he kept his hold on her.

'I should look at your dressings,' she said gently.

'Not yet. Give me a few more minutes. Talk to me.'

'You don't sound Belgian.' She said the first thing that came into her head. 'Which part are you from?'

'My mother was English. I was educated here. My father . . . we had a house not far from Bruges. A château, we called it, but it was really no more than an overgrown farmhouse. Pretty, though. Shutters. Two little round turrets. You know.'

'I know. I stayed in Bruges.'

He could not know that she was making him a gift, that

the months she had spent in that city were something of which she never spoke, never thought. Her reward was his open eyes, the pupils dilated with interest.

'You know Bruges? The Minnewater? The Beguinage?'

She nodded.

'Ja, mijn heere.'

His smile crinkled the corners of his eyes, banishing the tightly stretched look of pain suppressed.

'Een brave meisje! Et tu parles Français, aussi?' The shift in language had no power to dismay her, she was too used to the Belgian bilingual abilities. Nor, strangely, did the intimacy of the 'tu' seem anything other than natural.

'Oui, mais . . . but not as well as you speak English.'

'Oh, you English, so parochial, so insular. When will you learn to be Europeans?'

'When we've finished dealing with Herr Hitler, perhaps?'

He laughed outright.

'Yes – with a little help from Uncle Sam, maybe! Oh, I shouldn't laugh. You know that we are not ungrateful.' He lifted her hand to his lips. They were hot, and the part of her that was a nurse registered that he was feverish. The nurse, however, was in abeyance to the woman, and when he turned her hand over and kissed her palm her fingers curved by instinct to caress his cheek. The stubble, rough against her fingertips, made her skin contract in a shiver of pleasure such as she had never experienced before. She blinked, and saw his eyes fixed on her face.

'You should be sleeping,' she said inanely. 'Shall I fetch you a nice cup of cocoa?'

He allowed her to remove her hand, and tucked his own behind his head without lowering the steadiness of his gaze.

'You couldn't,' he said. 'A cup of cocoa, yes, but a *nice* cup of cocoa? A contradiction in terms, in this country. How you manage to make it at once watery, sickly and muddy is beyond my comprehension, but then, look at what you do to poor, inoffensive cabbages! It is nothing short of a massacre!'

'Well, I know it is no use to remind you that there is a war on, and I suppose your ideas of English cooking are based on your school food, which you must admit is hardly fair.'

'I will grant you that. Perhaps we had better not talk about food, or my blood pressure is likely to go sky high.'

'Then by all means let us not. Since you are so rude about our cocoa, you shall not have any. Will your English half allow you to enjoy a cup of tea?'

'It would, if you will have one with me.'

'There are other patients on the ward, you know.'

'All sound asleep, surely? If not, they may have a cup too, I suppose.'

'Kind of you!' She walked to the door, aware with every nerve ending that he was watching her.

She made the tea, and took a cup to Jimmy. But when she returned to the side ward he was asleep, his head turned to one side and his rough cheek cradled in the hand that had held hers. His lips, relaxed, were slightly smiling and she found her fingers curling in to touch the place where they had kissed her palm.

Ridiculous, she scolded herself. You are behaving like a schoolgirl. In the morning, he won't even remember who you are.

She left the tea beside him, so that he should know that she had come back. In the morning she glanced in, and saw it untouched on the bedside cabinet. Obscurely hurt, she made sure that she was busy at the other end of the ward, so that the staff nurse woke him. She did not see him again before she went off duty.

Chapter 8

What a strange courtship it had been, thought Frances. All very well for Amy, from a distance of all but fifty years, to find it romantic. At the time it had been frustrating, uncomfortable, and on her part at least, tense with the anxiety of being discovered by Sister.

When she came on duty the following night, she found him to be feverish. There was some fear of an infection in the amputation wound, and she was told to check him as frequently as possible, and report at once any rise in temperature, or change in his condition. She spent, in fact, most of the night at his bedside. At times he rambled, disjointed words in French, English and occasionally Flemish, and when the night sister learned that she had some familiarity with the other languages she was told to stay with him, and soothe him as far as possible.

She did not know whether to be glad or sorry. She had never had a boyfriend, and although she had been invited out with some of the other probationers to go to dances, or for a drink at the local pubs, she had never been in the least attracted to the young men she met. Older than the other girls, most of whom had just left school, she was seen to be prim and old-fashioned, her father's position making her, in their eyes, slightly holy and untouchable. For her part she found their jokes and slang incomprehensible, their language embarrassing, and their youthful brashness unattractive.

In spite (or perhaps because) of this she had begun to feel a gap in her life, a lack of something that made her an incomplete person. This, curiously, made her all the more inclined to withdraw from contact with an agreeable man. Life in a small country parish had shown her many of the pitfalls that could entrap an unwary woman, and she had no wish to find herself chasing a rainbow.

As a man, she would have shunned him. As a patient, however, he called forth both her compassion and her sense of duty. The sight of a wedding ring on his left hand, unnoticed the night before, scarcely made any impression on her.

For most of the night he was in a state of semi-delirium. Several times, as she sponged his face and body to cool him, he caught at her hand and called her 'Françoise', which was near enough her own name to fall very naturally on her ears. He spoke in French but she answered him in English, assuming it to be his cradle-tongue.

After midnight he fell into a heavier sleep, but roused later with a cry.

'Françoise! Françoise!'

He was struggling to sit up, and she ran to his bedside to restrain him.

'Hush,' she said as to a fractious child. 'Hush, now, and lie still.'

'Françoise?' His eyes were searching her face. For a moment the man of the night before looked at her, then his gaze clouded again with dreams and visions. 'Tu es là?'

'Yes, I am here.' She took hold of his hands, and as before he gripped her painfully. 'It's all right. The pain will pass. It will be all right. Hush.'

Her low murmur seemed to quiet him, his grasp relaxed, but when she would have withdrawn her hands it tightened again.

'Reste. Reste avec moi. Je dois . . . j'ai besoin . . . je regrette, oh, je regrette . . .'

'No regrets. No apologies. That is the past. Hush, now, the past is finished with, for tonight. You need only to rest.'

She scarcely knew what she said, it seemed not to matter as long as it was soothing, as long as she kept her voice steady and low. He breathed a long sigh, and turned his head a little into the pillow. Frances let her voice drop lower and lower and finally ceased speaking. His eyelids quivered, but his fingers were slack as she slipped her hands free of his. A movement of air and a whisper of starched apron behind her warned her of a presence, and she did not jump when the night sister came to the bedside and laid her hands on forehead and pulse. Frances fought an instinctive movement to prevent her, but he did not wake and after a moment the older woman withdrew her hands and gave a brisk nod.

'Fever's down a bit. Good girl,' she said in the quiet undertone that was less disturbing, in the silence, than a whisper. 'There's tea in my office. I think you can leave him now.'

'Thank you, Sister.' In the darkness Frances turned her head away and smiled to hear, in her own voice, the nervous obedience he had parodied the night before.

It was May, and by four o'clock the birds were already ringing out their chorus, a network of bright sound across the sky that seemed to summon the first light of dawn. Frances slipped back into the side ward. He lay as she had left him, but as she approached the bed he opened his eyes.

'Hello,' he said. 'Where's my cup of tea?'

When she returned with the two cups he had somehow managed to lift himself higher in the bed and was leaning back against the banked pillows, his face moist and pale as new cheese. Without comment but with compressed lips she set down the cups and fetched a towel to wipe his face.

'Thank you, Nurse,' he said primly, with a sideways glance. 'I'll be good now.'

'Well, you'd better,' she said. 'If you've disturbed the dressings, it's me that'll get the blunt end of Sister's tongue.'

'Don't worry. I'll protect you from the dragon.'

'Thank you, St George. Drink your tea before it goes cold.'

He took a sip.

'No sugar.'

'Oh, I'm sorry, I forgot, I'll go and—'

'No, no, you misunderstand. I don't like sugar in tea. How did you know? Everyone else brings me cups of syrup, and with sugar being rationed I never like to complain, it sounds so ungrateful.'

'I don't like sugar either. I'm afraid I always forget that other people might. My father thinks it decadent to put sugar in tea or coffee.'

'That must help make the ration go further.'

'Well, it would, only he insists on giving it away. He's a man of strong principles, you see.'

How odd, she thought. I never talk about my father to strangers.

'Admirable. But not very comfortable to live with?' He raised one dark eyebrow, and she smiled.

'Not very. Of course, my mother is used to it. And so am – was – I.'

'You don't have to tell me. I know. My wife, also, is a woman of strong principles.' He was looking down at his cup as if he could see into it like a crystal ball.

'Françoise?'

'Yes. I babbled, then? Nothing embarrassing, I hope.'

'Not at all. You just called for her. It's very normal.'

'And you answered? Thank you. I remember that she was – you were kind.'

'That's my job. And besides, it could almost have been me you were calling. My name is Frances, you see.'

'Frances. A boy's name.'

'Not when it's written down. Not as bad as Hilary. Or Vivian. You arrange these things so much better in French, though, with feminine endings.'

'Frances. I like it. It is a good name, a straightforward name. Better, I think, than mine, which is Jean-Pierre.'

'What's wrong with that?'

'It is so typical of the French not to be satisfied with one name. I could have been Jean, or Pierre, but no! They have to have that ridiculous hyphen tying them together. I mean, how many Englishmen do you know who are called John-Peter? There, you see? That makes you smile!'

'I'd never thought of it like that before. What did your English mother call you?'

'Oh, Jean-Pierre, of course. Having married a Belgian, against her family's wishes, and converted to Catholicism to boot, she cast off all taint of Englishness. Until it came to my education, that is, and then she reverted to type! But my father, who had nothing to prove, always called me Johnny.' He pronounced it with a soft J. 'Of course, I liked that no better.'

'What did they call you at school?'

'Froggy, naturally.'

'But you're Belgian!'

'Much the same, in the eyes of small boys. And really, when you think what they might have done with my surname, it's probably just as well.'

They fell silent, pondering the iniquities perpetrated by parents when naming their children.

'I was called Fanny,' she offered shyly. She had only recently discovered that this name, once so innocuous, produced raucous or embarrassed laughter from GIs. He glanced sideways at her, and grinned.

'Well, they *did* once start to call me John Thomas . . .'

The room was filled with a cool grey light that seemed to increase even as they spoke. She felt his eyes studying her, appraising, and felt a moment's regret that she was not in her summer frock instead of the starched calico apron that enclosed her like a carapace.

'Thank you,' he said, abruptly.

'For what? The tea?'

'For looking after me, I suppose.' For being yourself, he wanted to say. For not fidgeting with your hair, or your clothes, for your steady eyes and your unplucked eyebrows – yes, even those! – and for your wholesome kindness.

'It's my job,' she said again, knowing that it was inadequate. He closed his eyes and fell asleep, quite suddenly, like a child.

The following night she was kept busy with a young corporal whose stomach wound had become infected and who died, unexpectedly but not peacefully, in the early hours. Afterwards the ward was filled with the kind of silence that is noisier than a shout, and she could not go and hide in the sluice, as she wanted to, to weep away some of her anger. Jimmy caught at her apron as she went past his bed, his little eyes screwed up in a grimace that she knew was meant for a smile.

'You done your best, Nurse. Nobody couldn't have done more. You done your best.'

'Not enough, though, was it?' He jerked as if she had slapped him. 'Thank you, Jimmy,' she said, more kindly.

'You go and have a chat to your Froggy,' he said,

winking. She reflected rather crossly that there could be no privacy in a place like this.

'He's Belgian,' she said, stiffly.

'Same thing, near as damn it.' She thought of Jean-Pierre's schooldays, and smiled. 'That's the ticket. You take him a nice cuppa, when you've brought me one, there's a good girl. Froggy he may be, but he likes a nice cuppa, same as the rest of us. And you could do with one, and all.'

She shook her head and moved away. It would be better, she thought, not to visit Jean-Pierre again while he was in the side ward. Rumours were soon started in this inward-looking environment, and he was, after all, a married man.

Such good intentions were to be blighted by Sister towards the end of the shift.

'There's a specialist coming first thing in the morning to look at the Belgian in the side ward,' she said briskly. 'He'll be here early, so freshen him up and get him into clean pyjamas, Nurse Mortimer. At least you can communicate with him.'

'He speaks perfectly good English, Sister,' protested Frances, and received a baleful glare for her pains. 'Yes, Sister.'

It was a point of pride among the night staff to leave the ward ready for the coming day, with the patients arranged in clean, tidy beds. That sick men, most of whom had passed a restless night and had finally dropped into an exhausted sleep, might not benefit from a summary awakening and a cold, disinfectant-flavoured thermometer thrust into their mouths never seemed to occur to anyone. Frances went meekly to fetch a bowl of water, towels, and fresh pyjamas.

Jean-Pierre's eyes, with bruised shadows round them, were eloquent as he lay with lips clamped over the thermometer and watched her take his pulse.

'I can perfectly well wash myself,' he protested as soon as it was removed.

'Probably. But you're supposed to stay as still as possible.'

'It's so humiliating. And it's cold.'

'I'll be as quick as I can.' She, too, remembered the chilly bed-baths of childhood illnesses, the gooseflesh on damp skin that was always left feeling too soapy. 'You know I have to do as Sister tells me, and so do you.'

'I know. But I don't have to like it.'

The skin of his arms and body was pale and fine, the dark hair of chest and armpit showing stark against it. She soaped and wiped and dried briskly, impersonally. He lay still, raising and lowering his arms at her touch, his face turned to the glowing light of the window. She pulled the sheet lower, and found that he had an erection. She was neither shocked nor surprised.

He turned his head to look at her. Unusually, his face was calm, almost cold. He neither apologised, nor looked embarrassed, nor made a ribald remark. In the stillness of his face only his eyes were alive, holding her gaze. Moving slowly, deliberately, she put her hand on him and saw the quiver that ran through his body, the sudden contraction of muscles in stomach and thighs. She moved her hand, surprised by the physical combination of inner hardness with soft, almost velvety skin.

In a few seconds he climaxed. She had closed her eyes, hearing his harshly quickened breathing through the pounding of blood in her ears. Then he drew in one long, sobbing breath and was quiet. She opened her eyes, disconcerted to find his own gaze still fixed on her, knowing at once that it had been throughout. Without speaking she continued the bath.

When the painful business of putting on his clean pyjamas was accomplished, she began to clear up the cloths and towels. Neither of them had spoken, and she felt unable to look him in the face.

'Frances.'

The towels were all folded, there was nothing left to occupy her hands and eyes. He was holding out his hand. To ignore it would be an insult. She took it, half expecting that he would put it to his lips as he had done before. Instead he tugged on it so that she had to come nearer, and nearer still until she stood beside him, her apron crackling against the side of the bed. Still he pulled on her hand. She knew that if she made only one movement of resistance or withdrawal he would stop at once, but as if in a trance she allowed him to pull her down until he could kiss her lips. His own were dry, slightly cracked. It was a sexless gesture, such a kiss as a boy might give his mother or his sister. She could not raise her eyes above his mouth.

'Look at me.'

He knew that if she did not, shame and embarrassment would keep her from ever coming near him again.

'Look at me, Frances.'

The pupils in her eyes were tiny, unfocused, as if she had taken some strong narcotic. He saw that she was in a state, almost, of shock. What, he wondered wryly, was the correct thing to say, under the circumstances? An experienced man, none of his previous dealings with women had prepared him for a situation like this. Unnerved, he blurted out the first thing that came into his head.

'It's all right.' It sounded inane to his own ears, but it seemed to be the right thing to say. He felt the infinitesimal easing of tension in the hand he still held, saw the muscles round her mouth relax and her pupils dilate to normal. 'It's all right,' he repeated.

She did not say, as he had feared she might, 'I don't know what you must think of me.' She did not, in fact, say anything at all. He lifted his free hand and touched his fingers to her face, running them across the clear brow, round the hard curve of eye socket and cheekbone, across the smooth plane of her cheek to her lips. Before they moved on to her chin he felt the tiny movement that was the hint of a kiss, and smiled.

Frances went off duty in a daze. Part of her mind was scolding: haven't you done yourself enough damage, already, with one mad impulse of sympathy? Don't you know, yet, what harm such a man could do you? It scolded in her father's voice, and she blanked it out, like tuning out a radio station. She felt exhilarated, every nerve ending tingling, not knowing whether she wanted to dance, or weep, or sing, or laugh. She felt that she must look different, glowing, and was amazed that the other nurses in the canteen seemed to notice no difference in her as they queued up for pie and mashed potatoes, and bowls of stewed apple and custard.

Around her the hospital gossip flowed, rather like the hospital custard; unnaturally coloured, with indigestible lumps in its thin glutinousness, and the occasional tasty bit of skin. Complaints of aching feet, and chapped hands, and the biting things that Sister said mingled with the tiresome or amusing habits of the patients and the prospects of a dance on Saturday night. Frances treated it as she did the custard, picking out the parts that she wanted and ignoring the rest.

'You've done all right for yourself, then, getting your hooks into that Belgian with the leg.'

The nurse to her left, who shared her night duty, was a notorious gossip and Frances felt her skin contract, her mouth drying as if she had bitten into a sloe.

'There's a specialist coming to see him this morning,' she offered, as distraction from herself. 'About his leg, I suppose.'

'Well, I don't know why he should get all that fussing, private room and everything. There's plenty in this place worse injured than he is, and he's not even one of our boys.'

'Come off it, Murgatroyd.' A round-faced girl spoke from across the table. 'Anyone would think he was a German, to hear you carry on. The French are having a tough time, by all accounts. Don't grudge the poor chap a bit of TLC.'

'He's Belgian . . .'

'Same thing. Anyway, I heard he's a hero. Involved in some group that was helping our people to escape. Got I don't know how many of them back to England, before he was hurt.'

'How did it happen?' Frances, unable to resist asking, despised herself.

'Don't know. Why don't you ask him? You speaka da lingo.'

'He speaks English as well as you do.' Better, actually, she thought crossly. 'His mother was English, and he went to school here.'

'Oh. He's rather handsome, isn't he?'

'Do you think so?' Frances fought to keep her voice offhand.

'Don't you? I suppose you're too saintly to notice.'

'Too busy, that's all. Besides, he's married.' To her horror, her voice sounded plaintive in her own ears. She pushed away her plate and stood up.

'I shouldn't let that worry you. After all, she's over there, and he's over here, and who knows whether they'll ever even see each other again? You don't want to let a little thing like that put you off, not at a time like this. Not when there's a war on.'

Her father's daughter cringed, but the person she was learning to be heard the rough sympathy behind the crude morality, so she smiled.

'It's not me that's likely to be put off, it's him. I'm off to bed. Good night.'

'Sleep tight, mind the bugs don't bite. Sweet dreams, Mortimer. At least that's one thing they can't stop you from doing.'

'Sleeping?'

'Dreaming. You just get dreaming, girl. Seems to me you've been awake too long.'

Back in her room she undressed and stood before the mirror. The early morning sunshine flooded in, lighting her body so that the pale skin looked dazzlingly white. After weeks of picking at hospital food when exhaustion and nausea had killed her appetite, she was thin. Her stomach was hollow, blue-shadowed beneath her rib cage and between jutting hip bones. Against the luminous skin her nipples looked darker than she remembered them, puckered – the air was chilly – into deep pink points on breasts that were less full than they had been. She cupped them in her hands, surprised by the sensitivity of her nipples and by the shiver that ran down her back. Were they softer than before? Was that, and the pigmentation, something that happened when you had a baby? Would he . . . would anyone who saw her . . . know?

She moved her hands down to the concave stomach, remembering. Her navel was an indigo shadow: then, it had projected and been so sensitive that it had frightened her. She had felt that the slightest touch would damage it, that she would gush out blood and water from her distended belly. She stroked her hands – was the skin here, too, less elastic than it should be?

The triangle of her pubic hair looked dark, almost black, between the whiteness of her thighs. Her hands hesitated, moved, touched. There had been times, in the last few years, when she had woken from unremembered dreams to a throbbing warmth that she scarcely allowed herself to recognise as pleasurable. She could feel that warmth now beneath her questing fingers and, as she explored, a sharp stab of excitement that was so intense it was almost pain.

Outside, a cloud went across the sun and the light dimmed. Frances started and glanced at the window, almost expecting to see someone watching her in disgust or anger, though she was two floors up. A puff of chilly air came through the open casement and she shivered, her skin puckering into gooseflesh. Going to the bed she put on her nightdress, shivering again as the cold cotton slipped over her skin. She closed the curtains, climbed into bed, and lay on her back with her hands by her sides. Her feet were cold, but she did not move. Rigid with self-disgust, she clenched her hands into fists. Was she, as her father had said bitterly in his first anger, no better than a whore? A woman so lost to all sense of decency that a look, a smile and a kiss from a married man were enough to make her forget every Christian value she had been brought up to revere?

And yet . . . It's all right, he had said. It's all right. And she had believed him. Even now, with his voice echoing in her ears, she still believed him and was comforted. Maybe it was all right, after all. She relaxed. The bed was warmer now. Suddenly exhausted, she turned on her side, curled up so that her feet were in the nest of warmth her body had created, and slept.

Chapter 9

'Avoiding me?'

Frances hovered just inside the doorway. The night shift was almost over. The day before she had dreamed of him, as Nurse Murgatroyd had suggested, and had woken from those dreams sweating and horrified, unable to believe that her subconscious could betray her into such wanton behaviour.

'Yes.'

'Then don't. You are embarrassed, but why? An act of kindness, of generosity, no more. The action, if you like, of a nurse. Think of it, if you want to, as of no more significance than bringing me a bedpan.'

'Is that how you think of it?'

'Of course not. I have more respect for my body, and for you. But I do not wish you to be ashamed or uncomfortable. And I don't want you to think that I will take advantage – that wonderful old-fashioned English phrase! – of your kindness. I shall not be expecting it to happen again. And when – if – you look at me, I don't want you to see me just as that.' He gestured. 'That is only one part of my body. There are other parts, though fewer than before, sadly, as well as a mind and, I suppose, a soul.'

Frances came to the bedside.

'It's just that I've never . . .'

'No, I don't suppose you have. Not many women would

be so understanding of a man's needs, I don't think. At least, my wife wouldn't have.'

Startled, Frances' eyes flew to his face.

'Oh, but surely . . . I mean, under the circumstances? Your leg . . . ?'

'Françoise never touches me. Oh, she would nurse me, of course, as a dutiful Christian wife should. She would change the dressings, and wash me, and be all gentleness, all consideration. Do I disgust you?'

The abrupt question made her blink.

'No! No, of course not! And I'm sure she wouldn't be disgusted by you either. You're just upset about your leg.'

'No. You don't understand. She wouldn't mind about my leg. She would probably like it. She would like to see me as an invalid, someone she could care for like a child. It would be better than nothing, I suppose.'

His face was quite blank, but his voice was so bitter that the air seemed acrid with it.

'For you, or for her?' This was not new ground for Frances. It was not the first time that a wounded man had poured out his anger, his insecurity, even his hatred for those who were still whole and undamaged. Her brisk tone, calculated to deflate self-pity and lower the emotional level, had no effect.

'For her, of course. For me . . .' He shrugged, and for the first time she saw him as not an Englishman. 'For me, I would rather have her hatred than her pity. But I will have both, I suppose.'

'Come along, Nurse, it's time for Obs, if we're to get the ward straight before the end of the shift.' The staff nurse's brisk voice cut between them like a knife. Frances jumped, then automatically reached out for the thermometer in its container, shook it down, and pushed it unceremoniously into Jean-Pierre's mouth. His hot eyes glared at her as she laid careful fingers on his pulse, and with her other hand lifted the watch at her breast. The pulse was rapid; his temperature, when she removed the thermometer, up again. Without a word she marked his chart.

'Don't go.' It was spoken like an order, but his eyes pleaded.

'I must. Staff will be after me.'

'I want to talk to you . . .'

'Later.' There was no time, no time to talk or to listen. 'Remember the nuns? Our timetable is just as strict.'

'It's inhuman.'

'It's discipline. And I am subject to it. But I'll come back later.'

Frances came back at the only time that seemed possible, during the visiting hour. At three o'clock she walked nervously into the ward, along with a few other visitors who lived near enough, or who had braved the intricacies of wartime travelling in order to visit a husband or a son. It seemed strange to be out of uniform, and she had picked over her scanty wardrobe before selecting a simple cotton frock, not very new but of good, pre-war material and as well cut as the village dressmaker could manage. Her hair, long enough now to be pinned up under her cap, she left loose, curling the ends under with borrowed tongs. The girl who lent them generously offered a lipstick, but after a moment's hesitation Frances shook her head, smiling.

'Oh, go on! Everyone wears it now! It's a nice colour, too, just right with that frock.'

'It's sweet of you, but no. I should feel uncomfortable and silly, and then I'd look silly too. Thanks anyway.'

At the entrance of the ward, waiting with the other visitors, she wished she had said yes, and only the recollection that the other girl would by now be fast asleep stopped her from running back to the nurses' home. Turning her face away, she bit her lips hard. Her hands were damp with perspiration, and she took a handkerchief out to wipe them. The doors were opened, and with a little discreet shoving the other people pushed their way in, their feet clacking on the polished floor as they hurried. Frances followed more slowly.

His eyes were closed, his face turned away from the open doorway. Visiting hour is not an easy time for a man who never expects to get any visitors. She went in quietly, in case he was asleep, and when she reached the bedside he spoke without moving.

'Frances.'

'Hello, Jean-Pierre.'

'I hoped you might come, but I didn't think you would. When will you get some sleep? You'll be exhausted.'

'I slept this morning. It won't hurt, just this once. After all, people stay out late at parties and still go to work the next morning, don't they?'

'They do. But do you?'

'Well, I never have done. But that doesn't mean I never shall.' She reached down to look at his chart. 'Hmm. Temperature still up a bit, I see.'

At last he turned his head towards her.

'I shall try not to get too excited, Nurse,' he said primly, his eyes glinting. 'But I must say you look very nice, just the thing to send a poor invalid's temperature soaring. And how sensible of you not to wear any lipstick.'

'Why?'

As an answer he took her hand and pulled it, as he had done before. This time, however, his kiss was far from brotherly, and when she felt his tongue probing between her lips she started back in surprise. No one had ever done anything like that to her before; she had no idea whether it was a normal thing and was confused, embarrassed, and slightly disgusted. At once he let go of her hand.

'I beg your pardon.' The formal phrase was as hard as pebbles dropped on to flagstones. She resisted the impulse to wipe her mouth with her hand, flushing miserably.

'No, it's all right, it's just . . . the door is open.' She was glad of an excuse to turn away, push the door shut, take a deep breath to calm her shaking voice.

'Got a bit carried away, I'm afraid.' This time the voice was pure English public school. 'Won't happen again.'

This was not at all how she had meant it to be. This cold-voiced stranger was not the Jean-Pierre of the last few nights. Unsure of herself she walked back to the bedside, bent over him, and put her lips to his. She pressed them down, as she had seen in screen kisses at the cinema, but his mouth was flat and unresponsive. All she could feel was the hardness of his teeth beneath flaccid lips. Greatly daring, she pushed the tip of her tongue between her own lips and against his.

Her eyes were firmly closed but she was sure she could feel his eyebrows rise in astonishment. His lips firmed against hers and she retained enough self-command not to pull away as they parted. Bravely she pushed her tongue between them. What am I doing? she thought. Is this what everyone does, or is it some kind of perversion? Or is it something men do to women, and not the other way round? Am I making a complete fool of myself? Will he laugh at me?

Then his mouth moved against hers, and his hands were warm against her back and behind her head, firm and secure. And suddenly it was all different. Her tense muscles slackened and went as soft as warm toffee. His lips, which had felt rubbery against hers, were alive and demanding and his tongue was no longer sluglike but something that teased and caressed. Abruptly she ceased to be aware of herself, no longer watched herself from outside like an anxious mother peering through a classroom window on her child's first day at school. It's all right, she thought. It's going to be all right.

'We had an affair,' Frances heard herself say baldly to Amy. An affair. How brusque, how sordid, even. And yet, how to express what had happened? How to describe the slow, exquisite process of his seduction: necessarily slow, because of his leg, so that for a long time (or so it seemed to her, then) there could be no more between them than kissing and touching. How could a generation who, as it seemed to her, appeared to regard the sexual act as the inevitable and immediate outcome of a kiss, understand the glory of a look, a touch, of the gradual awakening of bodily sensations involved in the long-drawn-out mutual exploration, not just of the intimate parts of the anatomy but of hands and arms, cheeks, necks, ears, shoulders, knees, feet?

Amy's expression was carefully controlled, but Frances was too well accustomed to dealing with young people not to see the hidden astonishment, dismay, even disbelief that she was feeling. Impossible, she supposed, for this child to imagine her as a young woman, to see her as anything but a retired schoolteacher in sensible tweed with her hair in a bun. The idea of passion, when connected to the elderly, can only seem grotesque to a girl of her age.

Goodness, thought Amy. It must be true, of course, but it's so – so cringe-making. And one of his legs only a stump, too, which must have been sore. Does that mean that she . . . that he couldn't . . . Oh, I wish I'd never started this. What can I say?

'Have you got a photo of him?' The words seemed to come from nowhere, summoned by her mental images that, try as she might, she could only see in black and white, flickery as an old film.

'Yes, I have. Not very many, only four or five. Do you want to see them? I'll get them out in a minute.'

'Want to see him? Of course I do! After all, that's why I'm here, in a way.'

Frances went to the drawer of the small table near the window. The cardboard box had once held soaps, and still gave out a faint waft of clove carnation that was the ghost of its former spiciness. She riffled through the photographs, picking out the small squares.

'They're not very big, I'm afraid, but that one is quite clear. I always liked it the best. I did think, at one time, of having it enlarged so I could put it in a frame, but then it seemed a bit sentimental, somehow. It was something very private, too, and people would have asked . . .'

Amy peered at the small square, scarcely bigger than a book of stamps. The man's face was distanced not only by size and the fading of time, but by a kind of old-fashioned appearance. Like the film stars in old black and white movies, he had the face that suited his era. Impossible to imagine him now, in jeans and a sweatshirt, for instance. She stared intently, waiting for some spark of familiarity or of recognition, but the image remained shuttered, remote.

'He looks nice,' she said flatly.

'But not what you expected? I thought him good-looking, but I don't suppose that was a particularly unbiased opinion.'

'I thought there would be something . . . something familiar, something to recognise. But he's just a face.'

'Familiar? Why?'

Amy stared at her.

'Because . . . surely he was my grandfather, wasn't he?'

'Your grandfather?' Frances felt a bubble of laughter rising like a monstrous belch inside her. 'My dear child, of course he wasn't! Don't you know how old your mother is? She was born in nineteen thirty-seven, long before the war even started. Didn't I tell you this was nineteen forty-three?'

'Oh.' Amy blinked at her. 'Of course. How stupid of me. It all seemed so long ago, and I never thought to work it out. But when you said to call you Mée, and that it was the Belgian for Granny, I thought . . . it seemed obvious . . .'

'Oh dear, yes, it must have done. I'm sorry, my dear. I didn't mean to mislead you. And I suppose when I told you to call me Mée, it was a kind of subconscious wish that Jean-Pierre had been the father of my baby. And I do wish that he had been. But it wouldn't have been possible, and if it had been, it wouldn't have happened. I mean, we'd probably never have had an affair.'

'I don't understand.'

'I'm sorry.' Frances gave a hysterical little laugh, then drew a breath and tried to pull herself together. 'I'm sorry. I didn't mean to be cryptic. But Jean-Pierre couldn't have fathered my baby. Any baby. He was infertile.'

'How do you know? I mean, mightn't he just have said that, to – to reassure you?'

'He might, but he wasn't that kind of man. No, in a way that was at the heart of the whole thing. He'd had mumps, you see, just a few weeks before he married Françoise – his wife. You know the effect that can have? In children it's no problem, but in an adult man the swelling can affect the testicles, and make him, not impotent, but infertile. He had known there was some risk, but he hadn't discussed it with Françoise, and the wedding went ahead as planned.'

'He should have told her.'

Amy spoke with the unconscious arrogance of the era of political correctness. Frances smiled.

'Of course he should. But such things were not freely spoken of in those days. Françoise had been brought up in a strictly Catholic household, educated at a convent. While it was not exactly an arranged marriage it was certainly one that suited both families, and was encouraged by them. Even as an engaged couple they were scarcely ever alone together, and she was very shy, prudish, even. And so terribly innocent. She knew nothing about sex, before her marriage. Nothing at all.'

Amy looked horrified, shifted in her chair as if the idea gave her physical discomfort.

'You hear of things like that, but it's so hard to believe. In Victorian times, maybe, but in this century! It's – oh, I can't find the words. I can't imagine it.'

'My own mother, who was the kindest and gentlest soul alive, told me nothing,' said Frances. 'When my periods started I would have been terrified, only we had a maid who talked to me, told me what would happen. And I didn't believe her! Poor Violet, I told her it couldn't possibly be true, that she'd made it up to frighten me. Of course, a few months later, I found out she'd been right, and I was almost too ashamed to tell her, and say I was sorry.'

'And did you ask your mother about it?'

'Never. It seemed impossible to connect her with anything like that. I believe, deep down, I thought it only happened to people like maids, and I was rather ashamed that it was happening to me.'

'My mother gave me a present, when I started,' said Amy thoughtfully, her fingers straying to a bracelet of fine gold links on her left wrist. 'This. She said it was something to celebrate, a turning point in my life. I thought that was lovely.'

'It was. You were very lucky. Luckier than poor Françoise, who knew nothing at all of turning points until she had passed them, and it was too late. She didn't greatly care for being touched, Jean-Pierre told me, and she found the physical side of marriage distasteful, something to be endured only because it would bring her babies. Only, of course, it didn't. And when she understood that it never would, that she could never bear a child of his, she had what I suppose would now be considered a nervous breakdown.'

'I'm not surprised.'

'Nor was he. He took her to Switzerland – I say took, though she could not bear him to be anywhere near her, and he had to keep out of her sight all the time, as far as possible – and paid for the best help, medical and psychological, that was to be had. She recovered, after a fashion, she even forgave him. But it was a cold forgiveness.'

'She wouldn't sleep with him?'

'Never. Not even in the same room. Nor be near enough to touch him, or he touch her.'

'Not a very Christian kind of forgiveness. I thought you said she was very devout?'

'So she was. But the Catholic faith, so she said, ordained that the sexual act should always be performed with the intention of creating a baby. It's the main argument against contraception. And since there could be no babies, there must be no sex.'

'It doesn't sound to me as though the specialists in Switzerland did a very good job.'

'That's what I thought, when he told me. But he was so racked with guilt, he couldn't see it, or at least admit that he saw it. He felt, you know, that he had failed as a husband, and as a man. When the war came along, and Belgium was occupied, he took terrible risks. It was amazing that he survived at all, and I don't think he expected or even wanted to.'

'That's probably why he did. But he was injured.'

'Yes. Though that was nothing to do with his work with the escape route. Or at least, only indirectly. He had cycled out into the country, to a farm where they sometimes hid people. Only this time it was just to collect some food –

they'd a whole lot of stored apples hidden there, and he wanted some for Françoise. On the way back a German patrol car skidded on a bend, and knocked him down. His leg was crushed. It was ridiculous. The driver knew it was his fault – he'd been going much too fast – and felt bad about it, so he loaded Jean-Pierre into the car and rushed him off to the military hospital. At least, he tried to, but the car had been damaged and broke down. While the driver went for help – he was alone – Jean Pierre managed to drag himself out and into the fields. He hid in a ditch – don't ask me how he managed it, or why he didn't die of exposure or an infection – for twenty-four hours before some of his friends came looking for him.'

'He couldn't just have gone to the military hospital?'

'No. He was in the wrong place, with the wrong papers, and if there had been any kind of suspicion . . . he knew too many names, too many hiding places. He had to get away. A doctor treated him as best he could, and they got him out in a submarine that night.'

'Goodness. Just like a film.'

'Yes. Only not really exciting when you're living it. Just frightening, and lonely, and endless stretches of time doing nothing but keeping still and trying to bear the pain. Impossible to imagine, really.'

'And he never went back to Belgium?'

'No. He died in nineteen forty-four. We had less than a year together.' Frances saw that Amy did not like to ask what happened. 'He was in London. They'd fitted him with an artificial leg, and he was getting on well. I'm not even very sure why he was in London, he wasn't allowed to say. Something to do with identifying someone, I think. It was just at the time of the Doodlebugs – you know?' Amy nodded. 'Horrible things. You'd hear them coming, and wait for the noise to stop, hoping it wouldn't. Only this time, it did. A direct hit. Only a few seconds of fear, hardly any time, really. And then quick. Very quick. No pain, probably. At least, that's what I always told myself. Tell myself.'

'I'm so sorry.' Amy's eyes were filled with tears again, though she thought she had wept them dry already.

'Yes. It was – I don't know – terrible, sad, all of that. But there were so many people in the same boat, and I was busy . . . I thought I should never be able to bear it, but I did. And now – as I told you – I hardly ever think of him. As if it all happened to somebody else. As I suppose it did.'

Was she really somebody else, that young woman who had fallen so rapturously into love that summer? Frances had thought so, had believed it forgotten, but now it came back to her as clear and fresh as if it were still happening. Their first attempt at lovemaking – clumsy, because of his leg and her ineptitude – had not been a success. She had been terrified of hurting him, and he had suffered from similar inhibitions because he had thought her a virgin. Afraid that he would think less of her she had not told him: indeed, in every respect other than the purely physical loss of hymen, she was. In spite of all this, on their second attempt he managed, with a skilled gentleness that she was too inexperienced to appreciate, to bring her to a gasping climax.

'Oh!' she said breathlessly, moments afterwards. 'Oh, goodness! I had no idea! I mean, that it was like that! So . . . so lovely! Of course, I knew men liked it, but . . . is it always like that? For everyone?'

He ran his hand down her spine. They were in a grassy hollow on the far side of the small copse that marked the beginning of the open countryside. It was her afternoon off, and she had wheeled him sedately out in his wheelchair, her face flaming, sure that everyone would know. Because of his leg he had persuaded her to take the dominant position, straddling him as he half lay, half sat against the warm banked-up turf. Now she had slipped carefully off him and lay curled against his good side.

'It should be,' he said, amused and touched. 'Of course, most people find they need a great deal of practice, but then you have had an exceptionally gifted teacher.'

'Yes,' she said seriously. 'Is it something you have to learn, then? Like a language?'

'Not so difficult,' he answered lightly. Except, his mind whispered, except . . . He pushed away thoughts of the future.

'I want to learn,' she whispered, turning her head to look up into his face.

'And I want to teach you.'

As the year moved into full summer, and then into autumn, they spent every moment they could find together. Jean-Pierre was moved to a convalescent home, mercifully only a few miles away. His stump healed, he was fitted with an artificial leg that Frances, because she found it so unbearably sad, treated as a joke, giving it pet names and fussing over it as if it were a teddy bear, or a pet. Still considered unfit for any kind of war work, he rented a small cottage near the hospital, travelling occasionally to London for meetings that he could not discuss with her. That was as much planning as either of them felt able to do.

They lived, necessarily, in the present. Afterwards, Frances was thankful that this had been the case. For them there had been no 'after the war', no 'when I am fit again', above all no 'when we can be together'. She knew, they both knew, that he neither would nor could leave his wife. Nor, she knew, would he stop loving her, though some perverse kind of loyalty always stopped him from telling her that he did.

Frances, in her turn, snatched hungrily at every moment, every chance of happiness, but made no demands and asked for no reassurances. Nor, though afterwards she wondered why, did she discuss her past with him and he, respecting her reticence, did not ask. Perhaps, she thought now, it was because talk of the past carried with it the awareness of a progression of time, held the embryonic future within its grasp.

So, when it happened and the joyful present shattered into the mirrored fragments of her tears, she was in truth able to contain it, to wrap it up and enclose it in a protective shell. As if it had been the picture of a perfect sunlit day she put a frame round it, protected it with a sheet of glass, and put it into the cupboard of her mind to be examined in secret, smiled over, mourned over. Less and less often, as time passed. Yes, she thought, it was true to say that the woman in that picture was not the same person.

'It happened to me, but not to the me you see here and now,' she tried to explain to Amy. 'It was too long ago, and I have lived too much life since then.'

'Yes.' But Frances saw that Amy did not believe her. Or did not believe that time could heal her wounds, though others might find solace. Frances sighed for her youth. Who was it, she thought, said that youth is wasted on the young?

The clock struck ten, and Amy yawned suddenly, her jaw cracking, her teeth white and even and unmarked by flaws or fillings.

'Oh, I'm sorry! I didn't mean to be rude!'

'I know. I'm tired too. Let's get your case out of the car, and go and make up a bed for you.'

'But we haven't, I haven't . . .'

'Tomorrow,' said Frances firmly. 'Tomorrow.' And in the morning, she thought, I will make you telephone again, call your mother, tell her . . . what? That you're all right, at least. That you're safe.

Amy had slept at once, like an exhausted child. In

Oxfordshire, in the bed made up for Amy, Robin had lain wakeful, knowing his mother was not asleep. There was a feeling of tension in the house, like static or the build-up of pressure before a thunderstorm, but he respected her wish to pretend that she was. Unfortunately, it also prevented him from getting up and prowling down to the kitchen, though he knew there was a scarcely touched bottle of Scotch in the larder, and he longed with every fibre of his being to drink quite a lot of it and so sleep, whatever the subsequent effect.

In Gloucestershire, too, his nephew Charlie was awake. Only he didn't think of himself, ever, as Charlie. Charlie was a stupid name, that meant a stupid person. Someone had once called him a right charlie, to his face, and he had never forgotten it. Charles, then, lay with screwed-up face and clenched fists under a duvet in a cover made to look like a sports car. He would not cry. Crying was for babies, like William. So he would not cry, and tomorrow, tomorrow he'd show them all. And then they'd be sorry they hadn't listened. He had tried to tell them, tried to talk, but it was like communicating with creatures from another planet. Well, Gammy would listen to him. She wasn't busy, like Mummy, or worried about money, like Daddy. He could talk to her, and she would put everything right. He pulled in a deep breath and relaxed, beginning to lose himself in the pleasure of planning his adventure.

Chapter 10

The morning, which should have brought wiser counsel, seemed instead to conspire to keep Charlie to his plan. Already old enough to be aware that the things which seemed unbearable at night usually shrank to insignificance with the light of a new day, he also knew, and perhaps deep within himself relied on the fact, that the reverse was true: plans that appeared possible when viewed from the safe haven of his bed were likely to become as lurid and insubstantial as cartoon films in the ordinary surroundings of the breakfast table. On this Bank Holiday Sunday, however, it seemed that matters were arranging themselves to make it impossible, without loss of self-respect, for him to back out.

He woke later than usual, having fallen at last into a heavy sleep after lying awake for some while making plans which had grown progressively wilder as the hour advanced. The Sunday morning smell of fresh coffee and toast made him sniff appreciatively and pull on his clothes as quickly as possible. He did, however, take clean jeans and T-shirt from his cupboard, as well as clean underwear – he needed to look respectable for his journey, and for when he arrived at his grandmother's. Young though he was, he was aware of the value of at least an appearance of respectability.

A quick glance in the bathroom mirror showed him looking unnaturally tidy apart from his hair, which being aggressively curly always looked wild unless it was very short. He disliked his red hair very much, being very bored with the various unoriginal variations of 'Carrots' and 'Gingernut' he received at school, and had already been known to look longingly at the bottles of hair colour in Boots. His face was too familiar to be worth a second glance, but an outsider would have seen that behind the appealing freckles and the slight outdoor tan from cricket he was paler than he should be. He seldom smiled, mainly because he was very late shedding his first teeth and he considered them small and babyish. He wet his hands under the running tap and pushed his fingers through his hair, trying to flatten it.

Downstairs William was smugly shovelling up the last of the packet of Cocoapops, his eyes glued to the television. His father raised his eyes from the Sunday paper to smile a welcome. The table, as always, was properly laid with a pretty cloth, matching table napkins, and jams put out in cut-glass dishes.

'But Edward, you *can't* have forgotten the Harrisons' lunch party! I know I told you about it weeks ago!' His mother, pretty in a pink flowered dressing gown, turned from the cooker where she was timing boiled eggs. 'Good morning, Charlie. Did you brush your hair this morning?'

'Yes,' he lied sulkily, as a matter of course.

'Well, you didn't make a very good job of it. Come here and I'll do it again.'

'Don't *fuss*, Mum.' He wriggled away from her embrace and from the hairbrush she had produced from the oddments drawer. 'It's only breakfast.'

'If it's not done now, it never will be. And don't call me Mum,' she added.

'I don't remember anything about the Harrisons' lunch party,' his father said without lowering the business section. 'In fact, I don't remember anything about the

Harrisons, either. Do we have to go? Wouldn't it be nice to stay at home with the boys, as it's half-term?'

'We did that yesterday, and it's a Bank Holiday tomorrow, so you won't be at work. And you do know the Harrisons. She goes to my bridge class, and their oldest boy is at school with Wills. He's something big in the City, and I thought he might be a useful contact for you.'

Hovering in the air, invisible to the engrossed William but clear to Charles and his father, was the clear statement that since Edward wasn't 'something big in the City' then he should be grateful to his wife for finding him a potentially valuable acquaintance. Edward sighed.

'Well, if you've accepted it's too late to get out of it now, I suppose. What about the boys, are they invited too?'

'Wills is. Several of his schoolfriends will be there, and Jane says they'll be having lunch in the playroom, with the nanny. She said we could bring Charlie as well, but I thought he'd prefer to go to Sam's. We can drop him off on the way, the Harrisons live just outside Cheltenham. You did remember to ring Sam, didn't you, Charlie?'

Charles felt his insides contract. He had rung Sam the day before, but though they had talked for half an hour about their own ploys he had completely forgotten to ask if he might visit today. His best and oldest friend, they had played at one another's houses all their lives, and their mothers stood on little ceremony with one another. Feeling that he was being controlled by some invisible puppeteer, he raised limpid eyes to his mother.

'Oh yes. Sam's mother said it's fine. And can I stay the night?'

'May I. Yes, all right. Though it would have been easier to pick you up on the way back.'

'If you invite Sam to come here tomorrow, you can get his mum to bring them in the morning,' said William thickly through a mouth full of brown sludge.

'Really, Wills, how cynical! And how many times do I have to tell you not to say mum?'

'Don't call me Wills, then,' said William, but in a mutter.

Hardly able to believe that this was really happening, Charles went about his preparations as if he were in a dream, or taking part in some make-believe fantasy. Into the small rucksack he used as an overnight bag went, not only spare pants, socks, shorts, T-shirt and wash things, but a carrier bag with half a French loaf, three bags of crisps, a packet of biscuits, some cheese, and several apples, all filched while his mother was dressing. The carefully hoarded savings in his money box came, he was impressed to find, to nearly ten pounds, a princely sum that must surely be enough to pay his fares, with some over for drinks and sweets at the bus station.

As they left the house he looked behind as he was careful never to do when going back to school. Home stood there, with its aura of warmth and safety that he conjured up, sometimes, in the dormitory, and for the first time he saw that the building he had always taken for granted was beautiful. His eyes filled with a rush of tears, but at that moment William put out a foot and tripped him. Sentiment was lost in the urgent need to show his younger brother his place, and put him firmly in it, and their tussles lasted long enough to call down parental displeasure which was severe enough to banish the fleeting thought of confession.

Sam's house in Cheltenham was in a one-way street, and as they often did when he visited, Charles' parents did not go round the inconvenient one-way system, which would have taken them through a maze of side roads where the parked cars, particularly on a Sunday, made driving space restricted. Instead they dropped him on the corner, waited a moment to see him reach the gates, then drove off. Charles, who had carefully positioned himself before the entrance to the drive where he was screened from the house by hedge and shrubs, let the arm he had raised in a wave fall to his side. For a moment he hesitated. He peered through the bushes at the house, still only half believing that he was going through with his plan. But there was no car on the sweep of the drive, every window was closed, and it exuded that indefinable air of emptiness that reminded him that Sam had spoken, vaguely, of a visit to London for the day. That was it, then. He, Charles Edward George McKenzie, was running away. Hoisting his rucksack to his shoulder, he set off towards the bus station.

The journey was straightforward, if not as easy as he had thought it would be. Luckily one of the geography projects this term had been centred round using timetables, so he was able to work out which bus he needed to take for Oxford, and what time it would leave. What he had not taken into account was the reduced Sunday service. Although he knew that his parents, by now, would be safely into their second pre-lunch drinks, it was still difficult to have to wait around for an hour. While he was certain that no one he knew was likely to be at Cheltenham bus station in the middle of a Bank Holiday Sunday, he still felt conspicuous. He bought himself a can of fizzy lemonade, but managed to resist the urge to eat all his food as a way of filling up the time. If the journey was all this slow, he would be more hungry later. In the end he sat down near a family with several children and took out his Walkman. The earphones would be enough to discourage anyone from speaking to him, and the familiar tones of Michael Hordern reading *The Lion, the Witch and the Wardrobe* were comforting and safe.

All the same, he was glad when the bus arrived and he was able to get on it. With the kind of good fortune that seemed to be nudging him every step of the way, the family he had been sitting near were also going the same way.

Charlie got on after they did, and sat just behind them so that others might assume he was part of the group. No one gave him a second glance, and since the bus was half empty he had the row of seats to himself. He kept the earphones on with the sound turned low, and sat hunched in his seat, his face turned towards the window but his eyes glazed and unseeing.

In his head he heard, not the serene, grandfatherly tones of Michael Hordern, but the voices of his schoolmates. Shriller than in real life, mocking, hard. Accusing him of things he understood as little as they did, things he felt were untrue but was unable to defend or refute. And, worst of all, he saw again how his erstwhile friend, Simon, turned away from him. They had started school together the previous September, had encouraged one another through the first anxious weeks, given comfort in the inevitable patches of homesickness in the bleak second term, and visited one another's houses during the holidays. It was the first betrayal of Charlie's short life, and the unexpectedness of it still made him clench his hands into fists and tied his stomach into knots.

Charlie shook his head to clear the memories from it. He could not possibly have told his parents what was happening to him, but Gammy would know what to do. Calm, unshockable, always-the-same Gammy. He blinked away the fuzz of tears that the thought of her brought to his eyes, and resolutely sat up straighter, turning the Walkman louder. They must be nearly at Oxford, by now. He had not long to wait.

From Oxford, he knew from Mrs Baxter who had once been his grandmother's daily and who still called in, from time to time, for a cup of tea and a chat, he could get a bus to the village. After his experience with the Oxford bus he was a little worried, but he reasoned that even on Sundays they must run some buses on the country routes. He was right, but it took him a long time to find the right place to catch the bus, and he waited for nearly an hour at the wrong stop before someone put him right.

'You're not travelling all by yourself, are you, dear?' The motherly woman he had finally nerved himself to ask was concerned; he thought he saw a hint of suspicion on her face.

'Oh, no,' he said, opening his eyes wide. 'I'm with my brother. My big brother. Only he went to get some sweets and told me to find out about the bus stop. I'll go and find him now, and tell him.' He felt the woman's eyes on him as he trotted down the road and round the corner. Luckily there was a newsagent's there, and it was open, so he went in and spent some time choosing a packet of sweets. When he emerged, cautiously, the woman had gone.

It was nearly six o'clock by the time he reached the village where Persephone lived. Climbing down from the bus his legs trembled a little from tiredness and relief. Never had he been so pleased to see anywhere, even the pavement felt yielding, almost soft to his feet. It was nearly a mile's walk to the cottage but each step was a pleasure, a few feet nearer his grandmother's familiar, safe presence.

The garage doors were open, the space inside empty. He halted at the gate, dismayed. Never, in all his calculations, has it crossed his mind that Persephone might not be there. She was Gammy, she was always there when he came. No, of course she must be there. The car, he told himself, would have gone for a service. He would knock on the door and she would open it, smiling and surprised and welcoming. He shifted the rucksack on his shoulder, feeling the ridge where the strap had cut into his flesh, and went up the path.

As soon as he rang the bell, he knew. Something in the quality of that sound, echoing round the silent house, told him that it was empty. He rang again, and a third time, keeping his grubby hand pressed over the button until the fingertip was white and dead. He pushed open the flap of the letterbox. A waft of air, faintly scented with the rose geraniums from the conservatory, came through as he peered inside. The smell, speaking so poignantly of unattainable comfort, was the last straw. He felt his mouth twisting and opening to the square shape of a crying baby. Stuffing his fist into it he hunched his head down between his shoulders and ran to the side gate. It was bolted, but he knew from past games that the gap at the bottom was deep enough to admit him. Sobbing gustily he pushed his rucksack through, then lay on his stomach and inched his way underneath. He felt his sweatshirt catch and tear on a splinter of wood, and took a perverse satisfaction in the damage.

At the foot of the garden was a shed, rather large for the small garden, where Persephone stored garden tools and kept a stack of logs for the fire. During their last visit, he and Sam had spent a happy afternoon rearranging the logs to create, in the middle of the pile, a space big enough for both of them to hide. Moving doggedly, Charlie climbed over the barricade of logs and looked. Their camp was still there. An old duffel coat, too decrepit even for gardening, shrouded the lawn mower. Charlie dragged it up with him and used it to line the floor of the camp. It smelled musty, of old damp wool, and in his despair Charlie thought the smell the very essence of desolation. In an effort to distract himself from his misery he ate the last bag of crisps, and put the Walkman on again. The familiar story soothed him, and though one or two tears still trickled down his cheek he relaxed. Pillowing his head on the rucksack, he slept.

Robin returned from Oxford tired, irritated, and profoundly depressed. Like his nephew he had slept late into the morning, waking to find that however much he hurried he would inevitably be late for his appointment. Cursing, he stamped through to the bathroom where he dropped the soap in the shower, banged his head on the shower control when he bent to pick it up, and cut himself shaving. Downstairs the bread jammed in the toaster and sent up a cloud of black smoke, and the milk he poured into his coffee was sour. On the table his mother's note was affectionate but uninformative. 'Darling,' she'd written in her familiar untidy scrawl, 'sorry not to say goodbye, will ring this evening.'

The road to Oxford seemed to be full of learner drivers, tractors, and little old men in hats driving shiny Morris Minors at a careful twenty miles an hour. By the time he had managed to park his car he was an hour late for his appointment, and only the fact that the man he was meeting had once tutored him saved him from a wasted journey.

'This, I suppose, may be put down to the fell influence of the BBC. You were, as I recall, reasonably punctual as an undergraduate.' Professor Jones spoke with dry precision, raised eyebrows seeming to pull his glance up so that it could peer over the top of his glasses. Robin remembered the habit. It had always seemed to him that the Professor took delight in playing the part allotted to him, and lived up to his stereotyped image with all the enthusiasm of an amateur dramatics buff. And his own part, obviously, was the feed man. Well, so be it. If the powers above him demanded a genuine Professor of History to act as adviser for a second-rate historical drama, they might as well have one that fulfilled their expectations.

By the time he had painstakingly argued his former tutor through numerous pettifogging objections and treated him to a long and expensive lunch at the Randolph – Professor Jones was not the man to stint himself on someone else's expense account – Robin was exhausted. They parted with expressions of mutual esteem, the Professor keeping up to the last the pretence that he was still in two minds about the agreement he had made. Robin, who was acquainted with the scales of remuneration offered by the University, knew very well that his adversary had no intention of allowing the generous fee to slip through his fingers, particularly when it involved so little effort.

Knowing that he was returning to an empty house, Robin was in no hurry on the return journey. Out of perversity he had eaten only salad at lunch time, a ploy which had disconcerted Professor Jones not at all, and now in spite of himself he felt ravenous. There was a pub just off this road, he remembered, that had attracted an eccentric chef who liked to cook, but didn't want all the worry and fuss of a smart restaurant. The turning came and without a second thought he swung into it.

As soon as he walked into the pub he knew it had been a mistake. This had been their place, his and Harry's – the place they had come to for celebrations, birthdays, anniversaries. The smell, a blend of wood fires, beer, cigarettes and adventurous cooking surrounded him as he walked in, and he was actually reaching behind him for the door to leave again when one of the waitresses, an elderly countrywoman with a face like a cottage loaf and a figure to match, surged into the lobby.

'Well, how lovely to see you, dear! It's been so long . . .' Her eyes, small and kindly, were already going over his shoulder, searching the empty space behind him, seeing and understanding the implacably closed door. 'Just a quiet meal, is it? We're very full, with the holiday and all, but there's a little table I can give you, dear, down by the terrace and nice and private . . .' Impossible to reject her kindness, her unspoken sympathy. Harry, of course, would have done so, with never a second thought and without even an attempt at an apology, but Robin found himself swept along in her wake, buffered by her brisk goodwill against the looks and greetings of other, equally familiar, members of staff. Still in a daze he let himself be seated, and allowed her to tell him what he wanted to eat, like a docile child with a good nanny.

The food came, and he ate it, surprised by his own enjoyment. Careless of the future he ordered a good bottle of wine to go with the main course, an extraordinary concoction of turbot and crab cooked with lime leaves, coconut cream and pickled ginger that was so delicious that he had finished it, it seemed, almost moments later. With unashamed gluttony he used his spoon to scoop up the last puddle of sauce, abandoning the plate with regret when it was scraped clean. Almost as soon as he had laid down the cutlery the plate was whisked away, and to his amazement a portion identical to the one he had just finished was laid in front of him. The waitress – Ivy, he suddenly remembered – briskly gave him a clean knife and fork.

'But . . . I've already had that course,' he objected.

'Never mind, dear, have another one. You look as if you haven't had a square meal in weeks. Daft girl over there ordered it, then changed her mind at the last moment. Chef's tearing his hair out in the kitchen, so I said, give it to Mr Hamilton-Knight, at least he knows good food when it's put in front of him.'

'It's extraordinarily kind of you, Ivy. I must admit, I didn't realise how hungry I was. I'll pay, of course . . .'

'Get along with you, dear! Chef was all set to throw it in the bin, before I snatched it out of his hand! You eat it and enjoy it. Things never look so bad when you've got a good meal inside you.' She trotted away, so that he need not answer her. Robin smiled wryly, and picked up his knife and fork.

This time he ate slowly, savouring every light and fragrant mouthful. By the time he had finished, the small dining room was beginning to empty. Out of habit he had a portion of sticky toffee pudding, tooth-achingly sweet but as light as a cloud, and sat back with a sigh. Ivy, busy clearing the tables, gave him precisely the right amount of time to savour the remaining toffee flavour in his mouth, then came to his side. Like many large women she had small, pretty hands and feet, and even at the end of a busy evening her walk was light as a dancer's.

'Coffee, dear? And a brandy?'

'No brandy, I'm driving. Coffee would be lovely. Do you still do Turkish? Will you have one with me?'

'With cardamom? Yes, dear, of course. But not for me, thank you, though I wouldn't say no to a nice strong cuppa.'

She was soon back with a tray, refusing to allow him to pour her tea for her ('I know how I like it, dear') and sitting opposite him with a sigh of pleasure.

'Well, I needn't ask if you enjoyed your meal. Properly cheered up, Chef was, when he saw you'd eaten all that second portion. Well, you know him, dear. Temperamental as they come. It's the lifestyle, of course. Still, we're all as God made us, and as I say to Stan, he may be a bit of a devil but he cooks like an angel, and that's good enough for me.'

Robin, who remembered that the chef was a (mostly) reformed drug addict with a ponytail and a nose ring, could only agree.

'Artistic temperament, Ivy. I have to deal with it all the time. And at least he really is an artist. Not like some of the mob I come up against.'

'Yes, I thought you looked a bit harassed, dear. And on your own? What's become of that nice American friend of yours?'

So direct and sympathetic was her curiosity that it was robbed of any offence.

'He went back to the States. We had a row, I'm afraid. A pretty trivial one, or at least about something trivial, but isn't that always the way? I wanted him to give up smoking.

For his own good, of course, and also . . . well, you know how it is. I got sick of the smell of smoke, and the dirty ashtrays. It seemed – it still seems – such a pointless and revolting way of spending a lot of money. He'd started as a boy, mainly to annoy his father I think, and I used to tease him about it, hoping to persuade him . . . I suppose I went on about it too much, but he used to cough . . . it worried me. Then I was having family problems as well, and I wasn't careful enough, spoke my mind too freely, and Harry – well, Harry was never one for compromise, or forgiveness. He said he never wanted to see me again, and took the next flight. I had to pack up his things, and ship them after him. It took me days, he was a terrible hoarder, and I didn't dare throw anything away, because if I did it was sure to be some vital keepsake that he couldn't live without.'

'What a shame, dear. You always looked so happy together. You must miss him.'

Her matter-of-fact acceptance of the situation was balm to his soul.

'Yes, I missed – miss – him dreadfully. It's like having had an arm or a leg amputated. I was all unbalanced, and then I kept forgetting he'd gone. I thought I was getting used to it, moving on, but . . .'

'Something's happened. He's coming back to England, perhaps? You've heard from him?'

'No. As I told you, Harry never backed down, never compromised. No, I heard it from someone else, someone who knows us both. He's ill. He said he's got . . . Oh God, I can't say it!' He sucked in a mouthful of coffee, thick and spicy, felt the grounds like soft sand between his teeth.

'Cancer?' He shook his head. 'Aids, then.'

There she sat, solid and unperturbed, sipping her tea. Robin glanced at her sideways.

'Aren't you shocked, Ivy?'

'In my time I've lived with four brothers and three sisters. I've had three husbands, and raised four children of my own and two steps. Takes more than that to shock me, dear. So what is it worrying you? Do you think you might have it too?'

'I was always careful. I knew he hadn't always been – faithful – and I knew the risks. I've had tests, and they're clear. No, it's him. Harry. He's all alone out there. His family won't have anything to do with him, or rather, he won't have anything to do with them, and he's quarrelled with most of his friends.'

'You're not responsible for him.'

'No. And he'd be the first to say it. But I can't help feeling that I am. When you've loved someone, still love them, you can't just write them off. I can't, at least. I can't leave him to die alone. Even if I didn't still love him.'

'So what do you want to do? Go out there? Can you afford it?'

'I can afford the fares, but I can't afford to throw up my job. No, I want to go and fetch him, bring him back here.'

She was silent, thinking. In the end she folded her hands on the table in front of her, and looked at him.

'He won't thank you for it. The kind of man you say he is, he may hate you. They may say it's more blessed to give than to receive, but in my experience it's a sight more difficult to receive. There's nothing worse than having to be grateful to someone all the time.'

Robin smiled.

'Tell me about it! Our family knows all about that.'

She leaned across the table to pat his hand, then began to stack her tray methodically.

'Well, you'll do what you have to do, and whatever it is will be right, and so you must make up your mind to believe. There's your bill, I must be getting on with my work. Come in again, some time, if you can. It can be easier to talk to strangers, but sometimes it's better if they remain just that.'

Robin laid a pile of notes on the bill, stood up, and leaned down to kiss her cheek. She smelled of clean laundry, and lavender cologne, like an idealised Victorian grandmother.

'Thanks, Ivy,' he said. 'I'll be back. And that's a promise.'

He drove back to the cottage feeling empty of all emotion, exhausted but elated at the same time. The very act of putting into words what had happened made it easier to think about and accept. Now, he thought, he would be able to talk to Persephone, to make up his mind, and to act.

He garaged the car. The telephone was ringing as he opened the front door, and he remembered with a guilty pang that Persephone had said she would ring that evening. When he picked up the receiver, however, it was not his mother's voice he heard, but his sister's.

'Robin? Where have you been, where's Mother? I've been ringing and ringing . . . Robin, you have got Charlie, haven't you?'

'Charlie?' He felt completely at sea. 'Your Charlie?'

Her voice was sharp.

'Of course my Charlie! Oh Robin, don't tell me he's not there! I was so sure . . . Is he with Mother? Yes, that must be it. But why didn't she ring me? She must have known I'd be worried sick!'

'No, hang on a minute, Sarah. Ma's been gone since first thing this morning, as far as I know. She went down to Sussex. Charlie can't be with her.'

'Oh God! Where can he be? I must ring the police!'

Robin felt the sickness rising in his throat, hot and sour. This was the sort of thing that happened to other people, people on the news. Not to him, not to his family, not – oh please God – not to Charlie.

'I've only just walked in the door,' he said, subduing the panic and pitching his voice low and slow. 'You'd better ring the police straight away, and meanwhile I'll hunt around. You thought he was here? Did he leave a message?'

'No, it was Sam told us. His friend Sam. He said Charlie was desperate to see his grandmother . . . Oh Robin, I can't bear it! My baby!'

He heard the hysteria in her voice.

'No time for that,' he said crisply. 'Ring the police. I'll call you back when I've had a good look round.'

The cottage was dark and silent. Robin went from room to room, switching on lights, calling, even looking under beds and in cupboards. The place was, at his insistence, very secure, with locks on every window and an infrared burglar-alarm system. No child could have found a way in. The garage, he knew, was empty for he had put his own car in it, and every corner had been brightly illuminated by his headlights. The shed? He snatched up a torch and ran down the garden, his heart pounding. The wall of stacked logs was solid and unbroken, the garden tools undisturbed in their serried ranks. Robin went back indoors and dialled Sarah's number. Engaged. And again. And again.

After the fifth try he made himself go to the conservatory to wait for a few minutes. He sat at the table, where the night before his mother had slept, and put his head down on his arms where hers had been. Images that he could not dismiss flashed before his eyes. Charlie, terrified, struggling with a stranger, hurt, molested, murdered. The soft tapping took several moments to penetrate his nightmare, then he lifted his head. A small white face, with two starfish hands on either side of it, looked in, just high enough to be framed in the lowest pane. Robin stood up so quickly the chair crashed to the ground. The window, of course, was locked. Unable to think straight, he fumbled in the drawer for the key, unlocked it, and his nephew was only just quick enough to duck as the casement was thrust wide. Robin leaned out, careless of the geraniums he was crushing. His hands closed round the skinny body, and Charles was hauled up through the window and into his uncle's arms.

Chapter 11

Even the telephone was no longer making an engaged tone, as though conspiring to prove that everything would now turn out happily, that even the innate malignancy of inanimate objects was in abeyance.

'Mummy . . .' Charlie, his lower lip wobbling, spoke into the telephone as instructed.

'Charlie! Oh darling, are you all right? Where are you? Has anyone . . . were you . . . are you all right?' Sarah's voice, high-pitched in its urgency, came clearly through to Robin. Charlie raised frightened eyes to his uncle, his unstable equilibrium thrown further off balance by the extreme emotions he had stirred up.

'Tell her you're all right. Tell her you're here.'

'I'm all right, Mummy,' Charlie parroted obediently. 'I'm at Gammy's, with Uncle Robin. I'm sorry, Mummy. I didn't mean . . .' His voice dried up, and the corners of his mouth turned down.

'Oh, thank God, thank God. Oh darling, how could you . . . I mean, why? Why run away? What did we do?'

Charlie hiccuped on a sob and shook his head speechlessly. Robin took the telephone back.

'Sarah? Listen, it's too soon to question him yet. No, he's fine, honestly, just tired and dirty . . . don't worry, he's fine.'

'But where . . . why . . . ? Oh no, I'm going to be sick

again . . .' There was a clatter as the phone was dropped in haste, and another clatter as Edward picked it up.

'Robin? He's really all right? You're not just saying it?' He sounded like an old man, his voice hoarse and strained. Once again Robin reassured, calmed.

'I absolutely promise he's fine. He got here hours ago, and fell asleep in the shed. I'd looked in there, but I didn't know he'd made a camp at the back, in the middle of the log pile. Look, I can bring him back at once, put him straight in the car, but I honestly think the best place for him is bath and bed. He's in no state for questions and fussing.'

'Nor are we.' There was a ghost of a laugh in Edward's voice. 'Hang on, Sarah will be back in a moment, but I'll have to go . . . ooh!' He ended in a sound that was half gasp, half groan.

'What on earth's the matter?'

'We've both got bloody food poisoning. Went out to lunch today, there was a seafood starter . . . Oh hell, I don't even want to think about it! Thank goodness young William didn't have it, of course – he's gone down the road to his friend's – but we're both feeling like death, and with this on top of it . . . oh God, there's the doorbell, that'll be the police. I'll have to go and let them in . . . here's Sarah.'

'Robin? Sorry, did Edward tell you?'

'Yes, you poor things. Well, the drama's over now, you ought to go straight to bed. Have you called the doctor?'

'No. It's beginning to ease off a bit now, but the stomach cramps come in waves, it's agony, only I scarcely noticed it once we realised Charlie was gone. I rang his friend's house, you see, to say we were ill and ask them to keep him tomorrow. There was no reply until about nine o'clock, but I wasn't very worried, just thought they'd gone out and taken Charlie with them. But when they said ... Oh, Robin!' Her voice rose to a wail.

'I know, I know,' he soothed. 'You must have been frantic.'

'I just prayed he was with Mother, as Sam had said, and when there was no reply I kept expecting her to turn up with him. Oh God, the police. How embarrassing. They'll think we're quite mad, or the world's worst parents, or something.'

'Don't be daft, you sound just like Granny. What does it matter what they think, and why should they criticise anyway? You did the right thing calling them, and they'll be only too happy that Charlie's turned up safe and sound. Now, I was saying to Edward, do you want me to put him in the car and bring him back to you? Truthfully, I think he'd do better to go straight to bed, and so would you, but if that's what you want ...'

'Oh dear, I don't know. Part of me needs to see him, to know he's all right, but ...'

'But some parts of you are still causing trouble, aren't they? Look, give your doctor a ring, tell him what's been happening. I'm sure he'll come out and give you something to settle you both down, and I honestly think you need a few hours' sleep before you take on anything else. All right?'

'All right.' She was unusually submissive, which told him more clearly than anything else would have done how badly she had been affected.

'Here's Charlie to say goodnight.'

Sarah's voice was calmer, and Charlie was visibly happier when he handed the phone back to Robin.

'It's Daddy, he wants to talk to you.'

'Robin? Thanks, old man. You're quite right not to bring the poor little chap back at this time of night. Sarah's a kind of pale green colour, and I don't suppose I'm much better.

I've sent her up to bed, and I'll call the doctor as soon as we've finished talking. But I just wanted to say,' his voice dropped, 'if you can, try to give Charlie a chance to talk to you, will you? Obviously something's bothering him badly, this kind of behaviour is completely out of character, and I blame myself for not noticing. Ten to one it's something to do with school. Mothers always think their children will tell them everything, but I reckon Charlie might find it easier to talk to you than to us. Not so much emotional pressure, eh?'

Robin agreed, rather ashamed to find how surprised he was by Edward's good sense. He had been guilty, he saw, of one of the most common pitfalls of an artist, in thinking that anyone who made his living in the sordid world of business must necessarily be insensitive. Rather humbly he agreed to do what he could, and put the phone down.

Charlie, with the rapid recuperative powers of the young, had taken himself to the kitchen to forage in the refrigerator. When Robin joined him he turned round, his dishevelled and grubby self brightly illuminated in the light from the open fridge door. He had a carton of fruit juice in one hand, and a biscuit in the other.

'Hungry?' Robin was amused.

'Starving. There's some super bacon in here, the sweet-cure kind. Do you suppose . . . ?'

Robin, nauseated by the thought of more food after his mammoth meal, stiffened his courage.

'Bacon and eggs do you? And some fried bread?'

'Oh, yum. Are you sure you don't mind?'

'At the moment we're all so glad to see you, you could probably ask for caviare and get it.'

'I've never tried that. Is it nice?'

'Delicious, but beyond my means and your palate, I suspect. Out of the way, and let me at the frying pan.'

Later, Robin sat and sipped at a brandy, watching his

nephew tuck into a plateful rich in cholesterol and saturated fats, washed down by Coke. Sarah, he reflected, would have insisted on hand washing at the very least, but he himself was unperturbed by the grimy fingers that were carefully picking up the crunchy bits of bacon that wouldn't stay on the fork.

'This is great,' said Charlie thickly. 'Mummy never gives us this sort of food.'

'It's not very healthy, but once in a while won't hurt.'

'When I'm grown up,' his nephew said, with a trace of belligerence, 'I shall eat like this every day.'

'Well, that's your choice. A happy life, but a short one.' This hardly seemed the moment for arguing about dietary fibre. 'More Coke?'

'Yes, please. Can I try some of your brandy?'

'No, it doesn't go with bacon and eggs.'

'OK.' Charlie seemed to accept this gastronomic dictum with equanimity. He wiped a piece of bread round the empty plate, and pushed it away with a sigh of repletion that turned into a yawn.

'Right. Bedtime for you. But a bath first, don't you think?'

Robin spoke with calm indifference. Opposite him, an extraordinary expression flitted across Charlie's face. A look compounded of embarrassment, shame and – fear? Robin blinked, keeping his own face neutral.

'I suppose so . . .' said Charlie warily.

'You'll sleep better after a bath, you know, especially when you're very tired. Sometimes when you're really tired it's difficult to get to sleep.'

'Yes.'

God, thought Robin. I'm out of my depth here. I know boys of his age hate soap and water, but I've never known him react like this before. Jesus, has he been hurt, has he got bruises on him he's frightened to let me see? Has someone – oh no, not that, please not that. I should have taken him home. I wish Ma was here. What the hell do I do, what do I say?

'No rush,' he said easily. 'You had quite a long sleep in the log shed, after all. It must have been quite an adventure, your journey.'

'Not really.' Charlie appeared to seize on the topic with relief. Whatever had happened to upset him, it was not during the journey. 'It was rather boring, actually.' He spoke with the casual blasé voice of a world traveller. 'The buses don't go nearly so often on Sundays.'

'No, you probably didn't know that. Still, it was jolly clever coming here without getting lost. I couldn't have done it, at your age. As a matter of fact, I'm still hopeless at timetables, they're a complete mystery to me.'

'We did them in geography, last term. I could show you, if you like.'

'I'd appreciate that.' Unsure how to continue, Robin fell silent, looking down into his glass. To question was, he felt, to invite a rebuff, and yet without asking, how to find out? Charlie stirred in his chair.

'Will they be very cross with me?' His voice was small, the man of the world vanished.

'No. Well, they're bound to be a bit cross. That's how parents are. They're cross with you for putting yourself in danger, and giving them a fright. And, frankly, for behaving rather thoughtlessly. Don't be upset. All you have to do is explain to them why you did it. They'll listen, you know they will.'

'Yes, but ... but I *can't*!' There was a world of desperation in his cry.

'You can't tell them?' Charlie shook his head, two fat tears rolling down his cheeks. 'Believe me, old son, I do remember how difficult it is to tell things to parents. Even when you're grown up ... But if you don't, you'll be hurting them even more. All they want, you know, is to help you, to keep you safe and happy. And they can help, though it probably doesn't look possible from your end. If there's something wrong at school . . .' He left the sentence hanging, and like a trout rising to a fly Charlie came to the bait.

'How did you know?'

'I didn't, it was a guess. Are you being bullied?'

'No, not really. I mean, they don't hit me or anything. It's what they say.'

'The masters? Or the other boys?'

'Not the masters.'

'Do the masters know about it?'

'I don't think so. I said something, once, and all he said was "sticks and stones". I don't know what he meant.'

'It's a saying – "Sticks and stones may break my bones, but words can never harm me." Stupid, of course, because words can be much more painful than being hit, and much more difficult to deal with.'

'Yes.' Charlie looked at him with doubtful gratitude, pleased to be understood. ''Specially when it's someone who's . . . who was your friend.'

'Yes,' said Robin in his turn, bleakly. He looked across the table, seeing someone he had thought of as scarcely more than a baby, and realising that he was a person with a world and a life all of his own. He was silent, pondering. 'Can you tell me what it was they said?' he asked gently. Charlie shook his head, and once again the look of shamed wariness came over his face. Robin felt a sick feeling in the pit of his stomach, took a gulp of brandy. There had been, somewhere deep down in Charlie, a look of accusation as well. 'I think I can guess,' he said. 'Was it – something to do with me?'

A tide of scarlet ran up Charlie's face. His eyes fell. He nodded.

'Oh, Charlie. My dear, dear Charlie. I'm so sorry.'

Charlie's head came up, his lower lip jutting.

'It's not your fault,' he said belligerently. 'They're just stupid, and – and babyish.'

Profoundly moved, Robin longed to be able to pick his nephew up and hug him. Such an action, he thought sadly, would have been possible before, but might never be possible again.

'Well, it is "sticks and stones" as far as I'm concerned, at least. Let's hear the worst of it, then. Tell me what they said.'

Charlie drew in a long, wavering sigh. 'It was Jamie Rivers,' he said. 'He's in the third form. He said he heard his dad talking to someone, about you, and that you had a nephew at school. His dad was joking about it, saying he hoped you didn't come and visit ever. And Jamie knew it was me, because we'd listened to that play you did last term, and I'd told everyone you were my uncle. And it was a brilliant play, everyone said so,' he added defiantly.

'Well, I suppose Jamie's dad didn't know he was listening,' said Robin. 'It doesn't really matter, you know. They'll soon forget about it. Everyone has a few funny relatives, and nobody thinks any the worse of them. I'll just keep a low profile, as far as school's concerned, and by the time the summer holidays are over, it'll all be forgotten.'

'But I wanted you to come to Sports Day! I'm in the relay, and the hundred metres. And anyway, I told Jamie Rivers his dad was a prat and a wanker, and didn't know anything about anything. And Jamie said . . . Jamie said I must be a homo too, and that nobody should get too near me in case I had Aids.' The final words came out in one great rush. The anger fizzed inside Robin's head.

'Now that,' he said furiously, 'is pure spite. That is completely out of order. Surely none of the others took any notice?'

'Well, it started as a kind of game – you know?' Robin nodded curtly, remembering how an inexplicable craze could sweep through the enclosed world of a boarding school like a forest fire. 'But Jamie kept it going. His dad,' he explained with sudden and touching maturity, 'has gone off with a young girl from his office, and Jamie hardly ever sees him any more. He cries about it sometimes, at night.'

'Oh, bleeding hearts. That doesn't mean he's allowed to take it out on you.'

'No. But you see . . . it's not just Jamie. Or even Simon, though I really thought he was my friend . . . I mean, after half-term it'll probably be different, but . . . I can't stop thinking about it. I don't know, you see. I mean, it might be true. How can I tell?'

Trusting, pleading, he fixed his eyes on Robin's face.

'Oh, Charlie.' Helplessly he shook his head. 'What can I say? You shouldn't be worrying about this sort of thing at your age – except that you are worrying about it, of course. I don't think I felt any different, at your age.'

'I don't really like girls,' said Charlie sadly.

'So what? Do any of the others?'

'No, none of them. They all say girls are wet, and boring.'

'That's perfectly normal for eight-year-olds. You've got several years yet before hormones rear their ugly heads.' Charlie nodded, understanding the meaning if not the words. It was one of Robin's great charms, in his eyes, that he never talked down to him but spoke in the language and vocabulary of adults. 'I don't believe you're any more likely than anyone else to end up finding you're gay. Not all that many people are, you know. And if, by any chance, you decide when you're grown up that you fall in love with men rather than women, it's not the end of the world. I'm not saying it's easy – but then grown-up relationships never are. What matters, in the long run, is that you should be honest with yourself and other people, treat them fairly and with respect, and don't use them or allow them to use you.'

Robin paused. Opposite him, Charlie was no longer looking at him. His eyes had been eagerly fixed on Robin's face, but now they had dropped and not only his face but his whole body were eloquent of resignation. Robin gave a wry smile.

'Sorry, Charlie,' he said. 'I'm going on like an agony aunt, aren't I? I know this isn't helping you right now – though I hope one day I can say it to you again, and better. Look, old son, nobody can say what sort of a person you or any of your friends will grow up to be. But it doesn't come from outside you. You have a say in the matter, too. You don't have to be anything you don't want to be.'

The boy looked up again.

'Don't I? Promise?'

'I promise, Charlie.' And may God forgive me, he thought. And make it true. His reward was in the lightening of his nephew's eyes, and the look of trust and gratitude that he gave him. Charlie slipped off his chair, and came round the table. As he had always been accustomed to do in the past he put his arms up to hug Robin, and as he held the skinny body close Robin felt a pang of sadness that he would never hold a child of his own, tempered by relief that this crisis, at least, they seemed to have survived.

The grandfather clock, its sonorous tones magnified by the small room, tolled midnight.

'Well, Charlie, it's tomorrow. Time you were in bed.'

'All right. Uncle Robin . . . ?'

'Nephew Charlie?'

'I don't really like being called Charlie.' The confidence was made shyly, and Robin was flattered. He stood up, lifting the boy easily in his arms as he had often done in the past.

'Don't you? Fair enough.' The red head lolled against his shoulder. 'What do you want to be? Charles?'

'I don't know. I suppose so.'

'It's rather stuffy, isn't it. What about Chas?'

'Like jazz?'

'If you like. It's usually spelled with an s.'

'Chas. Chas.' Charlie rolled the name about in his mouth. 'I like it.'

'Good. And while we're at it, being called Uncle makes me feel about a hundred and ten. Don't you think you're old enough now to call me just Robin?'

Charles – Chas – fell for this not very subtle flattery as Robin had hoped he might.

'Just me? Not Will? He's only six.'

'Then he's still too young.'

'What will Mummy say?'

'Nothing to do with her,' said Robin subversively.

Chas made an indeterminate sound of satisfaction and awe. Twenty minutes later, clean and still slightly damp around the edges, he was fast asleep in Amy's abandoned bed.

When the telephone rang, Robin was almost glad. Lying in Persephone's bed staring at the darkness above him, sleep had been as far away as the moon. The brandy, on top of the strong black coffee, had stimulated him to the point where just lying still required as much effort as climbing a mountain. He had found himself imagining scenarios – arriving in New York, finding Harry, saying – what? And, more to the point, what would Harry say to him? He knew only too well the danger of such daydreams. In the past, as a form of comfort, he had taken refuge in them, planning out the meeting, the reconciliation, feeling for a few minutes the joy of it. But even as he had revelled in the emotion, he knew that the Harry he saw so clearly in his mind was not a real person, but the creation of his own needs. When, in his mind, the two of them talked over the past and resolved its problems, the dream Harry listened, understood, and reasoned where the real Harry would have shouted, his mind closed to all words and feelings but his own, and ended up retreating into what he doubtless thought of as dignified silence, but which Robin always saw as sulking.

As a form of escapism, though, it was dangerously seductive. Robin told himself that so long as he hung on to the knowledge that it had no foundation in reality it did no harm, and helped him to bear the pain of parting. Now, with the memories brought back by the meal and his talk to Ivy, followed by the intense anxiety and equally intense feelings of guilt and sadness for Charlie, he tried yet again to decide what, if anything, he should do about Harry. Though they were much the same age Robin had always felt himself the older, and he had always acknowledged that the love he felt for Harry had a strong element of parental, even motherly, emotion. In his more elevated moments he had told himself that if Harry's happiness could only be bought at the cost of his own misery, by never seeing him again, then it was a price he was prepared to pay. He wanted to think it was true, but the next moment he found himself picturing disguising himself with wig and false beard, and haunting the street outside Harry's apartment just to get a glimpse of him.

Pushing aside the fantasy, he set himself to picture the real Harry. Not just his appearance – though even now the image of his brown eyes beneath the finely marked eyebrows and shock of dark curly hair, or the memory of his rare smile, could strike him like a knife – but the person behind that undoubtedly handsome face. The Harry who was, to him, infinitely lovable not in spite of, but because of, his flaws.

And that, of course, was what Harry had been unable to accept. Outwardly confident and aggressive, Robin believed that at some time in his childhood Harry had found the world to be a frightening, potentially painful place, and had constructed for himself a shell. A hard, prickly shell, hung with signs saying 'Keep Out', 'Leave Me Alone', and 'Why Should I?'. As time went by the shell had calcified and hardened. Harry, unwilling or unable to compromise, had forged his way into the adult world, making friends easily and losing them even more easily. The slightest hint of disagreement or criticism signified, to him, the end of a relationship, and former friends were discarded and written out of his life as if they had never existed.

Robin, with a crusading zeal that he had never known before, had set himself to break through that shell. Early on, when he and Harry were scarcely more than acquaintances, Robin had seen him relax, and smile. Suddenly, Harry's face had been open, vulnerable, with a kind of surprise to find himself feeling happy. That, for Robin, had been a revelation. Profoundly moved, he had set himself to bring that smiling Harry, the Harry as he should have been, into the world. Like an anxious mother hen he had tried to incubate Harry in the warmth of his love. Now, he wondered sadly whether Harry hadn't been better off in his shell, where he was safe from the harsh realities of the world. In the anguish and worry of his grandmother's suicide he had, if not turned his back on Harry, at least failed to give him the support he needed, and at once the cracks in the shell had sealed, thicker than before, and he found himself among the ranks of those Harry had turned his back on.

Now, though, how was Harry managing? He had, Robin knew, fallen out with most of his friends. He would be too proud to contact any of them now. Nor would he turn to his parents. Robin had only seen photographs of Harry's father. Large, bearded, red-faced, he looked rather like Henry VIII in his later years, and Robin could well believe that Harry both disliked and feared him. His mother, whom Robin had met a few times, seemed pleasant, even friendly. It was only on the second or third meeting that he realised he had got to know her no better than he had in the first five minutes. Outwardly cheerful, even outgoing, she hid whatever she might be thinking or feeling behind a smile and a bright, high voice: her eyes met his look directly but without any give and take, revealing nothing unless it was a kind of blanked-out desperation.

Robin turned over, burying his face in the pillow that was faintly scented with the reassuring smell of his mother's perfume. He was in Persephone's bed, having given up the spare room to Charlie. Should he telephone Harry? Write to him again? He had written once, apologising, trying to explain, assuring him of his love, and had heard from friends that Harry had laughed at his letter, showed it around. Since then he had written several letters, not intended to be sent but simply as therapy to unburden himself of the thoughts and feelings he could not contain, but could not discuss with anyone. Harry, he knew, would probably have laughed at them too. Did he need to risk putting himself through that again? But against that, could he bear the thought of Harry alone, ill, in pain? In the dark, his hand reached out to the telephone, and as he did so, it rang.

The harsh clamour of the telephone bell – it was an old-fashioned kind, not the fake saccharine birdsong of the modern variety – jolted him into a sweating panic. Worried about waking the sleeping boy he grabbed for the receiver, trying to find it by feel in the darkness of the unfamiliar bedroom. Who on earth could be calling at this time of night? Involuntarily his mind sped across the Atlantic, automatically checking what the time would be there. Early evening. Oh, God.

'Hello?' His voice croaked, he swallowed and tried again. 'Hello?'

'Oh, darling, it's so late, I'm sorry. I tried to get you earlier, but first there was no reply and then it was engaged. I should have waited until morning, but . . .'

He took a breath, tried to make his heartbeat slow back to normal.

'It's all right, Ma. I wasn't asleep. Are you all right? Did you find her – your, um, your mother?'

'Yes. I mean no. Oh dear.' She sniffed, she who so seldom cried. 'Sorry. I drove down first thing, well, you know that. And then I thought, she might not want to see me, or she might be busy and put me off until tomorrow, so I went to Lewes again and got a room in a hotel, like last time . . . the Crown Hotel, in the High Street . . . and then I wandered round the town a bit, you know . . .'

'I know. Putting it off. I don't blame you.'

'Well, I do. It's so *feeble*. Anyway, by the time I got my courage up it was afternoon and I waited a bit longer, because I thought, she's an old lady, after all, she probably has a rest . . . and when I got there, oh Robin, Amy was there!'

'What? There in the house? So that's where she went. What did you say?'

'Nothing,' said Persephone bleakly. 'It was her car, you see. I saw her car, parked outside the house. And I ran away. Drove away. Oh, bugger it.' He heard a tearing sound as she pulled a tissue out of a box, then the violent blowing of her nose. He waited while she drew in some deep breaths. 'Sorry,' she said again.

'Don't be daft. Where are you? Lewes?'

'Yes. The Crown Hotel.' She repeated the name of the

hotel, like a talisman. The force of her not asking came over the line like a sledgehammer.

'I'll come down tomorrow. Not first thing, there's something I have to do first, tell you about that later. But I'll be there by late morning. Have a lie-in, go and visit the sights or walk round the bookshops or something, and we'll have lunch together before we beard the lioness in her den. Both lionesses.'

'Oh Robin. Would you really? I'm sorry to involve you in all this, but I would be grateful.'

His mind seized with relief on the distraction of his mother's problems.

'What do you mean, involve me? Really, Ma, this is my grandmother we're talking about here, after all! Allow me some human curiosity! And don't worry about Amy. She's much tougher than you think.'

'Yes, but . . .'

'But me no buts,' he said firmly. 'Go to sleep, Ma, and don't worry. After all, I'm the man of the family now. Kind of.'

Persephone reacted to the implied insecurity exactly as he had known she would.

'Yes, of course you are. Oh thank you, Robin darling. It's so lovely to be able to rely on you. Are you sure . . .'

'Sure I'm sure. Now go away, Ma darling, and let me get my beauty sleep.'

'Don't be camp.' She was returning to normal, now, and he smiled into the receiver. She knew as well as he did the rules of the game they were both playing. 'Goodnight, darling.'

''Night, Ma.'

Obscurely comforted, he turned his head into the pillow, and slept.

Chapter 12

'I *do* like your car, Unc – uh – Robin.' Charlie stroked the rounded curve of the wing, looked with dismay at the dirt on his hand and the even brighter red patch of paintwork his touch had revealed on Robin's cherished Alfa Romeo. 'I could wash it for you, if you liked?' Harried though he felt, Robin grinned at the crafty offhand offer.

'And pay you, no doubt?'

'No!' Charlie, caught in an unconvincing lie, grinned back. 'Well, not much, anyway. And we wouldn't . . . I mean, there's no hurry, is there?'

'Worried about getting home?' Robin abandoned his mental check list – boiler off, food in the freezer, burglar alarm on, windows closed and bolted, doors double-locked, note for the milkman – and glanced searchingly at his nephew as he fished in his pocket for the car keys. Charlie scuffed the toe of his trainer on the ground, hung his head, then lifted it again.

'A bit.'

'You needn't be. I've spoken to them, they won't go on at you any more than you deserve. They're bound to scold a bit, you know that, don't you? Because you frightened them half to death.'

'Mm. Yes. I didn't mean to. I just didn't think.'

'They understand that. They're only upset because they love you, you know that.'

‘’Course I do.’

Robin unlocked the driver’s door.

‘No point pulling on that handle.’ He leaned across to undo the passenger door. ‘No central locking. I don’t know, you lot with your plush cars. Electric windows, heated seats, you don’t know you’re born.’

‘I like yours better. Can we have the top down?’

Robin was already undoing the levers to release the black soft top, an action so automatic that he did it without thinking, unless it was really raining.

‘Of course. Breathe in the lovely fresh exhaust fumes. Just give that lever a pull, would you, Chas?’

With an affectation of nonchalance that marked his deep gratification, Charlie complied. He looked with reverence at the softly polished black leather of the seats.

‘Can I really sit in the front?’

‘You probably shouldn’t, but there aren’t any seat belts in the back, and not much room, either. It’s what you might call a selfish car.’

‘Why?’ Charlie sat up as tall as he could, fastening his seat belt.

‘No room for extra passengers, or their luggage, or their shopping. Just for me and . . . one other person.’ He turned the key in the ignition, felt the familiar satisfaction as the engine caught and purred.

‘Like Harry?’ Charlie’s question came out with no visible embarrassment. Robin schooled his face to reply.

‘Like Harry? You remember him, then? It’s quite a while since he went back to the States.’

Charlie was scornful.

‘Of course I remember him! I’m not a *baby*. Anyway, I liked him; he was really cool. He made me laugh. And he was brilliant at card games. I wish he hadn’t gone. Why did he?’

'Well, it's where he came from, after all,' said Robin carefully. 'It's his home, really.'

'But he always used to say he hated it, he liked England much better. Perhaps he'll come back.'

'Perhaps. Anyway, I'm glad you like my car,' said Robin, hoping to change the subject. 'Even if it *is* selfish.'

'I don't think it is. After all, there's room for me.' He thought about what he'd said, and laughed. 'I suppose that's selfish, too. But so what? You don't need more than this. I mean, you haven't got children, or anything, have you?'

'Or anything,' Robin agreed, carefully. Sublimely unaware of having said anything tactless, Charlie stroked the dashboard lovingly. Robin wondered, as he had done once or twice during the night, whether his nephew had any real idea what being gay meant. Beyond, he supposed, the cruder physical aspects which he had no doubt that dormitory gossip had informed him about. He tried to think back. How had he felt at Charlie's age? Had he felt, even then, different? He didn't think he had, not really. And why should he have done? At that time, sex was as remote and unreal as his own death – something that everyone assured him would happen eventually, but which had nothing to do with the here and now apart from smutty talk and giggling. He sighed as he reversed out of the garage and stopped to lock it again.

For the first half of the journey, Charlie kept up his usual chatter to which Robin lent half an ear and responded with suitable grunts or monosyllabic exclamations. When his nephew turned quiet he shot a sidelong glance at him. He was staring sightlessly down at the hands clasped on his lap, the nape of his neck where the short red curls crisped childishly tender and vulnerable.

'Chas? Don't worry. It'll be all right, you know. I'll talk to them.'

Charlie swallowed.

'Yes, I know. Only . . . what are you going to tell them?'

'What do you want me to?'

'Nothing!' It was a cry from the heart. 'Nothing,' he repeated hopelessly, knowing it was impossible.

'They'll have to be told something, or they'll worry even more.'

'I know. But I don't want . . . they might come to school, say something, you know . . .'

Robin, remembering, did know.

'It's what parents want,' he tried to explain, reaching in imagination beyond the level of his own ignorance. 'They need to protect you, look after you. They want to help.'

'But it *won't*! It'll make it worse!'

'Perhaps. Not necessarily. Look, Chas, what do you imagine they'll think if I refuse to tell them anything, and you do too?'

He waited while Charlie digested this. After a few minutes the boy gave a sigh that was half a sob.

'What, then? What do we tell them?'

Robin sighed too, with relief.

'The truth, of course. But I think . . . I think I'll just tell your father. He'll understand, I promise you.' After talking to Edward the previous evening, Robin was pleased to find that he actually believed what he was saying. 'Look,' he said, glancing at the hopeless scepticism on the young face, 'nobody believes this about their own parents, but he was your age once, too, and went to prep school. We don't have to tell him the details, just that they were teasing you about me, that we've talked it over and you're not worried about it any more. Fair?'

'Fair,' Charlie admitted reluctantly. 'But you will make sure he doesn't tell the Head, or anyone? Promise?'

'I promise. But you must promise something back. Promise that if you have any more trouble, or if anything like this worries you again, you'll tell your father, or me, straight away. I really mean that, Chas. No more not telling people, and running away, and stuff. OK?'

'OK. I promise. At least they let us use the phone, now. If anything happens, I'll ring you. But I don't think it will. Everyone will be talking about what they did at half-term, and cricket, and where they're going in the summer.'

Remembering the short attention span of most eight-year-olds, Robin was inclined to agree.

'What about the boy that started it all. Jamie, wasn't it?'

'Yes, Jamie Rivers. He'll have got bored with it too, probably. Anyway, he's got Common Entrance soon, and then they don't do proper lessons after that, just special leavers' courses, so he won't be around much.'

'And your other friend? Simon?'

Robin thought this was more delicate ground, but Charlie shrugged.

'Oh, he'll be all right. I know he doesn't really think it's true, what they said.'

'So he'll apologise, and you'll make it up?'

Charlie looked at his uncle as if he'd just landed from another planet.

'Apologise? No, of course not. He won't do anything, because he'll be embarrassed. He'll just say "Hi", to see what I do, and if I say Hi back he'll know it's all right. And I'll get Daddy to buy me some extra tennis balls and take them back with me. Simon's good at tennis, but his parents aren't interested in games so he never has very good kit. Sometimes he borrows my racquet.'

Robin blinked.

'So you don't feel angry with him, or hurt?'

'Not really. I did before, but . . . I know he didn't really mean it. He's a friend, you see.'

Robin glanced at his nephew. He sat in his clean T-shirt and shorts with one leg twisted up beneath him, displaying its bony knee. With a grubby hand he picked absently at the scabs on it. His face was still pale, with bruised shadows beneath the eyes, but it was tranquil beneath the wild mop of red curls that neither of them had thought to brush. Talk about out of the mouth of babes, thought Robin.

'What's the matter?' Hastily Robin returned his attention to the road, mercifully traffic free this early on a Bank Holiday Monday morning.

'Nothing. I was just thinking.'

'What?'

'That you should probably be running the country. Or the United Nations. Or the world. Don't pick that, you'll make it bleed.'

Charlie latched on to the only part of what Robin had said that made any sense to him.

'I know it will. But don't worry,' he added soothingly, humouring the peculiarities of the adult world, 'I won't let it get on the seat.'

Charlie's arrival home was less stressful than even Robin had dared hope. Sarah, whose maternal anxieties he had feared would lead to some kind of full-scale inquisition, was still in bed. The food poisoning, aggravated by anxiety, had hit her badly and in spite of the doctor's treatment she had been ill for most of the night, only subsiding into heavy sleep at dawn. Edward opened the door, greeted his son with matter-of-fact cheerfulness, and took them through to the kitchen.

'Mummy's still asleep, so we mustn't disturb her. She was pretty poorly in the night.'

Charlie looked anxiously up at him.

'Is she all right? Is it my fault?'

Edward picked him up, holding him so that they were face to face. Robin saw, quite suddenly, that in spite of Charlie's vivid colouring they were facially very alike, and would resemble one another closely when Charlie grew into manhood.

'Of course it isn't! She ate some bad shellfish – we both did – at the Harrisons'. Everyone was ill, not just us. We were worried about you – very worried – but we'd have been ill anyway. Now, let's hear about yesterday. You had it all planned, did you? To go to Gammy's.'

He sat down, keeping Charlie on his knee. Forgetting his grown-up status Charlie snuggled into him.

'Yes. And it worked really well, except that there weren't very many buses,' he said, with a certain amount of pride. 'I was perfectly safe, honestly, Daddy. I wouldn't do anything stupid, you know that.'

'I know you wouldn't. It wasn't what you did, it was that you didn't tell us about it. If I'd known you wanted to go to Gammy's, I'd have fixed it for you. I'm not sure I'd have let you go on the bus on your own, but I might have let you do it some of the way.'

Charlie leaned away to look up at him.

'Would you really? Honest?'

'Yes. I want you to be independent, to learn to do things for yourself. But – and it's a big but – not without discussing them with me first. Right?'

'Right.'

'OK. Gimme five.'

They slapped hands with all the solemnity of a religious vow, and Charlie put his arms round his father's neck.

'I'll tell you why I went, if you like,' he whispered.

'Only if you want to. Of course I want to know, I always want you to tell me if something is worrying you. But I know it isn't always easy.' He glanced swiftly at Robin, who was leaning against the worktop watching in pleased admiration. Robin nodded quickly. 'If you'd rather, Uncle Robin can talk to me about it.'

Charlie considered.

'No,' he said in the end. 'Robin and I talked it over last night. I feel all right about it now.'

'Robin, eh?' Edward raised an eyebrow at his brother-in-law.

'Now I'm eight, I'm a bit old for "Uncle", Robin says. Not William, though. Not until he's older.'

'What about "Daddy"? Do you think you'd better start calling me Edward?'

'Oh, *Daddy*!' Charlie correctly interpreted this levity. Robin thought that his presence was increasingly unnecessary, and said so.

'You're welcome to stay,' said Edward, recalling his duties. 'I haven't even given you a cup of coffee, and I'm sure Sarah would like to see you. I'm not sure what the arrangements are for lunch, but you'd be very welcome . . .'

'Good of you, but I must get going. I promised Ma I'd go and join her in Lewes. In fact . . .' He glanced at his watch, and made his farewells. If he hurried, he thought, he'd have time to call in at home, and put a phone call through to America. It would be early morning, but Harry was like him in preferring to wake early, he would probably be awake. Whether he would just slam the phone down again was anybody's guess, but Robin knew, quite certainly, that he must at least try. Whistling, he drove towards London.

Persephone floated up out of sleep. Floated, quite literally, for in her dream she was in Cornwall again, swimming in the sea. A sea warmer and bluer than any waves that ever washed against that granite shore, but still Cornwall. The water rocked her, carried her gently along. For a few moments she was aware that she was dreaming, knew that the knowledge meant that she was about to wake. She held on to the dream, willing it to remain, able for an instant to direct it so that she could turn, and see the face of the person who swam beside her. She knew, of course, who he was, but she needed quite desperately to see the face that she had forced herself to forget so that now, when she needed it, it was gone from her. For a moment she saw him, and he smiled. Oh, yes, she thought. Yes, now I remember. Of course. Then the bubble burst, and she was awake.

For a second she screwed up her eyes, then knowing it was pointless she let them open. The room, at first, was utterly strange. Simple, functional pine furniture and pleasant neutral colours, with an occasional rumble of traffic through the open window. The daylight coming in round the curtains was bright. Her body felt limp and warm, she knew she had slept for a long time. Her arm was heavy as she moved up her watch from the bedside table; even so small an action was an effort. The watch wasn't there, and the arm seemed to be dressed in a sweater sleeve. She fumbled with her other hand, pushing the sleeve up to see the watch she still wore. Half past nine. Not so very late, then, and it was Bank Holiday Monday too, she remembered. That accounted for the Sunday morning hush of the town.

All the feelings of panic she had experienced the day before had vanished, as if the warmth of her long sleep had evaporated them. Without them she felt empty and drained, but oddly peaceful, willing to let the future take its course and carry her along as the tide, in her dream, had drifted her towards the shore.

Her stomach growled and she laughed, suddenly aware that she was ragingly hungry. The afternoon before she had fled from the sight of Amy's car, had driven in a panic back to Lewes and then, on reaching it, had been unable to face going back to her hotel. She had gone, instead, down to the coast. Without really knowing how she had done it she found herself at Seaford, dimly aware that she had followed the signs because they contained the word 'sea'. She took a turning by a motel, eyeing the soulless building with something like pity for its ugliness, went under a railway bridge and found herself on a long stretch of road that ran beside, and level with, the pebbly beach. On the other side, houses gave way to a patch of empty land, scrubby with grass and salt-stunted bushes. It had a desolate look which was wonderfully unthreatening, and she slowed the car to a crawl.

The afternoon, which had at no time been particularly warm, was now discouragingly chilly, and the beach was deserted but for a group of teenage boys skimming stones with practised flicks over the pewter-grey water, and three people walking their dogs. Persephone parked her car, and got out.

The pebbles shifted beneath her feet, hard and uncomfortable through the thin-soled summer shoes. A cold wind cut through her cotton sweater and she was vaguely aware of her skin puckering into gooseflesh. The salty air whipped her hair into her eyes and she blinked, but strode down to the water's edge before turning to walk along the shore. Even here there was no sand, but at least the shingle was finer and easier for walking.

The boys and the dog-walkers ignored her. She walked for about a mile, until she neared the town proper, then turned and retraced her steps. Her mind was empty. Her feet came down heavily, with a scrunch as satisfying as the feel of scissors cutting through hair. She counted her steps, stopping at a hundred and going back, pointlessly, to one. When she reached the place that was level with her car she turned again, and set off once more towards the town as if performing some bizarre sentry duty.

It grew colder, the light not precisely dimmer but somehow thinned, like watercolour. The beach was deserted. The harsh calling of the seagulls seemed the only sound, other than the crunch of her marching feet and the hiss of the receding tide. Still she counted, clinging to the numbers as a shield against thought, memory, or decision. Her eyes watered, her breath was searingly hot against cracked lips and dry salty mouth and throat. Every time she thought of Amy, or the woman she found her mind unable to name, she pushed them away from her with so physical an effort that she could feel the thud as something like a mental up-and-over garage door slammed down against them.

Nearing the end of the third circuit she sidestepped to avoid the wave, and slipped. She fell heavily, not even thinking until it was too late to put out her hands to save herself, and lay for a few moments, winded. She had fallen away from the sea, but even so the shingle was wet enough to seep almost at once through her clothes. The sea smell came to her, the iodine tang of seaweed and the sharp salt of the water, evocative, heartbreaking. Her ankle gave a protesting throb as she struggled to her feet, and for the first time she felt a twinge of fear that she would not be able to walk. It was curiously reassuring, that fear; it showed her that she was still functioning, still living in the real world after all. Cautiously she put some weight on it, relieved to find that though she had twisted it in falling it was not sprained. Carefully, realising quite suddenly that her whole body was shuddering with cold, she picked her way up the beach and back to her car, lone and deserted in the empty road.

She found she had no idea which way she had come, couldn't even remember from which direction she had approached. She began to drive towards the town, but found to her dismay that the road was a dead end, finishing among bleak buildings. The railway bridge was faintly familiar: when she saw the motel it was almost an old friend, and she had half a mind to drive up to it, lose herself in its anonymity. She told herself sharply not to be a fool, that her luggage was in Lewes, that there were signs.

By the time she reached the hotel it was dark. It had no

car park, but the little public car park behind it was only half full. The warmth of the car heater had dried her clothes and stopped her shivering, but even so it was bliss to push open the door and walk into the safe fuggy smell of the bar. On her previous visit she had stayed at the Shelley, but though she had driven there first that morning she had found herself alarmed, suddenly, by its faded grandeur, its pillared hallway and large rooms that seemed filled with the ghosts of wedding receptions, and Round Table dinner dances, and Glyndebourne visitors. The White Hart, too, had looked formal from the outside, and it was not until she found the Crown, inconveniently set on the crossroads and with neither garden nor car park, that she had felt comfortable.

She crept inconspicuously past the bar and through the double doors behind. Ahead of her the dining room and conservatory beckoned, from the kitchen came inviting cooking smells. But when she ventured into the conservatory and looked through the windows into the dining room, the sight of tables filled with people eating, talking, laughing, drinking, made her throat close up and she retreated, stumbling up the stairs to her room. She had meant to undress, have a hot bath, perhaps ask if she might have a sandwich in her room, but she sat down on the bed to telephone Robin and, when there was no reply, fell almost at once into sleep. She woke suddenly, later, to find that her feet were cold – she had retained enough sense to kick off her shoes before lying down. Wide awake again, she dialled her own number, worried as always by having difficulty remembering the code. Robin's voice soothed her at once. With his promise to come down the following day still in her ears she pulled the covers over her as she lay, and subsided once more into sleep.

Now, in the morning, she pushed aside the bedclothes and sat up. Still in the jeans and pullover of the day before, she felt sticky with salt and sweat, her mouth dry and foul. Catching sight of herself in the mirror she laughed again, amazed at the youthful sound coming from this pale, crumpled woman with salt-stiffened hair.

Three-quarters of an hour later, bathed, freshly dressed in a flowing cotton jersey skirt and a long loose cardigan over an old striped shirt of Amy's, she strolled downstairs. The dining room was empty of guests when she looked into it, but a middle-aged woman looked up from polishing a dulled silver teapot to smile at her.

'Am I too late for breakfast?'

'No, of course not, my love.' Her voice held a lilt of Irish. 'Will you not sit out in the conservatory, now? It's a shame to be indoors, this time of year – not that that's out of doors, precisely, but still there's the plants, and all – and what shall I bring you? Continental, or full English, will it be?'

'Full English, please, if it's not too much trouble.'

'No trouble, no trouble. And will you have tea, or coffee?'

'Tea, please.' Bemused, her mouth already watering and her head practically swimming at the thought of food, Persephone obediently went to a table in the conservatory. The room was long and narrow, slightly shabby like the rest of the place; she thought it might once have been a small courtyard that had been roofed over. The air was heavy with the scent of the jasmine that climbed above her head, framing the painted wall where a couple in Edwardian dress, oddly short and stout, seemed to be stolidly promenading round a sundial in the middle of a lawn, surrounded by flowers. As an attempt at *trompe-l'oeil* it was flat, two-dimensional, but it had a naïve charm of its own and Persephone let her eyes rest on it in delight.

By the time she had eaten her breakfast it was quarter to eleven. Her friend from the dining room came to clear away her plates, and offer more tea.

'All alone, are you?' Her eyes flickered to Persephone's left hand with disarming curiosity. 'Nice little Bank Holiday break?'

'Sort of. But my son's joining me here, later on. We're visiting . . . family . . . a few miles away.'

'That's nice, that is. There's nothing like family.'

'No, there isn't, is there,' agreed Persephone without irony.

'And you can have a lovely walk round the town, till he comes. Have you seen the castle? Opens at eleven, that does, beautiful, if you don't mind the steps.'

'I don't want to miss Robin – my son.'

'Oh, never worry about that. I'll keep an eye out for him, tell him where you are. Bit of fresh air, put some colour back in your cheeks.'

Rather to her own surprise, Persephone found herself obediently turning right out of the door and walking up the empty High Street. She missed the little lane leading to the castle, for her eye was distracted by the buildings on the other side of the road, so she carried on. Words, here and there, leaped into her mind. A plaque on an elegant house-front: Dr Gideon A. Mantell, FRS, Surgeon and Geologist. An unlikely mixture, she thought vaguely. Who would call on the services of a Surgeon and Geologist? Someone with kidney stones, her mind replied facetiously. She looked again, saw that it was a memorial to a man who had lived there in the eighteenth century, not an advertisement as she had foolishly thought.

Further on, across the road, a legend lettered across a timbered building – In this house lived Thomas Paine, Writer and Revolutionary. Writer and Revolutionary? You'd be even more unlikely to call on his services, though presumably the media would have loved him. Guest appearances on chat shows? Trenchant articles for the Sunday supplements? Still, at least I've heard of *him*, she thought, rather proudly. She reached a corner that clearly marked the end of the High Street proper, realised that she had gone too far, returned.

The little museum shop was just opening as she arrived, so she bought a ticket and crossed the narrow street, overshadowed by the barbican tower, to push open the iron gate into the castle garden.

It was, as she had been warned, a bit of a climb, the brick-edged steps uneven and the rail, an iron strip, quite open underneath so that it almost asked for small children to tumble beneath it and over the edge. Still, she told herself, I'm beyond the stage of having to worry about that. The garden below was a neatly mowed lawn, edged with flowers, but the sides of the hill were thick with the aggressively healthy growth of ground elder, through which a few tenacious bluebells had managed to push their way.

At the top the remains of the keep, though well preserved, seemed empty and oddly dead. Impossible to imagine their church-like purity sullied by coarse soldiers, in spite of the faint and inevitable tang of urine that hung about them. In the centre, a circular bench round a pollarded lime tree beckoned, but after a few moments Persephone felt cold and went down the first few steps, breathing in the heady scent of self-seeded wallflowers growing in crannies of the wall. There a wooden frame against the flint wall supported a low roof of S-shaped tiles, their terracotta glowing like a little patch of Tuscany, sheltering two wooden seats.

Persephone sat down. Out of the breeze the sun was hot; she spread her hands on the soft green jersey of her lap, turned them palm up as if to capture and cup the warmth. From the garden below the sound of children's voices came, shrill as the seagulls of the day before, but she kept her eyes lifted. In front of her the barbican stood as if it had grown, stone by imperceptible stone, from the ground beneath, its walls curved as naturally as the whorl of a seashell or the rough round trunk of a tree.

Behind it the roofs spread, and her eyes drifted over them, filtering out the unsightly grey of some factory-like sheds and the distant movement of cars on the main road to rest on the chalk cliffs and the rolling face of the downs against the sky. One or two fields already showed the acid chemical yellow of flowering rape. Farmers are going in for rape, she thought idly.

Beyond them, she dimly supposed, was the sea – that sea she had walked beside the night before. Not the sea of her dream, not the sea of Cornwall. Cornwall. Like a cat in the sun she drowsed, and let her memory take her back to Cornwall once again. It was time, at last, to remember what she had spent so many years forgetting. It was not, as she had thought, over and done with. Soon, today, she would have to face her daughter, and tell her why she could not marry the man she loved. Of the meeting with her own mother she scarcely thought. Oh Amy, little love, dearest child, will you forgive me? Can I forgive myself?

Chapter 13

That summer holiday in Cornwall. Persephone realised with a shock that she had not thought of it for years. In the early days it had been something she had cherished in secret, to savour with guilty joy. Needing to be able to think about it she had for several weeks afterwards immersed herself in cosy domestic tasks that gave her body the semblance of activity and left her mind free to drift back. Every word, every moment stood out in three dimensional Technicolor, brighter than any reality could possibly be. Kneading bread, stirring jam made from the fruit in the freezer – picked in that grey, fuzzy BEFORE time – she would let it run before her eyes like a favourite old film, smiling a gentle, abstract smile that even George, never a perceptive man, thought made her look different, somehow. Prettier, even beautiful.

'What a little nest-builder!' he had said, indulgent, patronising, as he tucked into slices of fresh bread with new jam or chunks of home-made pâté, slices of cake, puffy rolls of brioche with chocolate embedded in them. 'Mmm. I'm not complaining, of course. But you'll need to watch your weight. You got yourself nice and slim, these last two years. Don't want to go putting it all back on again.'

She had not bothered to point out to him that she seldom ate the things she had made. Nor did she mention that he, himself, was beginning to sag here and there, to bulge softly over the waistband of his trousers. When, eventually, her stomach began to round out, he had been noisily smug until she told him the reason.

'Another baby? But – but the other two are grown up!'

'Hardly that, surely.' She kept her voice mild, as ever. 'Sarah may look eighteen, but she's only eleven, and Robin is still only eight.'

'Nearly nine. Off our hands, anyway. Well, off at school, at least. And that's another thing. What about the school fees? It's bad enough now, with Robin at prep school, but in a few years he'll be at public school, and you must have some idea what that costs! And with another one to see through all of that . . . My God, pre-prep, prep, public school, another eighteen years of it . . .'

His voice was rising. Persephone put protective hands over the mound of her stomach.

'Mummy will help,' she said calmly.

'Yes, it's all very well to say that, but will she?'

'She has done up to now.' In spite of her care a little edge crept into Persephone's even voice.

'Oh, yes, and hasn't her ladyship let us know it,' he said, bitter for once about the necessity to accept help from his mother-in-law. 'Carol service, sports day, founder's day, every bloody day her ladyship has to be there, checking on her investment. I'm lucky if I get a glimpse of their reports, even.'

'She's very proud of them, and she likes to see them.' Helplessly she listened to her pleading voice defending Sarah, stifling the nagging little creature inside her that agreed with what he said. 'Anyway, if you don't like to let her help, there's always the village school. It has a very good reputation, you know.'

'Maybe, but after that? The local comprehensive?' He sounded as appalled as if she had suggested selling the child to a white slaver. 'Never. No child of mine shall ever . . .'

No child of mine. In spite of her control, the phrase was like a physical blow. She gave a snort of nervous, hysterical laughter. It was so out of character that for once he cut himself off short.

'What's the matter? Don't get yourself all upset, now. You'd better sit down. Do you want something . . . ?' He looked helplessly around, his face brightening as his eyes fell on the kettle. 'A cup of tea?' Like a child showing off his skills he bustled about the kitchen. Faced with a choice of tea caddies he picked the Earl Grey. The perfumed steam that rose from the pallid cup he brought her made her stomach heave, but she forced herself to smile and sip at it. Later she was to wonder how she had found the courage, how indeed she had carried it off without even a twinge of guilt. At the time she thanked him, assured him that she was all right, and watched him begin to preen himself as the first shock wore off and the possibilities for a bit of office boasting began to assert themselves.

'I'll book up a game of squash for next week,' he said casually, unconsciously sucking in his stomach and pulling his body straighter. 'Two games, maybe. I'll need to keep fit, after all, with a new baby in the house. Keep us all on our toes, that will.' Suiting the action to the word he rose to the balls of his feet, miming a few thwacks with an imaginary racquet. Persephone followed the progress of the invisible green ball as it bounced off the dresser to rebound against the wall above the hob and return to his bobbing, crouching figure. He hit it again, and this time it was a baby that flew across the empty air, curling up to push off from the window frame like a swimmer doing a racing turn. Neat and athletic in its babygro, it spread its arms like a bird, like a diver, and swooped among the hanging bunches of dried flowers. She closed her eyes.

George preened himself, his eyes glancing sideways to his reflection in the dark glass of the French window.

Persephone thought of Sarah's early years, and Robin's, and how he had never been home before eight or nine in the evening ('Social contacts, you know – very important to keep up with these people'), how his weekends had been filled with golf and tennis and squash, ('Have to get some exercise in – mustn't get flabby'). 'Of course, you realise I'll never hear the end of this in the office, don't you?' he asked with feigned resignation, turning a little to get himself at a better angle in the glass, pulling in his stomach still further. She saw that he was preening himself, ready for 'you randy old dog' comments from his friends.

She was reminded, forcibly, of a five-year-old Robin in the Batman costume she had made for him, and for the first time she felt a twinge of guilt. At once, as if in answer, she felt the unmistakable fluttering deep inside her, the first stirring of the cuckoo child that was to be hers, and hers alone. Quickened, she thought. My baby has quickened. There was a kind of magic in the old word that moved her; her eyes filled with tears and she blinked rapidly behind her glasses. What is it they say? The quick and the dead; well, it has to be the quick, after all. She smiled again, that inward-looking smile that George had remarked before, and agreed cheerfully that a couple of games of squash with the lads, every week, would be an excellent idea.

Cornwall. A bucket-and-spade holiday, George had called it.

'Not really my sort of thing, old dear,' he had said. 'I mean if it had been Rock, now . . . lots of people go to Rock in August. But Mousehole . . .'

'The children love it. And so do I,' she had pointed out. The conversation was too familiar, she did not need to think about it since the conclusion would be the same as always. And, sure enough:

'I could come down for the first few days, I suppose. Just to see you settled in . . .'

'That would be lovely, if you're sure you can get away from the office.'

'Well, I expect I can. If nothing turns up.' And in the event, as she had known it would, something did turn up, and once again she took the familiar roads to Cornwall without him.

'I'll try and pop down . . .' His kiss was perfunctory, his mind already turning to – what? She realised that she had no idea, and thought a little sadly that she didn't really care. They had made love the night before, the first time in – how long? It seemed dreadful that she couldn't remember, more dreadful that she didn't really care about that, either. He had been, as always, conscientious in a perfunctory way, worried that she should reach some kind of orgasm more, she thought resignedly, for the sake of his own ego than for her pleasure.

Then she told herself that she was being unfair, that he did at least try to ensure that she enjoyed it. It could only be perversity on her part that made her sometimes wish he would just get on with it, a bit of Wham, Bam, thank you Ma'am instead of this suffocating insistence that it must be perfect for her which led, of course, to her not infrequently having to pretend. She was fairly certain that there were times when he had been unfaithful to her. Staying late at the office, returning full of loud bonhomie and smelling, faintly, of strange perfume. At such times she was careful not to ask, not even to allow herself a hint of suspicion. She didn't want to know, and she was horribly afraid that if she were to discover he had been unfaithful she would feel, beneath the hurt and the resentment, a tiny well-spring of relief that would destroy such relationship as they had more than any anger could do.

Five miles down the road Persephone had forgotten George completely. In the back of the car Robin bickered cheerfully with his schoolfriend, Michael, a taciturn child who seemed to regard all adults as potentially threatening but who was perfectly happy if ignored. Persephone, who had spent her own childhood in strenuous defence of her mental privacy, was content to do just that.

The cottage was one she had known since childhood. Belonging to an elderly great-aunt, she had stayed there from time to time with her mother. Lady Singleton had never cared for it: like George she found it too small and too lacking in the kind of social life she liked. But to the child Persephone the village had all the charm of a toy town: the narrow winding streets where cars seldom came, and the grey stone cottages that even when picturesque had a kind of rugged self-sufficiency that resisted any attempt to make them 'olde worlde'. Fairmaids Cottage had passed now into the ownership of a cousin, and Persephone rented it for two or three weeks every summer.

This year, as always, Lady Singleton had offered to take them abroad.

'The South of France, darling, or what about Portugal? Or Italy? Tuscany is delightful, and we could take the children to see Florence . . .'

'Don't you think they're still a bit young for that?' Persephone thought with a pang that there were not many more years that she would be able to say that.

'I suppose so. And so hot in the summer. It would be a pity to put them off. But the South of France, now? My friend Clarissa – you remember the lovely couple I met last year, in Philadelphia? – well, she has a villa just outside Nice, and she would *love* us to go there! You know she has a daughter the same age as Sarah, they could have a wonderful time together.'

'Yes, but what about Robin? You know how he hates being with people he doesn't know, and he's already invited Michael to come to Cornwall with us. They've been planning all sorts of adventures.'

'Which one is Michael? Have I heard of him? I don't believe you've told me about a Michael. Is he at school with Robin?'

Lady Singleton spoke in a sharp, suspicious tone that seemed to imply that her daughter had been secretive, even underhand, in not keeping her up to date with Robin's life. Persephone felt the usual shiver of anxiety brought on by that particular tone of voice, with its invariable accompanying flood of irritated resentment. She knew that her mother had met Michael several times, but knew equally that to remind her of this would only make things worse.

'Oh, he's a nice boy,' she said with hearty enthusiasm. 'He's in Robin's class at school – very bright, probably going in for a scholarship,' she added, knowing that this would be approved of. 'His parents have just split up, poor little fellow. His father's in the army and his mother is up to her eyes in trying to sell the house, and sort everything out, so he's rather at a loose end.'

'Oh, *that* Michael. I didn't realise you meant him. Of course, we're old friends.' Persephone relaxed, smiling inwardly as she pictured Michael's appalled face if he had heard himself referred to as an old friend by Lady Singleton. 'Well, I suppose if you've already invited him . . . but maybe Sarah would like to come to the South of France. It would be lovely to have some time with her . . .'

Yes, thought Persephone. Yes, it would be lovely to have some time with my daughter. She's growing up so: I hardly feel I know her any more. Sarah had no qualms at all about accepting her grandmother's extravagant generosity, indeed regarded it as no more than her right. Persephone had often thought that she was exactly the kind of child her mother would have liked her to be. It was, she supposed, better than nothing. In that, at least, she had given Lady Singleton what she wanted.

'Why don't you ask her? It's half-term next week.'

An indulgent laugh.

'As if I didn't know that! You know I always put all their holidays and exeats down in my diary, as soon as you know them! I thought I'd come for a few days, if it's all right? Now, what can I bring? Some smoked salmon, of course. Sarah does so love smoked salmon. And what about a nice piece of fillet steak? That's nice and easy to cook, I know how busy you are. And I'll get some of those special chocolates that Robin is so keen on . . .' I should stop her now, thought Persephone, knowing that she would not. I shouldn't allow her to turn up here like some kind of Little Red Riding Hood in reverse, with baskets of goodies. But how can I? When it gives her such pleasure, when she can afford it ten times over without even thinking about it? And I'll tell the children, again, that they mustn't take it for granted. As they do.

Sarah, who had been unable to find any friend who would be available to spend three weeks in Cornwall with her, had been jubilant.

'The South of France? Oh, yes, please, Granny! Helena's going to the Caribbean, and Emily and Lucinda are going to Portugal, and of course I love Cornwall, but . . . You don't mind, do you, Mummy?'

Persephone, who minded quite a lot, looked at her daughter's glowing face, and weakened as she always did.

'Of course not, darling. I know you've rather grown out of Mousehole. What fun for you – we must go and look for some new swimming things, and some thinner tops to go with your shorts and skirts.'

'We could pop up to London tomorrow,' said Lady Singleton, an order rather than a suggestion. 'I think it will be quite smart – we ought to get you two or three nice things for the evening as well.'

Sarah's face had lit up, and as usual Persephone found herself unable to say or do anything to dam the flood of generosity.

Driving to Cornwall, wondering a little wistfully whether Sarah was missing her and hoping, as mothers do, both that she was and that she wasn't, Persephone felt the lightening of her spirit that she always felt on that road. She was unable, at that moment, to admit it to herself, but deep inside her a kind of hippie Persephone was singing a song of freedom. Behind her, Robin and Michael were happily, and slanderously, dissecting the masters at their preparatory school. Persephone began to hum, until without realising it she was singing aloud. The boys, astonished and affronted, exchanged a glance eloquent of disgust at the embarrassing ways of adults, then pointedly resumed their discussion. Persephone sang on.

They stopped for lunch at a Little Chef, a traditional visit that Robin regarded as the height of luxury and sophistication. Afterwards, full of food and milk shakes, they fell asleep. Persephone muted her singing to a hum, glancing at them affectionately from time to time. Knowing that they would probably feel sleepy she had put a couple of old cushions in the back of the car, which would in any case be useful for the beach and for picnics. Now they lolled like a pair of sticky bookends against their doors, looking as always in sleep much younger and astonishingly innocent.

Even so, she thought she could see something in Michael's face, strain, or sadness. She had noticed that he rarely smiled, even when playing with Robin, certainly never when talking to her. Although he had several times visited their house Robin had seldom been invited back, though Michael's mother had been very apologetic about it.

'It's all such a muddle,' she had sighed when, having run in to collect Michael she had succumbed to the lure of a glass of wine and was slumped on a kitchen stool. 'Ian's been sent off to Germany, I can't get hold of him most of the time and there are a hundred and one things to sort out.' Her voice, with its attractive Australian lilt, sounded despondent, and Persephone, who scarcely knew her, leaned forward to top up her glass as being the most practically sympathetic thing she could do. 'Michael doesn't say a thing, not a word, but I know he minds a lot. Not, between you and me, that Ian's been particularly close to him. He has this dreadful tendency to treat children as if they were Other Ranks to be trained, you know? But still, a father's a father, isn't it?'

'What are you going to do? Go back to Australia?'

Sue Macdonald pushed her hair back from her forehead.

'I suppose so. My family are there, and I'd like to be nearer them, at least for a while. But Michael . . . if only I knew what he *thought* about everything! Whenever I try to discuss it he just looks through me, you know how they do, those big brown eyes of his just blanked out, and says he doesn't mind. And if I try to push him, he makes an excuse and slides out of the room. He doesn't seem to like being at home at the moment, either. Too many memories, I guess. He loves coming to you, though. I hope it's not a nuisance – I'd have him back like a shot, but he doesn't seem to want that and I'm afraid I'm rather inclined to give in to him at the moment.'

Looking at the sleeping child, Persephone remembered this conversation. Michael and his mother would definitely be going back to Australia, she knew now, probably quite soon after his return from Cornwall. Was he unhappy about it? Would he, perhaps, be a problem on this holiday? Her mind ranged over possibilities of bed-wetting, homesickness, aggression or just plain unhappiness. Poor little fellow, she thought. I hope he has a happy time. I hope he'll be all right. And behind the thought was the sneaky one she always felt guilty about, on hearing of other people's troubles; thank God it's not me, not my children.

The cottage welcomed them. As always on opening the front door there was a waft of musty air, a smell of damp that in a London basement would be bleak and depressing, but which here was all part of the holiday atmosphere. Robin, festooned with bags and carriers containing the inevitable last-minute additions to the packing, squeezed past Persephone's legs as she stood inside the doorway, head back, inhaling.

'Come on, Mike! This is our room, it's downstairs, and the living room's upstairs!'

Michael followed more slowly. Persephone saw his face twist into an involuntary grimace as his nose wrinkled.

'It smells a bit damp, doesn't it! We'll open all the windows and doors, it'll soon be better. The downstairs walls are so thick, they never really dry out. This bit of the cottage wasn't really built for living in, it was for storing pilchards. That's what "fairmaids" means, it's a local word.'

'Pilchard cottage! Yuck! I hate pilchards.' Robin was bouncing on the bed. 'We have them for supper at school, with horrible icky tomato sauce round them, and disgusting crunchy bits of bone.'

'Well, actually, I hate them too. But they were very important to people here in the old days. They salted and pressed them for food in the winter, and used the oil for lamps and things, so you see . . .'

Persephone saw that Michael was still standing in front of her, his face lowered and his whole body eloquent of patient resignation. She had, she realised, been guilty of that well-known childhood scourge, Didactic Conversation, and he was too polite – or too lacking in confidence – simply to escape into the bedroom. She fished in her pocket.

'Here's the other key. Would you go up the outside stairs and unlock the top door, please?'

'Not fair! I wanted to do that! Wait for me!' Robin was too slow. With an inarticulate mumble Michael had glanced warily up at her, taken the key, and was already going up the old stone steps two at a time. Watching him, she saw that even in his haste he was careful not to tread on the small flowering weeds that had seeded themselves in the cracks between the stones.

Persephone smiled, and went into the boys' bedroom to open the windows chiselled like tunnels through the walls. Downstairs was a large twin bedroom, a bathroom, and a utility room that housed all the essential paraphernalia of seaside holidays alongside the washing machine and freezer. Upstairs, reached by a wooden staircase as well as the picturesque stone steps that went up the outside of the front wall, was a large living room with a corner kitchen, a bedroom, and a little shower room. With all the doors and windows open, the wild crying of the gulls came in with the fresh air, an almost tangible waft of excitement.

Once the car was unloaded, Persephone sent the boys off so that Robin could show Michael the village, the harbour, and the delights of the beach. She had no illusions about their being willing to unpack anything at all, except perhaps their bathing things, and knew that having been confined in the car for most of the day the pent-up energy would be rumbling like a volcano within them, demanding outlet. Privileged children brought up in beautiful country surroundings, to them it was the height of wonder to be allowed to roam the streets alone, spend their pocket money on ice creams and sweets, and sample the heady delights of independence.

Besides, having the cottage to herself was bliss. Compared to her own spacious house it was so tiny it was almost like playing in a Wendy House. Once again she was enraptured by the workmanlike little kitchen, as neatly functional as a galley, from which she could watch television with the boys, or gaze dreamily over rooftops to the harbour and the sea beyond.

'You see that window? That's our bedroom. We can climb out if we want to.' Robin's voice, in what he fondly imagined was a conspiratorial whisper, carried up to her from the lane outside.

'Won't your mum mind?' Michael sounded dubious, wary of an unknown adult.

'She won't know, dumbbell. We can go out first thing in the morning. We could go out at night, too, if we wanted . . .' Persephone smiled to herself. Robin, she knew, was still scared of the dark. He might talk of it in the safety of the daylight, but nothing in the world would get him out of that window into a dimly lit street.

Chapter 14

From that very first day, the holiday had a magical quality, gilded with seemingly endless sunshine, a time out of reality when everything she undertook, from baking to an outing to Land's End, was successful. The scones she made rose like clouds, and they spread them with home-made strawberry jam and clotted cream, picnicking on the rocks looking out over the Atlantic. Persephone leaned back on the sun-warmed rock and watched the two boys as they clambered perilously on the cliffs. Their voices rang in the clear air, weaving a pattern of sound with the soaring gulls.

Three times she opened her mouth to call out 'Be careful, darlings!' but each time she closed it again with an effort of will. If nothing else, she thought, she could give her children what she had never had, the freedom to explore their world and find their own place in it.

Driving back to the cottage, their insides full and their outsides sticky from scones and ice creams, Persephone thought she had never been so content. If I were a cat, I'd be purring like a dynamo. She hummed, then sang. To her amazement, after a few lines of 'Green Grow the Rushes, O', a voice chimed in from the back of the car. Startled, she flashed a glance in the reversing mirror. Robin, who had a voice like a corncrake, lolled half asleep against the door, but Michael, sitting with his knees up to his chest and his feet on the seat, was singing. His eyes were fixed dreamily on the drystone walls that edged the narrow lane, and his thin, clear voice soared effortlessly above Persephone's alto. Careful not to look at him again, Persephone continued to sing.

By the time they had reached 'I'll give you seven, O' they were singing well together. Persephone, though she had never achieved the solo performance her mother would have liked, had nevertheless been well taught by her school choir mistress. Tentatively at first, she moved into an alto harmony. To her intense pleasure, Michael put his feet down to the floor, sat up straighter, and carried the tune, his eyes meeting hers in the mirror for a moment as they had seldom done before.

Reaching the final verse, they launched themselves with gusto, emphasising each number as they went backwards through it, holding the high note on 'rivals' as Persephone conducted with her left hand, and finishing with a pronounced beat on 'One is one and all a-lone, and ev-er more shall *be so*!'

'Great!' said Michael. He smiled into the rearview mirror as they looked at one another, sharing the moment. 'That was great.'

'Yes, it was. I didn't know you could sing. As well as that, I mean.'

In the past, any direct question more personal than 'Would you like some more?' had invariably resulted in an instant and prickly withdrawal, and as she spoke Persephone wondered if he would do the same thing now. But Michael glanced at Robin who was now fast asleep with his mouth open, then lolled forwards on folded arms against the back of the passenger seat.

'My mum and I sing together, at home. When we're on our own. Without Dad, I mean.'

'Your dad isn't musical?'

'No. He thinks all music is wet, except brass bands.'

'Occupational hazard,' suggested Persephone in a carefully neutral tone.

'What's that?'

'Something that happens to people who do a particular kind of job. Like vicars liking church music, for instance.'

'Oh.' He fell silent, withdrawing into his thoughts. Persephone concentrated on driving, trying not to be disappointed. His face was suddenly irradiated by a grin. 'Or miners liking rock music?'

After a stunned pause, Persephone put back her head and laughed until her eyes watered. Michael leaned the side of his head on the top of the seat back and watched her, his eyes bright with satisfaction and a kind of astonished pleasure that made Persephone want to stop the car and hug him. Instead she reached back and lightly ruffled his dark hair.

'Oh, Mikey!' She caught herself up. 'Sorry, Michael, I mean. That's brilliant. I haven't laughed so much for ages.'

He suffered the caress without flinching.

'I like words. I like the patterns they make.'

'Goodness. I thought just now you ought to be a musician, but perhaps you'll be a writer. And I'll be able to say, Ah, I knew him when he was young, I was the first person to spot that he was a genius!'

'And I could put a bit in the front of my book, with your name.'

'Oh, a dedication! "To Persephone Hamilton-Knight, without whom this book would never have been written." How grand. I should feel so important. I'd buy copies for all my friends, and pester you to sign them.'

'And I'd do one of those squiggly signatures that nobody can read.'

'Perhaps you'd better start practising it.'

'Mm.' He let his arms flop over so they hung down over the front seat and rested his chin on the top. 'I don't mind, actually,' he said shyly.

'Don't mind what?'

'If you call me Mikey. Dad always said that it's babyish to shorten people's names, but I don't have to take any notice of that anymore.' His fingers, scratched and grubby, picked at the leather seat back.

'Well . . .' What do I say now? she wondered.

'Mum calls me Mike, or Micky, sometimes, but I don't like that. Mickey Mouse, Dad used to say. Anyway, what does he know? His name's Ian.'

'Difficult to shorten that,' Persephone agreed. 'Ee?'

He giggled, and his fingers stilled.

'Yes. Or Un.'

Distracted, Persephone let her attention flicker between his profile and the road. An unnoticed figure sitting on the narrow grass verge startled her when he got to his feet, sticking out a raised thumb. Persephone swerved to avoid him.

'Bloody idiot,' she muttered, but Michael had pulled himself upright and was staring back.

'That was Hugo,' he said.

'Was it?' said Persephone, who had no intention of stopping for a hitchhiker even if he was someone the boys had met on the beach. 'Hugo who?' She thought he would enjoy the sound of that, but he was still craning to see out of the back window.

'My brother, Hugo,' he explained matter-of-factly, as if unknown brothers materialising out of the hedgerow were a normal holiday hazard. Persephone braked sharply. Behind her the figure, already subsiding hopelessly back into the grass verge, started after them, running lopsided because he was hauling an enormous rucksack along in one hand.

'Are you sure?' she asked, as he came nearer. It was, she knew, a singularly inane question, but she had always thought he was an only child.

'Yes, of course I am.'

'I didn't even know you had a brother.' Oh dear, she thought, I sound quite accusing.

'My dad was married before,' he explained in an offhand voice, still watching the approaching figure. Persephone eyed Hugo warily. Her experience of teenage boys was minimal. She found the thought of them rather alarming, and was secretly dreading the onset of adolescence in Robin.

'Hugo's nice.' Michael's voice was defensive: she cast a startled glance at him, rather dismayed by his perceptive remark. Until then she had assumed that because he rarely looked at or spoke to her, he was unaware of her as a person. I should have known better, she thought. Children always see more than we want them to. She was very glad, suddenly, that she had sung with Michael. Short though it had been, the little episode had been a tremendous advance.

Remembering his smile, his pleasure at her calling him something special, and above all his air of surprise at their shared enjoyment, Persephone felt an upwelling of love for Michael. Though less intense, it reminded her very powerfully of how she had felt on first holding her babies in her arms, and she knew that for the rest of her life Mikey would have a special place in her heart. And as for his brother, if Mikey liked him, she would like him too. Acne, moodiness, and all.

Hugo was near enough now for Michael to hang out of the open window.

'Hugo! Hugo, it's me!'

'Hey, little bro! What are you doing down here? Don't say the Aged Ps have come chasing after me! I thought I'd thrown them off the scent by telling them I was going to Wales!'

His voice was pleasant, deep for a boy, and he sounded pleased to see Michael, which she liked. Not every teenager wants to be friendly with a half-brother so much younger. Persephone studied him as he came up to the car. His tall, thin figure was dressed in the regulation jeans and sloppy jumper, his dark hair was shoulder length but looked, to her relief, very clean. He bent down to Michael's window, reaching in to ruffle the boy's hair as she had done. His face was bony, attractive, the skin tanned but (she noted) free of spots. Beneath uncompromisingly straight dark brows his eyes were a clear light brown, like run honey. They met hers easily and openly: he certainly had none of Michael's withdrawn shyness.

'Hello! I'm Hugo – Hugo Macdonald, Mike's brother.'

Persephone reached across to unlock the front passenger door.

'Persephone Hamilton-Knight.' He opened the door and leaned in to shake her offered hand. 'I'm sorry I nearly ran you over – Mikey and I were talking and I'm afraid I didn't see you until you stood up.'

The line of his black eyebrows was raised, and he gave her a look of approval.

'Talking, eh? Think nothing of it. It was stupid of me, and lucky nothing was coming the other way. Of course, when I saw you, I knew you wouldn't stop. I mean, I don't blame you. Women on their own never do – at least, not for scruffy herberts like me, in Dad's charming phrase.'

'Well, no. But of course this is different. The boot's unlocked, if you want to put your rucksack in.'

'Thanks.' He did so, then folded himself neatly into the front seat.

'What are you doing in Cornwall? Have you been camping? Where are you going?' Michael bounced on his seat, more animated than Persephone had ever seen him. Her decision to like this boy – or young man, she hastily revised – was scarcely necessary, for she found herself liking him without any effort.

'Hey, slow down! One question at a time, *if* you please! And how about introducing your friend? Rip van Winkle, I presume? Or Sleeping Beauty?'

'Oh, that's Robin. He's my friend. He's asleep,' added Michael unnecessarily.

'I'm afraid once Robin's asleep, he's asleep,' Persephone said with a smile.

'A clear conscience, obviously, lucky chap.'

Persephone drove on down the narrow lane.

'Where were you heading for? This isn't exactly the busiest road in the world to hitch down.'

'No, I'd been sitting there for half an hour. I set out to walk it, but to be honest I was fairly tired, so I thought I'd try for a lift. No particular destination – I thought I'd leave it with the gods, and go wherever my lift took me.'

Persephone glanced at him. She had already noticed the bony face, but now she saw that it was too thin, and that beneath the healthy outdoor tan he was pale, with shadows beneath his eyes.

'Well,' she said comfortably, as if he were no more than Robin's age, 'you might as well come back and have supper with us. There isn't another bed, but the sofa's long and I suppose you've got a sleeping bag in that rucksack? Or Mikey and Robin could sleep head to tail, and leave you the other bed.'

'Oh no, the sofa's fine. In fact, even the floor would be luxury! You've no idea how extraordinarily lumpy even the smoothest-looking patch of ground can feel at three in the morning! That is,' he hesitated, his direct gaze fixed on her face, 'if you're sure? And what about Mr Hamilton-Knight? He might not be very delighted to have someone like me messing up his holiday.'

'I wouldn't have asked you if I wasn't sure. And my husband isn't with us. He's very busy at work, and not very keen on Cornwall, though he's going to try to get down next weekend.'

'Thanks.' His smile was delighted, infectious. 'Talk about leaving it with the gods! I feel like one of those Greek heroes, carried off to Olympus!'

'Hardly that,' she laughed. 'Only Mousehole. And with my name you might just as well find yourself carried off to the Underworld.'

'I thought women were less the carriers than the carryees – is that a word? – in the myths. Perhaps I've come to rescue you.'

'From the terrible monsters? What a happy thought.'

'I'm not a monster!' Robin's indignant voice made them both laugh.

'I thought you were asleep! Faking, were you? Well, you know what they say.'

'No, what?'

'Eavesdroppers never hear any good about themselves. What a pity you spoke up – I'm sure your mother was about to tell me all about your dreadful behaviour. Warning me, you know.'

'She couldn't.' Robin's voice was odiously smug, playing to the gallery. 'I make sure she doesn't find out about it.'

'Oh, Robin, you revolting boy! There's still time to change your mind, Hugo. I'd quite understand if you decided you'd rather sleep in a field full of rocks and cowpats.'

'Well . . .' he drawled, 'I would, of course. But I'm far too polite to say so. What did you say was for supper?'

Persephone felt her spirits spiral upwards, whirling her

into a world she had glimpsed, in the past, staying with schoolfriends. The families of several sisters and brothers, bickering, laughing, teasing, fighting and making up – it had all seemed exotic to her. She had hovered on the fringes, terrified to be noticed and yet fascinated. And now, at thirty-one, she was suddenly there.

'Supper . . . ?' She pretended vagueness, as if the word was unfamiliar. 'Let me see, I don't think we were having anything much, were we . . . ?'

The boys, who knew there was a large pan of pasta sauce, and a treacle tart of mammoth proportions, waiting to be heated up, broke in with loud protestations. They were still arguing about the relative merits of ice cream or clotted cream with the tart as Persephone parked the car by the harbour.

'What do you think, Hugo?' asked Robin, who had obviously taken the new addition to their number well in his stride.

'Both.' said Hugo succinctly. 'Now, then, you two, help carry the picnic things. Or would you rather take my rucksack?'

Indoors he asked if he might have a bath, and, rather shyly, if he could put his clothes in the washing machine. He arrived at the supper table in swimming trunks and a T-shirt, disarmingly well scrubbed and with his hair still wet, looking as though it had been painted on his head.

'I'm afraid everything else is in the washing machine,' he said. 'I meant to find a launderette, but they're a bit thin on the ground in these parts.'

'That doesn't matter. This isn't a dressing-up kind of holiday, anyway, and it's such a warm evening you won't be cold. Would you like to open the wine?' On her own with the boys she had scarcely touched the bottles that George had put in the car for her, but in Hugo's honour she had taken one out. 'I'm sorry I haven't any beer. If you want to go and get some from the pub . . . ?'

'No, wine's fine, thank you. Tom and I – Tom's the friend I was with – got through a fair bit of beer, one way and another, since we got to Cornwall. Celebrating finishing A levels, leaving school, and all that. Joining the human race.'

'What happened to Tom? Did you fall out?'

'No, he had to go home. His parents were taking him to Barbados, lucky bugger. Oh, sorry.'

'What? Oh, I see. Don't worry about me, as you see I didn't even notice, and I'm sure Robin and Mikey are well acquainted with more rude words than I am. So, you thought you'd carry on camping? And told your parents you'd gone to Wales?'

He grinned, shamefaced.

'Yes. We've got an elderly cousin there, and I knew they wouldn't fuss if they thought I was with her. Dad, that is. My mother doesn't fuss much – she's too busy with her own life, really. But Dad . . . well, it's not so much that he worries about me – I'm not a child, after all – but he always wants me to have some kind of rigid timetable. You know the sort of thing: 9.17 a.m., depart St Ives. 11.52 a.m. arrive wherever. 12.30, drink pint of shandy. I've had years of that at school, and I just wanted to be free, to wander on or stop where the fancy took me. So I remembered Cousin Gwen. She's completely dotty, never answers letters, and she's not on the phone, you see . . .'

Persephone laughed.

'How enterprising! I wish I'd been as brave, at eighteen. You are eighteen, I suppose?'

'Yes. Nearly nineteen, in fact, but don't tell anyone. I had pneumonia very badly when I was fourteen and missed two terms, so I'm a year older than everyone else. I know it's not a long time, but sometimes I feel much older than them. Just born geriatric, I guess.'

Persephone eyed the enormous second helping he had just started to eat. He caught the direction of her gaze, and grinned.

'I've been living on cornflakes and bread,' he admitted. 'Spent too much in pubs when I was with Tom. I thought I'd get a job, but I haven't had much luck yet. I expect I'll pick something up, though.' He saw the question in Persephone's eyes. 'Dad would help, if I asked him. I just don't like to ask him.'

Persephone thought rather wistfully that he was lucky to be able to achieve so much independence, so young. Then she looked at him, and saw a kind of hopeless sadness in his face, and thought again.

'I suppose men like their sons to learn self-reliance,' she offered tentatively. Hugo glanced at Michael, who was deep in discussion with Robin and paying them no attention.

'Rather the opposite,' he said bitterly. 'He takes his duties as a father very seriously. My future was all mapped out for me, you know. Sandhurst, the Regiment, following in his footsteps, all that. Only I don't want it. I don't know what I do want to do, but I'm perfectly sure that it doesn't involve the army, in any shape or form. I'd tried to tell him before, but he just didn't want to hear it. I finally got it through to him at the end of last term, and he was furious. Well, I suppose I can't really blame him. He went to a lot of trouble for me, and under the circumstances I suppose I should be grateful. Well, I am grateful, but not to the extent of having my life run for me. I don't think anyone should be expected to be that grateful.'

Persephone, who had passed all her life believing the reverse, was stunned.

'But don't you think, when someone owes someone else a lot . . . a parent, I mean . . .'

He looked at her, and she was surprised how cold his amber eyes could be, like splintery chips of bottle glass.

'No, I don't. And I'm damned if I'm going to be made to feel guilty. I didn't ask him to look after me. I've never asked him for anything. As far as I could, I have always tried to please him. If that's not enough . . . well, it's too bad.'

'Goodness.' Persephone thought of her own life, her constant striving to repay her mother by doing and being what she wanted. 'You are brave.'

'Not really.' His eyes warmed again. 'As a matter of fact, I'm terrified. But I thought I'd better have a go at surviving on my own – financially, that is. In every other way, I've always been by myself.' The words were dour, but his tone was cheerfully optimistic. 'And here I am. Only I rather feel that this is cheating, letting you feed me and give me a bed, or rather a sofa, for the night. But it was just too tempting to turn down.'

'Perhaps it was fate. The Fates. You can't refuse their gifts, you know.'

'Well, whatever.' He put down his fork and leaned back in his chair, raising his glass. His hair had dried, and he brushed it back from his face with the other hand. 'To the Fates, and Persephone. May they continue to smile.'

After supper, to Persephone's astonished pleasure, he dragooned Robin and Michael into helping him wash up by promising to play Monopoly with them afterwards. Persephone, whose evenings had been rendered hideous by their insistence on this latest craze, found herself able to curl up on the sofa with a book and the rest of the wine.

The following morning he slept late. Persephone, creeping through to the kitchen to make herself a cup of tea, saw him sprawled on the sofa. He had draped the T-shirt he had been wearing neatly over the back of a chair and with his bare torso, ending from the waist down in the twisted sleeping bag, he looked rather like a very masculine mermaid. His face in sleep still retained some echo of the child he had lately been, the dark lashes lying sweetly as a girl's against the smooth plane of his cheek and contrasting almost shockingly with the dark tuft of hair revealed by his upflung arm. He was, as she had thought, too thin, the lines of his ribs clearly delineated beneath the tanned skin.

The weather performed in a predictably English fashion, changing overnight from brilliant sunshine to heavy cloud and outbursts of violent rain. Persephone made hot soup for lunch and a casserole for supper, her hands automatically chopping, mixing and turning as she watched the two boys playing endless games with Hugo. At one point during the afternoon he made polite suggestions of moving on, but was shouted down by the boys. And somehow, by the following day, it had become taken for granted that Hugo would stay with them.

The weekend came and went. George telephoned and said that he was too busy at the office, sorry, to come down. Persephone, who sometimes wondered who it was at the office he was busy with, said that she quite understood.

'We have another guest – Michael's older brother has joined us. The boys get on very well with him, he's a great help, so you don't need to worry about us.'

'Splendid,' said George heartily, having been quite unworried in any case. 'Splendid. Keep up the good work.'

On Monday they went to St Michael's Mount for the day. Though naturally suspicious of any attempt to have outings of an educational nature, Robin and Michael fell under the spell of the little island. The weather was kind, and they picnicked on the wide sandy beach of Mounts Bay, the boys industriously attempting to dam the little stream that meandered across to the sea while they waited for the retreating tide to reveal the causeway. Once on the island they climbed the steep paths at a pace which left Persephone puffing behind them, clambered happily over the cannons, and even admitted to finding the castle itself interesting. By the time they had finished the tide was in. Persephone firmly vetoed their suggestions of (1) swimming back to shore or (2) camping on the island until the tide went out and the causeway reappeared.

'The boat trip's just as much fun,' Hugo pointed out. 'Then you know you've been on a real island. And I might, I say I just might, be prepared to stand you each a go on the funfair by the car park. Only one go, mind.'

This put the seal on their day. By the time they returned to the cottage the boys were yawning, and for once they put up little resistance to the idea of bed fairly soon after supper.

Persephone pottered over the washing-up, listening with half an ear to Hugo's voice as he read a chapter of an adventure book to them, by now a nightly ritual. After a while she heard his feet on the stairs, glanced round to smile at him.

'Coffee?'

'Yes, please.' He seemed slightly out of breath, but she thought with pleasure that he had lost the pale, drawn look she had seen when he first arrived. 'Don't worry, I'll get the kettle.'

He brought it to the sink, and she shifted slightly to let him reach round her to the tap, continuing to scrub a scorched pan. The water pressure was low, and trickled slowly into the kettle as he held it out, his arm against hers. When his other hand touched her shoulder she scarcely noticed: the space was so small there was hardly room for him to stand behind her as he was doing, let alone get past her. Then she felt the warmth of his breath as he bent, and gently kissed the nape of her neck.

She felt an extraordinary frisson of shock run down her spine. The muscles in her stomach clenched involuntarily, and she plunged her hands into the soapy water to hide their tremor. I must say something, she thought. It's nothing. After all, Robin kisses me sometimes, without any warning. He's just being friendly. I hope. Don't I?

'Goodness, Hugo,' she said lightly. 'If you go around kissing older women like that, you'll either get arrested or raped.'

'Good,' he said, and she felt his hand tighten as he bent to kiss her again. His lips lingered, hot against her skin, moving round to the side of her neck where it joined her shoulder.

'You want to be arrested?' I should be stopping him. I should tell him not to. Kindly, but firmly.

'Well, no.' The kettle overflowed, and automatically she reached out to turn off the tap. She felt his lips part, the soft warmth of his tongue as he touched the hollow above her collarbone, the shock of cold on damp skin as he took his mouth away. Her heart thudded as if it would burst. 'As a matter of fact, I was rather hoping to be raped,' he said.

Chapter 15

'Oh, Hugo!'

It was not, she realised belatedly, an adequate remonstrance. He put the overflowing electric kettle down in the washing-up bowl, where Persephone was to find it, ruined, the following morning and shake her head over it with a smile. His now free hand came up to cup her other shoulder, but so gently that she did not feel herself constrained. She could not move out of the kitchen area without pushing past him, but although he was so much taller and, she supposed, stronger than she was, she felt no alarm. Though he continued to kiss her neck he made no attempt to make her turn round and his hands stayed where they were, the thumbs gently massaging her shoulders. While eagerness would have disturbed or even frightened her, his diffidence was, by its very lack of sexual aggression, appealing. To her dismay she felt her nipples tingling, her breasts engorged and heavy. She drew in a deep breath.

'Hugo, don't.' She tried to say it firmly, but it came out as a plea. He lifted his head, but his hands still held her.

'Why not? Don't you like it?'

'Yes. No. Yes. But that's got nothing to do with it. You mustn't.'

'But you do like it?' He nibbled gently at her ear. 'What about that? Is that nice?'

In the confined space she was pressed against him. She hoped that his own excitement, so unmistakably hard against her lower back, made it impossible for him to feel how her heart was pounding. She eased herself away from him. At once the slight pressure of his hands relaxed. Somehow his instant acceptance of her rejection made her feel guilty, as if she had been cruel. She lifted her hands, wet and wrinkly from the cooling washing-up water, and laid them on his which he turned so that, with thumbs underneath, he was holding hers.

'I'm sorry,' she said carefully, 'but you must see it's impossible. I'm . . . I'm married.'

Even as she said it, she acknowledged that it was not, for her, a reason for refusal. True, she had never been unfaithful to George, had never even been tempted, but there had been no opportunity. Busy with pregnancies and babies, her married life had been enclosed and surrounded just as her girlhood had been, so that sometimes she wondered whether she was living at all, or was merely an extension of her mother's experience. George, she knew, had not always been faithful to her, and the thing that saddened her most about that was to find how little she minded, so long as he was discreet.

Her experience of sex was confined to a few adolescent fumblings in cars or taxis during her London season, and George. Though he had, initially, been gentle and careful enough, she had at first found the process both embarrassing and absurd. She soon learned, however, that George could see no possibility for humour in their couplings. Once, when she had been unable to stifle a giggle, he had turned away from her at once. She had, he said, put him off, and it was true that her caressing hand found ample evidence of this when, rather daringly she thought, she touched his limp penis. Mortified, he had pushed her hand away and hunched his back to her, huffily refusing to speak. They had never referred to the incident again, and she had learned that, whatever advice books and magazines might give, any attempt to discuss their sex life would be bitterly resented by him as a criticism.

As a result, on the occasions when she climaxed (as opposed to faking it) it was more by luck than anything else. Persephone was inclined to think of herself as sexually inept, and if not frigid at least not very highly sexed. She never expected the men she met socially to find her desirable, and on the one occasion when a colleague of George's, rather too full of sherry at a Christmas drinks party, made a pass at her, she fell into a fit of giggles which had much the same deflating effect it had had on George.

But this was very different. She had, she supposed, closed her eyes to Hugo's masculinity, distancing herself from it by treating him as a child. Now, suddenly, one touch of his lips on her neck had set the blood fizzing in her veins. She felt alive and aware as she had never been before. Her upbringing taught her that such feelings were wrong, but beneath that superficial layer of respectability the long-repressed desire to rebel was bubbling up.

'I'm Robin's mother.' There, that was better. Would that not put her back into the place where she belonged?

'Yes, of course you are. But that's only part of you. You're you as well. Persephone. Lovely, lovely Persephone.' His low voice lingered on her name. She could not help remembering how George invariably called her 'Perse', and how much she had always hated it.

'I'm too old. I'm over thirty.' She remembered how, at eighteen, thirty had seemed to her unimaginably ancient.

'You mean, I'm too young. But I'm not! What is there between us? Twelve years, thirteen? If it were the other way round, if you were a man and I a young girl, nobody would think twice about it. I'm not a child, not Mikey's age. I'm old enough to make my own decisions, lead my own life, learn about love . . .'

She remembered how she had watched him asleep, that first morning. Had she not felt, then, an obscure stirring of desire? She thought, now, that perhaps she had, though at the time she had not understood it. She had been so careful to think of him as just another child, older than Mikey and Robin, but still a child to be fed and indulged.

'You don't love me, Hugo,' she said sadly.

'No.' To her surprise he agreed with her. 'No. Or at least, I do, but not for ever. I'm not romantically "*in* love" with you. I don't want you to leave your husband and children, come away with me, spend the rest of our lives together. Not that kind of love. But I do love you, and like you, and desire you . . .' His hands gripped hers, but he did not kiss her or allow his body to touch hers. His honesty disarmed her; in a curious way she found it more moving than any passionate protestation. 'I want to know, to be sure, to . . . oh, I don't know, to live!'

She knew that later – tomorrow, next week, next year – she would perhaps feel guilt, even self-disgust, but it was distant and unreal. Never, in all her life, had she done something merely because she wanted to. She felt how her own body ached with a longing she had never felt before. And it was to her body that she spoke, as if it had been a child begging for a gift, rather than to Hugo.

'All right.' She sounded so calm, so matter of fact in her own ears. Scarcely believing what she was doing she pulled his hands forward, crossing them so that his arms lay hieratically on her breasts. She leaned back against him, realising as he dragged in a deep sigh that he had been holding his breath, and let her head fall back against his shoulder, turning her face to meet his kiss.

A child's kiss at first, such as Robin might have given her, his lips dry, touching hers lightly. She waited, respecting his hesitation, recognising an inexperience that was not far from her own. After a moment his lips parted. With memories of assault-by-tongue from her younger days she steeled herself not to flinch, but his touch was so tentative that she relaxed. His mouth tasted of toothpaste, and she realised he must have gone to clean his teeth after reading to the boys. The thought was both amusing and touching: she let go of his hands and turned within his embrace, holding him off with her hands against his chest.

'What's the matter?' She saw how vulnerable he was, realised that, like her at eighteen, he had passed his life under the domination of a strict parent, and confined within a single-sex boarding school. For the swinging Sixties he was remarkably inexperienced.

'Nothing.' She leaned against him, looking candidly up into his troubled face. 'I'm a bit nervous, actually. I've never done anything like this before. I mean, only with George. And that was, well, a bit boring, really. Oh dear, I shouldn't say that, how disloyal of me.' She looked as dismayed as she felt, then realised that such a minor disloyalty paled into insignificance beside the major infidelity she was about to commit. Her lips twitched, and try as she might she could not help laughing.

For a moment he stood stiff and silent. Persephone choked back her laughter.

'Oh, I'm sorry, Hugo. I wasn't laughing at you.'

To her relief his bony, intelligent face creased into an answering smile.

'I know.' They both laughed a bit wildly, clinging to one another. Persephone recovered first.

'Oh dear, I'm sorry. I shouldn't be laughing like this.'

'Why not?' His hand smoothed down her back, slipped up beneath the baggy sweater she was wearing and caressed her bare skin. 'I thought this was meant to be fun?'

'Yes, I suppose it is.' Her tone was surprised and Hugo, who for one reason and another had formed a low opinion of George, revised it downwards.

'Well, it looks like this is going to be the blind leading the blind, Mrs H. I warn you now that my knowledge of sex, though extensive and well researched, is purely theoretical. Yours, I suspect, is heavy on the practical but light on theory. Am I right?'

'Yes. Oh, Hugo . . .'

'Don't worry. We'll work it out. It'll be all right on the night. Now, what do you prefer, passion and discomfort on the kitchen floor, or removing ourselves to the bedroom?'

'Definitely the bedroom. But I'd like to go and clean my teeth first, please.'

'Yes, I stole a march on you there, didn't I?' His tone was lightly smug. This time, when he kissed her, there was no withdrawing, no hesitation for either of them.

Much later in the night she woke. She had forgotten to draw the curtains, and the moonlight streamed in, edging their tumbled limbs with silver. His lean body lay sprawled, relaxed in sleep. One of his hands lay on her where it had fallen from her breast. Gently she lifted it back, and even in sleep his fingers caressed its curve, his thumb passing over her nipple so that it hardened. He stirred, murmured her name, and settled back into sleep.

She looked at her own body as if she had never seen it before. Critically at first, as she thought Hugo would have seen it. Mercifully free of the silvery scarring that pregnancy stretch marks inflicted, it was not so very different from how it had been at her marriage. Regular swimming and riding, mostly to exercise Sarah's ponies over the years, had kept her muscles firm. Two years ago she had found her weight creeping up, and after some pointed remarks from her mother had taken a look at her diet. Rigorously cutting out the comforting chocolate biscuits at coffee- and tea-time, and refraining from picking at the chips the children insisted on, had been enough to slim her down again.

She ran an exploratory hand over her thigh, up her stomach to her breast, trying to feel it as he would have done. Smooth and firm enough, she thought, except perhaps for the breasts which the feeding of two children had softened a little. Even so, she did not need to be ashamed for him to see her. He had wanted to undress her, but seeing her embarrassment had not insisted, allowing her instead to huddle beneath the sheet before slipping off her nightie.

Even the touch of her own familiar hand made her skin tingle, her flesh tighten. Her body had responded to Hugo in a way that was more astonishing to her than to him. His almost innocent curiosity had been subtly exciting, his exploring touch and, above all, the murmur of his voice, were revelations. George, apart from an occasional groan at the height of passion, had been silent in his lovemaking. Hugo, on the other hand, commented and complimented, questioned and exclaimed. His words seemed to Persephone to bring her to life as she had never been before: his delight in her body and his need to have her tell him how she felt made her aware of sensations that were new to her.

At first she lay quite passively, enjoying his caresses and explorations, so stunned by the feelings they evoked that it never occurred to her to touch him. His hands, his lips and his tongue were the only part of him she was aware of. Afterwards, remembering his youth and inexperience, she realised that it was the best thing that she could have done, making it possible for him to excite her to the point where, when he could no longer control his need, she was as eager as he.

'I can't wait any longer,' he whispered, drawing away from her and closing his eyes as if to blank out his body's clamour for a moment. She reached to embrace him, her leg over his hip, her body seeking his.

'Don't wait, don't wait, I'm here . . . Oh, oh, Hugo!' She exhaled on the aspirate of his name, the breath leaving her body for an exquisite second as if he had punctured her with the thrust as he entered her.

'Too quick. I'm sorry.'

'No! No, not too quick. It was . . . Good God, Hugo, I didn't know. I didn't know it could be like that. It was – so easy.'

'Like learning to ride a bicycle, and finding you could do it?' She heard the smile in his voice.

'More like jumping off the Empire State Building, and discovering that I could fly,' she said, quite seriously. He lifted himself up, and looked down at her face. His eyes were black in the moonlight, his face almost completely shadowed by the curtains of hair that fell forward round it.

'That was just the beginning. Wait till we jump off Mount Everest,' he said.

The next few days passed in a kind of fevered dream. Time, Persephone discovered, behaved quite differently under these circumstances. In the morning, waking alone because Hugo made sure, for her sake, that he left her bed and returned to his sofa at dawn, she would stretch luxuriously, feeling that the day ahead would be as long as eternity but would still fly by. During the day he was Mikey's big brother, helpful, amusing, companionable, never hinting by word, look or touch that he was only waiting, as she was, for the night. They were meticulously careful not to give any hint of intimacy in front of the two boys. Both Robin and Mikey, fortunately, were sound sleepers, and the long active days in the open air meant that they were generally asleep even before their evening reading was over. The creaking wooden stairs gave ample warning, should one of them have woken and come to find her, but in the event they never did.

There was a heady excitement, she found, in living this kind of double life. She felt that she was quite literally two people: by day Robin's mother, concerned with their meals and their pleasure, disinfecting cuts and scratches, providing an admiring audience for swimming, castle-building, games. By night she was the young girl she had never had the chance to be; free of restraints and inhibitions, taking pleasure in her own body and in her lover. Because they kept the two elements so separate there was never any hint that Robin and Mikey – inhabiting as they did a world of their own where adults, even friendly ones like Hugo, had only a peripheral place – noticed anything out of the ordinary.

Then, quite suddenly between one moment and the next, she realised that the holiday was over. The following day was the last, and they must leave early on the morning of the next day. That night their lovemaking was different: more tender, a gentle, lingering farewell. Persephone felt a kind of distant sadness mixed with something akin to relief. She had been living like a teenager – every emotion taken to the extreme of pleasure and pain. She was exhausted, mentally if not physically, and though she found the thought of saying goodbye to Hugo unbearable, it would be a relief, she knew, to return to her usual prosaic existence.

'No regrets?'

They lay side by side, holding hands like children. Persephone turned her head to smile at him.

'No regrets. And no recriminations. It was . . . wonderful.'

'Yes, it was.' His agreement was uncomplicated. Already his eyes looked beyond her, away into the future. 'I'll never forget you. You'll always be . . . the special one. Oh, Persephone . . .'

His lip trembled like a child. She laid her fingers on his mouth.

'Hush. Remember what you said. Love, but not in love. It's not finished, it's complete. Perfect. But it can only stay like that if we don't try to carry it on.' She paused, amazed to find that the words she spoke to comfort him seemed so true to her.

In the bustle of packing and cleaning the cottage there was no time for emotion. When everything was in the car and he was standing, rucksack on his back, by the door of the cottage, Persephone gave him a maternal kiss, and put an envelope in his hand.

'Thank you,' he said automatically. 'What is it?' he added, with dawning suspicion.

'Emergency fund.'

He looked appalled.

'No. I couldn't.' He pushed the envelope back at her. She closed his fingers round it.

'Don't be silly,' she said firmly. 'I can't send Mikey's brother off into the wild blue yonder without a penny to his name. I know you'll get a job, but it might be a few days, so just take it. You've earned it, anyway, helping with the boys and the house. Think of it as – as a kind of *au pair* job, if it makes it any easier.'

Under the steady gaze of two pairs of youthful eyes he could do no more than grin ruefully and push the envelope into his pocket.

'Thanks,' he said gruffly.

'And if you run into any problems . . .'

'I know.' He ruffled Michael's hair, punched Robin gently in the ribs. 'Behave yourselves in the car, monsters.'

They watched him stride off up the lane. At the corner he looked back and waved, then he was gone. Persephone blinked hard and swallowed, heard an answering swallow from Michael. She put an arm round him, and after a second's instinctive stiffening he relaxed against her, pushing his head into her side.

'He'll be all right,' she said, as much to herself as to the boy. 'He'll be all right, Mikey.'

'I know. It's just . . .'

'Yes,' she said, into his silence. 'It is.'

Back at home, the world resumed its accustomed patterns and colours. Sarah was still in the South of France, for Lady Singleton had declared that there was no point in their going for less than a month. Persephone felt she had been granted a respite that she scarcely deserved. For two weeks she drifted round the house in a dreamy, semi-vegetative state. Robin was occupied with his own concerns, busy with building a camp in the wooded part of the garden, alone because Mikey's parents had sold their house. Mikey's mother had promptly whisked her son off to Australia, flying back to home and family and shaking the dust of an unsatisfactory marriage from her without ceremony.

'I just can't wait to get away,' she said when she collected Mikey on their return from Cornwall. 'I mean, I've never felt at home here, y'know? And since Ian and I fell apart, I find myself noticing how *cold* it is, all of a sudden. It didn't seem as bad as this, at first . . .' The upward lilt of her voice was belied by her shiver.

'Robin will miss Michael. So will I – he's a dear little boy.'

'He doesn't want to go, of course, but what can I do? I can't stay here, I just can't. But he'll be right, once he's had time to settle. 'Stralia's a great place for kids to grow up. He'll love it.'

'Yes, of course he will,' said Persephone with false enthusiasm. In her mind's eye the oceans round Australia teemed with sharks just as the land teemed with snakes and deadly spiders. It was, she knew, a ridiculous exaggeration, but her heart quailed at the thought of Mikey, her only link with Hugo, going to the other side of the world.

'And what about . . . Hugo?' Her voice was so casual that her visitor didn't hear the question, and Persephone was forced to repeat it, stooping to stroke the cat to hide her heated face.

'Hugo?' Mrs Macdonald's voice was blank. 'Oh yes, Hugo. I forgot, he landed himself on you in Cornwall, didn't he? I hope he wasn't a nuisance.'

'Not at all. He was very helpful. I enjoyed having him.' Persephone smiled primly, ignoring the fizz of laughter at her unconscious choice of words.

'Oh yes, he's a nice boy. Of course, I've never seen a great deal of him. He lived with his mother most of the time, and under the circumstances . . . well, you know how it is. Ian always did his best for him, of course, but . . . Still, if he should come out to 'Stralia, I told him there's always a welcome for him there. Can't say fairer than that!'

No, thought Persephone. From a not very involved stepmother, one couldn't ask for much more. She felt Hugo, and Cornwall, and Mikey, slipping away from her like water ebbing through wet sand. A wave of exhaustion washed over her and she closed her eyes for a moment.

'Hey, are you all right?' She opened her eyes to find her visitor eyeing her anxiously. 'You've gone white as a sheet!'

'I'm fine,' she said, drawing in a breath to subdue a pang of nausea. 'Bit of a bug, I expect.'

Rather to her amusement, the possibility of a bug drove Mikey's mother from the house at top speed, pulling a reluctant Mikey with her.

'Can't risk catching anything, y'know,' she explained briskly. 'Flight's in two days, after all.' Persephone agreed, but two days later as she was thinking of Mikey and his mother on the plane to Australia she felt another rush of sickly tiredness. She sat limply at the kitchen table, waiting for it to pass, her eyes falling idly on the calendar that hung on the wall by the telephone. As usual during the school holidays she had rather lost track of time, frequently being surprised by the advent of a weekend. Now she stared at the neat chequerboard of dates with dawning suspicion, searching her memory, counting weeks on her fingers. Five weeks, nearly six? Surely not. Once again she counted back, knowing as she did so that it was unnecessary, remembering how pleased she had been to have finished her period the week before leaving for Cornwall. Now she, who had always been as regular as clockwork, was two weeks late.

It had not even occurred to her, in Cornwall, that they ought to take precautions. The joyful pleasure they had taken in each other had seemed quite different, to her, from the purposeful acts which had been undertaken, with carefully timed planning, to start both her previous pregnancies. In the early years she had been on the pill, but after Robin's birth she had decided that the health risk was too great. She had experimented with a cap, but found it messy and awkward, and an IUD had been uncomfortable and given her furiously heavy periods. In the end, since with two young children she was nearly always too tired and their sex life had diminished, she had asked George to use condoms. He had grumbled a bit at first, but the routine was soon established.

As a result she had lost the habit of worrying about pregnancy. Feeling, as she did, so much older than Hugo, it had never crossed her mind that they should do anything about it. And he, presumably, had assumed that she was experienced enough to take care of things, and thought that she was on the pill like most younger women. How, she wondered, could she have been so naïve? With her conscious mind she knew very well that at thirty-one she was still very fertile, and yet she had perversely ignored the danger. Or had she? Her initial response to the realisation had been pure, unadulterated joy. Had her subconscious, wiser than her intelligence, acted to suppress the thought?

Her breasts tingled, as they had done when Hugo kissed her neck. Good God, she thought, I'm pregnant. What do I do? Nothing, she answered herself at once, feeling the flood of joy that filled up an empty space in her heart that she had scarcely been aware of. Somehow she never doubted that it was Hugo's baby, although the pregnancy could have been started by George the night before she left. Nor did it ever occur to her not to go ahead with it, or that she should tell George that she was carrying a child that was not his.

Instead she sailed through the ensuing months serenely, at peace with herself and the world, silencing even Lady Singleton's criticisms with a blank, uncomprehending look. None of her pregnancies had caused her much discomfort, but apart from the dizzy spells at the beginning she felt healthier, bearing Amy, than she had ever done in her life, as if she had finally achieved a physical state that she had always aimed for, but never quite managed. Her skin glowed, her hair shone like polished copper and curled more softly, losing for a time its tendency to frizziness.

The birth was equally simple; even the pain seemed distant and unreal compared with the triumph of producing this child. George, as before, was too squeamish to be present. Once she had been disappointed, even resentful; now she welcomed his absence and forgot him almost before he had walked out of the ward. He was glad to leave: not only did he find the process of birth alarming and disgusting, but he was deeply affronted that suddenly, out of the blue, Persephone had insisted on going to the maternity ward of the local hospital, instead of the private nursing home where Sarah and Robin had made an expensive appearance.

'But, Perse, your mother *likes* to pay for you! What will she say? What will everyone say? They'll think you're mad!'

'Will they?' Persephone's voice was vague. 'Oh, well, never mind.'

'Supposing something goes wrong?' He thought this a very cunning argument, but she smiled at him as at a foolish and fractious child.

'If something goes wrong, they're better equipped in the hospital than in the nursing home. All the real emergencies get whizzed in there by ambulance, didn't you know?'

Silenced, he had left her to Lady Singleton. She, however, had been so astonished by having her decision questioned that she scarcely knew how to argue with this serene stranger who simply clasped her hands over the dome of her belly, and smiled.

When they put Amy into her arms, Persephone looked down at someone who was, miraculously, already a person in her own right. She did not need to see the straight dark brows, so ludicrously adult on the newborn face, or the eyes that so quickly changed from newborn blue to a familiar golden brown, to know that this was Hugo's daughter. Sarah and Robin, so deeply loved and wanted, had for the time of their babyhood seemed more like extensions of her, as she always felt herself an extension of her mother. Now this tiny scrap stared at her from beneath the dark eyebrows, so unlike the invisible down of most babies, and appeared already to be forming her own judgement of the world. Persephone felt so triumphant she could have shouted aloud. By creating Amy, so unique and so much her own self, she had somehow managed for the first time to feel she had validated her own identity. At last, she thought. At last I am real. A real person, with a real baby that no one else has any claim to. I'm free.

A hand on her wrist.

'Ma! Ma?' Persephone blinked, coming back from a world of certainty to where freedom was, as ever, a mirage that she now suspected was not even worth chasing after. Robin bent over her, a dark shape against the fitful sunlight. 'Are you all right?'

'Yes,' she said, automatically. 'Hello, darling.'

He stooped to kiss her then sat on the bench beside her, his hand still lightly gripping her wrist as if to tether her like a partially filled helium balloon.

'A woman at the pub greeted me as if I were a long-lost relative, and told me that me mother was up the Castle,' he said lightly.

'Yes. She told me to come up here, so I did.'

'Obedient creature. You shouldn't do everything that other people tell you to do, Ma.' He was only half joking, and she sighed.

'No, I know. Habit of a lifetime.' She fell silent. Beneath his fingers Robin felt her pulse pound and the tendons in her wrist move as her fingers clenched. He took her hand in both of his.

'What is it, Ma? Is it the business about Granny, and Amy going to see your – to see that woman?'

'No. I can cope with that. At least, I think I can. It's something else.' Her throat tried to close up, she passed a dry tongue over lips that seemed numb, and drew in a deep breath. 'Do you remember Hugo, Robin? Mikey's brother, who stayed with us in Cornwall?'

'Hugo? Yes, of course I do. Why?'

She tried to withdraw her hand, dreading that when he

heard what she would say he would drop it in disgust. He held it in a warm clasp. She turned her face to look in his eyes, trying to read his soul.

'He's Amy's father,' she said baldly. 'I don't know what to do, Robin. How can I tell her? She can't marry Michael, he's her uncle. She'll never forgive me. Oh, Robin, what am I going to do?'

'Good God.' He looked stunned. Whatever he might have expected, it was not this. He thought back, remembering the holiday, remembering Hugo and thinking of him, now, from the perspective of a man much older than Hugo had been then. It had been, he remembered, a particularly happy holiday, and it had been largely thanks to Hugo that this was so. Hugo, organising games, teaching them swimming strokes, reading to them. Hugo, devoting his days to their amusement in a way which he had taken for granted, then, but now saw was exceptional in a young man of, what? Eighteen? Nineteen? And his enjoyment in their company had been real, he thought, not just a cynical ruse to ingratiate himself with Persephone.

How do I feel about this? he wondered. My mother was unfaithful to my father, slept with a boy more than ten years younger than her, had his baby and foisted her off on her husband. It sounds . . . sordid. *News of the World*, here we come. But this is Amy we're talking about here. And Persephone my mother, and Hugo. Nice people, good people.

Somewhere, deep down, a small child cried out for the inviolate image of motherhood that spelled security. Hush, he said to the child. Go back to limbo. How does it harm you? Amy, perhaps. My father, certainly. But can I really blame her? What, over all the years of their marriage, did he give her? Not fidelity, that's for sure. And not happiness, either, except in the sense that he never went out of his way to make her *un*happy.

I have to respond, he thought, aware of her tension as she sat beside him. He knew that his face would have expressed nothing of his thoughts. It's all right. This is something I can deal with. Something I must deal with, so that I can help her and Amy. I'll worry about it later, sort it out in my head. For now—

He let a smile twitch at his lips.

'Good God, Ma,' he repeated, and his tone was awed, even, she thought, impressed.

'It's not *funny*, Robin!'

'No, no, of course it isn't. It's just . . . I had no idea! I mean, you never expect your mother to . . . Oh, Lord, I'm saying all the wrong things, aren't I? Come on, Ma, don't look so Greek Tragedy. It isn't the end of the world.'

'It will be, for Amy. Oh, Robin, do you think it would be better not to tell her at all? Just keep it quiet?'

He thought.

'Would you have preferred not to find out about Granny adopting you? If it hadn't been for that piece of paper, you'd never have known.'

'No.' Her immediate response surprised even Persephone herself. 'No, I wouldn't. Oh, at first I thought just that, wished I'd never found out. But afterwards . . . I don't know how to explain it, but it felt right. I felt more at home with myself, more real, if you know what I mean.'

'I know exactly what you mean. Rather like when I admitted to myself that I was gay.'

'Oh, Robin. So, I have to tell her, don't I?'

'Yes, I'm afraid I think you do. No more hiding, no more lies. I'll come with you, pick up the pieces if I can. That is,' he added scrupulously, 'if you want me to.'

'Yes, please. You mean, now, today? There, at . . . her house?'

'Why not? Bring all the skeletons out to rattle about in the daylight. Poor things, they'll probably enjoy a bit of fresh air.' He let go of her hand, but before she had time to feel bereft his arm was round her in a comforting hug. 'Come on, Ma. Let's get it over with.'

His voice was relaxed, even cheerful. Since that morning, nothing seemed able to dismay him. The memory of his telephone call to Harry wrapped round him like a suit of armour, only infinitely more comfortable. Silent at first, Harry had at least listened, had not merely slammed the phone down. He had sounded – what? – different. Quieter? Gentler, even? Noncommittal, but to Robin's sensitive ear pleased to talk to him. I'll call you later, he had said. Thanks, he had said.

'What kind of treatment are you getting?' Robin had asked carefully, not sure whether this might be taken as too pushy. Harry, however, had only sounded surprised.

'Treatment? Oh, the usual.'

'Oh.' What, Robin wondered, was the usual treatment? 'I didn't know they had come up with a specific way of dealing with it yet,' he said, noncommittally.

'Oh yes.' Harry's voice was matter of fact. 'Chemotherapy, radiotherapy, all the usual stuff. My hair started coming out, so I had the whole lot shaved and got a wig. Well, more like three wigs.'

'Chemotherapy? Radiotherapy? For *Aids*?' Robin was appalled. Was Harry being given the wrong treatment?

'Aids? No, I haven't got Aids. Who told you I had? I bet it was Bob.'

'Yes, it was. Oh God, Harry, he only just told me a few days ago. I was so worried . . .'

'Idiot.' Harry's voice sounded warm, almost affectionate. 'You might have known I'd have let you know myself, if it had been that. No, Bob came round on the scrounge, you know how he is, comes for an evening and stays for three months. He saw I looked ill and I told him it was Aids, to get rid of him. No, it's Hodgkin's disease.'

Robin felt his eyes fill with tears. Not Aids, after all. No the ultimate death penalty.

'Harry. Oh, Harry, I'm glad. I'm really glad.' There were no words, as things were, to express how he felt. Hodgkin's was bad, he knew that, but it could be treated, could often be cured.

'Yeah, well . . . no need to worry, now. No need for blood tests.' The words were cynical, but he spoke them gently, as if probing for a splinter.

'Harry . . .'

'I know. Out of order. I know. Why do you have to be so bloody *nice*, Robin?'

'Just made that way, I guess.'

They had talked for nearly half an hour, communicating with increasing ease. Robin could scarcely contain his joy and his relief. It was, he thought happily, a beginning. It had even been better than he had dared to hope. He had always known that the main problem, the thing that would be most difficult to overcome, was that Harry had behaved unreasonably. He had, as so often in the past, taken umbrage at an imaginary slight and overreacted. Robin had seen it happen before, if less finally, and knew that the one thing Harry found impossible was to back down, to admit he had been wrong, to apologise. And the worse he had behaved, the more he could not do it. Unable to forgive himself, because he refused to confront what had happened, Robin suspected that deep within his macho exterior was someone so lacking in self-confidence that he did not really expect anyone else to forgive him either. So, rather than risk the possibility of that rejection, he preferred to move on, cut out that bit of his life, by ignoring it make it not have happened.

Now, however, the whole misunderstanding over the nature of his disease had eased the way, and Robin's obvious pleasure seemed to have gone some way towards healing the breach. If only, thought Robin, he will let me help him. I could, I know I could. Even if he's ill, really ill, even if he doesn't get better. I would have looked after him if it had been Aids, if there had been no hope at all. If only he will let me.

Chapter 16

Sunday morning.

Frances crept downstairs to make her tea. The creeping was, she found later, unnecessary. Unversed in the habits of the young, her own teenage years had been passed in an age, and a family, that regarded lying in bed in the morning as a dangerously luxurious habit morally permissible only in the sick or the infirm. Her sleep patterns had been further fossilised by the discipline of nursing shifts, and it had never occurred to her that a generation accustomed to staying up late, if only to watch videos, must necessarily be used to sleeping on until late morning.

She laid her tea tray with two cups and drank her own with her ear cocked for sounds of stirring. At seven thirty she washed and dressed, thinking that a girl of Amy's age might require to use the bathroom for some lengthy beautifying rituals such as she had dimly taken in from glossy magazines in the dentist's waiting room. At half past eight the silence in the house was so profound that Frances suddenly formed the idea that Amy might have run away from her in the night, as she had done from her mother the night before.

Opening the door of the spare bedroom she was relieved to see a mound under the bedclothes, amused and touched to find that Amy slept, curled like a dormouse, with her head almost hidden beneath the duvet. The cat, who was generally put out every night, had presumably come up the wisteria and through the wide-open casement, for he was curled into a comfortable cushion shape in the hollow behind her knees. He looked up, assessed her presence and the degree of his own hunger, stretched, and dropped with a thump to the floor. Frances backed out of the doorway to let him past, but a creaking board betrayed her attempt at silent withdrawal, and Amy emerged blearily from her nest.

'Mmmaah,' she groaned. 'Oh, good morning, May. Is it late?'

'Half past eight,' said Frances, who wasn't sure whether this counted as late or not to someone of twenty-three.

'Good,' said Amy. 'Shall I get up?'

'Only if you want to. Do you want a cup of tea?'

'Yes, please, but not in bed or I'll fall asleep again and drown in it. What do you usually do on Sundays?'

'Go to church, I suppose. Then I garden, or read the papers, or have friends round – the usual things, really.'

'Great. May I have a bath?'

'Yes, of course, there's plenty of hot water. I'll see you downstairs. No hurry, just take your time.'

By the time Frances had made porridge, laid the breakfast table, and peeled some potatoes for lunch, Amy was in the kitchen. She smelled of flowers, a subtle mingling of scents like a sophisticated country garden, and her freshly washed hair hung against her cheeks, chestnut dark with damp.

'Oh, you've done everything. I meant to be down in time to help with breakfast. Sorry, May.'

'It's only porridge. You can make the toast if you like.' Frances was feeling awkward. On the rare occasions when she had friends to stay, she was in the habit of taking them breakfast in bed, on a tray. Her guests were loudly appreciative of this luxury, and Frances would accept their gratitude with becoming modesty, not telling them that she did it to keep them out of her way. A leisurely breakfast, reading her current book, had for many years been the high point of her day, a reaffirmation of her freedom from the bonds of childhood. Even in her teaching days she had preferred to get up an hour earlier and enjoy that little oasis of calm, the memory of which returned to solace her when beset by fractious children, temperamental staff or over-reacting parents.

Her mind and her emotions churned up by the events of the previous day, she had slept little and restlessly. The tea she had drunk in bed had been sour in her mouth, too hot and then, almost at once, too cold. And her book, once again, had failed to draw her into its world so that, for the first time in her life, she had abandoned her beloved Trollope in mid-novel and taken up a Dick Francis. Even this safe refuge, to which she fled when beset with influenza or toothache, had turned its back on her and refused to let her in. Now she felt tired and bruised, her eyes gritty and her head full of grey fluff. If only, she thought, I could sit quietly over my breakfast, try *Barchester* again, perhaps I would be able to face the rest of today.

Amy took a childish pleasure in making toast on the Aga, putting the slices of bread between the long-handled wire-mesh holder and laying them on the hot plate. As usual the cat was in the way, but she leaned across him without bothering to move him.

'This is nearly as good as doing it on a toasting fork by a fire. Can I have that burned bit? I love burned toast, and this burns it so much better than a toaster. How many slices do you have?'

'Two.'

'I slept so well, it was wonderful. I've never had a sleepless night before, and it was awful, but it's almost worth it to sleep so deeply the next night. Did you sleep well, too?'

'Not very.' Frances hated herself for speaking so shortly, and opened her mouth to apologise, but Amy turned round, the bell of her drying hair flying out round her face. She subjected Frances to a swift but shrewd examination.

'No, of course, and it's my fault. I'm so sorry, May! And here I am wittering on, when I expect you'd like a nice quiet breakfast. Do you have a Sunday paper? Or can I get one of your books, and read while we eat? I know it's not very good manners, Granny hated it, but Mummy always let us because she liked doing it too. I'm very experienced, and never get marmalade on the pages. Would that be all right?'

Frances felt a huge bubble of relief rise in her, burst and spread through her body like a soothing balm.

'Of course it is. As a matter of fact, I always read at breakfast, though my mother would have been horrified. Um, the toast is burning again.'

Amy swung back and lifted the lid of the hot plate, enveloping herself in acrid smoke.

'Oh dear, even I can't eat that bit!'

'Never mind, I'll put it outside and open the back door for a minute, while you go and fetch a book, if that's what you want to do.'

The cat, much affronted by the smoke, shot out of the door. They spoke no more, signalling acceptance of a cup of tea or the passing of the marmalade only by a look, a nod, a raising of the eyebrows. The familiar words of her book, though they did not take her away from the anxiety of the present, at least managed to smooth and order Frances' tangled thoughts. By the end of breakfast she felt calmer, more ready for the day. What were they to do? she wondered. Amy, of course, wanted to hear the truth about her mother. For most of the night Frances had been trying to put the past into words, into a narrative form that she could communicate, but she felt no nearer being able to than she had the day before.

She was terrified of doing it wrong, making what had been quite a simple matter into something sordid, or frightening, or just plain ridiculous. There was also a slight sense of discomfort, a feeling of wrongness, in telling Amy first. Surely Amy's mother, as the person most involved, had a right to that? Frances felt that she needed more time to decide what was the right thing to do.

'Could I come to church with you?' They were washing up, and Frances rested her hands in the hot water for a moment, surprised. She had expected Army to want her explanation as soon as possible, that immediately breakfast was over they would settle down in the sitting room for the heart-to-heart session she had been dreading. Glancing at Amy, she realised that the girl was almost as nervous as she was, that she was no more ready to hear than Frances was to speak. Church, at least, would provide an excuse for them both. And, who knew, perhaps by some divine intervention the words she must speak would be given to her?

'Yes, if you'd like to. That would be very nice.'

'I used to go with Mummy,' said Amy, polishing a plate that she had already dried, 'but she doesn't go very often, now. You don't have to introduce me,' she concluded in a rush, her head bowed over the plate so that her hair fell forward to hide her reddening cheeks.

'Introduce you?'

'To your friends. I mean, if you go every week, they all know you, don't they? You don't want to tell them who I am. I could be . . . someone you used to teach, or the daughter of an old friend, or something. I don't want to make things embarrassing for you.'

'I see.' This aspect of things had scarcely dawned on

Frances, who had not been expecting to go to church anyway. 'Do you mind? But I suppose it's embarrassing for you, too.'

'Not really. But it's different for me, isn't it? And I haven't got to go on living here, meeting them every week.'

'Well. I suppose so. We'll see, shall we? I must get ready, we need to leave in ten minutes.'

'Am I respectable enough?' Frances eyed her granddaughter who was dressed as she had been the day before, but for a different shirt. She herself had dressed, from habit, in the conservative tweed suit she kept for Sundays and trips to London.

'We both do. Half the choir wear jeans under their robes.'

The old church welcomed them with that indefinable ecclesiastical smell that was as unmistakable, Frances always thought, as the smell all schools have on the first day of term. They smelled of polish, disinfectant, and the ghosts of old plimsolls; the church of dust, old hymn books, mothballs (mothballs? Mrs Etherington must be here again, she registered on one level), and old polish, through which a tantalising whisper of scent from the flowers threaded itself like bright ribbon through hessian.

Since the advent of a new vicar, the congregation had been gently eased into the (to some) embarrassing and pointless modern affectation of sharing the peace. Stiff with resentment, the older worshippers smiled coldly and offered a limp handshake to people they intended to greet with proper pleasure at the right time, which was the end of the service. The choir, well drilled, portioned out the pews amongst them like synchronised swimmers, darting back to their places at a given moment with a flick of a surplice and an instant vanishing of insincere smiles.

Usually Frances, who was English enough to find the whole thing deeply inhibiting, muttered her 'Peace be with you' and touched hands with the person next to her, then stood staring at the ground until it was over and they could get on with the opening prayer. Now, for the first time, she found herself actually welcoming the moment. Acting from instinct rather than reason she did as she had seen other families do, bending down to Amy to kiss and be kissed. And Amy, to whom the expression of physical affection was as normal as breathing, responded without surprise or awkwardness, lifting her face and smiling a wide and uncomplicated smile.

Amy, Frances was relieved to find, knew her way around the Alternative Service that she herself disliked, still hearing weekly echoes of the old prayers whispering sadly through the updated milk-and-water flatness of modern prose. She sang the hymns with gusto, her clear soprano rising like a bird to the high notes Frances had to strain for, and folded her hands neatly throughout the sermon, never fidgeting. As they knelt side by side at the communion rail Frances found herself offering a prayer of gratitude to the God she still, after all these years, was unsure that she believed in, for sending this child to her.

The final prayer, the blessing, the last hymn, a moment on the knees when nobody, surely, actually prayed but which allowed time for worldly concerns to return – will the joint be dried out? Did I peel enough potatoes? – and they were hanging up hassocks, collecting handbags, gathering hymn and prayer books. The vicar was at the open door, Frances and Amy were among the first few to leave.

'Miss Mortimer, good morning. And you have brought a visitor with you, how nice.'

'Good morning, Vicar. Lovely service. This is my granddaughter, Amy.'

The words were out, sprung from her lips like birds escaping from captivity, fluttering round the church among the heads of the congregation.

'Your granddaughter, how lovely.' His words, too, came from his mouth without thought, a stock response. As he shook Amy's offered hand with both of his in priestly welcome, he heard what they had both said and his eyes flew back to Frances who met them blandly. He might have been in the parish only two years, but he knew very well that Miss Mortimer, regular communicant, frequent member of the Parochial Church Council, and staunch supporter of parish fêtes and sales, had led a blameless spinster life of devotion to her pupils and had never, to the best of anyone's knowledge, produced even a niece, let alone a child to be parent to this granddaughter. A ripple of silence flowed over the surface of the chat behind them, followed by a wave of the same chat in louder, more clearly articulated tones to show that no one, no one at all, was saying anything about the extraordinary thing they had just heard.

'What a beautiful church, Vicar,' said Amy brightly, 'and my grandmother didn't tell me you had such a good choir. And the flowers . . . my mother helps with the flower-arranging, at home. I can't wait to tell her how pretty yours are.'

'Thank you. Er,' he said, bereft of all the platitudes he might have offered in return. 'God bless,' he fell limply back on, a benediction that Frances found peculiarly aggravating in its telegraphic style. Amy scattered a smile like confetti over the people queuing to leave, and followed Frances down the brick path between leaning, lichen-splashed gravestones and beneath the ancient yew that was so old that, rather like the church it represented, it had to be propped up.

'Wow!' she said quietly. 'That's let the cat out of the bag

and put it among the pigeons, all right.' She giggled. 'Did you see his face? And that tall woman in the hat, her ears were out on stalks and if she'd moved I swear she'd have tripped over her jaw. Will they ever speak to you again, do you suppose, or will they cut you dead? I hope not.'

'Of course they won't,' said Frances robustly, hoping it was true. 'They'll be too eager to find out where on earth you came from, and the only person they can find it from is me. I'd better get in a stock of chocolate biscuits, they'll all be happening to drop in for coffee, or tea, or to bring me a recipe they promised me last year.'

'It was very brave.'

'Honesty,' said Frances sententiously, 'is the best policy. Actually, I was showing off, I think.'

'Great.'

'Roast lamb for lunch.'

'Even greater. May?'

'Yes?'

'Could I ring Michael? Just to say where I am – I don't want to go into long explanations on the phone. But if he could come down tomorrow? He was going to come home, to see Mummy, but . . . I'd really like you to meet him.'

'So would I.' Frances' voice was gruff with pleasure.

'Good. And we could get on with the books this afternoon, if you'd like.'

Frances, who would rather have gone for a walk, saw that Amy wanted to earn her keep.

'That would be a great help. It's much easier with two.'

So here I am, thought Frances on Monday morning as her tea went cold in its cup and her book lay abandoned beside it. Half the village, if not all of it, buzzing with surmise and gossip about me. Half my books packed away in boxes that I will now have to do something about. A young man, of whom my unknown daughter disapproves so strongly that she has behaved with what is obviously unprecedented violence, is coming to meet me and if he stays the night, do I put them in the same room? Or not? And if I do, am I supporting something that may be very wrong? Amy says she has never known her mother to behave so irrationally – may she not have some very good reason for disliking Michael? Am I interfering? How can I not?

Amy had had a long talk with Michael the previous evening. She had also, on Frances' insistence, tried to telephone her mother. Several times during the afternoon Frances had driven a reluctant Amy away from the piles of books, but each time the phone rang unanswered, to Amy's visible relief.

'I know I've got to talk to her, and I will. But not yet. I'm not ready. When I've seen Michael, perhaps it'll be easier. When everything is sorted out . . .'

She meant, Frances realised, when she, Frances, had told her everything she had to tell. It was the closest they came, all through the day, to mentioning it. By tacit mutual agreement they did not speak of it, though Frances told Amy more about her own parents, her childhood, and her later life as a nurse and, after the war, as a teacher. In return, Amy told her of her own childhood and adolescence, about school and holidays and friends and, endlessly, about Michael, needing to feel his name on her lips and hear it spoken. His intelligence, his humour, the fact that even at the advanced age of thirty-one he was still so enthusiastic and unstuffy . . . Frances listened and refrained from smiling, agreeing with becoming seriousness that it was amazing that with eight whole years and half the globe between them, Michael and Amy should have so much in common.

As a result, when Michael arrived in the middle of the morning, Frances felt that she already knew him quite well. Amy, who was suffering intermittent pangs of guilt, between the flashes of joy that she was going to see Michael soon, had tried to insist that she take them both out to lunch.

'Really, May, you must let me. After all, I turned up out of the blue, landed myself on you, disrupted your life and destroyed your position in the village.' ('Steady on,' murmured Frances, but was ignored.) 'Now I've invited another perfect stranger to your house. Lunch is the least I can do.'

'There's nowhere much to go, unless we drive miles,' Frances said sensibly. 'I've got plenty of food in the freezer.'

'I saw several pubs on the way here, that do food. Couldn't we go to one of them?'

Frances, who as a single woman had never acquired the habit of going into pubs, had no idea what they were like. Pubs, to her, meant an atmosphere thick with stale beer and cigarette smoke, filled with loud manly bonhomie. She hunted for an excuse.

'We could, I suppose. But . . . I'd rather not. There are bound to be people in there that know who I am, and . . . well, after my little exhibition in church yesterday, I'd rather keep a low profile.'

'Oh dear, of course. I never thought. Sorry, May.'

'Not that I'm ashamed of you, of course. I'd just be more comfortable if we were here.'

'Let me do the cooking, then. I'm not brilliant, but I can do a good spag bol if you've got some mince in the freezer.'

'Plenty, but what on earth's a spag bol?'

Amy laughed.

'Sorry! Spaghetti bolognese to you. At least, some kind of pasta with sauce. Is that all right?'

'Of course. And if there's anything you need, the village shop is open between ten and twelve thirty.'

Amy accordingly disappeared down the road at five to ten, returning with packets of herbs and spices and a huge bag of spaghetti, as well as two cakes and several packets of expensive biscuits.

'For the neighbours,' she said, with a grin.

'Amy, you ridiculous girl, I was only joking. What am I going to do with all this cake?'

'Feed it to us, and put the rest in the freezer,' said Amy succinctly, rolling up her sleeves in a purposeful fashion and tying an apron briskly. 'Where are the onions?'

When Michael arrived she flew to open the door, opening it wide and throwing herself into his arms. Tall and thin, he hugged her in one arm, smiling over her head at Frances and holding out his other hand. Frances was relieved to see that in spite of his advanced age his dark hair was neither greying nor receding. She thought at first he wore it quite short, but as he turned his head a little she saw it was tied back in a neat ponytail. Goodness, she thought. I've only seen actors and pop stars like that. Still, it's tidy, and clean – and if he looks like an actor in a historical drama, so what? I'm in no position to criticise. He was watching her, and she wondered if he could read her thoughts. His brown eyes crinkled attractively at the corners as he smiled.

'Hello. I'm Michael Macdonald.' Amy, recalling her manners, struggled from his embrace.

'Oh, May, I'm sorry, this is Michael. Michael, this is my grandmother, Miss Frances Mortimer.'

Michael, who had been told no more than that Amy was staying with a mysterious new relative who wanted to meet him, took this on the chin without a blink.

'How do you do, Miss Mortimer?'

Frances responded, shaking his hand.

'Did Amy tell you about me?'

'No, I'm afraid not. I thought Amy's grandmother was

dead, but I suppose that was the other one. Are you her father's mother, then?'

'Far from it. I'm her mother's mother. Her natural mother, I suppose I should say. Persephone was adopted at birth. I never knew her.'

His face expressed fascinated interest, but no more.

'Goodness! I had no idea. Amy never mentioned any of this, and nor did Robin, come to think of it. Perhaps he didn't know, in those days. It was a long time ago.'

'He certainly didn't know. In fact, he probably still doesn't.' Amy leaned against him, pressing her cheek into the blue-grey flecked wool of his jumper. 'I only just found out myself, on Friday night. She never even told me.'

Her voice betrayed her hurt.

'Some things are difficult to talk about,' he said gently. 'So you came and found your grandmother – Miss Mortimer – for yourself? What an adventure.'

He looked at Frances again, his eyes asking a question. Frances gave him a little nod.

'Miss Mortimer doesn't feel quite right, under the circumstances,' she said. 'Why don't you call me Frances, or May, like Amy does?'

Amy and Michael held a short silent communication with their eyes.

'Thanks.' There was, Frances noticed, a trace of Australian in his vowels, pleasantly reminiscent of overheard scraps of soap operas. 'It's good of you to invite me, May. I'd been beginning to get worried about Amy, when nobody answered the phone at her mother's house. I don't know what you've been up to, Amy, but thank goodness you've turned up again, is all I can say.'

'Oh, Michael, it's been so horrible!' Amy's voice gave a suspicious wobble. 'I was telling you last night, how I told Mummy about you, and . . .' She stopped, hearing her own voice rise and reaching for control. Michael put his arm back round her and she leaned against him for a moment before pulling herself upright again. 'There's so much to tell you,' she said, more moderately. 'I scarcely know where to begin.'

'Hold on, there, give a bloke a chance. Didn't you say something about lunch? I'm starving.'

He grinned at her and then looked across at Frances, including her in their give and take. Frances found herself smiling back. Surely, she thought, whatever Amy's mother objects to in this young man, it can't be the man himself.

'Quite right,' she said briskly. 'Amy's made us a spag bol. Why don't we go and see how it's doing?'

'Sounds good to me. And I've got a couple of bottles of Australian Shiraz in the car, too. Go nicely with spaghetti, I'd say. I'll fetch them in.'

He did so, returning from the car with not only the two bottles, but a flowering plant and a box of Belgian chocolates.

'Goodness, Michael! How generous!'

'Well, to be honest I bought them for Amy's mother, originally.'

'Buying her favour?' Frances glanced at Amy's back, but she was frowning over the concoction of an ultimate salad dressing and not listening. Michael grinned, pulling the cork from the wine with a satisfying pop.

'Too right! Well, in a way. But I do know her, sort of. Amy's brother Robin was a friend of mine, way back when. I went on holiday with them, to Cornwall, when I was about eight. Never forgotten it, either. It was a bad time for me, my parents had split up and my mother was set on taking me back to Australia with her. Persephone was – well, she was kind to me, I suppose. No, more than that. She treated me as a real person. I was pretty well off adults at the time, everyone seemed to be rearranging my life so drastically, without any reference to me. I really appreciated how she listened to me. Not everyone does that with little kids, you know.'

'I know. I spent many years teaching in a primary school. Teachers see and hear a lot more than people realise.'

He poured the wine, handing a glass to Frances and taking another to Amy.

'Come on, I reckon this deserves a toast of some kind. A new grandma, and Amy and me getting together – or should it be Amy and I, I never can remember.'

'Not if Mummy has anything to do with it,' said Amy bitterly, remembering her grudge. 'She says I can't have anything to do with you.'

'I know, you told me all about it last night. I must say I was a bit shaken, but I think we should wait and see. You're not a child, after all. In the final analysis she can't really stop us, can she? I remember your mother pretty well, you know. She's not possessive, or hysterical, or an idiot. She must have some reason for what she said, and I bet it's no more than an honest mistake.' He raised his glass. 'To us,' he said.

Frances and Amy repeated the words and drank, but Amy's eyes suddenly focused past Michael. She took a gulp of wine, and choked.

'I hope you're right,' she spluttered to Michael as he thumped her on the back.

'I always am. Right about what?'

'About Mummy. Because a car's just stopped out in the lane, and it looks awfully like hers.'

Moving very slowly, as if she were encased in heavy armour, Frances put her glass down on the table, choosing a place for it with as much care as if she were making a subtle move in chess. Then she turned round. Through the open kitchen door she could see into the hall. Framed in the window next to the front door a blue car was reversing carefully into the drive – ready for a quick getaway? her flustered mind wondered – and parked in front of Michael's. If anyone else turns up, she thought numbly, they'll have to park in the layby down the road. The driver's door opened, and her heart gave a great thud so that her sight blurred. When it cleared she was confused to see that a man, not a woman, had emerged. Then the passenger door opened hesitantly. A head, crowned with red curls that were instantly familiar. Alastair Johnson, she thought. Oh, my goodness. After all these years.

'Who's that with her?' Michael's voice was calm, but she heard his glass clatter against a plate as he put it down near hers.

'It's Robin!' Amy sounded relieved.

'Robin! Good God, so it is!' Uncomplicated pleasure rang in Michael's voice. He stepped briskly into the hall, opened the door. 'Robin! Hey, Robin, man, how are you? Where've you been hiding all this time? Come on in!'

Chapter 17

'Michael! I might have guessed you'd be here too. Where's that little sister of mine?'

'She's here.' Michael's tone was still friendly, but he stood foursquare in the doorway, shielding Frances and Amy with his tall body. 'Hello, Mrs Hamilton-Knight. Or may I call you Persephone, now that I'm grown up?'

'Of course you can. Oh, Mikey, is it really you? Yes, of course it is. I'd have known you anywhere.' Persephone, holding on to Robin's arm as if he were providing her only motivating force, like an outboard motor, reached up absently to kiss him. Her legs felt like rubber. 'Goodness, you've grown,' she said, idiotically. 'Is Amy all right?'

'Yes, she's fine.' Michael stepped back, and stood holding the door. Amy and Frances waited, side by side but about a yard apart, at the far end of the hall. In the doorway Persephone, with Robin behind her and down the steps so that they were almost the same height, stood framed. Nobody moved or spoke. Like a tableau of waxworks they froze.

Goodness, thought Frances, this is awful. This is the most awful thing that's ever happened to me. She had often thought that social embarrassment was more difficult to deal with than real tragedy, which has its own set of rules, and now she knew with hideous clarity that she had been right. Well, someone's got to do something. If only I were the kind of person who fainted. Or a heart attack would be nice. A stroke, paralysis, unable to talk. Can I fake one?

For God's sake, you're over seventy. Pull yourself together. It's no use expecting these children to extricate us from this quicksand. No use waiting for Amy to say: Mummy, this is your mother; May, this is your daughter. I'm the oldest; I'm the one who started all this, I suppose you could say it's all my fault. So I'd better do something.

She stepped forward to the doorway, offering her hand.

'Frances Mortimer,' she said, her voice sounding preposterously stilted and loud. 'How do you do?'

From force of habit Persephone took the offered hand, unaware that it was icy cold and not very steady, because her own was frozen as well. Unable to look Frances in the face, she fixed her eyes on her left ear.

'Persephone Knight. Hamilton-Knight, really, but I . . . How do you do? And this is Robin. My son.' They nodded at one another, unable to shake hands since Persephone stood as if bolted to the step between them, still clutching Robin's right forearm with her left hand.

'Hello, Robin. Won't you both come in?' Frances found that she had somehow started talking just like the vicar, in hearty and rather plummy tones. Heavens, she thought, I sound like a scene from a second-rate amateur dramatics production. Any minute now I'll break out with 'Anyone for tennis?' or burst into a bit of Gilbert and Sullivan. '*Iolanthe*,' she said, involuntarily.

'I beg your pardon?' Stepping over the threshold, Persephone came to a halt and blinked at her in bewilderment. Robin, behind her, gave a sudden crack of laughter.

'"This lady's my mother"!' he sang. A collective shudder ran through everyone. 'Well, not quite, but close. Hello, Grandmother.' He bent to kiss her cheek, as if it were the most natural thing in the world. Another shudder.

'Robin,' Persephone pleaded faintly.

'Well, she is, and we all know it. At least, I suppose Michael knows it by now, so why pretend? Trust me, Ma, I know about these things. When you come out, do it properly.'

'I did,' said Persephone, seeing herself sitting in miserable silence at a débutantes' tea party. 'And I survived that,' she murmured to herself.

'Of course you did,' said Robin, who was talking about something quite different. 'And so did I. Perhaps I should tell you,' he turned to Frances with a kind of stately nineteenth-century courtesy, 'that I am a homosexual. That used to be *my* guilty secret, but then I thought, why hide it?'

'Why indeed, Robin.' I like this young man too, thought Frances with relief. Her icy body suddenly burned hot, she felt the prickle of sweat starting on her skin, her mouth was dry. The first hurdle overcome, what do we do next? she wondered. A nice cup of hot sweet tea? No, alcohol. 'Michael brought some wine with him. Why don't we all have some? And there's lunch, too. Can the pasta be stretched a bit, Amy?' How ridiculous, to be thinking of food at a time like this. And yet, why not? It's something to do, and even if none of us can eat a mouthful it will get us sitting down, and give us something to do with our mouths other than talk. Besides, it's lunchtime. The show must go on. Are we back to *Iolanthe* again? Shut up, she told her mind. Can't you just keep quiet for a few minutes?

'Of course. Hello, Mummy.' Amy took one step forward, and stopped. Persephone dragged her eyes away from not quite looking at Frances. 'I'm sorry, Mummy. At least, I'm sorry if I worried you, but . . .'

'No, darling, it was my fault, I'm sorry I said what I did, but . . .'

'Not now,' said Michael.

'Wine,' said Robin in the same moment. In silent

complicity they swept the three women through the door to the kitchen. It was a relief to move, to have something to do. Frances produced two more glasses while Amy tipped another tin of tomatoes and one of sweetcorn into the sauce, and washed another lettuce to add to the salad. Persephone stood helplessly by the table, trying not to look at the house in case she appeared intrusive, trying not to look at Michael, trying above all to keep her eyes off Frances.

'Perhaps we ought to eat in the dining room,' suggested Frances, with extra cutlery in her hands.

'No, no.' Amy seemed anxious to stay in the kitchen. 'It's more friendly in here,' she explained. 'There's plenty of room. How much pasta should I put in, Mummy?'

'The whole packet, I should think,' answered Persephone automatically, without noticing that it was a strange question for Amy, who frequently cooked for her friends, to ask. This is ridiculous, she thought. A family lunch on Bank Holiday Monday. Good God! She took another mouthful of wine, grateful for its soothing warmth as it slid down her throat like velvet and curled up like a friendly cat in the unquiet darkness of her stomach. A real cat, a portly ginger creature, came out from under the table and twined himself round her legs with ineffable condescension. She bent to stroke him, soothed by his touch. Amy, watching her mother while appearing to fuss with the food, saw the infinitesimal signs of relaxation and smiled quietly to herself. She had long ago learned that her mother was calmed by any call for assistance, however trivial.

'Can I do anything to help?' asked Persephone, wanting to be doing something.

'Work out a seating plan?' suggested Frances drily. 'The table's a bit small for five.'

Persephone looked helplessly at the table. The thought of sitting down at it and eating seemed bizarre, unreal.

'Michael and Amy next to each other on one side – they're not going to complain about being squashed together,' said Robin briskly. 'Me opposite, Ma that end, and – what do I call you?'

'Amy calls me May,' said Frances. 'From the French – Belgian – for grandmother. Or you could call me Frances. Or whatever.'

'Not whatever. May sounds fine to me, short and sweet. How does that seem, for seating? And where can I get another chair?'

Belgium, thought Persephone. I was born in Belgium. Of course, she knows that. She was there at the time. Why did I come here? This is grotesque. I refuse to sit and eat a meal in this house, with this woman, as if everything were perfectly normal.

'Robin, I . . .'

'That's right, Ma, you sit here.' His hand was on her shoulder, his arm round her exerting a pressure that she could not find the strength to fight. Weakly she sat and he filled her glass again.

Under Robin's direction they found themselves sitting round the table with plates of pasta steaming in front of them. Persephone decided that eating was easier than looking across the table at her mother, and plunged her fork with determination, concentrating on spinning the strands into a controllable ball, like dealing with unravelled knitting wool.

'When I was a child,' remarked Frances conversationally, 'I spent hours sitting holding skeins of wool over my hands so that my mother could wind them into balls. Really, one needs to do the same with pasta.'

Now she's reading my mind, thought Persephone. How dare she! She tried to cast a venomous look across the table, but was unable to lift its weight further than the top button of Frances' blouse. No one else said anything.

'Delicious,' said Robin into the brittle silence. 'Your cooking's improved no end, Amy. Have you been taking lessons?'

'No, just natural genius.' Amy gulped her wine. Her throat was so tight that the food seemed to stick in it. Her pleasure in being with Michael had evaporated into worry about her mother. She had seemed pleased to see Michael, hadn't she? Kissed him? Was she going mad, then? Had the other evening been a kind of nervous breakdown? Was suicide hereditary? But no, Granny wasn't her mother anyway, was she? Amy chewed and chewed on pasta that seemed to stay in her mouth like gum, unswallowable.

By mutual consent Robin and Michael constructed a conversation in the midst of this female silence rather as they had once built Lego models together, piece by piece. Robin's work, Michael's writing, filling in the gaps of their adult lives, saw them through some while. Inevitably, though Robin tried to steer away from it, their talk drifted into the past.

'I can't believe it's so many years since that time we were in Cornwall,' said Michael idly. 'It was a good holiday, wasn't it? One of the best I ever had, I've always thought, and so did Hugo. D'you remember my brother Hugo, Robin? He stayed with us for a while. We made that huge wall of sand on the beach, remember, and tried to hold back the tide. And those model sailing boats we used to race, with winkles as cargo. I kept mine for years, in fact it's probably still gathering dust in the loft of my mother's place in Australia. Twenty-three years, or is it twenty-four? Why, Amy wasn't born, or even thought of, the last time we met.'

He successfully negotiated a forkful of spaghetti into his mouth, looking up to find Robin's and Persephone's eyes fixed on him like rabbits confronting a weasel. The air between them was so charged that he thought it would crackle with blue sparks if he stretched his hand into it. Then, as if recalled to life, they simultaneously dropped their eyes to their plates, being careful not to look at one another. Michael glanced at Amy beside him. Untouched, unmoved, she picked at her salad. The gold chain bracelet round the fine-boned wrist of her right hand gleamed in a ray of fitful sunshine. He thought of the star sapphire he had already mentally chosen for an engagement ring, how its chatoyant light would show elusively on her finger. As if feeling his look she turned her face to him and smiled, her dark eyebrows that made so fascinating a contrast with the burnished glow of her hair lifting a little in the way that he loved before she looked back at her plate. Her eyes were their usual clear, untrammelled gold, warm as run honey as they rested on him. An unusual colour, lacking the greenish tinge of hazel, looking as if they had been especially created to blend with her hair. He had only ever known one other person with eyes that colour, but Hugo's hair, of course, was as dark as his eyebrows . . .

His gaze travelled from her clear profile to Persephone's shuttered face, and back. Suddenly enlightened, he remembered that at their very first meeting Amy had seemed in some way familiar. He had put it down to his old friendship with Robin and later, romantically, to the recognition of kindred souls finding one another. Though he had taken it with outward calm, he had been dismayed to hear of Persephone's reaction when Amy told her about him. Dismayed, and hurt, because she had remained in his mind as a kind of fixed point, an understanding adult. Surprised, too, because in all modesty he knew that he was the kind of man – successful, intelligent, neither too old nor too young – that mothers of girls like Amy would usually welcome as sons-in-law. During the night he had puzzled over it. Since Amy had assured him that her mother was not, had never been, possessive, he had been unable to come up with any answer.

Now he saw, quite suddenly, the resemblance that it had never occurred to him to look for. It was there, not just in the eyebrows and the eyes, but in the bone structure as well. He thought back, mentally counting up years and months. Yes, it all fitted. And Hugo – Hugo had so often, over the years, asked for news of Persephone, and been so surprisingly disappointed each time that Michael had admitted, with regret, that he had no contact with her or the family.

He thought that enlightened was the precise word to describe how he felt: it was as if his whole body had been lit from within, every particle of his physical substance shining like phosphorescence, an unearthly self-generated light that did away with all doubts and shadows. Saint Paul, he thought, on the road to Damascus, must have felt like this. But I am not blinded: I see, I see it all. So simple, and so easy. Thank God they gave me time, didn't blurt it out too quickly.

'Hugo,' he said, using the name with the precision of a surgeon making the first cut, 'is living in Australia now, Persephone. Settled there, about ten years ago. Funny, really – he's out there, and I've moved back to England.' Persephone's face was bone-white, and Robin was trying to catch his eye across the table, but Michael turned to Frances as if politely including her in the conversation. 'Hugo's my brother. At least,' he explained conscientiously, 'I've always called him that, and thought of him as a brother, though he isn't really.' From the corner of his eye he saw Persephone lay down her knife and fork and lift her napkin to her lips with hands that trembled. Robin sat with his fork halfway to his mouth, unmoving. 'My father married his mother when he was a baby. She was a widow, and his father had been in the same regiment as mine. He was killed in some kind of accident during a training exercise – I never knew what happened, but I've sometimes wondered whether my father felt himself to be in some way to blame. Anyway, he married her a few months later, and insisted on Hugo taking his own surname.'

Frances, drowning in her own maelstrom of emotions and future explanations, scarcely heard him.

'That was good of him,' she said, wanting to keep some semblance of conversation going.

'It was typical of him, really. Duty, the Regiment, all that kind of thing. He did his best to be a good father to Hugo, though he never really cared for him, I don't think. Resented him, probably. I don't think he really wanted to marry at that point, but because she had been left with a baby to bring up, and no other family to help, he felt some kind of obligation. He did his best for Hugo, of course. Even when the marriage broke up he still kept up his responsibilities, saw Hugo through school, had him to stay from time to time, tried to get him to follow in his footsteps and join the army. My mother said she always dreaded Hugo's visits, not because she didn't like him but because Dad behaved so oddly when he was there.'

'Poor Hugo.' Persephone had lowered her napkin. Her lips trembled and behind her glasses her eyes were blurred with tears. 'I never knew,' she said simply. 'You called him your brother, and I thought . . . We didn't talk about his family much. Or the past. Or even the . . . the future.' She took off her glasses and wiped her eyes. Amy watched her, surprised, hardly taking in this talk of things that had happened before she was born. Robin put down his fork at last and breathed in a sigh so deep it seemed it would never end, before lifting his glass of wine. He caught Michael's eye and nodded, raising the glass in silent tribute.

'Believe it or not, nor did I until I was older,' said

Michael. 'My father always referred to Hugo as "your brother" to me, and it wasn't until years later that my mother happened to mention the truth. I was going through a heavy teenage rebellion phase, and she was trying to explain to me why she had found my father impossible to live with. She said that, in the final analysis, he was unable to see beyond his own conception of duty. It mattered more to him than anything, more than wife or family or love. It made him inhuman and, in her opinion, the most self-absorbed man she had ever met.'

'Like Daddy,' said Amy without rancour. 'Self-absorbed, I mean,' she added, looking up into another pool of silence and finding her mother regarding her with a peculiar mixture of guilt and worry. 'Sorry, Mummy, but you know he is,' she insisted. 'I'm fond of him, and all that, but you can't really get close to him, can you? As a father, he's more or less a dead loss,' she concluded cheerfully.

Persephone looked at Robin, and then at Michael. They glanced at one another, then looked back at her.

'I should tell her,' said Robin.

'You might as well,' said Michael. 'You don't really have to, but I think it would be better to have everything out in the open, don't you?'

'What everything? Tell who what?' Amy looked alarmed. 'Is this something to do with May?'

'Nothing at all,' said Frances, who had just woken up to the fact that something momentous was taking place. 'So much so, that I think I'd better go out of the room and leave you to it.' It would be a relief to go: in fact, the only difficulty would be in stopping herself from leaving the house altogether and disappearing, preferably without trace, into the countryside. For Frances, accustomed to her peaceful solitude, having four strangers sitting round her lunch table without much warning was already novel enough to be stressful. She was grateful for that: it helped to insulate her from what was happening. She felt as vulnerable as a crab that has shed its shell but not yet grown a new one. For the first time the barrier she had built to shield her inner self, not merely from the world but from her own external mind, was being breached. In both directions, which made it more difficult. Not only must she suffer the intrusion of others into her painfully secreted past: she must also open it to their view, offer it to them, re-examine and display the memories she had worked so hard to deny.

The only thing that helped her was knowing that later, even if it must be a great deal later, she would be glad of it. She had carried the burden of her secret for so long that she no longer felt it as such, its weight was so accustomed that she never noticed how it stifled her. The process of discovery must inevitably be painful, but in the end it was a healing pain, the lancing and cauterising of an infection so old that it had callused over so that it appeared to be healed, while still festering far below. She drew in breath, content to husband her strength for now, willing to stay or go as her daughter wished.

They looked at Persephone. This is it, she thought. The thing I have been dreading more, so much more, than finding out about her, my mother. Thank God it's here at last, and thank God, even more, that nothing is as bad as I thought. If I had only known before about Hugo, none of this need ever have come out. No one need ever have known. But . . . no. That's not how I want it. I want an end to the secrets, even if none of my children can ever think of me in quite the same way again. At least it will be *me* they are thinking of, the real me, not just a whitewashed false front. Goodness, is this how Mummy felt? Is that why she kept those documents, knowing that one day I would find them, when she could have burned them years ago and no one would ever have been any the wiser?

For the first time since Lady Singleton's death she felt a extraordinary warmth and closeness for the woman she ha always thought of as her mother. Now, quite suddenly, sh had something in common with her, something she coul relate to. The feeling of relief was so great that even th task of telling Amy seemed, if not easier, at least les appalling. And this other woman, her natural mother, wa she too feeling this relief? Persephone rather thought tha she might be. She looked at Frances for the first time, an in that shared moment each acknowledged something i the other that she recognised in herself.

'Only if that's what you want,' she said, surprised a herself. 'But I rather think this is tell-the-truth-and-shame the-devil day, don't you?' Amy saw the look, and relaxe slightly. Whatever the revelation might be it was not obviously, as bad as her mother had feared.

'Of course you mustn't go, May,' said Amy. 'After all remember church yesterday? May introduced me to th vicar as her granddaughter,' she explained generally. 'I was wonderful, there they all were with their ears flapping trying to pretend they hadn't heard. So go on, let's get it ou in the open. I suppose it's something to do with me an Michael? Why you were so upset about him?'

'In a way. More to do with you than with Michael really.' Persephone sat up straight and looked her daughte in the face just as, if she had known it, Frances had looke at the vicar yesterday. 'I'm afraid, darling, that Daddy isn' your father. Hugo is.'

'Hugo? You mean, Michael's brother?'

'Yes. Only not, as it turns out, his brother.'

Amy thought about it. She found it hard to look at it sub jectively. Even the loss of a father seemed insignificant, fo had she ever had him? If so, she had effectively lost him since the divorce for she had noticed she frequently forgo his existence, and had to remind herself to send him

Christmas and birthday cards. His role was irrelevant: it was her mother that mattered. Her mother, watching her with such loving anxiety, who must be soothed because, for her, this was only half of the story. For Amy the worst was over: she knew that nothing could keep her and Michael apart any more, and because of that all the rest was bearable. She swallowed the tight feeling in her throat and closed her eyelids for a moment to force the tears back from her eyes, in the same way that she pushed from her the regret for an aspect of her childhood that she had lost, locked away until she could examine and deal with it. She felt slightly dizzy.

'So you thought – you thought I was going to be marrying my uncle! Oh, poor Mummy!' She gave a helpless gasp of laughter that managed, somehow, not to be a sob.

'I'm glad you find it funny.' Persephone's back was ramrod-stiff. She could feel all her muscles tensing up: inside her shoes her toes were tightly clenched.

'Oh, Mummy!' Amy jumped up and ran to her mother, bending to hold her as if she were the adult and Persephone the hurting child. 'I'm sorry, I'm not laughing, not really, it's just I don't know what to say. I don't even know how I feel.' That was true enough, and now more than ever before it seemed important to say nothing that was not true. 'It's a shock, of course it is. But nothing like as bad as it might have been, or as bad as the things that you've been having to cope with. It must have been awful for you, knowing you had to tell me that.'

'It was, a bit.' Persephone rubbed her cheek against Amy's shoulder. 'I'm so sorry, darling. I never thought anyone would need to know, least of all you.'

'Daddy? Oh dear, I suppose I shouldn't really call him that. It seems so awful that I don't mind more. Poor Daddy. There I go again, calling him Daddy.'

'I don't see why not. No, he never guessed. I should have

felt guilty about it, but I'm afraid I didn't. I honestly didn't feel it made any difference to him. At least, though, he didn't have to pay for your school fees, or anything.'

'Well, he didn't for any of us, did he? Granny coughed up,' Robin put in.

'For you and Sarah she did – and incidentally, you weren't supposed to know about that – but I wouldn't let her for Amy. I used my own money, that my father left me.'

Amy rested her cheek on the top of her mother's head. Her red hair mingled with Persephone's curls, making them look pale and faded.

'I'm glad you told me.'

'So am I, now. Thank you, darling.'

Amy kissed her mother and went back to her chair.

'It's rather romantic, isn't it?' She looked speculatively at Michael. 'Is Hugo . . . is my father married?'

He laughed.

'Yes, and happily too! No retrospective matchmaking between your parents, my girl! He married an Australian, which is why he lives out there now, and he has three young sons.'

'Little brothers, what fun! Only . . . will he want to know about me? Or shall I just be your girlfriend?'

'Not so much of the "just", if you don't mind.' Michael reached out to hug her briefly. 'I think he'd like to know. And I know he'd like to know you. Janey – that's his wife – well, she's not the possessive type. He had a lot of girlfriends before he married her, and he stayed friends with quite a few. She's not going to see you as a threat.'

Persephone looked down at her plate. Impossible to imagine Hugo over forty, a married man with sons. She was glad and relieved to know that he lived in Australia, safely on the other side of the world. Her Hugo could remain enshrined in the little corner of her heart that was his, young and carefree and laughing. And Amy . . . Her heart illed with gratitude and wonder that neither her daughter nor Robin had shown any feeling of revulsion or disgust at what they could, not unfairly, have seen as a sordid episode n their mother's past. It was a lesson for her, she thought oberly. As they had dealt, so must she with her own nother. She hoped that she could find within her the same olerance, the same willingness to accept without blame or ecrimination.

Frances, the outsider, watched them all. They had orgotten her, forgotten for the moment who she was and what she represented. The other skeleton in the cupboard. She wished, now, that she could stay in that cupboard, noulder quietly away in the darkness, hidden and inviolate. Let it end here, she thought passionately. Let this be he happy ending, the new beginning.

Even as she thought it, their eyes turned back to her. She ried to gather the tattered rags of a hostess round her, as protection.

'Pudding?' she enquired brightly. 'Or rather, as there sn't any, coffee and cake? Or tea?'

Persephone stood up. She felt light and full of energy, as f newly made. In her present euphoria she felt she could bear any revelation.

'I know how you feel,' she said, 'but it can't be put off, can it? I'll put the kettle on, and make coffee or tea, if you ike.'

'I'll get the cakes,' said Amy. 'What a good thing I bought them. It must have been a psychic flash.'

Michael stood up and began collecting the plates.

'Is it our turn to offer to go away? Perhaps we should eave the two of you alone for a bit.'

'Oh no! I don't want to miss it! That is . . .' Amy looked apologetic, 'if you don't mind?'

'This isn't some kind of soap opera, sis,' said Robin repressively.

'Come off it! You know you're as eaten up with curiosit as I am! You don't want us to go away, do you, May?'

Frances looked at Persephone. Once again their eye met, with less strain this time.

'No, I don't. It won't be any easier for either of us to b alone together. In fact, it might even be impossible. It ha to be told: better to tell you all, now, while we're together And then . . . well, we won't look any further than that, fo now.'

Chapter 18

Frances sat like a statue while they moved around her. Amy and Persephone made tea and coffee, put out the cakes, working together without fuss and with an economy of speech and movement that showed how attuned they were. Robin and Michael cleared the table, rinsing and stacking the plates. It was a strange experience for Frances to sit while others did the chores she was accustomed to do for herself.

She tried to collect her thoughts, but found she could not get beyond the events of that day. She had tried to remain uninvolved in Persephone's story. It was not for her to judge, after all, and certainly not for her to condemn. She would not permit herself to feel any dismay that her unknown daughter had been unfaithful to her husband, had foisted another man's child upon him. From the little that she had heard, his own behaviour had been very far from perfect. Persephone's children, at least, had shown no sign of resentment on their father's behalf.

Now it was her turn. The precious moments were ticking by; already the pots of tea and coffee were steaming on the cleared and wiped table, cups and saucers, clean plates for the cake, milk in a jug were all set out ready. The time she should have spent searching for the right words had gone, and she must find something, anything, to say to them.

She raised her eyes and looked round the ring of their faces. None of them was looking at her: they had all found some means of occupying their eyes by pouring or cutting or passing. But she knew that their attention was focused on her and that they were aware of every breath she drew. She accepted a cup of tea from Amy and set it in front of her. She would not allow herself to procrastinate by waiting until it was drunk. She squared the cup on the saucer, put her hands in her lap, glanced up at their politely averted faces and addressed an area of space just over the middle of the table.

'I don't know where to begin. For so many years it's been something I pushed out of my mind, a hidden area of my memories. I still can't believe this is really happening.' She turned her face towards Persephone. 'How did you know? I mean, is it something you've always known, that you were adopted?'

Persephone shook her head very slightly, her eyes fixed on the untasted slice of cake. It still seemed hard to Frances to connect this mature woman with the scarcely glimpsed baby of so long ago. And yet the baby was there, too. As Frances was aware of the many aspects of herself, going back to her earliest memories as a toddler, contained within her, so that infant existed still beneath the adult exterior. It was to the baby that she spoke.

'I didn't want to part with you, you know, but I couldn't keep you. It just wasn't possible, you see. I'm sorry.'

Persephone looked up at her. Her eyes were open, unshadowed.

'I know. Things were different then. I do understand that, and I'm not blaming you. Not for anything.' She leaned forward. 'But I need to know what happened. Because I didn't know, you see. Not that I was adopted, or anything. She never told me. My life was a pretence, a lie, but I never understood that. I felt that something was different, not right, but I thought it was me that was wrong. I felt I had failed her. Then, after she died, I found out. All those years of keeping it a secret, but she left it for me to find. I wondered, before, whether she had simply forgotten, whether the lie had after so long become reality to her. Now, I'm not so sure. She was always so careful, so precise. All her papers, her will, her financial affairs, were left meticulously in order for us. I can't believe that when she was organising them, she wouldn't have given thought to that other document. So I have to assume that she meant me to find it. I found that thought unbearable, before. It seemed so cruel, so unnecessary. Now, I'm not so sure . . .' She said no more, unable to express the sense of relief she had felt that she no longer had to hide anything.

'The document?' Frances was confused by the formality of the word.

'The paper you signed. That's how I found out. Don't you remember? Saying that you gave up all right to me, that you'd never try to see me, or even mention me, never try to find out her name or mine. All of that. And your signature at the bottom, quite clear. That's how I found out your name.'

'Of course I remember. I remember every word, I could probably repeat every line of it, even now. That was the only time I met her, face to face, apart from . . . the day you were born. They made me hold you, hand you to her. The nuns. I begged and begged. Either not to see you at all, or at least to have the chance to hold you for a little while, on my own. On our own. But they wouldn't.'

'How cruel.' Persephone's voice was scarcely louder than the soft purr of the Aga. The others were so silent they scarcely breathed: Amy pressed up close to Michael, their hands touching but not clasped, her eyes fixed on her mother; Robin looking down into his cup as if seeing the past portrayed in it. 'Why were they so cruel?'

'They didn't mean to be. They were nuns, what did they know? It was her, you see. She paid for me to be there. Girls like me – fallen women, they would have thought – didn't go to them usually. It was a very expensive kind of nursing home, in Bruges.'

'Why Bruges? I mean, I know she was living in Belgium then, because of my father – I'm sorry, I don't know what else to call them – but why were you there? Were you living in Belgium too?'

'Not at first.' Frances clasped her hands together in front of her, examining her interlaced fingers as if she had never seen them before. 'When I first realised I was pregnant – and it was my mother who guessed it first, because I was so stupid, so innocent that I had no idea what was happening to me – my father was . . . destroyed. Not so much angry, though he was, very angry, but damaged. As if I had stuck a knife in him, or chopped off one of his legs with an axe. He felt it was an attack on him personally, you see. That I had struck at him, his beliefs, everything he stood for, and done it with intent. He simply couldn't see it any other way. And he couldn't bear to see me, even to have me in the house. I was sent away, the same night, to stay with an old servant of my grandmother, my mother's mother, on the other side of Sussex, near Arundel. My mother took me, made all the arrangements.'

'My mother came from Sussex.'

'Yes, that's how it happened. I didn't know it then, of course. My mother never spoke of it at the time. It wasn't until her last illness, in the final few weeks of her life, that she mentioned it. She talked about it, but as if I wasn't there. As if she were speaking to some invisible third person – it's hard to explain. I think my father had probably forbidden her to tell me anything, but she couldn't bear that I should know nothing. Such a small, whispering voice, flowing on and on about anything and everything, and now and then going back to those days. Never looking at me, never addressing me by name. In fact, I realised afterwards that she only ever mentioned the important things when I wasn't too near her, too obviously present. Poor Mother, she was so loyal, such a good wife. It must have been hard for her to go against him, but I'm so grateful that she did.

'She – your adoptive mother – had been told, I suppose, that she was unable to conceive, would never have any children. I don't know why, she probably didn't know herself. Doctors didn't tell you much, in those days. She was desperate, obsessed. She had some connection with the village where I was sent; I believe she had been brought up by some old ladies in the big house there. Anyway, she heard about me.'

Frances smiled wryly.

'Of course, in those days adoption was a relatively simple matter, not like it is today. Before the pill, before the days of family planning clinics and everything it was only too easy for an unmarried girl to get "into trouble". There were plenty of babies given up for adoption – single mothers were unheard of. So she would have had no difficulty in finding a suitable baby. *But* – and it was a big but – she wanted more than that. She didn't want to admit to adopting. She wanted to pretend that the baby was hers. Not, presumably, to her husband, but to everyone else. It sounds bizarre, but she was so determined. The most determined woman, my mother said, that she had ever met.'

Frances' mouth was dry. She lifted the cup of tea to her lips, surprised to find that it was, if not hot, at least still fairly warm. She drank thirstily, and Amy reached wordlessly for the cup to refill it.

'Yes,' said Persephone. 'Determined. If anyone could have made such a hare-brained scheme work, it was her. And she did, by heaven. She fooled everyone.' She sighed.

'She couldn't bear to fail, you see. Not at anything. She was careful, of course, not to attempt the impossible, but when at times she didn't manage something she had set out to achieve, it, well, it frightened her.' She ran her fingers through her hair, the red curls springing back wildly as if with a life of their own. 'To find that she couldn't perform this simple function, couldn't do what women all around her were achieving all the time, couldn't fulfil what she still saw as a woman's most important role – it would have been unbearable for her. Shame, humiliation, a complete loss of self-esteem. She wouldn't have been able to accept it. She would have done anything – and she did.'

Frances nodded.

'She certainly did. She sent someone to look at me, to see whether I was the right kind of person, find out about my background. My class, I suppose.'

'Pedigree.' Persephone's voice was bitter. 'Like buying a dog.'

'A bit. I can't say I blamed her. Such things mattered more, in those days. Anyway, I was deemed suitable. She went to see my parents, told them she would adopt the child if it proved healthy, that she would give it a life of comfort and luxury, that no one would ever know I had borne it. The comfort and luxury my father might have thought inappropriate, but that no one should know – that was what persuaded him. She said I would be taken to Belgium, settled in a suitably discreet home where I could pass the rest of the pregnancy, that the birth would take place abroad and I could then return. They could say that I had been studying abroad – she even offered to arrange for teachers for me – or that I had been to a sanatorium for my health. It was all taken off their shoulders, she would pay for everything, see to everything. So, of course, they agreed. And I went to Bruges.'

Her mouth was dry again. She saw to her surprise that

there was another cup of tea in front of her, and she took a sip. It was cool, had even formed a slight skin on the surface, but it was reassuring. She put the cup down carefully.

'I was happy in Bruges. Happier, almost, than I had ever been before. That must sound strange to you, but I had never been abroad, never even been to anywhere but London once or twice. I had lessons in French, and I picked up some Flemish from the family I boarded with. And they were kind, oh, so very kind to me. I saw a kind of family life, there, that I had never even dreamed existed. Their children were younger than me, but we played together, they treated me as an older sister. I suppose that was why, in the end, I went into teaching. That, and the evacuees during the war. It was like a holiday, and I was young enough to enjoy it day by day, not to look at the future too often. I was well, and although I knew that I had behaved wrongly I didn't feel wicked. Surprising, really, with the upbringing I had had.'

'I know. I know what you mean,' said Persephone. 'I felt the same about Amy. But at least I knew I was going to be able to keep her.'

'And I knew I wouldn't. But it didn't mean anything to me then, you see. I couldn't imagine how it would be. Although I felt the baby moving inside me, I couldn't believe in it – you – as an actual living creature, a separate person. I'd never even played with dolls very much, as a child. I never thought about the birth itself. The thing I most dreaded was having to go home again. I was only seventeen. I had no idea how I would feel.

'She used to come and see me. Your mother. I wasn't supposed to know. She didn't come to the house, but watched me when I went out. Most afternoons I had a walk, after my rest. I'd see her in the distance, be aware of her eyes on me. I would smell her perfume, often, and know that she was watching me go by. She was always beautifully dressed: couture clothes, though I didn't know that then, wonderful hats, furs, shoes . . . I thought she was beautiful. The funny thing was, she looked as if she was expecting a baby too. She got bigger, as I did. That was why I first noticed her. Because she looked like I did, only with those wonderful clothes, and I used to envy her. I wondered why she watched me so much, but never spoke to me, never came too near. She was older than me, of course, but I thought one day she would speak, that we might even become friends.

'Then, a week or so before I was due to have the baby, she came to see me. At the house. Everyone went out, I was alone, and she came to the door. She hardly spoke to me, didn't look at me though she had stared so much in the past. She handed me a piece of paper, told me I was to sign it. I didn't understand, at first, what it was all about. Because I didn't know she was the one, you see . . . I still thought she was having a baby too, and I couldn't understand why she wanted me to sign. All she would say was "Sign it. Sign the paper." So I did. What else could I do? I knew the baby was going to be adopted, and that I would never see it again. In those days, adoptions were final, not like today. It didn't seem to me to make much difference whether I signed or not.

'When I went into labour, they took me to the nursing home, and she was there. Not all the time. It was a very long birth. They didn't give you anything much for pain, in those days. I remember one of the nuns bending over me, when I cried out, and hissing "You didn't expect it to come out as easily as it went in, did you?" I hardly knew what she meant. I'd seen lambs born, and puppies, but I had no idea, really . . . She sat in the corner of the room. Your mother. She didn't speak to me, but I was glad she was there because at least she was English, and a bit familiar.

I suppose I was rather confused, I still didn't really understand.

'Then she was born. You, I mean. And I heard you cry, such a little, forlorn wailing, saw you held up in the nun's hands. And then, suddenly, it was as if some kind of barrier that had been coming between me and reality disintegrated, and I understood. This was a baby, a human being, my baby that had grown inside me, that I had felt, that I knew. When you cried again, I felt my breasts hurt. I wanted, more than anything, to hold you in my arms. But to hold you and keep you, not to have you taken away. So I shut my eyes, because I couldn't bear to see you, and turned my head away. They must have wrapped you up, because when the sister came and called me, shook my arm, I opened my eyes and she was holding you right beside me, offering you to me. They had wiped you clean, wrapped you in a white shawl, and even then you had little spikes of red hair, already drying. Your eyes were open, you looked at me as if you could see into the depths of my soul, and I was so ashamed. I begged the sister to take you away, but she wouldn't. She said I must hand you to the English lady.

'I'd forgotten she was there. I turned my head, and she was standing at the other side of the bed. I asked her, pleaded with her to take the baby now, if she must, but she said no, I must give her myself, so that we should both know that it was freely done. Freely! There was no freedom in that room for any of us. In the end it was like signing the paper. I took you in my hands. I wanted to kiss you, just once, but already her own hands were out to take you. "Give her to me," she said, "she's mine." So, I did.'

Frances' eyes were dry as she lifted them to stare blindly out of the window. The pain was there still, the pain she had for so many years encapsulated. Like a little phial of cyanide hidden about her, never quite forgotten, hovering, waiting for the moment when she would pierce the protective covering and release the twisting agony. How could she ever have thought she had buried the memory? Each passing year had added another microscopic layer, like the formation of a pearl but without its beauty, to that covering until she had come to think herself safe from it. She had thought that it was something she had learned to live with: instead she found it was something she had refused to acknowledge.

Dishonest even with her own self, she had never allowed her mind to examine why, even now, the sight of a new baby made her step back, rather than forward. Why, when teaching, she had always refused to touch the baby brothers and sisters brought for the schoolchildren to admire, had withdrawn with finality from any offer to hold them. Her many friends, she saw now, were friends on the surface only because they did not know, had never been told of this fundamental turning point in her life. Her withdrawal into the world of books, too, was all part of her attempt to escape from that single unbearable moment. All her life since then had been a denial and now, at last, came the moment to see that and with it, to affirm.

Persephone gave a wrenching sob. For her the pleasant, old-fashioned kitchen had disappeared, and she was seeing her own birth in terms of her memories of giving birth to Amy. She remembered the pure, uncomplicated joy she had felt when she first looked into the baby's face, remembered feeling that this child was hers alone, that no other person could come between them for a few years, at least. In her imagination someone was tearing her baby from her. At that moment she would have forgiven Frances anything at all, for the sake of what she must have suffered then.

She looked across the table. Looked at this elderly woman with the prim hair and the stiff, old-fashioned appearance, who was her mother. In that moment she saw in the unlikely figure an aspect of motherhood that tied them, and her other mother, in a common bond. She stood up and walked round the table. Frances did not move. Persephone laid her hand on the bony shoulder. It was scarcely a caress – it was too soon for that – but it was a sharing. Frances lifted her own hand and laid it on Persephone's.

'She didn't know,' Persephone whispered, apologising for the mother who had raised her. 'She only felt her own needs. She never did understand about other people. And so she always got what she wanted.'

A shiver ran through Frances' body.

'Not always.' She spoke with subdued triumph. 'There was one thing I kept. No one ever had it from me, and nor did she. I never told her who your father was. No one knew. Some of them thought they knew, but they were wrong. I was the only one. So I kept it, and now I can give it to you. The only gift I have ever given you, the only one I can give.'

Chapter 19

Iis name was Johnson. Alastair Johnson. He was a rmer, he owned a big farm, the most important in that rea, with a beautiful old farmhouse that had been in the mily for a long time. He had red hair, like yours. righter, perhaps, but curly.'

Persephone put her hand up to her hair.

'Mine used to be brighter. I am older, I suppose, than he as. Much older.'

'Not much. Ten years, perhaps, no more.'

'He was older than you?'

Persephone spoke stupidly, rapidly revising her mental nage. A young man, tanned and muscular, the smiling land face of a picture book she had had as a child (Here is ne Farmer. He grows food for us to eat. The farmer has ome cows) crowned with her own youthful red curls. He aded away with a regretful expression into his brightly oloured landscape, and was replaced by an older version. his one, so dimly coloured as to be almost monochrome, lso seemed to have a patched shirt, and was distinctly uddy to boot. Unshaven, even, with reddish whiskers. Vas this change, she wondered, the result of a generally arnished image of modern farmers? She wanted to giggle, nd understood Amy's laughter of a few minutes earlier. Ier mind could only cope with the reality of this situation y skirting around the edges and mocking it.

'Yes, much older. I was sixteen then, and both h children were older than I was. Well, his daughter w twenty, quite grown-up in my eyes, and his son, Rober was two years older than me.' She paused, looking ba as if down a long tunnel. 'We were friends, in a wa Robert and I, I mean. He'd always been kind to me eve as quite a young boy. We went to the same dancin classes and parties, and he used to let me ride h ponies.' She smiled reminiscently, and sighed. 'He was very good-looking boy – beautiful, even. I used to thin he was like a film star. I thought he was wonderful. Th red hair his father and sister both had was darker in hin a kind of deep auburn. The sort of colour, nowaday that you'd think was dyed. His eyes were grey, quite dark grey, not blue.'

'Like Mummy's,' said Amy wonderingly. Her moth looked at her as blankly as if she had never seen her ow face in a mirror.

'Yes. You have something of him, too, in the shape your nose, and your mouth. When you arrived her standing on the doorstep, you looked familiar. I couldn think what it was, at first. It was only later that it came me, that you look a bit like Robert.'

'But he wasn't . . . it wasn't him . . . ?' Persephone wa puzzled by this long description.

'No. He wasn't. Oh, he could have been, if it ha been up to me. I was foolish – and innocent – enoug But it didn't happen. He didn't like girls, you see. Not i that way.'

'He was gay?' Robin's voice was very quiet, tranqu even.

'Yes. At least, I didn't understand it at the time, but . . yes. He was gay. And it was – oh, how can I tell you? – disaster. A tragedy, in its way.' She looked at Robin. 'Yo kept it hidden, didn't you? Made a secret of it?'

Persephone stirred, as if moving to protect him from this intrusion. His reply came easily, however, and she sank back in her chair.

'Yes. At first, I needed time to come to terms with it. It was something I had been dimly aware of for some time, since early adolescence, but I kept thinking . . . hoping, I suppose . . . that it was a phase. A stage. Something I'd grow out of, like having spots. But I didn't.'

'Were you . . . ashamed?'

He frowned, but not, Frances was relieved to see, with anger.

'Not ashamed, exactly. Embarrassed, I suppose. Afraid I'd be laughed at, teased, taunted.' Oh, Charlie, he thought. Poor old Charlie. 'And I minded for my parents' sake. My mother. And my father, though thank goodness he wasn't one of the patriarchal kind, my son must follow in my footsteps, join the family firm, be a clone of me. But Ma, certainly. She took it very well, of course, when I did tell her.' He smiled wryly at Persephone. 'I knew you would. But you minded, didn't you?'

'Yes. But I wasn't ashamed of you. Not ever.'

He reached out and touched her cheek with the back of his fingers, a gesture he'd had since childhood. Persephone felt her throat draw tight.

'I know. Just the usual worries. Aids, prejudice, unhappiness. And . . . no grandchildren.'

'Yes! But not for me! I've got Charlie and William, and no doubt Amy's children too. But . . . oh Robin, you'd have been such a wonderful father! It's such a pity!'

Her heart was in the cry, all the pain she had suffered on his behalf, the sorrow of lost chances, vanished opportunities; the sorrow of a woman and a housewife for waste of any kind.

'I know. If wishing could change things, I'd change. But I

can't. And nor, presumably, could . . . Robert, wasn't it My uncle?'

'Robert, yes. And no, he couldn't. Even though h would have given anything in the world, I believe, to hav been able to. He died in the war, very early on. They gav him a medal, but I always wondered . . . that kind o bravery is a kind of death wish . . .'

There was a silence. Frances sat immobile, inward looking. Robin, too, was lost in his own memories. Amy' thoughts, and perhaps Michael's also, were turning inevit ably towards the discovery of her own beginnings. Onl Persephone, in the end, stirred restlessly. Frances looke at her, and came visibly back to the present.

'I'm sorry. You want to know what happened. But it wa relevant, about Robert. That was part of it, the reason fo it, if you like. We were together, you see. In the woods There was a clearing by a large pond, very pretty, I ofte went there on my walks. Robert liked it too – in fact, suppose that was why I went there so often, in case I migh meet him there. I had what we would have called then crush on him, which wasn't very surprising – he wa practically the only boy I knew, apart from the boys fro the village school . . . And that day – it was June, a beautifu June day, one of those perfect early summer days – he wa there. He'd been drinking, though I didn't realise at the time, I just thought he was more lively than usual. No drunk, though. Just enough to lose some of his inhibitions open up a bit. Just the person, he said. My only friend Come and sit down, come and keep me company, have some of this.

'I was so flattered. He'd always been kind to me, but more as an older child is kind to a younger one – never as equals. I'd have drunk anything he'd offered me, at that moment, without a second thought, though my father had never let me touch alcohol in my life. It wasn't spirits, though. Perhaps, if it had been, things would have been different: I'd either have hated it so much I wouldn't have drunk any at all, or I'd have passed out. Still . . .

'It was elderflower wine. Very light, flowery – my mother used to make a kind of elderflower fizz for special occasions. That wasn't alcoholic, and this tasted similar though stronger, so I drank it down quite happily. And of course it didn't take very much to get me tipsy. It was . . . extraordinary. I've never smoked pot, or anything like that, but it was how I imagine it would be, the euphoria, all the colours brighter, more intense; everything coming and going in a strange way; a feeling that I was somehow outside of myself but at the same time more myself than I'd ever been before. So of course I blurted it all out, that he was so wonderful, that I loved him. I don't know what on earth I expected him to do – propose marriage and produce a ring on the spot, probably, the state I was in. But I got more than I bargained for.

'He laughed. And before I had time to be hurt, I saw he was half crying as well. Then it all came out, that he didn't like girls, that he only liked boys. God help me, I didn't have a clue what he was talking about. I said, but you like me, don't you? That was different, he said, it wasn't the same thing at all. He said he'd tried talking to his father, but that his father was so angry that he would never forgive him, that the house had been passed from father to son all those generations, that he was unnatural, perverted, disgusting . . . He cried again, and we ended up in each other's arms, me trying to comfort him, to tell him everything would be all right even though I didn't know what that "everything" was. I suppose he thought maybe things could be different, maybe he could make himself be what he considered normal . . .

'He tried to make love to me. It didn't work, of course. After the amount of wine he'd drunk it probably wouldn't have done anyway, and besides I was a complete innocen Nobody had ever told me the facts of life, and though I' seen bulls and rams in service I had no idea that people . . It wasn't unpleasant or frightening, and I wanted to hel him, so . . . And then his father came, and caught us.'

Her eyes were fixed on the wood grain of the table Persephone sat with her own eyes half closed, as if trying t see the events on the inside of her eyelids.

'He was furious,' said Frances. 'Ragingly angry. And, realised later, pretty drunk too. After Robert had talked t him their reactions had been remarkably similar, only h had turned to whisky. Then he'd come looking for him, jus drunk enough to want to beat some sense into him, thoug he'd never lifted his hand to him in his life before. Then h found us. For a moment, perhaps, he thought it was all mistake, that Robert was a young man like any other youn man, perhaps a bit confused, but still ready to tumble willing girl. But Robert was crying that nothing ha happened, that he couldn't . . . I don't know what h thought would have been worse, that he had, or that h hadn't. His father knew, though. He was, oh, angry, bitter in torment. So he . . . well . . .'

'He raped you.' Persephone spoke through dry lips. 'M father raped you.' Her face twisted in disgust, she looked a though she would be sick. Farmers are going in for rape she thought numbly. And I thought it was a joke.

'No, no!' Frances cried out in dismay. 'No, it wasn't lik that! He wasn't violent, or aggressive, he didn't threaten me. You couldn't exactly say I was willing, because I didn' understand what was happening, and I was pretty drunk too, by that time. But I liked him, you see. I was sorry fo him, because I could see how unhappy he was, as unhapp as Robert. I didn't try to stop him, even. In my world, then young people did what adults said. It was wrong, of course But it was not cruel, not evil. Afterwards, he was horrified

More than horrified, desperate with remorse. And I said it was all right, it didn't matter, I was all right. I said I'd never tell anyone. And I never did.'

The smell of the elderflower, that was what stayed with her. The taste of it still in her mouth and memory, and the heavy, sweet musky scent from the bush above her head. As she lay there she looked up into it. The creamy-white heads were fully out, broad as soup plates among the bright green leaves. When a breeze rose and set them swaying, she could see a fine haze of pollen rise like mist from the curded heads, to hang in the warm air before drifting down on to her face . . .

In her daydreams, from time to time, she had danced with Robert, he had held her clasped in his arms and looked down at her face. In reality he was only two inches taller than she was, but with the latitude permissible in fantasy he became as tall as his father so that her head, that was so uncomfortably much higher than the level of other girls, could rest confidingly on his shoulder. She could feel cherished, secure in the knowledge that he would soon sweep her off her feet, carry her off to happy-ever-after land.

Now, in this real world, it was the other way round. She held him in her arms, his head was on her shoulder and it was she who cherished. And she had never been so happy. His whispered confessions were scarcely heard, still less understood. All she knew was that in his misery he had turned to her, that she was the one girl in the world whom he could talk to, confide in, trust.

When his hands tugged at her clothes, she did not object. Though brought up to be modest, even prudish, the heady mixture of wine and emotion was enough to lull her inhibitions. His touch, clumsy as it was, did not alarm her, she even welcomed it as a further sign of his feeling for her.

His weight, when he rolled on top of her, was slightl uncomfortable but not unbearably so. He pushed himsel against her but she was scarcely aware of his flaccid penis a the movement pressed the bones of her lower back into th hard lump of a tree root.

Neither of them heard the approach of Robert's father The first that either of them knew was when his hands strong workman's hands, grasped Robert by the back of hi clothes, pulled him off her, dropped him to the ground Frances lay stupidly, the skirt of her cotton frock rucked u over the whiteness of her thighs, scarcely aware of her grey schoolgirl's knickers with their elasticated legs and thei pocket, lying a foot away from her. Then, realising, sh pulled her skirt down and reached for the underclothes Impossible, in front of an adult man, to try to put them o again, so she pushed them out of sight behind her.

He was swearing, words she had never heard before. Th smell of whisky on his breath, familiar from occasiona visitors to the Rectory whose advent made her mothe hustle her from the room, drowned out the elderflower Robert lay for a moment where he had been dropped, o his back, his arms up to cover his eyes and shield his head

'I didn't . . . I didn't . . . Nothing happened!'

He rolled over to hide himself with a movement that, ha he been a mole, would have dug him into the ground.

'Well? Did he?' His eyes were hot and angry, glarin down at her. Dumbly, not really understanding but know ing only that she must protect Robert, she shook her head His face twisted as if he, too, would weep.

'It's all right . . .' she said helplessly.

'All right, is it? All right? My son, my only bloody son and he's a bloody pansy, a nancy boy, a . . .' He shook hi head like a bewildered bull. Robert crawled away from hin and got to his feet, breathing in dry, gusty sobs. He cast a scared glance at his father, who ignored him, then stumble away through the trees, crouching a little, like a wounded animal trying to protect its belly. Alastair Johnson ignored him. He looked down at the girl still lying at his feet with her skirt tucked decorously round her, then away towards where he could still hear Robert's halting retreat. He half sat, half fell to the ground as his legs no longer seemed able to support him.

With a low groan he buried his head in his hands then turned and rolled so that he was lying half curled up on his side. His mind was in turmoil. The discovery that his only son was the kind of man he had been accustomed, all his life, to regard with disgust and contempt had hit him in an area of vulnerability he had not even been aware of. He felt that it reflected on his own manliness, he felt diminished in his own eyes, but it was more than that. The farm, the land that he and his forebears had served for so long, the house that had sheltered them from cradle to grave, was at the centre of his life, the core of his being. To cherish it, to improve it, and to pass it on to the next generation, that was what he had been born to. From father to son it had descended, in a line unbroken until now. He was unable to accept that Robert would be fit to take on that trust, and certainly there could be no future generations after him. His whole life seemed suddenly worthless and without point.

A strong, self-contained man, who prided himself on his control, he had no idea how to bear the feelings that engulfed him. The unaccustomed whisky burned in his stomach and sent its fumes wreathing like smoke through his brain. He felt his eyes fill with tears, felt the slow gasping breaths that were not far short of sobs, and with that he hated and despised himself more than he did Robert. Engulfed in his own misery he had forgotten the quiet girl behind him. When her hand touched his shoulder he jumped.

'It's all right,' said Frances again. It was all that she could think of to say. 'Please don't mind so much. Everything's all right.'

'No!' It was a shout of despair. 'It will never be all right. Never. Never.'

With the words came the tears, gushing from eyes that had never wept since he left his childhood behind. Tentatively at first Frances patted him, then put her arms round him and held him. He scarcely felt her thin, childish arms, but the touch of another human being was comfort of a sort. The words she spoke to soothe him never reached his mind, but the warmth of her presence drew him and he turned towards her as if to the comfort of a fire.

Once again Frances found herself holding and comforting a man distressed beyond the limits of his endurance. Her mind, fuddled with emotion and with the effects of the unaccustomed wine, scarcely differentiated one man from the other. Sober, she would have been rigid with embarrassment at finding herself in such a situation with Robert's father, but now he seemed no more than Robert's *alter ego* as he sobbed against her shoulder. When, quieter, his hands reached to hold and caress her it was almost familiar, less alarming even than Robert's clumsy attempts because more experienced and assured. Pleased that he was calmer, pleased that she had somehow managed to help him, she made no move to prevent, said nothing to stop him.

His breathing grew harsh, and his weight when he moved on to her was greater than Robert's so that she felt her first pang of fear. Then he lifted up a little and, relieved, she moved slightly against him, a movement of accommodation and acceptance that she was not aware of but which seemed to his blinkered mind an invitation. It was so sudden, so quick, that she scarcely had time to move, certainly not to cry out. The sharp stab of pain when he burst into her made her gasp, but within a few moments it was over and he lay inert, collapsed on top of her.

A large man, and heavy, his weight seemed to be crushing her so that she wondered how she could still manage to breathe. She drew in the air carefully, slowly. Her ribs felt bruised, and her hips; compared to them the stinging soreness between her legs was no more than a minor discomfort. She looked up at the elder tree, surprised to see that it was unchanged, that the white umbels still floated luminous against the glowing green, that the sky beyond was the same kindly blue set off by fluffy clouds that looked young and cuddly, like newborn lambs.

Her ears hummed deafly, glugging as she moved her head. She felt a cold wet trail down the side of her face, running into her ears, and realised that her eyes were overflowing with tears and that her throat was swollen inside with them. Her nose, too, was as full of water as if she were drowning. Would she suffocate? She breathed in slowly, trying to pull air into her nostrils, embarrassed at the thought of her nose running like a dirty child's.

Her legs felt numb. She wondered whether she was paralysed, whether the hard ground had damaged her spine like the young man who, five years ago, had fallen from the top of a haystack, and had never walked since that day. She moved her toes, relieved to find that she could do it, carefully tried to shift her legs so that the blood could flow.

He felt the movement and lifted himself up on his elbows, looking blearily down at her. His face expressed blank amazement when he saw her, and she realised that he had had no idea who she was. His face filled with anguish, the horror of a man who looks at himself in the mirror, and sees that he is damned for ever.

'Oh God! Frances, little Frances! Oh God, what have I done to you? Oh child, child, why didn't you stop me? What have I done?'

He rolled off her, tucking himself with disgust back into his trousers, doing them up as though with speed he could go back to an earlier time, make things as they were, make it not have happened. She pulled her legs together, moving her feet and whimpering a bit as the pins and needles prickled in her flesh. His face averted, he picked up her knickers and pushed them into her hands. Awkwardly, catching the solid soles of her sensible shoes in the elastic, she started to put them on.

'There's blood . . .' She looked with dismay at the skin of her inner thighs, streaked with shiny red that was already drying to brown. She was wet, too, a sticky wetness that embarrassed her. Still turned away, he pulled a handkerchief from his pocket and passed it to her. 'Thank you.' She wiped her eyes and her smeary nose first, with real gratitude, then dried herself as well as she could, scrunching the handkerchief into a ball and pushing it behind her without looking at it. The starting of her periods had come as a complete and dreadful shock to her. Her mother had offered an awkward and incomplete explanation, but while she accepted them as an inescapable part of adult womanhood she still did not understand why they came. Now, though she knew her next period was not due for at least two weeks, she assumed that this was some kind of extra flow, and was ashamed that she should have blurted it out. She pulled up her knickers, glad of their warmth on skin that felt suddenly icy, and found that she was shivering, her hands shaking and clammy with cold.

Alastair Johnson sat with his back to her. His knees were bent up and his head bowed down on to them, his arms curled round his legs so that his hands came up to cover the back of his head, hiding it from the sight of a God whose all-seeing eye glared down from the brilliant sky.

Frances doubled her own legs up, hugging her arms round them for warmth. Her eyes felt hot and sandy, her nose swollen and thick with mucus. She tilted her head back to try to clear it. The sun was a benison on her face, warm, comforting, her closed eyelids glowing red as a winter fire. Gradually her shivering died away, her hands softened their rigidity as the cold stiffness gave way to warmth. Her body felt limp as she relaxed; she could almost have slept. The wood was very quiet, only the rustle of small creatures in the undergrowth, the cry of a pheasant, broke its silence with their familiar, unnoticed noise.

'Are you all right?'

His voice was hoarse, unrecognisable in its humility, thickened by tears. Frances realised with something like terror that he was as frightened as she, as uncertain what to do or to say. The realisation was almost more alarming than what had gone before. He was, after all, not merely an adult but a man admired and respected in the small village community. From a long line of farmers, he was known as they had been for his upright and straightforward dealing. He worked hard himself, and expected no less from his men and his beasts. Utterly unsentimental, his fields were tended, harvested and rotated with almost military scientific precision that was leavened by the long and close relationship of his family with the soil they tilled.

Her own father, she knew, considered him a good and worthy man, while deploring his neglect of spiritual matters and his erratic attendance at church. He knew, however, that while the farmer was seldom to be found at matins or evensong, he was open-handed in his gifts of produce, flowers or greenery at harvest, Easter and Christmas, and no appeal for someone in real need went unheard by him.

She put her legs down and moved forward on to her knees behind him, laying a tentative hand on his hard, muscled shoulder. Beneath the cloth of his garments his skin twitched and shrank from her touch, like an anxious horse, and she could feel that his whole being cringed fro her as if from a blow. She patted him gently.

'It's all right,' she said. 'I'm all right, honestly. I'm nc hurt, or anything.'

'I must tell your father. I'll do what I can . . .'

'No!' The cry burst from her, a sharp gash of sound. 'No she repeated more moderately, finding it hard to disagre with an older person. 'Please, no. There's no need. The needn't know.'

'They may have to, by and by.'

'No, no, really. It will be all right, I'm sure it will.'

He clutched his head more tightly as if he would crush i beneath his hands.

'If only it had been Robert!' It was a lament, a world o sorrow in his voice.

'It almost was,' she said, to comfort him. 'It could hav been. I'll say it was, if you like. If anyone finds out.'

'It's not right.'

'It doesn't matter. I don't mind. I'll say it, I promise. I they find out, but they probably won't.'

His hands relaxed fractionally.

'How old are you, girl?'

'Sixteen. Two years younger than Robert.'

'Sixteen. It's young, but not too young. It could be don . . . So you'd say that? Go through with it? He'd stand b you, I'd see to that.'

She scarcely understood what he was saying, but hear the germ of hope in his voice, and cherished it.

'Yes, yes, of course. I'll say it. But I don't think I'll nee to.'

'Sixteen . . .' He pondered. It was young to marry, bu not unfeasible. Then again, there might be no need Maybe, after all, she was more knowledgeable than he ha thought. Women had safe times, or at least safer times - was she telling him that this was one of them, that she was a ttle risk? With the thought came a surprising pang of egret, a moment of mourning for a child that would not be, child that could have been Robert's saviour and vindication, and his own hostage to an uncertain future.

He sighed, dragging the air into his lungs with the esperate energy of a newborn on its first cry.

'I'm sorry, Frances,' he said simply. 'I'm so sorry.'

She patted him again.

'It's all right,' she reiterated. 'It will be all right.' If she aid it often enough, it would be true. Already her memory f the violent events was retreating, dissolving into a mist of vilful forgetfulness, leaving only the scent of elderflower nd the memory of Robert in her arms.

Alastair Johnson stood up slowly, his joints creaking as if e had aged thirty years in as many minutes.

'I'd best be getting back,' he said gruffly. 'I must take you ome.'

'No.' Again she spoke with absolute definiteness. 'No, ou mustn't. They – everyone – would think it strange. And . . I'd rather be alone. You should go and find Robert.' still on her knees she looked up at him. 'Please don't be ngry with him.'

His face was wrenched with grief.

'How can I be angry with him? I'm ten times worse than e is. But I'll do anything I can for you, girl. Remember hat, eh? Anything I can, and more.'

'I'll remember . . .'

He was gone, his sturdy boots crushing the ripe pods of he bluebells that remained after the flowers were over. His read was heavy, she thought the earth must shake with it. she, too, stood up, aching in every limb. The stained andkerchief lay on the ground. Wearily she stooped, lawed a hole in the soft mould, buried it with an animal-ike instinct of secrecy. Then, slowly, she walked home.

As the days passed she put the event out of her mind,

pushing it back forcibly into its cocoon of darkne whenever it obtruded. No one said anything, asked an thing. Robert went away almost at once, fleeing for a whi from an unbearable reality where neither he nor his fath could bear to meet one another's eyes. Alastair Johnso kept away from the village, burying himself in the ha harvest as if his life depended on it. A few weeks later h sought Frances out when she was walking.

'Are you all right?' His eyes veered away from her. H had lost weight, the muscles stood out like whipcor beneath skin that had shrivelled where healthy fat ha melted away; his face was hollow, new-lined. Frances ha not noticed that her period was late, and would hav thought nothing of it if she had.

'Oh, yes, I'm all right,' she assured him. 'Is . . . is Robe all right? Is he coming back soon?'

'Not for a while, if it's not necessary,' he answere gruffly. 'You're sure, then? Sure you're all right?'

'Oh yes, quite sure.' She scarcely heeded his questio saddened that Robert would be staying away. He grunte and strode off.

Frances had no sickness, no indication of her state but tenderness in her breasts and an absence of periods. Th first she dismissed, remembering how tender they had bee when they first started to develop and assuming that the were growing a bit more, as indeed they did. The secon she found rather a relief, and thought she was lucky not t have the discomfort and inconvenience during the war summer weather. A slight thickening in her waist did nc concern her either, for she had a hearty appetite and ha never been encouraged to worry overmuch about he figure.

It was not until the fourth month of her pregnancy tha she felt a strange movement within her, and exclaime aloud. She was, fortunately, alone with her mother. At firs hey both put it down to an excessive indulgence in plums and a consequent upset digestion, but when a casual question about internal matters and the dates of her monthly cycle elicited a blithely honest answer, her mother looked afresh at Frances' budding breasts and the gentle swell of her stomach, and knew at once that every woman's worst fears for her daughter had somehow come to pass.

For a day and a night she kept her own counsel. Sending Frances up to her room to rest and keep out of the way, she struggled to find a way to deal with the problem, some means of keeping it secret from their neighbours and, most important of all, from her husband. Knowing, even as her mind scurried from one impossible scheme to another, that it could not be done.

The following evening, with Frances supposedly unwell and eating from a tray in her room, she told him. Like her, he went through the stages of disbelief, anger, grief and despair. The violence of his reaction did not surprise her, but his complete inability to accept what had happened did. She saw that in this crisis he, who had ruled the household for all of their married life, would be worse than useless, that she would have to deal with it herself and protect him, as far as possible, from the whole thing. She was dimly aware that this revelation was to mark a turning point in their marriage, that neither of them could ever be quite the same again.

Upstairs, Frances felt the atmosphere in the Rectory change and electrify. There were no raised voices, no shouting, but the silence reverberated like a bell. She knew, quite suddenly, that she could not lie outright to her parents. Her father, indeed, seemed to have no real wish to learn the truth of what had happened. That it must have been one of his parishioners seemed inevitable: the knowledge was a blow to him as violent as the discovery of Robert's sexuality had been to Alastair Johnson. Both men

felt threatened in some area of their lives that was vital t
them.

Frances retreated into a stubborn inability to name th
father, saying that she didn't know, couldn't remember
Her mother, quietly efficient, asked no questions bu
busied herself with arrangements and preparations. France
left that night, and did not return until she came back from
Belgium childless and, in every sense of the word, empty.

Chapter 20

But . . . the baby!' Persephone was unable to connect that ewly conceived foetus with herself. 'He must have realised t was his, why didn't he help you, do something?' She ould not believe that the man who had been her father had ot been aware of her.

'He didn't know,' said Frances simply. 'I didn't know I vas pregnant myself, until I was more than four months. Ie would have seen me around, everything the same as isual, no one worried or behaving strangely. He asked me f I was all right, and I said yes without even understanding vhat he was talking about. You must remember, my dear,' he endearment slipped out without either of them noticing t, 'that things were very different then. When I say that I ad never been told the facts of life, I mean that I had bsolutely no knowledge, none at all, of how babies were onceived. I didn't know even about periods, until mine tarted. I was terrified; like many girls of my generation, I hought I was bleeding to death. All my mother told me was hat it was normal, that it happened to all women until they vere quite old. And I accepted that, the more so because he made it quite clear that this was something one didn't peak of, something private and embarrassing.'

'My mother didn't tell me much,' admitted Persephone. She warned me against letting boys "do anything" to me, s she put it, but I had only a very sketchy idea of what "anything" might be. But we were taught about it at school so it didn't matter.'

'I must have been an extraordinarily unnoticing girl said Frances ruefully. 'Living in the country, with animal all around me, I still never made the connection wit human beings. I think I really believed that a girl wh wasn't married couldn't have a baby.'

'That says something about the moral standards of you village,' said Persephone drily.

'No, just about the extraordinary degree of protectio I was given from the realities of life. It was wrong, c course; wrong, and stupid, but done with such very goo intentions.'

'The road to hell,' said Persephone absently. 'If he ha known, what then?'

'He would have tried to marry me off to Robert. I realis that now. I do believe he was almost disappointed. It woul have been . . . fitting, in his eyes. A reparation, perhap Certainly a way of saving Robert, as he would have seen it

'Would you have done it?'

Frances paused, thought. Would I? she wonderec Possibly. Probably.

'I expect so. I still believed I was in love with him. Well, suppose I was. Young people can feel love just as poig nantly as anyone, more, probably. It might even hav worked, after a fashion, for a while. He would have been kind husband, a good father. But in the end it wouldn have been enough for either of us. Who can say? He migh still have died in the war and left me a widow, and yo fatherless. As it was, when my mother realised I wa pregnant I was sent away at once, as I told you, and then went to Belgium. By the time I came back, everything wa changed. Robert had joined the army. The war was there on the horizon, to the people who knew enough to see i Robert would never have been called up, of course rming was a reserved occupation – but he chose to go, and expect it was a relief to both of them. I never saw him gain.'

'Poor boy.' Persephone looked at Robin, thankful that ings were at least slightly easier for him than for his uncle. obin gave a little nod of acknowledgement and a smile, greeing with her thoughts. Amy and Michael sat very still, Iichael out of deference to a situation that he felt he was truding in, and Amy because she was living every second ith them, her involvement so intense that she had lost all elf-awareness.

'Yes. It was a waste. I would like to think, if we had arried, that he might have been happier, but maybe not. I on't know that one should even think too much of the ight-have-been. Perhaps things are better as they were. etter, maybe, to believe so.'

'Yes.' Persephone sounded forlorn. It seemed imporant, somehow, that she should explain how she felt, even ough she was not altogether sure what that was. The act f putting it into words might help her to find out, she ought. 'When I found that piece of paper, found out bout you, I felt as if I didn't know who I was any more. Oh,' she smiled angrily, beating one fisted hand into the ther, 'that sounds so trite, so corny, but I don't know any ther way to say it.'

'Of course,' said Frances. 'Things are trite because they re true. You must have felt that the foundations had isappeared from your existence.'

'Yes. I felt . . . incomplete. Or rather, I realised I had lways felt incomplete, and now I knew why. I thought, oday, that meeting you might get rid of that. Put me back ogether, like a jigsaw. Though maybe with a different icture.'

'And it hasn't.' There was no question in Frances' voice, o disappointment or guilt.

‘Yes, in a way. It’s strange, I feel I know my mother s much better now, just through meeting you. There didn seem to be anyone I could ask about her. She had very fe friends. A lot of acquaintances, a lot of people she calle “my friends”, but no one close. I never remember h talking to her women friends about anything persona Gossip, she would say. I can’t bear gossip. But she wa there, wasn’t she? In that prison?’

‘Yes, but she had you. Her secret was a happy one.’

‘Not always. I don’t think I was the kind of daughter sh wanted.’

‘Nor would a natural child have been, necessarily. N child is ever quite what parents expect.’

‘But in the end, she killed herself. I wasn’t enough t keep her from doing that.’

‘No.’ Robin spoke in a loud voice, positively. They a looked at him. ‘It wasn’t like that,’ he said more quietl ‘Believe me, I understood Granny. She used to talk to m you know. Because I was a boy, a male. Sarah was h favourite, because they liked the same things, but I wa always special. She always liked to see herself as th founder of a clan, didn’t she?’

‘Yes, I suppose so, but . . .’

‘And as her grandson,’ continued Robin, ‘I was t continue that clan. Poor Granny! She should have g together with your real father, they sound as if they’d hav had a lot in common. I used to see her as a sort of trib chief. She was the ruler, and to demonstrate that she gav us gifts. Valuable gifts, because that bound us to her, and a the same time displayed her power, her generosity, and h wealth.’

‘Really, Robin, you sound like a nineteenth-centur anthropologist,’ said Persephone rather crossly.

‘No, he’s right,’ put in Amy. ‘That’s just how it was. Sh didn’t like me so much because I didn’t want the things sh

vanted to give me. And I suppose because you hadn't let
er take me over as much as Sarah. Go on, Robin.'

'That's it, really. When Lloyd's took a nose dive, and
ll her syndicates started demanding money, she just
ouldn't cope with it. It was quite obvious that one or
wo of her syndicates were going to be long-term losses,
nd that the writing was on the wall. Total liability,
hat's what Lloyd's is all about, after all. She used to
oast about it, even. Not believing that it could happen,
ut liking to amaze people. "Total liability, of course,"
he would say. "If the worst came to the worst, they
ould take everything I possess." That was fine all through
he better years. She made losses from time to time, but
othing compared with the profits. She didn't even take
ut stop-loss insurance, said she had complete faith in
er managing agents. But the worst came to the worst.
he was going to lose her money, and with it her chiefly
tatus, her power source. She couldn't bear it. So she
ave us, she thought, one last gift. Not a rejection, but
he very opposite. The gift to end all gifts, one that no
ne could ever better. Not so much her life, but the
aving of her fortune. Or so she thought. The estate
rotection plan would pay out, we'd inherit all her millions,
nd everything would be back to normal. Oh, she wouldn't
e there to see it, but suicides don't always take themselves
hrough to the logical conclusion, you know. All she
ould see was that it would put her back on her pedestal,
er throne, and she would be Queen-Empress for all
ime.'

Persephone sat, letting the words wind through her
ead, waiting to see whether they made a recognisable
attern. The more she thought about what Robin had said
he more it seemed familiar and right.

'You really think that? You're not just saying it?'

'Of course I'm not. I don't do things like that, you know

perfectly well. Particularly not now, here, to you. She did for us. For you.'

Persephone shook her head, but not in dissent.

'I need to think about it. But not now. Because there still a piece of the jigsaw missing, one of those importa pieces in the middle that bring the picture together. I neve really knew my father – my adoptive father – at all, I w too little when he died. I didn't even mind very much, never seemed like a lack in my life. But, I suppose, since found out that I was adopted, there have been momen when I've hoped . . . he could have been still alive . . . m real father. But if he was so much older than you, it's nc very likely, is it? Still, as you say, perhaps it's better as it is

'He was a good man,' said Frances, very positively. know it doesn't sound like it, what you've heard today, bu you must believe it. A good man, in so many ways. He wa a strict father, I suppose, but that's how fathers were mostly, when I was a child. Or so it seemed to me. But in hi way generous, honest, even kind. I've often regretted that never had the chance to get to know him better.'

'And he never knew . . . about me . . .'

Frances looked down at the table, rubbing absently wit a fingertip at a knot in the wood.

'He did find out,' she said slowly. 'Later on. Afte Robert was killed. He'd never been a sociable man eve before that, he preferred to be out on the farm; I believe h liked the company of his animals more than that of people But after Robert's death he got worse. People would se him in the distance, standing staring out across his land, bu whenever they tried to approach him he would stride of pretend he hadn't seen them. He got over it, of course, bu it was a bad time for him . . . I was still living at home, it wa before I went off to nurse. I went for a walk one day, wen back to that place. The place where it happened. I was sti grieving, you see. Bereaved. It was about three years afte you were born, but there had been nothing to distract me, to take your place. And I had nothing, no photograph, or lock of baby hair, no little memento to weep over. So I went back there, on a cold November day, and he was there.

'We were both startled, to say the least. He was sitting on the trunk of a fallen tree, just staring out across the pond. It was . . . I felt it was a kind of gift from the Fates, that we should meet there. He was the only person, you see, the only one I could speak to. Having a secret like that, an unhappy secret, is like being in a kind of solitary confinement. It's so terribly lonely.' It was said matter-of-factly without a trace of self pity. Persephone nodded.

'I think he would have run away, if he could. He didn't, though. He just sat there, staring at me as if I had been a ghost. So I went and sat down beside him. Not too near. And then we both stared out over the pond.'

She shivered at the memory.

'It was bitterly cold. One of those November days when the air is so cold and wet it feels solid in your lungs, heavy on the top of your head. The trees had lost most of their leaves, just a few shrivelled brown rags hanging, damp, from the twigs. Everything brown and dead-looking, that had been so green and fresh. Even the water in the pond looked stagnant and gluey.

'He waited. I think he hoped if he didn't speak to me I'd give up and go away, but I just sat there. My hands and feet went numb, but I waited. In the end, he said: "Are you all right?" Just like he had before. But this time, I told him no, I'm not. I'm not all right.

'He was horrified. I suppose he expected me to say, like last time, that everything was fine. He turned and looked at me for the first time, and I told him everything. Belgium, the baby, the adoption. It all came flooding out. It was such a relief that I never even noticed, until I stopped talking, the look on his face. The pain. I had never seen anyone

look like that. It was as if I had stuck a knife in him, an
then twisted it around. He couldn't speak for a fe
minutes, he just looked at me as if he couldn't believe wh
he was hearing.

'Then – "Why didn't you tell me?" Just that, but his voic
. . . I don't think I'll ever forget how he sounded. I fe
dreadful, as if it had been all my fault. Of course I told hi
how it had been, how my mother had discovered I wa
pregnant when I didn't even know myself, and how I'
been hustled off the same night to the other end of th
county, and soon after that taken to Belgium. I told him I'
kept my promise, that I'd never told them who the fathe
was, how nobody had ever known. He groaned then, an
said if only I had told them, told him, told anybody. Bu
how could I have done? It never would have occurred to m
to write to him. I did as my parents told me – it seemed all
could do, when I'd hurt them so badly.

'He asked me about your mother. I think he may hav
had some kind of mad idea of getting you back, but I tol
him I had no idea who she was, where she came from
anything about her. I told him she lived in Belgium, and
think that was when he gave up. The Germans had overru
Belgium, you see, five months earlier.'

'She wasn't there,' said Persephone stupidly. 'She brough
me back, long before. Before the war started.'

'Of course. But what chance would he have had c
tracing you? And I – what could I tell him? Only that yo
were a girl, and that you had red hair. He smiled then, an
that was sadder than ever. I think . . . I'm afraid . . . that i
you had been a boy, he might have carried on with trying t
find you. Another of your dynasty-builders, you see.' Sh
smiled wryly at Robin. 'If he'd ever known about you . . .

'Lord help us,' said Robin, startled. 'Two of then
counting on me to found a family. And, let's face it, I'm no
exactly dynasty material, am I? Any more than poor ol

Robert was. But didn't you say he had a daughter, as well? Couldn't he have made do with her and her children?'

'No. That was why he was there, at that place. His daughter was married by then, and had just given birth to a little girl. A perfectly healthy child, but something went very amiss with the birth. She – his daughter – was desperately ill, nearly died. He'd just heard that she would never be able to have any more children. Not just that it would be dangerous for her, but that it was actually physically impossible.'

'He didn't want me for myself,' said Persephone sadly, like a child.

'Well, perhaps not,' Frances conceded, 'but then, he didn't know you, did he? And if he wanted you for what you represented, how does that differ from other parents who decide to have a child? Most of us want a stake in the future, and that's what a baby is, in the end. A little bit of ourselves, carrying on.'

There was a long silence. The sound of the Aga's rhythmic purr vied with that of the cat, who had settled in his usual inconvenient place in front of the Aga.

Frances thought, what is she thinking, this child of my body who is a middle-aged woman? How does she feel about me, about her father, her adoptive mother? Shall I ever get to know her, could we be friends? At this moment, I feel closer to Amy. Why does her age make her easier for me to relate to? Perhaps I think of her as a child, and I'm used to children. Or perhaps, because I've been spending so much of my time in the past, in my own girlhood, I have some kind of fellow feeling with her. I think we could be friends. I hope so. I like her young man. And Robin. I like them all. Would they like me?

It occurred to her then that she had been more alive, these last days, than she had been for years, perhaps even for the whole of her life since Persephone's birth. That, at least, had been real: so real that she had retreated afterwards, into the world of fiction that was controllable, ordered, and safe. Even Jean-Pierre, much though she had loved him, had been almost a figure of fantasy for her. Knowing that what was between them could have no future she had lived for that while in a world out of time, as separate from her everyday life as Barchester or Dickens' London. Nothing else, since then, had been as important, even as three-dimensional, as the worlds of the books she read.

For the first time she realised that this escapism was wrong. It was a denial of life, a refusal to allow her own mind and spirit to live and develop. By escaping into literature she had put herself into a prison, and it had taken Amy's coming to shatter the walls of that cosy padded cell. She shivered, knowing that she would never be able to withdraw into it quite so completely again. Life, with all its pains and pleasures, must be lived for whatever time remained to her. Suddenly her plan of moving into a sheltered retirement home appeared, if not impossible, at least premature. She was not ready for that yet, after all. Not just yet. If she could not manage this house she would find something smaller, with very little gardening. Somewhere, though, big enough for her to have her family to visit. If they wanted to.

Persephone's thoughts were less clear. Her mind was a jumble of images: a red-haired man, not much younger than she was now; a young girl, obedient and innocent and foolish, whose own life had perhaps been spoiled, ruined, by something that was not so very far from a rape. After all she had never married. Had her only experience of love been that, a schoolgirl romantic crush, and a violation by a man old enough to be her own father? And the woman she still thought of as her mother, who had taken her and tried to mould her, albeit unsuccessfully, into the daughter she so desperately wanted: could Persephone now, through her wn memories and those of her children, learn to know er? Could she fit that angular, awkwardly shaped piece ıto the puzzle that was her life?

Nothing, no part of her existence, could ever be quite the ame again. Was that a good thing? Could she bear it? She elt bruised. Perhaps she was not a puzzle at all, but a aleidoscope that some cosmic child had, with wilful bandon, taken up and shaken so that all the little coloured ieces were rearranged. And I, the plaything, must fit them ıto a pattern if I can. Without knowing what she did she ighed, and smiled, and shook her head.

Robin looked at the two women, his mother and his randmother. Now that he knew of the relationship he ould see similarities, small, subtle resemblances that were ound in the angle of a jaw, the shape of a skull, even the uance of a movement. Frances, he thought, was a person vho would not be easy to get to know, but who would try to neet one halfway. He thought it would be a rewarding rocess. He hoped, very much, that his mother would find ierself able to try it. As a son, his loyalty must of course emain with Persephone, but he was very reluctant to lose his new-found relative. She would not take Lady Singleton's lace: perhaps because he had understood her better than nost of them he had been genuinely fond of her. But he hought the whole family needed what she represented – a ink with the past, and a representative of her generation.

His mind, inevitably, strayed to Harry. How he would ıave enjoyed this! The drama, the emotion, the unfolding of their stories – to Robin, as a producer of dramas, the ppeal was irresistible. To Harry, who revelled in soap operas on the television and gathered up the life histories of hance acquaintances in every pub, it would have been a lice of heaven. He thought again of his telephone call arlier in the day. Would Harry come back? If he did, vhere would he live? He had said his treatments were finished, and that he was beginning to get over the effects them, that he was otherwise fairly well. He was st working, and no doubt could pick up the threads and t contacts of before, and find work in England. He coul Robin supposed, move back into Robin's flat, but th seemed to present problems now. Harry had alwa needed – would need more than ever now – a clear defined area of private space. It had been one of the thin that had caused friction before. Robin's little flat would n contain Robin, Harry, and the invisible third presence Harry's illness.

Perhaps he should move. Sell the flat, find a house in t country. As long as he was within reach of London, l didn't need to be on the spot. A little house, with a gard . . . he fell into a reverie.

Amy was conscious of Michael next to her. They s close, each unknowingly slightly inclined towards t other, but not touching. There was no need. They had qui early on moved beyond the hand-holding, leaning-agains one-another stage. Michael, being older, did not need th kind of reassurance, and Amy had soon learned the secr pleasures of a glance, the lift of an eyebrow, the slig shifting of posture that told her he was aware of her, rea to supply comfort and support if necessary, but leaving h to handle the situation in her own way. It was the thing sh most liked about him: he never trespassed on the integri of her separate human existence. The distance he p between them, which she might once have found chillin and insecure, somehow acted as a kind of moat against t rest of the world. Safe and inviolable within it, she kne that she could cross it whenever she chose.

The relief of hearing her mother's explanation had bee so profound that the rest of the family history had seeme of little relevance. Even the discovery that the man she ha always called Daddy was, in a sense, lost to her, was nall importance. The fear, unacknowledged but real, that er mother had inherited some germ of insanity from ranny, had been the most frightening thing she could ever emember. She was honest enough to admit that her main orry was that some taint of madness might have been assed down to her, but along with that was the fear, ore awful because unexpressed, that Persephone might e capable of the same act of self-destruction as Lady ingleton.

To find that her mother's violent reaction had a rational xplanation was enough to make her happy again. She new very well that if she had been forced to choose etween them, it must have been Michael she chose owever much unhappiness it might cause. Now it would ot be necessary. Her mother, at least, remained to her, nd what she had lost seemed insignificant in the light of aat gain. As for Hugo, she did not know. That she would ne day meet him was inevitable, given his relationship ith Michael. Whether or not she would claim him as a ather was something she was deferring. For now it was nough that she had a mother, a lover, and a new randmother with whom she felt so surprising an affinity. he was, she thought, wholly content.

She looked round the table. Robin, obviously, was miles way. In the glow of her own happiness she saw him more learly than usual. The marks of strain and old unhappiness eemed to stand out like knife scars, but that there had een the panacea of some new and hopeful development lso seemed clear. Was it Harry? She hoped so. With all his oodiness and aggression, there was something very ppealing and lovable about Harry. She thought she would ke to see him again.

Sitting opposite one another, to her right and her left, ersephone and Frances looked up at almost the same oment, and for the first time met one another's eyes without hesitation. It was the kind of long, searching ga that a woman might use when examining herself in a mirr for signs of ageing. Critical, hopeful, fearful, forgiving; mutual acknowledgement, a guarded promise for t future.

The telephone rang, startling them all. For a mome they all gazed at one another as if the strident sounds can from another world, inexplicable and frightening. Th Frances made a visible effort to collect herself, and sto up.

'Excuse me,' she said, with polite formality. Michael a Robin made the kind of polite lurch of well-brought- men, a token rising, then subsided. Amy met her mother eyes and smiled.

Frances walked into the hall, picked up the receiver.

'Hello?'

There was a pause. The distant quacking of a voice can through to them. They were aware of it, but uninterested

'On a Bank Holiday Monday?' Frances' voice w incredulous, rather brusque, like someone who thinks s is having a practical joke played on her. 'I thought solicito were strictly Monday-to-Friday-lunchtime people.'

Another pause. More quacking.

'Would you mind repeating that?' She sounded, anything, more incredulous than before.

'Oh. My goodness. Yes, as a matter of fact, she's . . . Ye Well, I certainly can, though I can't answer for . . . I thin I'd better ring you back.' She picked up a pencil from t notepad on the table. Electrified by her tone of voice, t others were listening with avid shamelessness. 'Yes, I' got that. And your name was . . . ? Well, Mr Prendergast, will telephone you in a little while. Er, goodbye.'

Frances put down the pencil carefully, then replaced t handset so gently it might have been an eggshell. She stoo for a moment contemplating the telephone as if it had ju ıetamorphosed into something bizarre, then looked up at ıe rest of them where they sat at the table, every face ırned towards her. She walked to the doorway and opped, leaning her hand against the door frame for ıpport. She spoke to Persephone as if they were alone ogether.

'That,' she said with careful precision, 'was a man called rendergast. Hugh Prendergast. A solicitor. He was, he ıys, solicitor to Alastair Johnson. And his friend. He has, e says, something to tell me. And you. You, particularly. Ie wants to see us both. He said, would one day this week ıit us.'

She drew in a breath. Strangely enough, the thing that truck her most forcibly at that moment was that she had aid 'us' about herself and Persephone. The word seemed ɔ carry a portentous significance.

'Something to tell us?' Persephone repeated the word. It ang like a bell round the room. 'What on earth . . . ?'

'Something to your advantage,' quoted Robin flippantly.

'Oh Mummy, how exciting! Perhaps there'll be a letter ɔr you!' Amy, typically, was less interested in the pos-ibility of financial gain than in her mother's peace of mind.

'He said – I'm sorry – that Alastair Johnson died quite ecently. I'm so sorry,' said Frances, for herself and to ersephone. 'If only . . .'

Persephone looked at her.

'I think we've had enough of "if only", don't you? But I hink we must go and see him. How extraordinary, to think hat if he had telephoned a week ago . . . Shall we go omorrow? Together?'

'Yes,' said Frances, her satisfaction too deep to express. Yes, tomorrow will do very well. We'll go together.'

They all looked at one another. From a set of disparate ersons they had become, quite suddenly, a group, melded ogether by the sharing of the past and by the sudden intrusion of the present. Robin pushed back his chai stretching.

'What I need,' he said, 'is some fresh air, and son exercise to work off all this excitement.'

'Good idea,' said Amy. 'What about you, Mummy? Ar May? The bluebells are coming out, I saw them the oth day. Let's all go. There's still so much to talk about, but don't believe I can sit any longer, I want to be moving, lik Robin.'

'Yes,' said Frances, pushing back her own chair decisive and standing up. 'Yes, that would be good. If . . . ?' Sh glanced enquiringly at Persephone.

'I walked miles on the beach yesterday, but I think could stagger on for a bit. As Amy says, there's still a lot t talk about. For one thing, Robin, what have you been u to? I know mothers aren't supposed to ask questions lik that, but you look different, today. Better, actually.'

'Yes,' he agreed. 'I am, much better. I couldn't bear t talk about it before, but now I think I can. I think – I hope I might be getting back together with Harry.'

'Oh, Robin! That's wonderful, I'm so happy for yo You've spoken to him? Is everything all right?'

'Yes.' Robin looked surprised to hear himself saying i His face lit up. 'Yes, yes it is. Everything's all right.'

Epilogue

ugh Prendergast leaned back in his chair and surveyed his sitors benevolently. The benevolence was not, of course, pparent to anyone but himself, for his face was as npassive as ever. Across the large mahogany desk his archment-coloured face, so smoothly shaved it was impossible to imagine any stubble daring to raise its head, ould have been carved from soapstone. The dignity onferred by the shelves of leather-bound, gold-tooled gal volumes behind him gave his stillness a hieratic air. e could have been some ancient high priest or god-king, ith the power of life and death in his hands.

He examined the two women before him. It seemed arcely believable that after all these years Frances fortimer was actually there, in his office. He had imagined is moment so often, particularly in the last few months hen his client had begun to look frail. He had tried very ard not to create an image of her, but the moment she had alked into the room he had decided that he liked the way e looked. With her well-cut, if dull, tweed suit, her severe airstyle, her un-made-up face with its direct grey eyes and ear skin, and her confident, upright carriage she was, to im, the epitome of what an Englishwoman of her generaon should be. He had not needed the memory of hearing er yesterday to know that her voice, too, would be clear nd pleasing.

Her companion – her daughter, of course – came as n great surprise to him. Her grey eyes looked anxiously a him through the glasses that she pushed, from time to time up the bridge of her nose in a gesture that was obviousl unconscious. And her hair! Unlike her cousin Angela's i colour owed nothing to the hairdresser's art, but the re curls, paled and streaked not unattractively with grey, wer so like Alastair's that he almost burst out laughing at th sight of her. Even the way they grew was his, and so was th well-shaped skull and bone structure beneath it.

Alastair's daughter, then. Surely, Alastair's daughte unless Robert . . . From the few things Alastair had let sli it seemed unlikely. Her summer dress with its contrastin jacket was expensive, if not very new, and though she di not seem at ease she had the innate social confidence an pleasing manner of a good upbringing. Her anxiety, whic showed only in the tension round her eyes and their expre sion, seemed centred not on him and what he might say, b on her companion, her mother. They were not at ease wi one another, he thought. Aware of each other's eve move, they interacted with the careful courtesy of stranger and there was a physical and mental gap between them.

He had stood to welcome them, sat them down, offere tea or coffee. His secretary, primed and ready, brought i tea and he saw Frances Mortimer's approval of the fin prettily flowered china, the home-made biscuits that Mar deeply intrigued, had insisted he bring in with him. She ha been almost as fond of Alastair as he had been, and whi Hugh would not have dreamed of breaking a client confidence the old man had himself informed her of th terms of his will, and relished her fascinated curiosity whi doing nothing to satisfy it. Mary, he knew, would appro of Frances, and be as amused by Persephone's appearan as he was.

The tea poured, the civil enquiries about their journe

ade, he put his fingertips together to make an inverted V histrionic mannerism much deplored by Mary but which nused him) and looked at them as if over the top of onexistent spectacles.

'I imagine you will have guessed,' he said to them both, hat you are beneficiaries under the will of my late client, lastair Johnson?'

'I suppose we did,' Frances agreed, 'although it isn't omething one feels able to speculate about, exactly. nder the circumstances.'

'Under the circumstances. Quite.' He paused. 'I should, erhaps, tell you that while I enjoyed a long and, I think I ay say, friendly relationship with my late client, he did ot confide in me the reasons for the disposition of his state, or the nature of the relationship, if any, that may ave existed between you.'

The younger woman, Persephone Knight, blinked be-ind her glasses and, he thought, relaxed a little, some f the tension ebbing from her. Frances merely looked mused, though whether by what he had said or the dry, wyerish way he had said it, he did not know. Both, he oped. He enjoyed playing his part, and enjoyed it all the nore on the rare occasions when he had an appreciative udience. Shameless old thespian, Mary called him.

'You don't know who we are,' said Frances with a winkle. He saw that she was able to discover the answering leam in his eye.

'I don't know who you are,' he agreed cordially, refusing allow his eyes to stray to Persephone's face that gave the e to his statement.

'Should you not be asking us for some kind of proof of ur identity?' Frances Mortimer was entering with gusto nto the spirit of the occasion. 'After all, we might be omplete imposters. The Titchfield claimants, you know. ambert Simnel. Or Brat Farrar.'

He allowed himself a small, tight smile.

'You forget that it was I who telephoned you, M Mortimer. Had you contacted me as the result of a print advertisement . . . But even so, I do not think I wou have needed to query Mrs Knight's identity, at lea So I suppose one might say that her presence valida you.'

Persephone looked first alarmed, then resigned. O hand lifted, as of its own volition, from adjusting h glasses to touch her hair.

'Yes, I suppose it does. How strange,' said Franc thoughtfully. 'For so long it was quite the opposite. An . . she hesitated over the word, 'an illegitimate child, someone of my generation and upbringing, would ha invalidated me as a member of society. Not in my ow eyes,' she added hastily, as Persephone made a sm gesture of distress, 'but in everyone else's. And yo if I had kept you, would have been as much an outca as I.'

'I know,' said Persephone. 'But I think,' she added wit little spurt of anger, 'that I'm a bit tired of being someo who validates other people. For all those years I was t daughter who validated, in your word, my adopti mother; now, I'm validating you. But am I valid? W validates me? My children? My grandchildren? I do want them to, I want them to be separate people in the own right.'

Frances looked stricken.

'I didn't mean . . .'

'My dear,' said Hugh Prendergast, 'you are, if I may s so, the most valid member of your family. It all hinges you. You are, if you like, the central point round whi they revolve: your adoptive mother, your mother, yo father, and no doubt your descendants also. No one trying to use you. Nor is there any coercion involved. Wh u inherit will devolve to you in any case, without your ving to do anything about it. It does not in fact come to u directly, only at the discretion of your mother, until her ath. You may walk away from this, if you choose, at any ne. Now, if you like.'

He waited. Frances also sat, not looking at either of em, examining the moulding on the edge of his desk if she had never seen anything so absorbing before. rsephone looked at him, at her mother, then as it were side herself. Then she relaxed, gave a small laugh, and ook her head.

'I'm sorry,' she said generally. 'What a ridiculous tburst! I'm afraid the events of the last few days have erwrought me, if that's the right way to put it. You don't alise this, of course, but I only met my – my mother for e first time yesterday. It's all been a bit . . . well, you can agine.'

'I can indeed. Traumatic is the word in current use, I lieve. If you like, I can just tell you the bare bones, and ave all the fiddly details for another day when you've had ne to get used to the idea.'

It was an offer he had to make, but he was glad when she ook her head.

'No, I'm – we're – here, now. Let's do this thing operly. I'm all right now and, to be honest, eaten up with riosity as well.'

'I think we are all that, in our various ways. Mine, of urse, is partly satisfied already, by meeting you both. As yours – I have taken the liberty of having the relevant ctions of the will of the late Alastair Johnson copied for u. The rest is concerned only with minor legacies and quests, which would be of no interest to either of you.'

He handed them the papers. Frances rummaged in her ndbag for her reading glasses, and Persephone waited urteously for her to be ready, as if they were about to start a meal. Hugh watched them reading. The ol woman kept her face impassive – she would make a go poker-player, he thought, not knowing that years teaching the most observant people on earth had train her to show nothing she did not want to – but her daughte eyebrows rose higher and higher as she read, and from ti to time she returned to an earlier paragraph as if unable believe what she was seeing.

The copies were simplified versions of the actual w shorn of unnecessary legal jargon and verbiage, and th meaning was quite clear and unambiguous. Frances laid t papers gently on her lap and looked up at him. Through t lenses of her glasses her eyes looked glazed.

'The house? That beautiful old house? But it's . . . it's t family . . . it's been in his family all these generations . .

'And it still will be. Your daughter is – must be – Johnson?'

'Yes, of course. She is Alastair Johnson's child, as y have surely guessed. But there must be others, legi mate . . . he had a daughter. What was her name, I nev knew her very well . . .'

'Joan,' he supplied.

'Yes, Joan. What about her? I know she had one child least, a girl. I mean, if my . . . if Persephone had been a bo I could have understood it, but . . .'

'I can't!' broke in Persephone. 'I can't take a fam inheritance like that, if there's a nearer heir. I've manag without a father all these years. I don't need a dead o now, ordering my life for me.'

He saw that she meant it, and his respect for her ros That's Alastair's daughter, all right, he thought. It's ju the kind of thing he would have said himself. How he wou have liked her. If only . . . But he could have searched f her before now, if he had wanted. What an extraordina business – she's young enough to be his granddaughte most. I wonder . . . no, don't wonder. Nothing to do with ou. Though perhaps, one day, they might tell me . . .

Frances said nothing, content to allow Persephone to ake up her own mind. She, he realised, would not try to fluence the outcome. While they could not be aware of e actual value of the legacy, they must realise it was onsiderable, and it pleased him that they were far from asping at it.

'I said before, no one can force you to accept this heritance. While she lives, your mother has the use of the ouse, and the income from the land, shares and other curities, but on her death you are free to dispose of it how ou will. Give it to Angela, or a home for three-legged cats, you like. He would have understood. Only I think his reference would have been for the cats.'

Frances judged it permissible to speak.

'Angela? Joan's daughter, I suppose? She couldn't have ny more children, could she? Is she still alive?'

'Joan? No, I'm afraid she died some years ago. Angela is ow Mrs Smith – Mrs Johnson-Smith, she would prefer me say. Her grandfather settled a large sum on her at the me of her marriage, many years ago, which is now worth a reat deal. Her husband, too, is extremely wealthy and bout to be more so.'

'That has nothing to do with it,' said Persephone swiftly.

'No, it hasn't. But what is to the point is that Alastair ohnson disliked Angela, and the feeling was entirely utual. She expected, naturally, to inherit his fortune, and ade it quite obvious that she was looking forward to doing as soon as possible. At no time did she show him any care r affection and, in my opinion, has not earned the right to ny particular consideration.'

'Nor have I,' said Persephone.

'Maybe not. But perhaps, simply by your very existence, ou have. This will was not written in a spirit of malice, or spite. I came to know him very well, over the years, an believe him to have been incapable of such an act. Angela had been in need he would have considered it duty to care for her. As it is, he regarded his will, he told the last time I saw him, as the payment of a debt, the char to make reparation for what he saw as the greatest wro he ever committed in his life. I never saw any need to de him that expiation. Angela, when I saw her, threatened contest the will, but I think it unlikely that any lawy would advise her to attempt it. She would be most unlik to succeed, and the costs would be prohibitive.'

'And she has no children? Angela, I mean?'

'None. If she had, it would perhaps have been a differe story. Though I am convinced you would still have been major beneficiary.'

'I have one son. He is a homosexual,' said Persepho baldly. 'He will not, as he puts it, be founding a dynasties.'

'He is not expected to. As I have said, the house a everything else will be yours absolutely, to keep or to se He was not trying to buy you, or to put you in shackles.

'There is nothing else? No letter, I mean? Or message, either of us?'

'Nothing. I asked him, but he refused.' His lips curved a reminiscent smile. 'He asked me if I expected him pontificate to a video camera, leave you a person message. He said that the will itself said everything that w necessary. He would not burden you with his actual wor or face, to haunt you after his death. It was, he said, clean like this.'

'It's a large house,' said Frances. 'And what about th farm? How are we supposed to run that? Or a house of th size, for that matter? Can we let it?'

'You can, of course. The remainder of the farm land let. Much of it has been sold. Some of it for building.'

'For building? But that kind of land sells for . . .'

Both the women were staring at him with something approaching horror. He permitted himself a smile.

'For a fortune, yes. You will not need to worry about the upkeep of the house, or anything else. You are, and you will be,' he bowed to Persephone, a courtly bend, 'extremely wealthy women.'

Frances blinked, and took off her glasses, as if bringing him into focus would make him easier to believe. Persephone put a hand up to her mouth, gave a sharp gasp, and fell into uninhibited laughter. Hugh eyed her warily; he hoped she would not turn out to be hysterical. Her laughter, however, was not wild: it was not shock, but a pure expression of merriment. He found his own lips twitching in sympathy.

'Ha ha ha! Oh! Ha ha ha!' He noticed that she articulated her laughter so that she was actually saying the words which are more usually just gusts of sharply expelled air. It was robust and oddly attractive: he was reminded of Alastair's sharp 'Ha!' of satisfaction. 'Oh, I'm sorry! Oh, poor George! Ha ha ha!'

Frances' own smile widened. The laughter was infectious and she thought she knew its cause.

'Her husband,' she explained. 'Or rather, her ex-husband.' She raised an interrogative eyebrow at Persephone, who had reached the stage of holding her middle and drawing in shaky breaths. Persephone nodded at her to continue. She took off her glasses and wiped her eyes with her fingers, like a child. 'He left her,' explained Frances, when her mother – her adoptive mother – lost all her money at Lloyd's, and died. Now, I imagine, she will be even richer than she would have been.'

'You are actually divorced?' Hugh's question was sharp. He would not like to see half of Alastair's money disappearing with an estranged and deserting husband.

'Yes.' Persephone had her breath back now. She put h glasses back. 'Yes, it's all quite finalised. Finished.' Sl spoke the word like a portcullis coming down. It sound good, so she said it again. 'Finished. Over and done wit Oh dear, poor George. He will be cross. If I were vindictive woman, I'd take the bequest just to spite him. it is, I believe I will take it anyway. It feels right, someho The right thing.'

'A new beginning?' Mary, he knew, would call th sentimental, but he wanted so much for it to be true.

'A new beginning?' Persephone sounded surprised, though the possibility had never occurred to her. 'Yes, suppose it is. And if Angela chooses to fight for it – we she's welcome to try. Welcome to win, even, if that's how turns out. It will be a new beginning anyway.'

Not just a new beginning, thought Frances. Perhaps, f me, it is *the* beginning. I have spent all my life in retrea hiding from reality. Now, at last, it has caught up with n with a vengeance, and given me more than I could ev have thought. More than I deserve, certainly. Will it work Will I live in that old house? Share it with them? Give pa of it to Robin, so that he can bring home his love? Have n great-grandchildren – how extraordinary – to stay with m buy them a pony and build a swimming pool? It could be disaster . . . but it's worth a try. All that guilt, all the takin and giving, the buying and the selling, will go on and exa its toll. And maybe, just maybe, a balance will be found. could happen. It could.

She and her daughter met one another's eyes agai without reserve. A long look that presaged, each believe the resolution of the past, and a hope for the future.

CATHERINE ALLIOTT

THE OLD-GIRL NETWORK

A SPARKLING FRESH TALENT FOR ALL JILLY COOPER FANS

Why didn't anyone warn her that the path to true love would be filled with potholes?

Dreamy, scatty and impossibly romantic, Polly McLaren is a secretary in an advertising agency, but the day a stranger on a train catches her eye, her life changes for ever. This American Romeo, who's recognised her old school scarf, begs Polly to help him find his missing Juliet. Over an intoxicating dinner at the Savoy, Polly agrees to play Cupid – St Gertrude's girls must, after all stick together – and her investigations begin. The last thing she needs now is trouble from the men in her life . . .

. . . like Harry Lloyd Roberts – Polly's madly attractive but infuriatingly elusive boyfriend. It's he who goads her into turning detective – on the grounds that it might give her something to do for a change. Not to mention distract her from his own lustful pursuits . . .

. . . and Nick Penhalligan – Polly's rude, arrogant and ridiculously demanding boss, who's not best pleased that her mind is everywhere but on her job. But even he gets entangled when the old-girl network turns into a spider's web of complications, deceit and finally, love.

FICTION / GENERAL 0 7472 4390 5

More Compelling Fiction from Headline

MASK OF THE NIGHT

MARY RYAN

Jenny knows her mother's face only through a portrait. She is a child when her beloved father is killed in a freak accident, leaving her alone with her grandfather to face the new century. But Jenny has her friends for company and, since her discovery of an old mask in the attic, a sinister stranger who comes to her bedside at night whispering dreams of the impossible . . .

On her visits home to Kilashane from her city life in the sixties, Dee is still fascinated by the big ruin of a house down the boreen and by the mysterious madman who haunts its grounds. And by treasures she finds amongst its shattered columns, a carnival mask, a gold signet ring and a faded leather diary telling of long-dead lives.

But these relics are only part of Kilashane's legacy; the passion and danger that come with them are more than Dee could ever have imagined. She and Jenny are linked by Kilashane's past – a history which casts shadows across generations, and across the seas and time from Venice to London to County Cork.

FICTION / GENERAL 0 7472 4521 5

A selection of bestsellers from Headline

LAND OF YOUR POSSESSION	Wendy Robertson	£5.99	☐
TRADERS	Andrew MacAllen	£5.99	☐
SEASONS OF HER LIFE	Fern Michaels	£5.99	☐
CHILD OF SHADOWS	Elizabeth Walker	£5.99	☐
A RAGE TO LIVE	Roberta Latow	£5.99	☐
GOING TOO FAR	Catherine Alliott	£5.99	☐
HANNAH OF HOPE STREET	Dee Williams	£4.99	☐
THE WILLOW GIRLS	Pamela Evans	£5.99	☐
MORE THAN RICHES	Josephine Cox	£5.99	☐
FOR MY DAUGHTERS	Barbara Delinsky	£4.99	☐
BLISS	Claudia Crawford	£5.99	☐
PLEASANT VICES	Laura Daniels	£5.99	☐
QUEENIE	Harry Cole	£5.99	☐

All Headline books are available at your local bookshop or newsagent, or can be ordered direct from the publisher. Just tick the titles you want and fill in the form below. Prices and availability subject to change without notice.

Headline Book Publishing, Cash Sales Department, Bookpoint, 39 Milton Park, Abingdon, OXON, OX14 4TD, UK. If you have a credit card you may order by telephone – 01235 400400.

Please enclose a cheque or postal order made payable to Bookpoint Ltd to the value of the cover price and allow the following for postage and packing:

UK & BFPO: £1.00 for the first book, 50p for the second book and 30p for each additional book ordered up to a maximum charge of £3.00.
OVERSEAS & EIRE: £2.00 for the first book, £1.00 for the second book and 50p for each additional book.

Name ..

Address ...

..

..

If you would prefer to pay by credit card, please complete:
Please debit my Visa/Access/Diner's Card/American Express (delete as applicable) card no:

Signature ... Expiry Date